D0180033

James Janko

The
Clubhouse
Thief

NO LONGER PROPERTY OF
SEATTLE PUBLIC LIBRARY

a novel

New Issues Poetry & Prose

Western Michigan University
Kalamazoo, Michigan 49008

Copyright © 2018 by James Janko. All rights reserved.
Printed in the United States of America.

First American Edition, 2018.

ISBN-13: 978-1-936970-51-3

Library of Congress Cataloging-in-Publication Data:
Janko, James.
The Clubhouse Thief/James Janko
Library of Congress Control Number: 2016919576

Editor: William Olsen
Managing Editor: Kimberly Kolbe
Layout Editor: Sarah Kidd
Copy Editor: Sarah Kidd
Art Direction: Nick Kuder
Cover Design: John Rappanoti
Production Manager: Paul Sizer
The Design Center, Gwen Frostic School of Art
College of Fine Arts
Western Michigan University

This book is the winner of the Association of Writers & Writing
Programs (AWP) Award for the Novel. AWP is a national, nonprofit
organization dedicated to serving American letters, writers, and
programs of writing.

Go to www.awpwriter.org for more information.

This book is a work of fiction. Names, characters, places and incidents
either are products of the author's imagination or are used fictitiously.
Any resemblance to actual events or locales or persons, living or dead, is
entirely coincidental.

James Janko

The Clubhouse Thief

a novel

NEW ISSUES

 WESTERN MICHIGAN UNIVERSITY

Also by James Janko

Buffalo Boy and Geronimo

Praise for *Buffalo Boy and Geronimo*

"A beautifully written first novel about the ugliness of war—in Vietnam and anywhere else...Folkloric in approach, it's sustained by prose that is often lyrical, though never self-conscious."

—*Kirkus Reviews* (starred review)

"Nothing in the publisher's biography of [James] Janko suggests he is a poet, but his book is what used to be called, admiringly, 'a poet's novel...' Leaving politics behind for the most part, Janko's book is about the universal absurdity of war."

—Gerald Nicosia, *Los Angeles Times Book Review*

"Set in Vietnam during the war, this simple tale achieves depth through its language and naturalistic detail...This book deserves to enter the canon of masterly, penetrating works about this still controversial era."

—*Library Journal*

"*Buffalo Boy and Geronimo* suggests that spiritual communion with the universe will enable us to transcend our differences, be they political, racial, or societal. Janko's novel also implies that all life should be treated with dignity and respect, and it challenges us to worship the very ground upon which we tread."

—*San Francisco Chronicle*

"Janko is an author to watch."

—*Hartford Courant*

"Out of great travail can come art that heals."

—*Seattle Post-Intelligencer*

"Janko keeps his two plots simple—men overcome obstacles in pursuit of love—both so as not to overburden his gorgeous, incantatory prose and to accomplish his more ambitious objective of bearing witness to the mute suffering of the earth and animals."

—*Kyoto Journal* #66

"Reading this book is a life-altering experience. It is exquisitely rendered on multiple levels simultaneously: the language is rich and flowing, the characters feel real, the story is compelling and the author brings the reader to a world that is sensually, emotionally and philosophically layered and unequivocal...This is a story of devastating wounds, on the scale of the individual, the culture and the planet. It also walks the reader to the brink of healing."

—Beth Jacobs, *Journal of Poetry Therapy,* 2016

"All wars leave an inherent trail of destruction. Few authors share their firsthand experience with the degree of sensitivity and reverence that Janko shows for the humans and animals, even the plants, that become victims of the war...From page one to the end of the book, we are held captive by his vivid descriptions of sights, smells, tastes—intimate details of every aspect of each character and scene involved."

—*Turning Wheel, The Journal of Socially Engaged Buddhism*

"One can revisit the Vietnam War in *Buffalo Boy and Geronimo*... It is not just its horrors that are recounted, but the thirst for beauty and nature, and the ecological damage that war inflicts on humans, animals, and the environment they share."

—*Bookviews*

"A boy who loves a buffalo, a girl who loves an elephant, a man who loves a tiger: These are the principals of *Buffalo Boy and Geronimo*, a poignant dance of preservation and destruction... Employing a restrained, meticulous style, Janko keeps the frenzy of war at bay, foregrounding the beauty of the natural world and the creative impulses of human beings."

—*Poetry Flash*, Number 301/302, Winter-Spring 2010

"*Buffalo Boy and Geronimo* is a stunning affirmation of the wonder of human joy and the importance of hope in the midst of the chaos, brutality and desperation of war...[It] is a spectacularly great achievement and one of the great dramas of good and evil in contemporary literature."

—Alan Miller
Author of *Gaia Connections: An Introduction to Ecology, Ecoethics, and Economics*

"To read *Buffalo Boy and Geronimo* is to realize the suffering of war, and the dearness of every life. An important book. A beautiful book."

—Maxine Hong Kingston
Author of *I Love a Broad Margin to My Life*

"This compelling novel has the ability to communicate village life in Viet Nam during the war and the way the whole of it—animals, people, the aged, as well as packed rice shoots—are moved through the forests, across rivers, as the Americans follow them in their business of destroying villages and imposing immense ecological damage. It's extraordinary."

—Grace Paley
Author of *The Little Disturbances of Man* and *Collected Stories*

For Chanpidor,

and in memory of

Robert Ray Boeskool, Harold "Jo-Jo" Bainsford, Sandy Taylor, and my mother and father

"What is poetry, which does not save Nations or people?"
    —Czeslaw Milosz

"I've heard a question, an echo, countless times in the span of my career—'Why can't you just play ball?' Well, I learned to play hardball on cracked sidewalks and cinders and broken glass. Wynton Marsalis wrote a song—'From the Plantation to the Penitentiary...' You know I got seven pen pals in jail? America has written off pretty much all the people in my Hood."
    —Arshan Azzam

"You're not going to reduce me to an entertainer."
    —Bill Russell, Five-time NBA Most Valuable Player

BASEBALL

Raise a cup to Auld Lang Syne, players long dead. Grover Cleveland Alexander, Emil "Hillbilly" Bildilly, Frank "Noodles" Hahn. In 1908, behind the pitching of Mordecai "Three-Finger" Brown, the Cubs triumphed in the World Series. As a boy, Mordecai lost part of his right hand in a farming accident, but a three-fingered grip improved his curve ball. In the old days, no rule prevented a pitcher from slathering the ball with spit, tobacco gruel, Vaseline, or whatever helped his curve. None of this mattered to Mordecai, who already enjoyed the advantage of a mutilated hand.

Only the dead might recall with clarity Chicago of 1908. I have worn photographs of horses and cobblestone streets, two-story apartment buildings scattered near the West Side Grounds, the home of the predecessors of the Cubs, the Orphans and Colts. Men sold apples and onions from wagons, or from baskets strapped to the backs of bicycles. I can't fathom how people filled their time, what they did after work. Imagine a town with no computers, no smartphones, no instant messaging, no TV. Imagine a game in which each play was seen just once by those present at the ballpark. Imagine the Chicago Cubs trouncing the Tigers, not once, but **twice**, in the World Series of 1907 and 1908.

*

Wrigley Field is a complicated park. On Clark and Addison, a theological seminary operated until 1910. Its history is unknowable, but probably involved an excess of soul-searching and tribulation. The property was owned by Charles H. Weeghman. A businessman, he tore down the religious buildings and put up a ballpark—Weeghman Park. On April 20, 1916, the first National League game was played at this site. The Cubs dazzled the crowd, beat the Reds 7-6 in 11 innings, and a live bear cub was paraded around the ballpark. In 1920, the Wrigley family purchased the team, and six years later Weeghman Park became Wrigley Field. Although the Cubs never won a championship for the new owners, they gave other teams and players a stage for glory. In Game 3 of the 1932 World Series, for instance, Babe Ruth supposedly called "the shot," pointed to the bleachers, and socked Charlie Root's next pitch for a round-tripper. The Yanks buried the Cubs in four games. Had I witnessed the rout, I would've said, "Wait till next year," a dumb parrot in a four-word cage.

In '69, when the Cubs were kings until they folded in September, I learned to suffer. At the time, I was a minor leaguer in the Cub system, a second-baseman in Des Moines. Nick Glouser, the Des Moines shortstop, the current Cub skipper, bought him and me two fifths of Old Crow the night the Mets clinched the pennant. In our shared room, in the dull glow of a night-light, Nick offered a toast so we could drink with purpose. "To the Mets," he said. "May their plane crash and burn before they play in the World Series." No smile lightened his words, nor did he smile later when he honed his hatred for Tommy Agee, the Mets' centerfielder. "To a murderer," he said, "a Cub killer, guilty as charged." Nick drank hard and belched. "Up to me, we'd tame

Tommy with a dose of strap oil, a hundred lashes. I'd say, 'Stop blubbering, boy, and take it. You know you earned every lick.'"

Nick tends to go to bed drunk and wake blurry-eyed and sorry. Our friendship, if I can call it that, spans fifty-three years, and I've never heard him censure or shame a black man in public. He's a Carolina cracker, proud and fierce, yet wily enough to keep hatred hidden. Only when drunk, alone with me, his confidant, the animosities of the ages blow through him like a biblical storm.

Nick made it to the Bigs, I didn't. He filled the slot of utility infielder for half a dozen teams, never sparkled, but was known as "a good head, a sharp strategist," and management liked him. I, a failed athlete, came with similar recommendations, and soon steered my career toward coaching and scouting. At age 36, I coached the Cub farm team in Boise, took a scouting job with Boston two years later, and for more than three decades, mired in loss, I gravitated back and forth between the Cubs and Red Sox. In 2003, a rough year for both teams, I was out of work, which was just as well. Drunk and alone, I went to Game 6 of the National League Championship Series at Wrigley Field. I hit myself in the face when Steve Bartman, a fan, deflected a foul ball that would've been caught by the Cub leftfielder. In the top of the eighth, the Cubs up three-zip, seemingly on their way to the World Series, the Florida Marlins began circling the bases like boys at a Sunday picnic. Eight runs in the eighth, no let-up. A hell-and-back pounding. By the time the game ended, I had a hankering to shoot myself. Bent over, beer cup in hand, I said, "Go on, Billy, blow your brains out. Do it." I own a Saturday night special, but the gun was at home. How can a man be so stricken by a game? Is baseball more than a game? Is it life itself? A blessing for some, a wound for others? These questions have hounded me all my life.

In 2004, I was back in the Cub farm system, a hitting coach for the Diamond Jaxx. After the Red Sox swept the Cardinals, won their first World Series since 1918, I had to wonder if I was the curse, if loss was my shadow. I mentioned this to Nick over drinks, secretly hoping he would disagree. He said, "Well, Billy, the cloud over your head holds some rain, doesn't it?"

I looked up.

"You can't win to save your ass."

Call me Billy the Curse. I was still in the Cub farm system when the Bosox won the World Series in 2007 and 2013. I seem to have a knack of sucking the life out of any organization that makes the mistake of hiring me. In 2016, when the Cubs won their first World Series in one hundred and eight years, I'd spent the season as the bench coach for the Portland Sea Dogs, a Bosox farm team that finished in last place in the Eastern Division. What's in store for me between now and the grave? More loss? More regrets? I've never had a lucky day let alone a lucky year.

*

So at age seventy-three, scuffed and scarred as a junkyard dog, I became the Cubs' bench coach, Nick Glouser's number one advisor. I don't really like the skipper, but somehow we're like brothers. We drink together, talk shit together, and try to believe in the promise of a new season. We're losers, though, and we know our history well enough to carry it to the present. What might it take for any team we're on to win a pennant, a World Series? Well, to whoever's listening I say, "Miracles, lottery luck, one in a million. It's like praying for peace in the Middle East. It's like praying for no one else to die in famine or drought or war. It's like praying to a God who doesn't exist for blessings that don't exist. It's like praying to somebody, anybody, "Please, please, just stop the dumb suffering! **Stop** it! Give us some shred of meaning before we leave this earth."

*

On the morning of our home opener, a day game, the team gathered at home plate for photos. The grandest scoreboard in baseball served as our backdrop, a mountainous slab that flirted with white clouds blown in off Lake Michigan. Posing with players, the diamond raked smooth behind us, the grass wet with dew, I told myself, "Billy, this is your last chance, enjoy it. You can't expect much else." Much else in my life, I meant, or the life of my team, or any life. Chin up, I stood in the last row and said, "All right, you guys know what to do. Everybody smile and say, 'Fuck the Cardinals!'" This got some laughs, but one of our relief pitchers seemed to be choking. He, too, had never been part of a winner, and had spent most of his career in the minor leagues.

Front and center, kneeling, were our stars, our tri-captains— Johnny Stompiano, Arshan Azzam (aka Azzy), and Jesús Mijango Cruz. Nick had asked Johnny to captain the team, but the Kid turned him down. "Tri-captains," he said, "three of us," and named his partners. Nick said it was undoable, but Johnny caused a fuss, talked to the media, and the publicity forced Nick to concede. Back then I was wary of anyone named Arshan, and Mijango sounded like a synonym for trouble. A whole season would come and go before the Cub captains would gather every opinion of mine, every stray thought, and burn it to ash.

After the photo session, our tri-captains gathered on the mound. Azzy, a hand on his brow, scoped the Waveland Avenue rooftops, some of which had seating areas for fans, and behind one of the roofs rose a jumbo billboard, a wordy ad that rivaled the height of the centerfield scoreboard. It was way up over the left-field foul pole, the words bold and black on a field of green.

I BELIEVE A LEAF OF GRASS IS NO LESS
THAN THE JOURNEYWORK OF THE STARS

As a boy I used to write poetry, even won a contest in 7th grade, but those days were gone. I thought I was viewing an ad for lawn fertilizer, greener grass, so I joked around and told the Cub captains Wrigley Field could never be improved. "No, they can go diddle themselves" I said. "The Friendly Confines can't somehow have greener grass or thicker ivy this year, next year, or ever." I tend to be depressive, but when I poke my head into a beam of light I sometimes swing the other way, exaggerate positives until they, and I, become silly. I would've kept jabbering about our All-Star groundskeepers if Azzy hadn't pointed to another attraction, a digital billboard that towered over the left-field bleachers. "Coach," he said, "look what we got here."

I pulled down my visor to shade my brow. The truth—contradictory, a play of opposites—stood in gold letters as tall as soldiers:

BASEBALL IS LIGHTNING.

—HENRY CHADWICK

...A LEISURELY GAME THAT DEMANDS LIGHTNING SPEED, A PASTORAL GAME THAT THRIVES IN CITIES.

—KEN BURNS

Well, why argue with facts? Why resist the truth if it knocks you on the head? I love most about our Game the contrasts: stop-go, pivot, held breath, fly, breathe, lunge, stop again, now run, slide, steal, score, run home, run all the way home. Fly, fly, fly.

I stiffened when Azzy lay a warm hand on my shoulder.

"You okay, coach?"

His hand bothered me somehow. "Fine," I said, and took one step to the side.

Johnny, who was standing on my left, said, "Hey!" and nabbed the attention of somebody in the press box behind home plate. "Fast forward," he said. "Show us the base-thief poem."

A moment later the board over the bleachers was a mess of words in fire colors, red and yellow. It took me a while to digest it, but I knew soon enough I was reading a poem tailored to a thief—Johnny Stompiano—the most daring base-thief in the history of the Game. By year's end, elderly Cub fans would claim he was smoother than Lou Brock, flashier than Rickey Henderson. The only thing wrong with this poem that climbs some forty feet into the sky is that it doesn't rise high enough. It prattles its praise for one way to steal, whereas Johnny has ten thousand. If you think I fluff things up, butter my bread on both sides, wait till you hear about Game 7 of the National League Championship Series. Yes, ten thousand ways to steal a base, and other ways undiscovered. On occasion, as in the poem, the Kid skitters, tingles, teases, hovers like an ecstatic bird.

POISED BETWEEN GOING ON AND BACK, PULLED
BOTH WAYS TAUT LIKE A TIGHT-ROPE WALKER,
FINGERTIPS POINTING THE OPPOSITES,
NOW BOUNCING TIPTOE LIKE A DROPPED BALL
OR A KID SKIPPING ROPE, COME ON, COME ON,
RUNNING A SCATTERING OF STEPS SIDEWISE,
HOW HE TEETERS, SKITTERS, TINGLES, TEASES...
HOVERS LIKE AN ECSTATIC BIRD,
HE'S ONLY FLIRTING, CROWD HIM, CROWD HIM,
DELICATE, DELICATE, DELICATE, DELICATE—NOW!
—ROBERT FRANCIS

Azzy draped a long arm over Johnny's shoulders. He said, "Coach, here's the scoop. When Wild Child"—that's one of Johnny's monikers—"steals a base, well, you'll see this poem or some other poem made for a thief. Coach, we got homerun poems, double-play poems, strike-three-poems—you name it. In some parks they shoot off fireworks after a homerun, but in Wrigley we'll fly a poem."

Fly a poem? Well, what could I say? I didn't say anything. I folded my arms to my chest.

Now Wild Child, ringleader as always, hollered up to some black guy in the press box, then gestured to yet another billboard, the digital board over the right-field bleachers. After these words appeared on the screen—

LEFT BEHIND

BY THE THIEF—

THE MOON IN THE WINDOW

—Johnny said, "Good, good," and turned again to the board in left.

He was testing things out, seeing how the boards looked, and Azzy and Jesús Mijango pitched in their two cents, and they all agreed the poems added "some color to the yard." I suppose anything goes on a digital billboard: poems, pictures, player bios, stats, line-up cards, ads, and so on. I more or less appreciated these poems, but at the same time they seemed out of place. I was more at home viewing names and numbers, statistics in black and white, or the parade of ads that used to fill most of the space. I don't take well to anything new.

Now Jesús Mijango jiggled his hips, tossed his cap in the

air, and barked something in Spanish. Sure as my name's Billy, the new poem on the left-field billboard was for him—Hector Jesús Mijango Cruz. That's his full name, his birth name, though no one calls him Hector. He's Jesús, or Jesús Mijango, or Bad Ball Jesús for his tendency to swing at bad pitches. He's our best hitter, though, give him that much. You should see him swing timber. A murderer itching for a kill.

I CAME HERE BECAUSE I WAS MEXICAN, A STICK
OF BROWN LIGHT IN LOVE WITH THOSE
WHO COULD DO IT—THE TRIPLE AND HARD SLIDE,
THE GLOVES EATING BALLS INTO DOUBLE PLAYS...
WHAT COULD I DO WITH FIFTY POUNDS, MY SHYNESS?
IN THE BLEACHERS I WAS BRILLIANT WITH MY BODY,
WAVING PLAYERS IN AND STOMPING MY FEET...
WHEN HECTOR LINED BALLS INTO DEEP
CENTER, IN MY MIND I ROUNDED THE BASES
WITH HIM, MY FACE FLARED, MY HAIR LIFTING
BEAUTIFULLY, BECAUSE WE WERE COMING HOME
TO THE ARMS OF BROWN PEOPLE.

—GARY SOTO

I doctored this poem in my mind. I changed the beginning (I came here because I was **American**, a stick of light), and the end (...coming home to the arms of **Cub** fans). Yes, I did away with brown people, and I also had a hankering to do away with Jesús, or at least silence him. I'm a better man now, but what irked me that day was the same thing that still irks half the world. Jesús, you see, is a homo, and had the nerve to come out of the closet

13

four years ago as a rookie. In my playing days we had these types, sure, but they knew enough to keep quiet. In Des Moines, on those minor league teams I played on, we'd have ganged up on a guy as brazen and brash as Jesús Mijango. Nowadays, the winds and the opinions they carry blow every which way. A manager, regardless of his prerogatives, has to let oddball players do as they please. I'll tell you a hard fact: nothing bedevils Nick more than having a homo on our team who shares the Savior's name. When the skipper goes on a bender, when the booze kicks in, he calls his best hitter "the Jackie Robinson of Faggots, the Cub Lord of Sodom and Gomorrah." He slurs his way through a whole litany of insults, one worse than the other. You're lucky you're too far away to hear.

*

The last poem I saw that day was devoted to the man some consider the finest pitcher in the history of the Game. Make you a wager: Azzy chose this one, and could have written it. A love poem to Satchel Paige.

SOMETIMES I FEEL LIKE I WILL NEVER STOP

JUST GO FOREVER

TILL ONE FINE MORNING

I'LL REACH UP AND GRAB ME A HANDFUL OF STARS

AND SWING OUT MY LONG LEAN LEG

AND WHIP THREE HOT STRIKES BURNING DOWN
  THE HEAVENS

AND LOOK OVER AT GOD AND SAY

HOW ABOUT THAT!

                                        —SAMUEL ALLEN

14

Well, I seldom glanced at these boards during the season, but just now I was curious. I asked whose brainstorm this was. Who paid to put poems on billboards? Would fans really read this stuff? Did they come to a game to read poems? Johnny said fans came to Wrigley Field "for more reasons than anyone can fathom." As for the brainstorm, he credited his fiancée, Janice Oyakawa, the prettiest girl in town, and smart too, a graduate student at the University of Chicago. I'd read about her and Johnny in the *Chicago Tribune*. I'd eyed Janice at banquets too, pre-season gatherings, but never met her face-to-face. A certain distance is desirable, even essential. Beside a perfect flower I hold my breath, afraid of muddying it up. Even from across a long hall, though, a man beholds beauty. Jet-black hair, dark eyes, fair skin, a face of light. What this highbrow sees in a rough-and-tumble ballplayer strains the imagination. Maybe anyone in the spell of love casts logic to a rabid sea.

As mentioned, I tend to be depressive, a sad sack, but sometimes I get ambushed by pleasure. Standing on the mound beside Johnny, the best base-thief in the Game, I sniffed fresh-cut grass and raw earth, the finest smells in the world. While Johnny sung praises to Janice, the brains behind the billboards, I pictured her perfect face, her black hair, and I learned that—according to these lovebirds—"jazz and poetry are twins." One night Johnny and his girl rode their bicycles[1] to Nicki's, a South Side club. They met up with Azzy and his wife Isha, Jesús Mijango and his boyfriend. Last November, it was, a few days shy of Thanksgiving. "Anyway," said Johnny, "we're listening to jazz, Sami Slyde, and

[1] The Kid doesn't own a car. He gives away so much money that he's the only star in the Bigs who isn't a multi-millionaire, or at least that's the rumor.

during a break Janice comes up with this idea. Why not buy up some billboard space at Wrigley and put up poems? Jazz poems. Baseball poems. Hip-hop poems. Whatever." He snapped his fingers. "Easy enough," he said. "Use a portion of our salaries and put up some poems. All right, so the next day Azzy and Jesús and I gathered at Janice's place to talk things over. Azzy learned that Satchel Paige poem by heart when he was five. I've known Whitman all my life, but we needed Janice to find the others." He shook his head. "Coach, you should see my girl's library. Poems in the Zulu language, poems in Swahili. Poems from your backyard and around the world." He wore his Cub cap backwards. Shaggy black hair curtained his ears, all but the lobes. He winked at the board over the left-field bleachers. "Well, there it is, coach, poetry on billboards, money well-spent. Janice thinks there are at least three good poems for anything that happens on the field of play."

My shoulders slumped. "Maybe she's right."

"Haiku," he said, "or epigrams. Just a few words to put a jump in your step."

I tried to rise to my full height, but my spine stayed crooked. "You know I once wrote poetry?"

Johnny shrugged. "Why stop, coach?"

"Well, it's just…" I shook my head. "I haven't written a damn thing since I was twelve years old."

Jesús Mijango said, "**Desafíos**, coach. **Canto hondo**."

"Huh?"

Johnny said, "This will be the year we wake the world with a poem."

*

Well, we blew the home opener, a heartbreaker, and played piss poor through April and May. Johnny was stealing bases, Jesús Mijango was hitting homers, but we got into the habit of throwing away games in late innings. June was a swoon. At the All Star break, we trailed the first-place Cardinals by eleven games. As in bygone years, when the word Cub was synonymous with loser, the Red Birds toyed with us, made us look like a bunch of rummies. After the All Star break, however, we woke as from a slumber and played better ball than any team in the Bigs. It wasn't till the end of the season, early November, that I came to believe some of our success had to do with a stranger, a person not on our team or any team—Khadijah Jamil. Nick said she didn't make any damn difference, but by then—and only then—I was strong enough to dissent.

Arshan "Azzy" Azzam is big and black and Muslim and loud and gentle and fierce and humble and impossible to ignore. He is—above all—a contradiction. He frequents Chicago's finest jazz clubs but refuses to drink. The ace of our staff, or **any** staff, he throws strikes that chip the corners of home plate at one hundred and one miles an hour. He calls his pitches "Bat Dodgers," "Blazers," "Sparks," "Trouble Balls," "Invisible Light." He echoes Satchel Paige, but he's also a close cousin of one of his other heroes—Muhammad Ali.

On September 6th, our post-season hopes fragile but alive, he entered our clubhouse waving the front page of the *Chicago Tribune*. A picture of gap-toothed Congresswoman Khadijah Jamil darkened the newsprint beneath a cautionary caption—PRESIDENTIAL? As always, the nation's politics were dysfunctional, especially at the highest level. Patricia Durgan, the democratic presidential candidate, suffered a stroke two weeks earlier and withdrew from the race. Democratic delegates, in an emergency meeting in Washington D.C., nominated Robert Pierson, a Missouri senator to replace Durgan, but he was immediately embroiled in scandals. In secret, or so he assumed, Pierson made sweetheart deals with the nation's four largest banks and vowed to do everything in his power to allow them to "grow large beyond limits." Leaked phone transcripts revealed his pledge to ExxonMobil to "reinforce and maintain a band-aid approach to climate change, and to prepare for a robust expansion of the energy sector." Because he'd cast himself as an environmentalist, this hurt him slightly, though it also filled his coffers. What sank Pierson was not the corporate shenanigans, which were bipartisan and expected, but his affair with an undocumented Guatemalan girl of questionable age, and lewd photographs that somehow reached the desk of the editor-in-chief of the *Washington Post* two days after his nomination. Pierson, calling himself "a devout Christian, a husband, a father, a grandfather," denied "any and all wrongdoing." When he failed to attend yet another emergency meeting in the capital, however, what was left of his party nominated Congresswoman Khadijah Jamil, a rabble-rouser educated at a community college in South Chicago. I am, at times, a gambling man. Hours after Jamil's candidacy was announced, I bet big money Michael J. Trent would be reelected by a landslide. This offbeat populist with a head of hair like cotton candy combed forward, with his Goldman Sachs cabinet, his Harvard-boy connections, would have four more years to make America great again. As for his policies, his schemes, I didn't give a damn. If Trent wanted to rule the world, let him have it. The last thing America would do was elect someone several shades darker than Barack Obama. Ms. Jamil is a black woman from a black mother. Sell that, Azzy. Go ahead. However mean this may sound, the world's meaner. I've been around long enough to know.

Azzy is young. Waving *The Tribune* at the TV crew that shadowed him around the clubhouse, he called Khadijah Jamil "the next president of the United States. Known her since I was eight years old," he said, "and living in that alley off Halsted. I called her Auntie Khadijah, still do, and she's been one of my mentors all these years. One thing I can tell you is she's for everybody, and I mean **every**body on this whole wide earth." He held up his arms like a preacher. "No, you don't know Khadijah like I know her, but you **will** know her down the stretch. Where did she go to school? Well, little Olive-Harvey College down on the South Side. My auntie's all Hood, no Harvard, no Ivy League. No big money stuffed in her purse. This woman **knows** the world, doesn't buy it or sell it. Presidential? Oh, yes. But like none we've ever known."

Azzy was too black to blush, but alas, not me. He said Ms. Jamil's daddy and granddaddy knew both Malcolm and Dr. King, knew them personally, and so what? In private, in the cramped corners of my mind, I said, "What in the hell are you, Azzy, a ballplayer or a soapbox campaigner?" Back then, I adhered to the Bible of Sports set in stone by Howard Cosell: "Rule number one of the Jockocracy is that professional athletes and politics never mix." **Never** is the right word, Howard, or at least I thought so. I'd believed this all my life.

Three years ago, as a rookie, Azzy—a rouser from day one—founded an athletic organization called **Live the Legacy: Tommie Smith, John Carlos, and Muhammad Ali.** Initially, all members were black or brown, but four years back Stompiano joined, and now—forty strong in both leagues and hundreds if you count athletes in other sports—they make a rainbow of rebels. They do not behave. They do not win endorsements from large companies. They invest money in ruined communities. They speak out. They get involved. They want their lives to matter. Azzy often tries to convince us "the Michael Jordan era's over and Ali's back, his tongue and punch no less sharp or sly or controversial." But most athletes still fall in line for lucrative endorsements. Azzy's referring to a few misfits, and in baseball most of them are Cubs.

Now Azzy waved the front-page news as though it were a

flag, some old symbol of might and right. Ms. Jamil has crooked teeth, a crooked smile, and she's damn near as dark as he is. Obama? Remember the man? He came to us copper-colored, bright as a mint penny, and spoke of "change," a nation undivided. Well, he rose twice to the presidency and the divisions widened. As for Ms. Jamil, her chances of stepping in the front door of the White House make for a simple equation: 0+0=0. Scorekeepers, close the books.

I slunk back a few steps. When Azzy, fanning his sweaty face with the headlines, quoted Dr. King, something about a mountaintop, then "Auntie Khadijah," who sounded like King, the problem wasn't so much the message as the delivery. Azzy's huge, 6'6". His blue-black face shone so keen and bright I felt diminished, dull, a pale shadow pinned to a wall. Today, as always, his off-field attire was preacherly, a dark suit coat and tie, crisp and clean, but the clubhouse was warm, or **felt** warm, and he'd worked up a lather like some grubber gathering his berries or cotton beneath a boiling sun. What good would he do "Auntie Khadijah?" Azzy would be wise to abide by the Bible of Howard Cosell.

I have a secret name for reporters—bottom feeders. Al Muscat, an ESPN variety, saw Nick and a few other coaches and players looking uneasy. He asked the skipper if he saw Congresswoman Jamil as a viable replacement for Robert Pierson. Nick shook his head and waved his cap in the air. "Well, you know the answer, no time for it. In case you haven't noticed, I'm trying to manage this team."

I was afraid Muscat would come for me, but he turned to Jimmy Lieski, our first baseman, a thirty-seven-year-old Christian fundamentalist. "And you?" said Muscat. "You got an opinion? Care to rattle the breeze?"

I knew what Jimmy would say before the words sputtered

from his mouth. "I re–respect Ms. Jamil, even ad-admire her, but she's Muslim. She doesn't know Jesus as I do."

Jesús Mijango piped up. "Yeah, she knows me better. We go fishing together."

Jimmy made a choking sound. "She's not suh-saved."

"Who says?"

"The **Bible**," said Jimmy. "Romans 10:9-10."

Nick held up his arms like a traffic cop. "Okay," he said, "show's over, and the encore," but it took around ten minutes to shoo Muscat and the other bottom feeders from the clubhouse. By then, I was sweating the way Azzy was sweating. My jersey clung like a wet towel to my shoulders, my back, the balloon of my belly. What I needed now was a stiff drink. I despised Azzy, this freak from the South Side who refused to play the Game between the clearly drawn lines of the field, and at the same time I admired him. Young and hopeful, he tried to make us relevant, to make the **world** relevant. In my own crooked way I cheered him on, though at the same time I wished he'd leave us alone. What did he want from me, or from any Cub? Mumbling to myself, I moped around the clubhouse, then made my way to the skipper's office and his stash of Old Crow. **Never drink before a game**—that was a hard-fast rule for players and coaches and even the skipper. I had just one before I shut off the lights and sat in a chair till the sweat cooled and my heart began to still.

*

But that day at the Friendly Confines Azzy Azzam and the Cubs made baseball look easy. Our ace struck out thirteen Red Birds. Johnny went three for four and stole three bases. Bad Ball Jesús turned on a pitch high and tight and planted it on a porch on Waveland Avenue. The Cubs set off on a four-game winning streak, lost one, then won five more, while the Cards did more losing than winning. On September 17th, Azzy celebrated his birthday by blanking the Brewers at Wrigley Field. In post-game interviews, he said he was "like Satchel Paige throwing Trouble Balls and such, throwing hot strikes burning down the heavens!" I have to admit he was man-mountain: splendid, bold, his dark peaks pointed at stars. All year long, till his arm gave out in early October, Azzy was the best pitcher in the Major Leagues.

Well, we passed the Red Birds, fed them some dust, but they snuck in the back door, the first of two wild card teams, and three games behind the Division Champion Cubs. They bested the Giants in the wild-card match-up, then trounced the Mets. We swept the Dodgers in round one, so it would be the archrivals—Cubs and Cards—for the National League pennant. No love lost between these teams. Bad blood and festering wounds for well over a century. I'll tell you the truth: I thought the pressures would be more than I could bear. Part of me wanted to quit, let the Red Birds hammer us, and slink away to hibernate all winter. I had that old feeling of worthlessness running through me, and sadness, too. A coach, whatever his age, should be a reservoir of hope, but I, in heart and mind, boarded a shipwreck, my own Titanic, and awaited the dark plunge into the familiarity of loss.

Success can knock a man off-kilter. After we won the first two games at Wrigley, insomnia plagued me. We dropped Game 3, a nail-biter in St. Louis, won Game 4, then dropped two straight for no good reason. Jimmy Lieski booted away Game 5 with the bases loaded and two outs in the bottom of the eighth. Game 6 was stolen by the home-plate umpire, Greg Safranski, a crab ass born and raised in St. Louis. Johnny Stompiano was safe, he usually is, but it's too late to argue. Game 7, do or die. Might the Cubs have a better chance if I wasn't on the team?

PENNANT

National League Championship Series

Game 7

Wrigley Field

Azzy Azzam, the finest Cub pitcher since Mordecai "Three Finger" Brown, would warm the bench. He begged Nick to let him start Game 7, but Franny Blair, the head trainer, convinced the skipper to rest Azzy and his ailing arm till Game 3 of the World Series. I spoke with Nick in the privacy of his office. "What World Series? Who's going to turn these Red Birds into dead birds?"

"Pray for rain. Pray we get lucky."

I told the skipper I hate that word—**lucky**.

"I know the feeling," he said. "Toss a coin and lose every time."

Dantel Hood, our thirty-year-old rookie, was scheduled to start Game 7. He's a giant, more or less Azzy's size, but he tends to be erratic. Muddy looking, black as a tire, wild, troubled—the mere thought of him made me cringe. I told Nick I didn't want the pennant riding on Hood's shoulders. "Azzy's our best bet," I said. "He's good for six or seven strong innings."

"If he were healthy."

"This is for the pennant, sport. You're trusting Dantel Hood with the pennant?"

"Well, what should I do? Put you on the roster? Let you pitch?"

I looked at the ceiling.

"Same old song," he shrugged. "Through hell and back, hell and high water. This is the story of our lives."

*

Long before game-time, Pete Carnes, the third-base coach, persuaded Nick to bar the press from the clubhouse. The skipper dimmed the lights, gave us a pep talk, and tried to make us feel comfortable, or perhaps invisible. Although we'd bid good riddance to the Cubs of old, legends of loss, personnel problems lingered. Jimmy Lieski, for instance, once a drunk, now a haunted evangelist; Matt Creighton, a failed seminary student, a drop-out, now a neurasthenic third-baseman; and Paddy Delaney, a forty-year-old middle reliever, a pleasant sort, except when he chattered about his feet.

Paddy conversed more with himself than his teammates. Before Game 7 he described his ailment in detail, the peculiar sensations, the way his feet sometimes felt lifeless, a couple slabs of meat, stiffened as by rigor mortis yet acutely painful. "Yeah, I know," he said. "Everybody's got a cross to bear, but I been walking on wounds forever." His face was yellowish, contorted; his feet were in a bucket of water. "It's a miracle I can put on my socks and shoes and walk out on the field."

Matt Creighton, hunched over in a corner, a hot towel on his neck, was talking on his cell phone. "No, I'll be fine," he kept saying, "I'll be fine. I don't want anyone to worry." Beside him, in a chair, Jimmy Lieski read the Bible aloud, his voice soft except for occasional pronouncements: "You already know...but let me remind you how the Lord, having once and for all delivered his people out of Egypt, later destroyed those who did not believe." Well, we had our tri-captains, talent and pizzazz, but we also had remnants of Cub tradition—heartache made visible, torment in poster colors. Lieski, Creighton, Delaney—how could they be winners? Born Again Jimmy raised an arm and recited: "There was a violent earthquake; the sun turned black as a funeral pall and the moon all red as blood."

*

Dantel Hood, ignoring Nick's advice, allowed himself to be interviewed in the Cub dugout. I followed him out there, a decision I would regret. Hood hung his head and told the TV crews he needed to stick with his plan. "I just got to throw strikes, keep us in the game." He dabbed his eyes with a hanky. "Who would've guessed I'd be pitchin' for the prize, a Chicago Cub pennant?" He rubbed his chin. "I just hope I can find my poise."

Long afternoon shadows edged the field. The sun, wintry and weak, would soon vanish. Hood hunched over on the bench, his hands limp between his thighs. "Pitchin' for the prize," he repeated. "This is sort of like a dream."

Asked how he'd approach Jason Ryder, Jr., the Cards' clean-up hitter, would he challenge him or pitch around him, he sighed, glanced over his shoulder, and took a deep and quiet in-breath. "Yeah," he said, "Ryder's tough, means business. Doesn't take losing for an answer."

The media, their mini-mikes clustered like grapes near his lips, pressed forward.

"So I best be careful," said Hood, "feed him junk-balls.

Pitch around him."

A reporter asked what he would do if he faced Ryder with the bases loaded.

Hood blinked. "Just hope I get lucky," he said. "Just hope somethin' goes my way for a change."

The same reporter began to stare at me. Let me tell you something: sports hounds double as ambulance chasers, rubbernecks, sadists. When this one said, "Coach, what do you expect from Dantel Hood tonight?" I wanted to say, "Screw yourself, fuck your mother." The great blubber of my heart was pounding like that of a sick and overworked dog.

"Dantel will pitch his heart out," I said. "I expect he'll keep us in the game."

Bent over, Hood cupped his hands to his belly. I suppose he felt some pain there, in his mid-section. He seemed to be having a hard time drawing a breath.

I blurted a civil farewell to sadists ("Gentlemen, we'll see you later"), and led our rookie down the tunnel to the den-like cavern and relative calm of the clubhouse. Hood's guardian, I sat him down in a comfy chair, padded arms, padded seat, but maybe what he needed was a padded cell, sides thick with cushions, good for skull slaps. A cell would've been good for me, too, a container for rising tension. "Forget the Cards," I said, "forget the reporters. Try to get your mind off the game."

Johnny Stompiano, in his skivvies, sauntered up with a ball and glove. "Ninth inning," he said, "Houdini-time. Bag of tricks." He did a little jig, tossed the ball in the air, and caught it behind his back. "Just like that," he said. "Baseball is easy and bright as a game of Sunday catch."

He underhanded the ball to Hood who bobbled the thing, then dropped it.

"Come on," said Johnny, "come on." He whirled and

jabbed Hood lightly in the gut. "Never mind the butterflies, the bad stomach. You look like the great grandson of Satchel Paige."

Azzy Azzam said, "Amen, amen. That's what I was thinkin', oh yeah. A bloodline to Mr. Paige."

He rose from a stool. A scuffed ball in his right hand, Azzy leaned over as for a sign, a pitcher gauging his catcher, awaiting the flash of fingers—cut fastball, hard slider, curve, change-up. I listened to him jabber about "Mr. Paige, the best pitcher of the previous century, or **any** century," a maverick barred from the Major Leagues till Jackie Robinson and the Brooklyn Dodgers broke the color line. By then Satch was thirty-something, forty-something, but he still had his stuff, a cocktail mix of curves, sliders and cut fastballs that made a hitter woozy. Azzy said to Hood, "He's your great granddaddy, and mine, too, in a way. Old as he was, he whipped hot strikes burning down the heavens. And he and Jackie helped blaze the black byways to the Major Leagues."

Our rookie, still seated, seemed oblivious. He looked around, his eyes vague and confused as though he'd just woke up and was trying to figure out what town he was in and for what reason. "Well, I guess I know a little about Satch," he said. "We've all heard a story or two. A pretty good pitcher even when he was old."

"Good?" said Azzy. "A man whips hot strikes down the heavens and all you can say is **good**?"

Hood blinked.

"Satch threw jiggers of moonlight, curved stars, hot light dipping and rising."

"Okay."

"He's the granddaddy of his team, so he sets up a rocking chair in the Cleveland clubhouse."

"I heard about that."

"Yeah, but did you hear about **this**? Before each game—picture it—Satch hunkers down for a snooze, dreams of how he'll paint the corners of home-plate with Bat Dodgers, Trouble Balls, Jump Balls—you hear me?"

The rookie didn't say boo.

"Sometimes a ballgame's a mirror of what a man believes before he walks to the mound to pitch." He poked Hood's right arm. "You believe you're less than Satch? Somehow less?"

"Well, I'm just..."

"Work on attitude," said Azzy. "Get your head right."

"I'm tryin'."

"You got to remember where you're from."

Azzy, still bent over like a pitcher awaiting a sign, said, "Take the mound for Satch. Take the mound for the blind man who can't see you."

Hood bobbed his head. "All right."

"Take the mound for your mama. Take the mound for Khadijah Jamil."

Hood gnawed on his lower lip.

"Remember," said Azzy. "Nobody we grew up with has enough money to buy a ticket for the World Series."

"I know."

"So pitch like you're throwing life-lines. Pitch for the brother shooting up in a dim hallway, a dead-end tenement."

Spittle hung from Hood's lips. He wiped his mouth. His hand shivered.

"Pitch the game for **him**," said Azzy. "And pitch for whoever's gone to jail, whoever's gone hungry, whoever's died for nothing."

"Pitch," said Hood.

"When you take the mound, your head high, you have one task. Deflect the light that shines on you toward all that's still hidden."

"If I can, sir."

"No, don't sir me. I ain't nobody's boss man."

Old Hood began quaking, his upper body a shiver of muscle.

"My words are yours," said Azzy. "I own nothing and no one."

"All right."

"So pitch the way the Prophet prayed," he said, "or the way Martin prayed. Hold back nothing for tomorrow."

Hood, his eyes clear, sat rod-straight.

"Yeah, you catchin' on," said Azzy. "No one on earth can do anything beautiful unless he's larger than himself."

*

No one on earth who looks like Hood can be beautiful. This was my silent sentiment, but a short while later beauty wore a new wrinkle. Pitching for the pennant, Hood took charge. No weak link in the Cards' line-up, but for six innings he weaved his way through with a cut fastball, a slider, and a change-up that had hitters rising on their toes, tweaking their bats at soft breezes. Each pitch made my blood jump. Hood's body and the ball lines of pure light, wriggling and writhing light, a thing our Cub captains might call a poem. In six innings he fanned eleven batters. Azzy kept reminding him to "pitch for Satch, pitch for everyone—hot strikes burning down the heavens!" The rookie seemed un-hittable. After he struck out Jason Ryder, Jr. the second time I yelled, "Bury 'em, Hoody, bury 'em! Lay these Red Birds in a grave!"

Someone in the stands blared a radio. Mel Torson, the voice of the Cubs, said, "We may be going down to the wire at Wrigley. Still no score, no runner has reached second. Ladies and gentlemen, we're locked in a pitcher's duel, a battle for the pennant: Dantel Hood versus Benjamin Reed."

I ducked into the clubhouse to relieve myself. All our TVs were on, so I muted them and sat on the crapper in silence. The Cubs—they gave me the heebie-jeebies. I'd seen too many sad times, mishaps, mutts in the manger. I remembered a Cub outfielder, Cal Durkey, who lost a routine fly ball in the moon. Cal said the ball seemed to flare away and vanish in strong light. He kept watching the moon and searching for the ball as the latter fell in front of him and bounced by him and three Diamondback base-runners headed for home and Mel Torson cried, "Wake up, Cal! Wake up! Sound the alarm!" Well, he woke as any loser wakes—too late. The bewitched outfielder blamed his bases-loaded blunder on the moon.

Tonight we were tied. If we surprised ourselves, stole the pennant, who would we meet in the Fall Classic? Boston's bums, the Bosox. The club that wins when I'm not on their payroll. Hope frightens me, but so does despair. In a whisper, eyes closed, I said, "Pitch, Dantel, pitch like a demon. Bury these Red Birds in a grave."

Somebody'd left a newspaper in the stall, the *Chicago Tribune*. The headline took up one-fourth of the front page— CUBS AND CARDS IN GAME 7! I riffled through Section A in search of distractions, anything but baseball. The presidential candidates had squared off in their second debate. Khadijah Jamil made a pitch for socialism, though she called it by other names. She wanted to popularize "cooperative systems, decentralization rather than globalization, a coming home to basics. I might be a new name to some of you," she said, "but I'm fifty-eight-years old. I've made it my life's work to serve the needs of communities rather than the strictly capital concerns of an international corporate elite. I don't know any bankers. I know the streets of South Chicago, the streets of D.C., the streets of LA where my brother lives, the streets of Harlem, where I have two sisters. I've seen the poor get poorer and more numerous. I've seen the nation's power gathered in a few fat hands I wouldn't care to shake. I'm not running for president because I like power or politics. I believe genuine human needs and the health of this earth are more holy than profiteering. How long will it take to change course? Dr. King would say, 'Not long, not long.' Nothing can be accomplished in isolation. 'Beloved community'—this was the Dr. King's phrase, but we'll borrow it. It's the only hope we have."

She might as well whistle Dixie to Cal Durkey. She might as well walk with this retired ballplayer hand-in-hand under the moon.

President Trent called her "a Muslim socialist, an outsider who despises her own country, a religious extremist who considers anyone who makes money a sinner." None of this meant beans to me. I browsed the news only to relieve some pressure. I had to wonder if Nick missed me, if anyone missed me. I'd been holed up here for a while.

I emerged from the stall and watched the game on Fox, no sound. Eighth inning now, still scoreless, one out, the Cards with runners at the corners and Jason Ryder Jr. striding to the plate. I found the master remote and flicked the TVs off, then on. Ryder was among the best clutch-hitters in baseball. Fearless, strikingly handsome, the guy had two World Series rings, money up the kazoo, and had long ago earned my hatred. Head down, I closed my eyes for maybe a minute. When I dared to look up the count was three balls, one strike, and Nick was on the mound jawing with Hood.

I knew more or less what the skipper was saying: "Don't challenge him. Nobody challenges Ryder, not even Azzy. Keep the ball down."

But Hood shook his head. The skipper issued an order, it seemed, jabbed a finger in the rookie's chest, but Hood kept

31

shaking his head. I turned the tubes off, counted to twenty, then turned them on. Hood let loose a hummer, a two-seam fastball, and all Ryder could do was snake the ball to Mijango Cruz—double-play, inning over. I gaped and howled and waved my arms. Our clubhouse is a cave, a round shadow beneath the ball yard. Overhead the crowd roared, bellowed, and I could feel the stands and the field tilt and sway, the movements as powerful as earthquakes. I weaved, stumbled, and held out my hands as for the reins of a horse. The sounds overhead quickened, the air thrummed. I waved my cap, put it on backwards, and strained my old man legs to hustle through the clubhouse and back to the dugout. I raised a fist and shouted, "Bury these Red Birds! Bust their backs and bury 'em deep!"

Wrigley Field is an open-air asylum first, a ballpark second. Crowd noise shook the rafters, the beams, the centerfield scoreboard, the brick walls covered with ivy. Dantel Hood, our Dantel, had notched eight scoreless innings against the Cards.

The rest still feels as if it's happening, as if it can't shift into the past and be something called history. In the bottom of the eighth, Cub fans are yapping and caterwauling like rutting animals. They quiet down after Dantel Hood fans on three pitches, then come alive again waving pennants and tossing programs and hats and beer cups when Johnny Stompiano laces a single to center. One out, one on. Jamal Kelsey makes his way to the plate.

Hood, Azzy's protégé, hollers, "Dig in, homey. Base hit for Khadijah and Satch."

Nick and I sit with bowed heads. I glance up to see Jamal take strike one. I mutter, "Don't choke, don't choke," but he lifts the next pitch in the air, an easy play for the right fielder. Two down now, Stompiano on first. Wrigley's pilgrims stand and applaud as Mijango Cruz beelines for the plate.

He steps in the box, digs in, takes a practice swing, and

taps his black bat on the plate. I close my eyes a little while. I hear the ball bang leather and the ump makes a sound like he's been gut-stabbed—"Humph!"—strike one. I stay in my dark till I hear Mijango rip the air. The crowd's screaming like somebody's been murdered, or else done something beautiful. My eyes open just wide enough to find the ball, a white spark skipping over the grass in right field. **Single, clean single.** That's what I'd say if I were announcing this game.

Stompiano cruises to third, and from the rattling roar of this crowd you would think we already won the pennant. Jimmy Lieski coming up, Jimmy bowing his head, forever praying. I'd never say it in public, but this Christer is the biggest choke in baseball. He gives me the creeps, too, the way he quotes Scripture before games: "There was a violent earthquake; the sun turned black as a funeral pall and the moon...red as blood."

The game slows to a dizzy crawl. As Carl Devon, the Red Bird skipper, trudges toward the mound, fans whoop and wail, shout taunts and dares, sassy as hyenas on a hunt. Carl, bent over, septuagenarian, plods through noise and frenzy. He might have an easier time walking head-on through a winter storm blown in off Lake Michigan. When he crabs his way up the mound, I don't know how Benjamin Reed can hear a word. Carl lifts an arm, calls for a left-hander to face Jimmy Lieski. The Cub Christer, for what it's worth, bats from the left side.

"Pinch-hitter," I say to Nick. "Drexel Rountree."

He can't hear me so I shout, "Rountree! Pinch-hitter!"

I give up when my voice wears thin. Nick will stay with Jimmy, his perennial favorite. The worst marriages end in death.

While the new pitcher warms up there's activity in the sky. Police choppers hover over Waveland roofs, dip toward the bleachers in left, then rise some five hundred feet above the centerfield scoreboard. All eyes are on Wrigley, minus mine, which sometimes close. You want an idea of how important this game is? Minutes before it started, the sky still light, a squadron of fighter jets treated us to an air show, a choreography of elegant loops and turns over Wrigley Field. You know something big's underway when they send in the planes. It's like a glimpse of war, but beautiful because those jets are made to bomb other people, not us. Faster than light, louder than thunder—they rule the heavens. I recall in my mind's eye the perfect symmetry of the craft, the bullet-gleam bodies, canted wings, the bright dips and turns and rises through a cloudless sky.

Mayberry, the Red Bird closer, finishes his warm-ups and rubs the ball as if his fingers can soften leather. He's lean, pale, delicate, but his first pitch—strike one—rocks the clock at ninety-six miles an hour.

The runners stray from first and third. Johnny slouches, loose and light, a hand on his hip, a guy without a worry. He has the look of a bum hanging out on a corner, a deadbeat with time to kill. Should someone remind him he's less than ninety feet from home and a Cub lead in Game 7 of the National League Championship Series? I hoot and holler, "Heads up, Johnny! Heads up!" I'm praying for a wild pitch, a pass ball, a hit batter. I'm trying to remember the last time Jimmy Lieski drove in the go-ahead run.

Jesús edges off first till he has a base-stealer's lead. Johnny's hugging third, still slouching, no more animate than a snail. My eyes are at half-mast. I'm thinking Jimmy has Out Number Three stamped on his forehead. If I pay attention, I'll see it. Baseball's mark of the beast.

Mayberry shoots Johnny a glance. He goes into his stretch, then side-arms a bullet to first. Ball and glove crack down on the spine of Jesús. Safe? Out? The ump waits a heartbeat before opening his arms—safe. I blink. I gape at Johnny speed-balling, flying home. The first baseman had turned, craned his neck to see the ump, read the call, and now he's got to pivot, plant his left foot before he can throw. Johnny's a blaze. He arcs and dives, his right hand and then his chest, his legs—all of him—skimming home plate. For what seems like minutes Wrigley Field is silent. Maybe our throats are corked, our hearts stopped, our breaths seared back to our lungs. The throw—high, late—can't catch Johnny. I start choking on a word...**safe, safe**. And now the ump, a black angel, wings his arms wide—**safe!** Johnny jumps to his feet, takes a high five from Lieski, and saunters toward the Cub dugout as if stealing home is an everyday blessing. I hear a voice in my gut, my heart: "Good Lord! Good God Almighty! The Cubs lead! The Cubs lead! The Thief stole home!"

The silence of the ballpark is splintered by shrieks. At first I can't hear myself hollering, only the crowd noise surging and rocking like cracked waves on a beach, like wind blasts and surf and ringing stone, the power of it shunting me up the steps of the dugout and lifting my arms skyward. If I'm out of my mind, I have no complaint. I hold my head and make a sound like an engine, a fighter jet at take-off, a burst of pure noise from a perfect machine. The vibration and the mad hum of machinery rush my throat, my lungs, and I'm ready to rise and soar till Jimmy Lieski pops the ball up to end the inning. Yes, I was right—the Christer had out number three stamped on his forehead. The inning's over, but so be it. We're winning. I wave my arms about, touch my chest, my throat, the sides of my face. Still some baseball left—three outs, three big ones. I start to think about this, gnaw on it: how the pennant can still be lost.

Okay, Hood on the mound. Face scared, cheeks sucked in, sucked dry, probably can't even spit. Grabs the resin bag, tosses it aside, looks in for a sign. The crowd's a blur of blue: Cub jackets, caps, pennants, Cub pilgrims straining forward as from the rail of a ship. Every man I see is standing and shouting. Fathers hoist children in their arms and point to the field and this game that is more than a game, this hallelujah or apocalypse that will mark their lives more profoundly than any praise or beating. I recall a painting of Abraham, the biblical father set to sacrifice his son, his knife long and sharp. I'm seething hot, bright fear. How many times have my teams been sacrificed? The Cubs, the Bosox. How many times? In crucial games, in late innings, any team I'm with offers its throat, paints an X on its jugular, and awaits the inevitable. I sit on the bench, head bowed, eyes glazed. I look up when I hear contact—leather and wood—a lazy pop fly floating down into the sure hands of Jesús Mijango. Azzy, half way up the steps of the dugout, hollers at Hood, "Chin up, homey. Now throw your Bat Dodger, your Trouble Ball. Let's take this game home for Khadijah and Satch."

The next hitter's a foul-ball freak. Works the count to 3-2, fouls back five straight pitches, then pokes a routine fly to Johnny Stompiano. The Thief drifts in and makes a one-handed grab, nonchalant, devil-may-care. He can't hear me but I yell up a storm: "Two hands, Johnny! Two hands! Goddamn!" He looks unflappable, lackadaisical. As if he's strolled out to shag a few flies, or join a pick-up game of softball on a balmy afternoon.

A pressure builds at the base of my skull. The next hitter, Mavis Blanton, has twenty-three homers on the season. My thoughts sing out warnings: "Easy, Dantel, easy...Paint the corners." Blanton takes a strike, lays off an outside pitch, then lifts a high fly along the third-base line. Matt Creighton sidesteps into foul territory. I'm at the rail of the dugout. I'm watching the ball, I'm watching Matt, my heart shooting bullets. The Cub third baseman is some five feet from the wall. Fans, remembering Bartman, lean back, arms folded to their chests, straightjackets invisible. Matt sets himself for the catch. He's there, glove raised, but the ball pops free, falls, and then he kicks it, boots it against the wall. Animal moans, yowls. Forty-two thousand fans squeezing their heads, keeping their brains from spilling. We believe it and we don't believe it. Out number three, a harmless foul fly, popped from Matt's mitt like a Mexican jumping bean. Deafening boos for our third baseman. Snarls and wolf howls. People kicking at themselves and each other, an ugliness brewing up that says the one thing we already know: **This blunder might cost us the pennant.** I try to yell encouragement but I can't, I'm done. I kick the bench. I hold up my hands. This pennant should be ours to celebrate. Cubbies should be storming the field, climbing up each other's back, weeping for joy. Instead there's a mounting pressure in my skull, a pressure that burrows into bone, into layers of cells. Into this thing called **me**, a sort of Grand Central Station for agony and loss.

Blanton works Hood for a walk. Dee Slater steps in, singles up the middle, so the Cards have the tying run on second, the lead run on first, and Juan Ortiz, pinch-hitting for Mayberry, stepping to the plate. I should be discussing the dilemma with Nick. Should we leave Hood in? Get him out? Let him face one more batter? Yogi Berra, the only Yank I was once friends with, said, "If you come to a fork in the road, take it." I look at Nick and shrug. I'm worthless as a three-dollar bill. I'm a scared sack of shit. I'm a lost little lad crying for his momma's titty. If I could whisper to Nick the one thing that is true, would he believe me? I would rush bullets, sacrifice my life, for my Cubs to win this game.

The skipper steps by me and sidles to the mound. He jaws with Hood, pats his right arm, gives the pitchers in the bullpen more time to get ready. Except for our third-baseman, the infielders surround their manager and pitcher as though to shield them. Matt Creighton? Straddling third base, he stares at the sky, opens and closes his glove, and kicks the bag every few seconds.

Nick takes the ball from Hood's hand. I can't see well, but I think he pulled hard to free it from the rookie's grip. I tell myself, "One more out, one more," but my throat slams shut as Paddy Delaney begins his long shuffle from the bullpen to the mound.

I slump against the rail of the dugout. Delaney moves in a special way. He doesn't really run or jog, but sort of skates over the ground, not putting too much weight on his pained feet. Watching from one eye (the other closed on its own), I estimate he'll need three minutes to make his way to the pitcher's mound. Dirk Rouda, hat in hand, remains in the bullpen. Rouda's our closer, a toughie, too dumb for bad nerves. In deep centerfield, Johnny Stompiano hugs his arms to his chest. Even the Kid, Steal Home Johnny, awaits grief and loss, an avalanche of heartbreak. But the crowd crows a thunder of thanks as Hood trots across the infield and into the dugout. I feel the man's heat now, his darkness—a force from which I need a certain distance. I sit on the bench, a bench coach on the bench, as Nick hands the ball and the game to Paddy Delaney. Moments later I stand, slurp water from the fountain, spit it back. My head seems swollen. I feel a pulse in my ears. Why Delaney? Why **him**? His crumby feet, his troubles. His habit of losing. Yet if Nick's lost his mind, who can blame him? He's facing the exact sort of pressure that turns brains into porridge. I sit my bum ass on the bench. I rise and rub my face. I try to shout, "Come on, Paddy!" but my voice won't work. I force myself to watch.

Delaney's first pitch plunks Juan Ortiz in the elbow. I feel a moan rise from my chest, an animal thing, a sound that tells of all things gone wrong, a low ghostly slur that echoes every sound I hear around me. Bags loaded now, Cubs in a jam—no room for mistakes. Nick should yank Delaney before he throws another pitch. I find my voice and holler, "Get him out, go on! What the hell you doing?" I look at Nick and point toward the mound.

Delaney shifts from one pained foot to another, his eyes as bland as those of a cow. I sit for a while with my face near my knees. Nick's beside me, close enough to touch. We're a couple chumps cowered in a corner. I waggle a hand to try to motion him to the mound. "Enough," I say, "put in Rouda," but he shakes his head. I look at him and consider putting an arm around him, holding him and telling him it's okay, win or lose it's okay, but I'm afraid we might come to blows right here in the dugout, grab each other's throat and jugular and whatever else keeps a man breathing. "Why Delaney?" I mutter. "Why? Just give a reason." Nick sure as hell hears me. The crowd's quiet, funereal. Someone over our dugout whispers, "Jesus mercy, Jesus mercy." I lean against Nick and say, "Why Delaney? Any special reason?" He might talk if I put a gun to his head.

I feel him shiver as Paddy lets go of a slider. Ball one to O'Leary, a hair outside. Paddy stoops, rubs his ankles, then wipes his pitching hand on his pant leg. He fires a change-up on the outside corner. He throws the next pitch harder than he's ever thrown, but O'Leary takes it the other way, whip-swings the bat and smokes one on the line to deep right-center. I'm holding my head and thinking double up the alley, triple, clear the bags, but Stompiano lights the field, the length of him fleet as a thrown knife, a lean blade moving in a straight line and then arcing for the blur of the ball, his glove and the white sphere meeting a thumb's width over the grass, the ball snapping leather and the second-base ump rushing toward him and pumping his fist, OUT, OUT! THE BATTER'S OUT! THE BATTER'S OUT! THE CUBS WIN THE PENNANT! Johnny freezes in the position of the Catch. He's stretched flat on his belly, his glove raised, the ball in the web of his glove. He holds the pennant in his glove, and in his chest that brushed home, stole home, and he keeps offering his glove to let the ump see and see again glove and ball, how they met, the great

39

arc of his body and glove and O'Leary's smash converging on one spot of green, one spot of heaven. Have I ever used the word heaven aloud? I doubt it. Nick, who never hugs anyone, hugs **me**. Heaven? No one can stand it for long. You're too damn happy to breathe.

It seems a week sails by before anyone can speak. At last I hear the roar of a radio turned up full volume. Mel Torson, the voice of our team, says, "Cubs win! Cubs win! Cubs win the pennant!" Paddy Delaney is jumping on the mound. Yes, he's jumping, hopping, forgetting about his feet, his chronic pain, decades of accumulated burdens. Matt Creighton lifts him off the ground. Jesús Mijango, arms wide, turns toward Johnny as the latter rises on his knees and waves the gloved ball over his head. I rear back and holler, "Johnny! Johnny! Hey Johnny!" He stands and turns to acknowledge the fans in the right field bleachers, the left field bleachers, and then the throngs along the third-base line and behind home and on down the right field line and back to the bleachers. He's our King bestowing graces, sharing his bounty, inviting his subjects to flourish. We want his heart, the marrow of his being. We want to kiss him, devour him, drain his blood into our veins. Every pilgrim wants to partake of something numinous, sacred, but what we see in right centerfield is Johnny's buck-toothed grin, his knees bending as he picks up his Cub cap and sets it on his head backwards. The puzzling thing is he seems ordinary. A kid with his ball and glove, his hat, his uniform. He doesn't yet know we would follow him off a cliff.

The lines of club-wielding cops and guardsmen have no chance securing this field. The first wave of pilgrims surges over the walls, then the second wave, the third, the fourth, and I am paralyzed by awe. While most fans are content to run around and holler, others create odd highlights. A white-haired lady who'd brought a bag lunch tosses chicken bones in the air. A Roman

Catholic priest, or somebody dressed as one, slides into second base and calls, "Safe! Safe! Safe by a mile!" A cripple hobbles around the pitcher's mound. He lights a book of matches, then another, and tosses fire toward home plate. The skipper squeezes my arm. He starts telling me why he called on Delaney in the ninth, but all I can make out is, "A hunch, a weird feeling." A woman older than I am comes down the steps of the dugout, crosses herself, then folds her hands to her chest.

I can barely move. I can barely breathe. I'm afraid people are so happy they'll lose their heads, beat each other up, burn down Chicago, tear Johnny Stompiano limb from limb. Two kids storm down the steps and shove me against Nick. He's blubbering, so am I, but I gather my strength and blurt my hosannas. "Catch of a lifetime! The Thief wanted that ball. Had to have it. Hijacked the pennant!" A woozy light encircles the field, a softness and warmth like a halo. I look out toward Waveland Avenue, a rooftop poem half way to heaven:

I BELIEVE A LEAF OF GRASS IS NO LESS
THAN THE JOURNEYWORK OF THE STARS

THE FRIENDLY CONFINES

"I hear a rumor," says Stompiano. "I hear the Bosox got bragging rights over in the American, earned themselves an appointment at Wrigley." He shrugs. "Well, then, mark your calendars, circle the date—October 27th, Wrigley Field." He tilts his head to imitate a thinking man. "I can't say for sure I'll steal home again, race lightnin' and win." Maybe a hundred cameras catch his wink. "Lightnin' might not show up," he says. "Lightnin' wants nothing to do with me."

Hail to Chicago's Royal Highness, our crowned King. Twenty-eight years old if I remember right, but with the mien of a teenage boy. He calls to mind the spit and sass and vinegar of memorable misfits: Braggo Roth, Rube Waddell, Noodles Hahn, Boys of Summer of the early twentieth century. He abides by no rules, except those he conjures for himself.

So bathe him in light, surround him with news hawks in this post-game clubhouse of high drama. "Hey," he says, and it's as if a great bell rang away some of the sadness of the world.

Jesús Mijango uncorks a bottle of champagne, aims a geyser at Johnny, then sprinkles some on Dantel Hood's kinky hair. Azzy rubs a paw over Hood's right shoulder. "Meet the man on the mound," he says, "the man who pitched us to the World Series."

Old Hood smiles a mile, big yellow teeth.

"Great grandson to Satchel Paige," says Azzy. "Winding up and throwing Bat Dodgers, Trouble Balls, one after the other."

Jesús says, "Nobody hits a Trouble Ball."

Johnny wings his arms through the air. "Whoosh! Strike three! Siddown. Shaddup. As Hawk Harrelson used to say, 'Sorry, Sam. Grab some bench.'"

Clubhouse TVs provide a bird's eye view of Wrigleyville: streets crammed with people, abandoned cars, apartment windows lit like Christmas, scores of pilgrims gathered on rooftops. Red lights mark the entrances and exits of Wrigley Field. Cops and firemen rush to douse a bonfire at Clark and Addison. Three guys in Cub caps get turned around, cuffed, shoved in a paddy wagon. The police have trouble driving off because rowdies stand in front of their vehicle with signs—THANK YOU JOHNNY! LOVE YOU DANTEL! I see an old man crying, his face in his hands. I see a black boy spread his arms and spin, spin, his face lifted to the sky.

Jimmy Lieski blurts, "Cu-Cu-Cubs win!"

Matt Creighton shakes his head and slumps in a chair near his locker. "No thanks to me," he says. "I did everything wrong."

*

11:20. I'm sitting on a stool between Jimmy Lieski and Matt Creighton when representatives of ballpark security and the Chicago Police tell us it's still too dangerous to leave the clubhouse. By now the press has vanished, we've taken our showers, changed into street clothes, and have begun to feel a tad edgy. In 2016, when the Cubs became world champions, Chicagoans surprised themselves and behaved, so what's with all the precautions?

Security won't tell us anything, except that it's best to stay put.

Old Jimmy asks who first described Wrigley Field as The Friendly Confines. The question is rhetorical, so I let Matt Creighton answer: "Ernie Banks, Mr. Cub." I tremble at the phrase—Friendly Confines—for what it suggests. A smile and a straightjacket. A wink and a scream. I give Matt a glance, then Jimmy. "Maybe you can spare me the Cub lore," I say. "Let's call Wrigley Field the home of the Cubs."

A moment later we discover Johnny Stompiano is gone. No one saw him leave, but he must have stole his way out of Wrigley Field soon after security officials issued their warning. I suppose the Kid donned a hat, sunglasses, and chameleoned his way into the crowd beyond the players' gate. I say, "Well, the Thief stole home again. Is anyone surprised?"

No one is.

"Goddamn," says Nick. "They should band him the way they band a wild bird."

Johnny's glove is behind him on a stool. An old Wilson, oiled and dark brown, a leathery map of wrinkles. Wouldn't surprise me if the Kid's been using this rag since Little League. I sidle in, grab the old mitt, and sniff the leather. No flower smells better than this.

*

Midnight. The skipper stands and is weaving a bit. "No hurry getting home, right? Fans could be raising hell, setting cars on fire, causing a ruckus. Security has given me the low-down. Play it safe, play it smart. Don't get mixed up with a bunch of goons."

So we hit the booze and watch the tube. I let out a cheer as they give us the last play of the ballgame. Old Paddy Delaney rearing back, throwing with all he's got and then some; O'Leary spanking the daylights out of the ball, drilling it on the line to deep right center. My head jerks when I see for the second time Johnny's sheer, stark speed. A blur as bright as a bullet, a perfect projectile. A muzzle flash lighting across the field.

After commercials, ten minutes or more, a Homeland Security official asks that "we remain vigilant and report suspicious activity to the proper authorities." Daily, and in dreams, we hear these words any number of times, but tonight they arrive with a footnote. The official, who is older than I am, adds that the Chicago Cubs won the National League crown. I wait for him to say something gracious, congratulatory, but instead he urges "all Chicagoans, in **all** neighborhoods—north, south, east, and west— to avoid crowds and celebrate indoors."

Why the hell all the worry? Nobody's raging, setting buildings on fire, blowing things up. I suppose the whole world's on alert, but little is happening. We know from TV that no bombs have gone off in Chicago or elsewhere. In asking us to hole up in the clubhouse till the streets are clear, park security and other authorities are erring on the side of safety. I'm outwardly calm, inwardly churning. Is this a celebration? Is this a party? We took the pennant from the Cards, literally stole it, only to be cooped like chickens in a clubhouse cave.

TV sucks at our eyes the way magnets suck metal. We're all watching now, even Jesús and Azzy. The Chief of Police, Dick Kowalsik, is giving his spiel. How we need to cooperate, how security is everyone's issue. Is this a public service announcement? If so, someone would do a service by stuffing a rag down the Chief's gullet. Every Tom, Dick, and Harry already knows Chicago and every other city is under surveillance. The authorities—let me tell you—have every gizmo the imagination can conjure. They aim an eye at every nook and cranny in the world.

A few nights ago I couldn't sleep. I watched a special on UAVs, Unmanned Aerial Vehicles, these contraptions that hover

over our cities to protect us from harm around the clock. We can't see what sees us, these hawks in the wild blue, watching and recording. They can, if those monitoring them wish, count the freckles on a girl's face as she walks east on Waveland Avenue. They can see the walkway beneath her shoes as she lifts her feet. In the same instant, they can zoom in on a madman palavering with his pecker. The cameras have catchy names like Global Eye. The UAVs on which they are mounted can, and usually are, programmed to rise above bad weather. The recording of data never ceases. The cameras house sensitive apparatus—radar waves, antenna—to shoot through blizzards, torrents of rain, sleet, dense fog, even foliage. They can map the ground beneath groves of dark trees. They can send an alert should anyone, animal or human, lurk or cower, or glance over his shoulder. Innovation is endless. Our legacy may be in the cameras that film every shadow and light beyond the time when human beings exist.

Chief Kowalsik congratulates "Nick Glouser and his champions, the Chicago Cubs."

"Sing it sweet," says Azzy.

"I'm pleased to report post-game festivities have remained civil, but let us pray they remain so." He squares his shoulders as the camera glides in for a close-up. "In two days, we'll open the gates at Wrigley Field when the Cubs face the Red Sox."

A cheer goes up in the clubhouse.

"As your Chief of Police, it is my duty to remind you that every fan is a patriot, a lover of God and country. Let this be the greatest, most unforgettable year in the history of our Game."

Who knows why we keep listening. Talking about our Game is not our Game. Spit and sass, dirt and grass, this is baseball. If you catch a ball, what happens? You feel the truth of it in your palm. If you throw, you feel the blood rush to your arm, your hand. If the ball moves fast, you hear the path it cuts through bright air. Baseball, baseball. What else is true anymore? Daily, I watch the tube, let it take every free moment, a watcher hooked on watching. Game shows, talk shows, sports, news, sit-coms, whatever. Only when I'm at Wrigley, near the field, the world takes a shape I believe. When Johnny steals a base, dives, muddies his jersey, I want to touch him. When Jesús lifts one toward the ivy and beyond, when he circles the bases, his body and the arc of the ball drive every last cell from Limbo. If I could live in the open air near the field, would I be happy? No, in close games neurosis sets in, fear of humiliation. My mind—what is left of it—teeters at the edge of a cliff.

Time passes. After the Chief paves the way to a Marine Corps commercial, Jimmy Lieski opens his Bible and reads in whispers. Matt Creighton is on his cell phone, probably talking with his mother. Azzy looks around and says, "Well, you guys can hang here till the sun comes up. I'm goin' home."

Jesús Mijango says, "Me too."

Dantel Hood gets up from a chair. "Long night," he says. "I'm more weary than Satch ever was."

Nick says, "Stay put. You can sack out in the trainer's room."

"No, thanks."

"Well, who's for another round of drinks? Security might not flash the green light till the last of the wee hours."

"They can flash it for themselves," says Azzy. "I'll be home by then."

"**Home**?" says Nick. "And what if you get trampled along the way? What if Stompiano got himself trampled?"

Jesús shakes his head. "**Olvídalo**."

"It could happen," says Nick. "You know it."

"Not to him."

"Oh? And what's Wild Child made of? Steel?" He tries

to stare down Jesús, then Azzy, then me, and succeeds with the latter. "Damn it," he says. "Let's hope Stompiano's not a piece of hamburger lying on the street."

My job, first and foremost, is to support the skipper. I say there's no hurry going home. We got booze. We got TV. We got everything we need.

Jesús, standing, raises his voice a notch. "I live nine blocks away," he says. "I got sofa space, floor-space. **Bienvenidos a todos.**"

"Nine blocks?" says Nick. "You ready to jump over how many thousand Cub fans? How many buildings?"

"**Millones.**"

"Well, I thought you were smarter than this, I was **sure** of it." In private, Nick says Jesús is dumb and dark as a Gullah nigger. "The trouble is, I can't keep you here, and maybe Security can't either." He shrugs. "The best I can do is air my concerns and hope no one gets hurt."

Commercials give way to Wrigleyville live, thousands of pilgrims still surrounding their beloved ballpark. The cameras zero in on a guy about foaming at the mouth. You don't have to be a skilled lip-reader to know what the lunatic is hollering: "Cubs! Cubs! Cubs!"

The skipper points to the large TV at the south end of the clubhouse. "Take a long look," he says. "Is this what you're ready to deal with? A world gone mad?"

Azzy's already at the door.

"I can't stop you," says Nick, "but I can warn you. Why not wait for Security to flash the green light?"

Creighton, his eyes on TV, an ear to his cell phone, says, "It's bad out there, believe me. It's way worse than it looks. I'm talking with a lady who lives a half mile from the ballpark. She says the chaos is ten times worse than what we see on TV."

Most players ignore him. Within minutes everyone has flown the coop except Creighton, Lieski, Delaney, the coaching staff, the trainers, the security personnel, the clubhouse manager, the chumps who stay. We chat and drink, watch the tube, but I feel a major depression coming on. Why can't I leave? Why can't I push myself up from a stool and place one foot in front of the other? It pains me to look at us, to hear us. Matt Creighton whispering his woes to a cell phone. Jimmy Lieski reading from the Bible, rubbing our noses in failure: "Babylon the great is fallen, fallen, and has become a dwelling place for demons, a prison for every foul spirit, and a cage for every unclean and hated bird!"

He describes well those of us who remain.

*

A long hour later Matt says, "It's a mob out there, a mob. Perfect for a suicide bomber."

Jimmy says, "And I saw the dead..."

*

Depression is often described as a veil or cloud, but it's more like a wall or an avalanche, a weight that restricts movement. On a given day, I manage to breathe a little, move a little, and call it a life. A few hours ago we stole the pennant from the Cardinals, but the heroics of Game 7 seem long over. If Security advises us to camp out in the clubhouse till tomorrow noon, we will oblige. We are remnants of old-time Cubs, legends of loss. Stuck in The Friendly Confines with no way to go home.

I wonder where Johnny is, what he's doing. I try to imagine a body as fleet as a thrown knife. Or as bright as a bullet blazing across a field.

ORPHANS

At 3:20 a.m., cops and security guards led us toward a fleet of limos in the staff parking lot off Waveland Avenue. Between ourselves and our fans, we still had a barrier, a chain-link fence about six feet high. News crews had been allowed inside to film the exodus of champions. Eyes down, shoulders bunched, I felt less heroic than some chump on the late-night news staggering out of jail, blinking at cameras. I saw myself as a loser because I was a loser. Any man with a morsel of moxie was already free.

Cubs sidled out two-by-two. Plagued with worry, Nick had organized a buddy system so we could help each other if pilgrims stormed the fences. Now, as when the field was mobbed after Johnny made the Catch, the fear was that boisterous fans would overwhelm Security and crush their heroes with embraces. Well, the mood on the streets was celebratory, but I saw no sign of danger. Pilgrims on Waveland Avenue chanted, "Beat the Bosox! Bury the Bosox!" I somehow managed to wave to the fanatics. Those familiar with depression know the condition sometimes seems to bear weight, corporeal substance. A pudgy paw can be as cumbersome as a corpse.

I was teamed up with Paddy Delaney. In case of a riot, we were to fend for each other, an ancient coach and an ancient player. As we neared the open door of a limo, he grabbed my arm and said, "Hold on, coach. Why go home? These people love us."

Love? He was talking to **me**?

"Come on," he said. "Let's get some air in our lungs. We've been holed up half the night."

Security tried to shoo us in the limo, but Paddy—me in tow—moved toward the street. "Use it or lose it," he said. "If we can't survive a few minutes, call the morticians."

I asked about his feet.

"What's to say? I'm walking on wounds."

"Then maybe—"

"Hell with maybe. I can hobble around the block."

A security official tried to dissuade us. Sure, the streets looked safe, the calm before the storm, but they might erupt—the whole town might erupt—at any moment. He painted the predicament in black and white. Thousands of crazies clogged the streets. Sane fans had gone home. What remained were the jackals, the rummies, the wolves. The most serious threat was a stampede. All it took was one lunatic getting roused up, swept away by hysteria. "You think I'm kidding," said the official, "but I've seen it—the power of one." He smacked his hands together. "One madman bumps another, the other bumps back. Fists fly, then more. People smell blood. Pretty soon you've got loonies smashing into each other, causing pile-ups, suffocations. I've seen this happen at a bar."

Paddy said, "This ain't a bar."

"Yeah, but—"

"What am I? Three years old? Afraid I'll pull a plastic bag over my head and suffocate?"

"Sir, the other concern is terrorism. Any time. Any place. Here. There. Everywhere."

Paddy shrugged. "Fuck the terr'ists. If we curl in a shell, too scared to move, we let the bastards win."

He nudged me in the ribs. "You with me, Billy? Walk out of here on our own steam?"

"I don't know."

He yanked my arm. "Come on," he said. "We'll salute this old ball-yard, hobble around the block, then call a cab."

The rest of the team left Wrigley Field in limousines. I suppose the vehicles were bulletproof, soundproof. No one could look in through the tinted windows. Each Cub was like a prize nut tucked safely in a shell.

Paddy said it might bring good fortune to walk clockwise around the ballpark. What baseball man isn't superstitious? "Clockwise for luck," he said. "Let's see how far we can stretch our luck."

The streets were calmer than what clubhouse TVs had suggested. Most fans were milling about as though they had no place to go, nowhere called home. At Sheffield and Addison, two boys hunched near a fire. A few twigs, scraps of paper, barely enough to warm the hands. The oldest, a brown boy, tucked a baseball glove beneath his left arm. Squatting, he rubbed his hands and held them near the fire. Three drunks chanted, "Cub pennant! Cub World Series!" as the boy tended the flames. He leaned in to take the warmth on his face.

The wee one, a white boy, raised his hands, and he too leaned toward the fire. I'm an old man, a spectator of the world, and an addict of the nightly news. Long before these boys were born I'd witnessed countless conflagrations, televised disasters, but when had I last seen the faces of human beings near the beauty of fire? The boys seemed oblivious to the drunks, the revelers. Their silence and small circle of shared light made a sanctum amid the crowd.

Paddy said, "Cub scouts up past their bedtime, huh?"

"They might be homeless."

"I doubt it."

I looked at them.

"West side's got the homeless," said Paddy. "South Side, too."

They remained calm as monks. After Game 7, win or lose, authorities feared that fans would build bonfires at major intersections, set a few buildings ablaze, turn over cars, loot stores, smash windows, dance in the debris of Cub joy or Cub sorrow. Thus far, however, nothing significant had happened. Just a bunch of fans wandering around like cows who had lost their bells. Now and then someone hollered, but with glee rather than menace. A teenager standing between me and the boys predicted that Johnny would steal the World Series, steal the Bosox blind. "That'll tell half the story," he said, "the Bosox struck blind. And the other half is that Jesús Mijango will hammer a homer every game."

I edged by him to be near the boys. Paddy, limping, sidled up beside me. "Feets are tired," he said. "Post-mortem."

"Call a cab."

"They can't get in here. I might have to walk half a mile before the crowd thins out."

"Ask Cub fans to carry you. Tell them you're on the team."

"Well, that's easy to say, but nobody will recognize me out of uniform."

"That puts you a notch or two above me. In or out of uniform, I'm anonymous."

"Yeah, but you're a champion, coach. No reason to hang your head on a night like tonight."

I lifted my head a little.

"Chin up," said Paddy. "No slouching."

"Okay."

"And be grateful you're not a gimp."

So Paddy shuffled away and left me with the boys. I wondered if they were motherless, fatherless, but they appeared complete, undiminished by loss. Still drunk, I said to myself, "Billy, you stand in the presence of the Huck Finn and Tom Sawyer of the 21st century." One white boy, one brown: a new Huck and Tom. They had neither raft nor river—who did anymore? But there remained the pleasure of a late-night fire built against the curb.

Law enforcement officials formed a cordon to prevent fans from approaching shuttered businesses on Addison Street. Three cops peeled off from a long line, their dark hats bobbing over the heads of pilgrims. A fire of any size would have been detected and reported at once. Cameras, computers—do they vie with light in contests of speed? Transmissions are instantaneous, but those monitoring them may have potbellies and legs made for waddling rather than running. "Police," I whispered to the boys. "Put out the fire."

The tall one smacked the flames dead with his mitt. The boys slipped into the crowd, anonymous, and so did I. Three cops, too thickset to move with ease, arrived late. I snickered and said to myself, "We ditched them! Let them sniff the ash!"

The police stood some twenty feet away. The stoutest cop, breathing hard, bent over his smart phone. I suppose he was surveying the street, seeing it from above, or from different angles, on a screen the size of his palm. He said, "Anyone seen two boys? The punks who started a fire here?"

Silence.

The cop still hadn't looked up from his phone. "Well, say something if anyone so much as lights a match to warm his hands.

You hear me?"

The teenager who spoke of Johnny stealing the Bosox blind said he would.

"Don't hesitate," said the cop. "One errant spark might be all it takes to burn this neighborhood to the ground."

Before the cops moved off, the stout one recorded a message on his computer: "Refer to case WF764 if need be; out for now."

The boys were beyond worry. They were too young to know how common it was to be hauled in days, weeks, or even months beyond the time when a crime was committed. Minutes ago, cameras and computers, hardware and software, had highlighted their faces, scanned their retinas, established their identities. If they lived in a home or a shelter, a cop could appear at their door tomorrow or next week or whenever the Czars of Security issued a warrant. The authorities would ignore a case this trivial, but they had a verdict if they wanted one—guilty. In a court of law, surveillance evidence is the near equivalent of blood, spittle, semen. DNA.

A common man may have uncommon wounds, a source of originality. I sometimes fear that our world is already dead. What is life? Have we driven it to the last corner? Can it flee our grasp? I am, in a word—predictable—as are most men, as were the Cubs tonight till Johnny stole home. But what might I steal? A friendship with boys? A memory of childhood? Johnny would say, "Shuffle the cards, include the jokers." I long to be less obedient than a well-oiled machine.

I followed the boys as they drifted with the crowd. A stalker? No, not at all. I couldn't have stated my goal, but I can state it now: I was attempting to salvage a fragment of my life.

"Boys," I called, "wait up. The cops are gone."

They turned.

"You ditched them," I crowed. "You made them dizzy."

The wee one consulted the tall one with a glance.

"Relax," I said. "You're out of the woods."

But they were afraid of me. Once, when I was four or five, I saw a deer at night when lightning struck a nearby tree. I'd never seen a wild animal up close, and I remember her better than the face of my father. The gleam of her eyes as bright as the rush of light that broke limbs. The way she bounded past me, leaped. And the tall tree that swayed in a swath of light before it thundered to earth at the fringe of a forest. The deer vanished, the storm, too. Lightning spent itself in one burst before yielding to darkness. All things turned black, black—the trees still upright, the tall grass near my father's tent, my body that grew wider and wider as the night let me in. My father broke the spell by talking about baseball, the Cubs, the Sox—who was worse? I've always longed to return to the night, the darkness. I've never known anyone who would understand this wish.

Worried the boys would see me as a scamp, some rotter trying to hit on them, I played my aces. I took out my photo ID, the one that identifies me as the bench coach and gets me in the ballpark. "Here," I said, "look. I'm a Cub." I wondered if Delaney, limping along on ruined feet, had the presence of mind to show his ID and inspire fans to carry him on their shoulders. Suffering flirts with madness when there's no sacrifice, no noble cause to explain it, when it claims us only because we are strange and lost and human. Delaney may fail to understand this, but he lives it. Showing my ID to two boys was a gross but necessary act.

They didn't recognize me, and why should they? I'm florid from drink, wrinkled. Hefty around the middle. Beady-eyed. Bald as a snake. More or less interchangeable with several coaches of forgettable teams.

I tried to smile. "The name's Donachio, but call me Billy."

"Bench coach?" said the tall boy.

"You bet."

He hesitated. "Sir, I'm not sure we've seen you before."

"Maybe you saw me but don't remember."

"When?"

"At a game," I snapped, "**any** game. But a bench coach stays on the bench."

I suppose I hung my head now. During a game, I am, at best, a shadow in the dugout. No more memorable than dust.

"You've seen Nick Glouser, right? The Cub skipper?"

"Every game, sir."

"Well, I'm his main man, his number-one coach. Sometimes we're on camera when they zoom in on the bench."

The wee one said, "I've seen you, sir. You sit near the manager."

I almost clapped my hands. "That's right!"

"You always look worried when the score is close."

Well, this lowered my sails, but at least he knew me. His face glowed. He said to the tall one, "Sam! Sam! This man is on the team!"

A while later Sam was pumping my hand. I asked the wee one his name and he said, "Jackie, Jackie Moriarty." He was maybe nine years old, Sam was twelve or so, and they kept smiling till I had to smile back. This was medicine. This was better than a session with a shrink, a round or two of Zoloft. I felt as if I'd lost a few pounds, shed some baggage. I climbed a little ways out of the dumps.

I showed the boys the Harry Caray statue near the corner of Waveland and Sheffield, but they'd already seen it "a million times." They wanted to know about the players, especially Johnny—what was he like in person? "Well, he's a ham," I said, "never shy of the limelight. And he happens to be the best base-runner since Cool Papa Bell."

They'd never heard of Cool Papa, so I told them he was the fastest man to ever run the base paths. "Played before our time," I said, "in the old Negro Leagues. You know of Satchel Paige?"

Sam nodded.

"He said Cool was so fast he could turn out the light and jump in bed before the room got dark."

Sam waved a hand. "But Johnny's faster. He stole home."

"So did Papa."

"Not like Johnny. Two outs in the eighth inning. Championship Series."

"Well—"

"Seventh game," said the boy. "Zero-zero score. You saw it."

"I did."

"How's anyone faster? How?"

"I don't know."

"If you blinked, you saw nothing. You missed it."

"That fast?"

His hands arced in front of him. "**There**," he said. "Faster than electric light."

Jackie said he didn't blink. "I saw him," he said. "Johnny dove head-first and the dust came up." He spread his arms wide. "Safe, stole home, and dust all over. Johnny's so fast he blew up all the dust."

Sam told me they viewed the game on TV. I'd guessed as much, for where would they get money for tickets? "You ever been inside Wrigley?" I asked. "Anyone treat you?"

Jackie shook his head. "Not yet, sir. We've never been in the park."

Sam told me they watched the Cubs from the streets, Sheffield or Waveland. Minutes before game-time, an old man on Waveland always set a TV on his steps, and a college girl on

Sheffield brought out a wide-screen computer. "Between innings," he said, "sometimes Jackie and me wander from one to the other. We were on Waveland once when Jesús Mijango hit a homer in the thirteenth inning. The ball almost hit the TV, then bounced up the steps and back to the street. The Cubs won 7-6, beat the Pirates. They always get lucky when Jackie and me are here."

Luck, the breaks. These words tell us more about the Game than all the great baseball books heaped together. I asked these urchins if they'd heard of Charles Victor Faust of the old New York Giants. Jackie thought he was a base-thief, but I said, "No, he fancied himself a pitcher."

"Was he good?" said Sam.

"The worst arm in history," I said, "Charles Victor. No one gave him a contract, he wasn't a real player, but that's not the story." I stooped to Sam's height. "Let me put it this way: Charlie was made of luck."

Early in the 1911 season, the Giants were in St. Louis. Charles Victor Faust, a fan, came out on the field during practice to inform John J. McGraw, the Giants' manager, that his club would win the pennant if he was allowed to pitch. Faust told McGraw he'd seen a fortune-teller in Kansas. "A clear sign," he said. "I need to take the mound for the Giants to win the pennant." A proper man of his day, Faust wore long coattails and a top hat. McGraw, as superstitious as any manager, said, "Well, let's see what you've got. Come on." The Giants' skipper grabbed a ball and two gloves and let Faust show his stuff. The guy's arm was so feeble McGraw soon caught him barehanded. He let Faust join the team, though, because maybe the fortune-teller was right.

I spun this story to the boys and then I posed a question: "Who won the National League pennant in 1911? Make a guess."

Jackie smiled. "The Cubs?"

"The Giants," said Sam. "The New York Giants."

"That's right, kid, thanks to Charles Victor Faust. Who needs talent when you have luck?"

I amused them with my imitation of Faust's pitching style. The old haunt would wind up like a windmill in a storm, his gangly arms whirling over his head, then down to his knees, black coattails flapping. Yes, he'd wind and wind, and finally let loose a pitch so slow you might study the stitching on the ball, read the trademark. Faust took the mound twice in 1911. In subsequent years—1912, 1913—he supplied luck and charm and the Giants kept winning pennants. I told the boys all this, but kept other thoughts private. Nowadays where are our fortune-tellers? Our diviners? Our spooks? Our wild men? I can claim that certain Cubs will never be tamed (you'll understand later), but most of us cower in corners, chased by the hard glare of a new century. Is there a light for every shadow? If not, will there be one soon? Only in baseball can a man still relish old stories and create new ones. The Game, which is now part of three centuries, has changed little since its inaugural year in 1876.

The Giants finished in last place in 1914. What happened to Faust? He got committed to a mental institution before spring training began, and died a year later of pulmonary tuberculosis. I know all about graves, cellar dwellers, haunts. But I made no mention of 1914.

I asked Jackie and Sam if they'd like to see a ballgame at Wrigley. "That's if I can scrounge tickets," I said, "a big if. Game 1 of the World Series."

Jackie, dreamy-eyed, peered up at me. Sam, two fingers down his throat, fired a whistle.

"Game 1," I said, "if there's still tickets. All you need to do is be my Charles Victor Faust."

I set the time and place to meet: October 27th, 2:30 p.m., at the southeast corner of Clark and Addison. "Game-time's seven,"

I said. "If I have tickets, you'll be the first ones in the gate."

Sam pounded a fist in his glove. "Call me Charles," he said. "Call me Victor."

"All right."

"And Jackie is Mr. Faust."

If these boys weren't street kids, they were up past their bedtime. "Charles Victor and Mr. Faust," I said, "you better head home now. Your mama's worried."

Sam shook his head.

"So where's home? Should I call a cab?"

Neither boy responded.

"Are you kids orphans? You know Johnny Stompiano's an orphan?"

Sam nodded. "We have a foster mom."

"She's old," said Jackie. "Almost old as you are."

"I see."

"Sixty," he said.

"Or eighty," said Sam. "She goes to bed around nine o'clock."

I found it odd that someone would foster a brown boy and a white boy. They were good kids, though, I could see that much. I didn't ask how often they snuck out of the house.

"You know Stompiano grew up in an orphanage?" I asked.

Sam nodded.

"An orphan from day one," I said. "But he's doing just fine, isn't he?"

Sam said, "A bunch of nuns took care of him till he ran off. He was gone so long they gave him up for dead."

Jackie grinned. "He fooled them."

"There were wild animals near the orphanage," said Sam. "One night he followed three coyotes to a field."

"Don't believe everything you hear."

"I didn't hear it, sir. I read about it."

"Okay."

"He followed three coyotes into a field near St. Mary's. They weren't afraid of him."

I winked. "Why not four?"

"**Three**," he said. "Three's the number."

"All right."

"And they watched over him," said Jackie. "They were his guardians."

"That's right," said Sam. "They lived in a ditch near some cherry trees in Aurora, Illinois."

People believe what they need to believe. Sam said the story about Johnny and the coyotes was "all over the internet." No doubt the boy had consulted various web sites born of imagination. Johnny said this and Johnny said that, but what was true? Well, he did grow up in an orphanage in Aurora, Illinois. The Kid ran away, sure, and enjoyed the adventures. Every time Johnny opens his mouth, though, another rainbow rises beyond the facts and washes the sky with colors. He rainbows so well you can almost see the lost colors of the world.

I said to the boys, "Johnny's the world's most famous orphan, and you're not far behind."

Jackie grinned.

"What about this foster mom? What if she wakes and sees you're gone?"

Sam turned away.

"She'll get mad," said Jackie, "but she won't hit us."

"That's good."

"She's nice," said Sam. "She doesn't hit us even when she should."

I asked if they lived nearby.

"Five miles south," said Sam. "The trains will take us

home."

These boys had spunk to spare. I wanted to venture beyond the Wrigleyville crowd to hail a cab, but they wouldn't let me.

"We've done this I don't know how many times," said Sam. "We'll be home before she wakes."

I had to ask him to speak up before I could hear his request. "Your phone number," he said. "Just so we can call you and make sure you have our tickets for the game."

I gave him my business card—home numbers, work numbers—and I would've given him and Jackie my address had they asked. "Call me," I said, "day or night, rain or shine." Did I have new friends? Did they trust me? I was already afraid they were too good to stay in my life for long.

JESÚS AND A DIAMOND

At 2:20 p.m., ten minutes earlier than scheduled, I met Jackie and Sam at Clark and Addison. The news was bad. I'd emailed the Cubs' ticket agent, the front office, offered three and four times what World Series tickets were worth, but none were available. Internet sales were grand larceny, as much as six thousand dollars for a seat in the bleachers. I promised the boys their day was nigh. "You'll have tickets for tomorrow," I said, "Game 2. The only coaches who got tickets for the opener put in orders before we beat the Cards."

Their eyes, beams of light moments earlier, dulled and darkened as though I'd flipped a switch. I opened a bag and brought out gifts. "Here," I said, "Christmas at Wrigley. Brand new Cub caps." They thanked me three or four times, but when they put on the caps they looked like losers. Jackie mumbled something, then pulled the brim down near his eyes. Sam, scraping the bottom of hope's barrel, said, "No tickets, sir? Nothing for tonight's game?"

"No, but tomorrow you're all set. Two tickets for the World Series."

"Thank you, sir."

"Come on," I said. "You might as well walk with me to the players' gate."

I stood still, though, and so did they, one on each side. We were across the street from Wrigley Field, its façade of cement and steel, its early-bird crowd straining against barriers. The sun beat down through shreds of cloud, but the afternoon had turned cool. A feather of wind seeped under my collar and spread a chill along my spine.

"Tonight I guess you boys will watch the game from the street. Am I right?"

Sam nodded. "Waveland or Sheffield."

"Well, take my advice," I said. "Be sure to duck in some storefront if you need to get warm."

I rubbed my hands.

"Come on," I said. "Let's join the crowd."

Wrigley's faithful, thousands of pilgrims, gathered at ticket booths, gates, will-call windows, and spilled over onto Clark Street. With the boys behind me, in the wake of my shadow, I barged a crooked path to Waveland Avenue and the players' gate. Loud-mouthed vendors hawked team photos, pennants, World Series programs. On this bright day, more than four hours before an ump would holler across the yard—**Play ball!**—pilgrims swarmed like fishes. If I bought mementos for the boys, would they consider me a friend? Don't ask, I thought. Just flash the money. Those vendors suckered me for forty dollars for souvenirs.

I was about to take my leave when a green taxi nosed into the entrance of the staff parking lot. Sam's eyes got big, then Jackie's. Two men had exited the cab.

Jesús Mijango Cruz stood some ten steps away. He held the hand of a man a few years his senior, a black man with a shaved head, a thin moustache, a hoop earring on his left ear. They say

Jesús' beau is a lawyer, imagine that. I'd met this sharpie at a pre-season banquet (in secret I called him Cue Ball), but I had no use for him. What's our world coming to? Just then I was afraid Jesús would hold him, kiss him, so I shouted, "Cruz! Mijango!" my voice an alarm bell. For Jesús and his kind, a kiss would be picayune. A small gesture, a way of saying farewell to his beau before he hurried toward the players' gate. If Jackie and Sam hadn't been with me, I would have tolerated the affront. As it was, a kiss—or even an embrace—seemed beyond what impressionable boys should witness. My shouts distracted Jesús. He turned, let go of his beau's hand, and came forward. Maybe he thought the white boy was in my family. A grandchild, cherub-faced, blue-eyed, with a slight apple-glow to his cheeks.

I met Jesús' smile with a stiff nod.

"Coach," he said. "How's it going?"

I caught a breath. "Fine."

"You look a little out of sync."

Jesús wears clothes the way a panther wears skin. Sleek and tight. No part of him, silk or skin, separate from smooth, hard muscle. Black silk is his preference, with accouterments of gold. Today he wore thin rings on three fingers. A band of gold circled his neck. A gold earring, a crucifix, hung from his left earlobe. The boys stood face-to-face with the Cub Lord, the man and his glory. Of course they'd never seen Jesús except on TV, in his baseball get-up. In person, he's prettier. Why deny it? His face is pockmarked, a bit oily, but somehow feminine. Jesús Mijango Cruz. A great, strutting panther of a queen.

Jackie and Sam echoed each other—"Jesús! Jesús!" The Lord took out a pen, slim and gold, and signed their programs. He shook each boy's hand, but didn't pat either one on the shoulder. Did he sense my concern? His beau still stood some ten paces away. In my mind I worked hard to raise a sky-high wall between these lovers and little boys.

Now a dozen or more fans were hollering at Jesús, so I told him to skedaddle. "No sense signing autographs till the moon goes home. You best get in there and get to work."

Ballplayers do work before games. Jesús, for instance, spends nearly two hours in the weight room, then another hour stretching his muscles. He's a worker, a powerhouse. Four years ago, as a rookie, he was frail as a teenage girl.

He strutted toward the players' gate.

"Hit a homer!" called Sam. "Hit a homer!"

"Two," said Jackie. "Hit **two** homers!"

Jesús, at the open gate, turned to us and waved. I began to wave back till he blew a kiss to his beau.

I watched Cue Ball stroll up Waveland Avenue toward Sheffield. I wondered how he fit in Mijango's world. He was short and slim, but walked with a swagger. Who was the husband? Who was the wife? I kept a close eye on him till he vanished in the crowd.

Sam traced a finger over the prize autograph on his program.

"Look," he said. "I thought he'd just dash his initials, but he wrote his whole name—Jesús Mijango Cruz."

I felt nameless, negligible, but I made an effort to sound upbeat. "Tomorrow's your day," I said. "I promise I'll get you in the yard tomorrow."

"Meet you the same time?" said Sam. "Two-thirty?"

"Two-thirty sharp, young man, Clark and Addison." I winked. "And I'll have two prime-time tickets for Charles Victor and Mr. Faust."

*

But I walked away miserable. I soon forgot about Jesús and his beau, for I had a more pressing concern—my life. On a given day, I lacked meaningful human contact. My one pal, Nick Glouser, was a fellow lush and loser. His predictability annoyed me, his inebriated rants, but who else might befriend me? No doubt the boys saw me as a deadbeat. I berated myself for failing to score two tickets for Game 1 of the World Series. The Cubs needed their Charles Victor, so did I. But even then—half-conscious—I knew my boys were larger than luck.

I remembered when I was Jackie's age and summer meant one thing—baseball. At age nine, though largely ignorant of the Game's lexicon, I knew a well-kept field, a sculpture of dirt and grass, white bases and lines, was rightly called a diamond. What other word was precise enough to describe the mound and the beveled dirt and grass of the infield? What other word was shiny enough to describe the outfield grass as bright as fire? My father, among other things, was the groundskeeper of several diamonds in Pekin, Illinois. As his assistant, I learned to take care of a ball field, sculpt the earth American. I lacked understanding, didn't look at a diamond and say, **This land is ours**, but it **was** ours and **is** ours when the eye is clear. Loyal to prescribed forms, guided by my dad, I drew white lines, boxes, and I helped raise the mound where the pitcher stood, the mound and the field the precise shapes of a boy's summer—symmetrical and sensual. I, a budding second baseman, made great efforts to sweep pebbles from the infield dirt. Each well-tended field reveals one thing—love of order—but herein lies the paradox. A batter faces nine players eager to catch what he hits. Once the ball is in play, all things under the sun and moon have permission to happen. A boy may hit a homerun or fall over trying. A thief, a base-stealer, may find his way home. An easy pop fly may bounce from the glove of a talented second baseman. How often is a game won or lost in the span of a moment? My father used to imitate Bill Veeck, a hard-nosed scrapper, who broke down once and muttered—"Baseball is a boy's game that makes grown men cry." My old man never cried, but he sure could moan. About the only time he stayed sober was when we were putting the shine on one of those diamonds in Pekin, Illinois. I'd like to show Jackie and Sam how to do that, get a field ready for players. Maybe I should have been a groundskeeper rather than a coach.

SPLENDOR

World Series

Game 1

Wrigley Field

Line-up Cards

Visiting Boston Red Sox

Home Chicago Cubs

SS Domingo López

CF Johnny Stompiano

RF Kaido Miura

LF Jamal Kelsey

CF Moises de Dios Ovando

2B Jesús Mijango Cruz

3B Bill Murphy

1B Jimmy Lieski

1B Maceo Mason

SS Rey Rodríguez

LF Preston Hollis

C Junior Parker

2B Jay McCreary

RF Terrence Gumbs

C Antonio Chévez

3B Matt Creighton

P Buster Levine

P Porfirio Guevara

First inning, no score.

Buster Levine, the best southpaw since Sandy Koufax, has thrown twelve pitches, eight strikes, but who's dallying toward first with a lead-off walk?—Johnny Stompiano. Levine glares (how'd he foul off all those good pitches?) as the praise of pilgrims wakes the ball yard. Everybody's whooping, calling on Johnny to steal second, steal third, steal home. Buster Levine has learned all he needs to learn about North Chicago: No one is more beloved than a thief.

Stompiano eases into his lead. Wings for arms, bird-like flinches. A sidewise step, another, and he crosses an unseen line to danger. His arms dangle, sway. Firecracker steps, sidewise jitters. Fourth of July. Old as I am, old as sun-faded bricks, rusted beams, I sense the electricity of a runner. The spark-quick muscles, the heat, the longing. I envy this man-child who is born to run.

Levine hurls one in the dirt. The catcher blocks it, but the ball pops free and Johnny dives into second—no throw. Rising, clapping his hands, he hollers at Levine and points to third. The Thief would mess with his mother if he weren't an orphan. Maybe he's telling the Bosox ace to be careful. Maybe he's saying, "Bus', this next pitch is mine. I'm running. How you plan to stop me?" Maybe Bus' can hear him, but all I hear is forty-two thousand fans, each as loony as the other. Over and over I hear one shiny word— "Steal! Steal! Steal!" Every chump from here to Hollywood wants to jump in Johnny's shoes and start running. My legs are cramping. My feet itch. And all I'm doing is sitting on the bench.

Kelsey looks to the dugout for a sign. Nick spits, touches his left ear, his right wrist. Kelsey has the sign to bunt.

The Thief, going on the pitch, is halfway to third when Kelsey lays one down. A slow roller hugs the first base line. The Bosox wait for the ball to roll foul but it teases the line, stays fair. Johnny's well around third when the first baseman pounces. The split second the fielder turns his back to the Thief, pivots to fire to first, I know what's coming. Have mercy on Maceo Mason—he's never played against Johnny. His throw needs a nick of time (a heartbeat) to reach first. Buster, covering the bag, needs a heartbeat to stop bobbling the ball, get a grip, another two beats to wheel and fire, shoot the ball home. Johnny slides by the catcher, snags the plate with his left foot, the slap-tag a heartbeat too late to matter. Nick, his hands in the air, lets out a whoop, a hallelujah. "Jesus H. Christmas! Ring up a run!"

*

Well, a ballgame goes nine innings, sometimes more. We miser that one-run lead till the Bosox seventh when Moises de Dios Ovando jacks a three-run homer into the first row of the left-field bleachers. All night the wind's been blowing in hard, knocking balls down, but it died some to let the ball reach the seats. Inside myself I'm cursing the sky, the elements—everything that's working against us. Does somebody up there like the Bosox? The wind picks up again after Dios Ovando crosses the plate.

Hope is a snare for slow learners. Jesús Mijango Cruz leads off the Cub seventh with a sharp single. Jimmy Lieski steps in, takes strike one, then three balls, each a smidge outside. Buster Levine is muttering in his glove. His next pitch, a hanging curve, splits the heart of the plate—strike two. Nick hollers, "God's sakes, Jimmy, swing the bat. That's what it's for. Use it." The thing to remember about Jimmy is his discipline. If he drives in a run, for instance, he often waits till we're around eight runs up or eight runs down. In close games, no one in professional baseball has a better double-play stroke than Jimmy. For now I'd like to see him hit by a pitch, hurt even. Enough pain that Nick has no choice but to remove him from the game.

But Buster throws the same pitch and Jimmy wheels. This is

a night game, no sunshine, a game for prime-time TV. Nonetheless, I hear the sun—split lightning—in the crack of the bat, the season made whole in an instant, the white blur of a ball arcing for the seats. I'm sure Jimmy's tied the game, his first clutch homer since Abraham spared Isaac, but the wind whips the ball down and Moises de Dios Ovando leaps, slams against the ivy, the ball a foot or so over his glove and off the wall. Moises scrambles as Jimmy and Jesús run, Jimmy a behemoth slogging on the turn around first, Jesús with long, thoroughbred strides and gliding for home. Look at Coach Carnes wind-milling his way up the third base line, a green light for Jesús. The Lord could come in standing but he slides, stirs the dust, and makes this a one-run ballgame. Old Jimmy's hit a double, but how do we bring him home? He weighs maybe two-hundred-and-sixty pounds. He moves like sludge, or someone depressed. I nudge Nick and say, "Put in Rountree, pinch runner. Jimmy's done his job."

Wild cheers, fervent as evangelical prayer, spread out over the ball-yard. I strain to hear the skipper's excuse, something about needing another at-bat from Jimmy in the ninth inning. "Fine," I say, "fine." But in Vegas I'd place one hundred to one odds that Jimmy won't get another big hit before the Seven Seas rise to a boil.

Trevor Doyle, the Bosox skipper, jogs to the mound and that's all for Buster. Pilgrims stand and wave fists and boo their farewells to the best starting pitcher in the American League.

I barely watch as Armando Atecas warms up. He doesn't just flip the ball, but throws diving and flaring bullets even in practice. I notice a police helicopter hovering over the centerfield scoreboard. All Chicago is watching, half the world is watching. I don't want to care about this game, or anything else. Whatever I care about always ends up in the dumps.

The rally sags when a long fly ball is caught in the right-field corner near the warning track. Jimmy tags and lumbers for third. I close one eye, watch him with the other. He slides too soon and halts in a heap three feet from the bag. The throw arrives a gasp later. Double play. Didn't I tell Nick to put in Rountree? He'd be wise to listen to me once in a while.

Well, we never rouse another rally. Mark it up—Bosox 3, Cubs 2. I've been a jinx all my life, so I sort of feel like I'm to blame. I mope around the clubhouse till everyone's gone. I watch three TVs, each on a different channel, but all is trivia. I drown some drinks and give myself a good talking to. "Now goddamn it, Billy, it's just Game One. Baseball is baseball. Anything can happen. Tomorrow's another night."

I'm barely smart enough to know there's something worse than a World Series loss—my life, or what passes for life. Is it a crime to live each day without meaning? Is it wrong to be born if one makes of birth a mockery? I tell myself as much truth as I can stand: "Billy, the world's fucked up and you're fucked up **worse**. You need something larger than a game, larger than a World Series. You need a revival that raises every Lazarus from every wasted pit."

For some time now I've been sitting in a plastic chair. I'd sit longer, sip from a bottle, but I notice a slip of paper on the floor near Stompiano's locker. It takes time and willpower to stand, gather it in, lean on a wall, and awaken a spark of curiosity. The paper—as small as a fortune folded inside a cookie—seems insignificant. When I raise it to my eyes, though, I see green ink, letters well-formed, an elegance no machine or font can duplicate. I read a note not meant for me, but I make it mine, I steal it. Sometimes the strangest thing can soften the edge of night.

Every now and then I have to reread Neruda's "Ode to My Socks" to orient myself to splendor. Johnny, we are alive in language and in our bodies, and who is luckier?

The remedy for the Cubs is as old as time: Winning and losing are dreams; live so deeply that you point toward nothing.

Steal a base for me, steal my heart. Love, Janice

*

Somehow this shoves a sliver of warmth into a corpse. Look. The girl wrote on both sides of the paper. She used it up. I nose about and spot a book in Johnny's locker, *Leaves of Grass*. I slip the note in a pocket and head on home.

A CUB IN CUSTODY

I heard about it around 2 a.m. Wakeful, lying in bed, I was watching a Charlie Chaplin movie when Channel 9 broke for news. The bottom of the screen read—STOMPIANO ARRESTED. For a moment or two the news seemed strange, then not strange in the least. The Boys of Summer, regardless of age, are America's children. As a father tends to open his heart to a troubled child, I open mine to a troubled Cub—Johnny Stompiano. Did he forget he's in the World Series? Should Nick or I have reminded him? I knew the roustabout was no stranger to the police, but I had no idea his criminality harked back to his childhood in Aurora, Illinois.

I switched to Fox News. Gayle Chan, TV's most beautiful late-night broadcaster, highlighted Johnny's arrest record. At fourteen, he pilfered an undisclosed sum of money from a priest, stole a harmonica from a music store, and ran away from St. Mary's Orphanage. Ms. Chan mentioned more serious crimes, including four burglaries. Yes, Stompiano was troubled. His lawlessness as a child was consistent with his lawlessness as an adult.

His teenage mug shot appeared on the screen. Spiked hair,

greasy and black. A devil's nest. Johnny looked like a two-bit punk.

I remembered Janice's note, her use of the word splendor. What did I know of splendor? It vanished soon after it arrived.

Ms. Chan said nothing about Johnny's most recent arrest. His mug shot remained on the screen as she posed two questions: "Who is Johnny Stompiano, and why has he brought to the world of sports a defiance not seen since 1968?"

The Fox camera crew played an old trick. A slow fade blurred Johnny's mug shot, and then he was gone. In his place, fuzzy at first, then microscopic, clear, two blacks stood on a platform, shoeless, fists raised, heads bowed, faces hardened with defiance. For a second I had no idea where Fox found this image. I needed Ms. Chan to remind me of the 1968 Olympics in Mexico City, "the silent gesture" of Tommie Smith and John Carlos, the winners of the gold medal and the bronze medal in the record-breaking dash of two hundred meters. As my head began to clear, then cleared completely, I remembered my own life in that pivotal year.

In the spring of '68, I quit Southern Illinois University before they could boot me out. A few administrators who didn't know me had made the mistake of giving me a baseball scholarship. I did pretty well on the field, but I cut too many classes and soon became "academically ineligible to compete." I was drunk most of the time, and depressed, but then the Cub organization—they didn't know me either—offered me a minor-league contract for eight thousand dollars! I'd never seen such a handsome pile of greenbacks. For a day or two, the depression lifted. My greatest dream was to be a Cub and play at Wrigley Field.

So in the summer of '68, in the minor leagues, I wrenched my shoulder diving into first base. I was laid up almost three weeks, and for part of that stretch I visited my family in Pekin, Illinois.

This was an emotional visit. I remember still the gossip about Tommie Smith and John Carlos, the great runners who became known on my block as "the Olympic niggers." The TV showed their stunt over and over. On the victory stand, as our National Anthem played, these hellions—who would've been heroes—stood shoeless, fists raised, and some say they relinquished their glory forever. My Uncle Lim was enraged, my dad less so, but we all got drunk on my dad's back porch and let out some steam. Lim, who was a sniper in Okinawa and a Purple Heart veteran, wanted "to line those boys up, one in front of the other, and shoot them both through the heart with a single round."

Sure, Lim was nuts, but who wasn't in '68? Now that misspent year once more threw back its shadow. As I stared at the screen, faces dark and unfriendly, I asked myself what Smith and Carlos had to do with a white base-thief, a Cub orphan, a twenty-first century hooligan. Ms. Chan, who seldom let anyone wonder for long, connected miscellaneous dots with a straight line.

Smith and Carlos remained front and center as she outlined the work of current professional athletes and their organization—**Live the Legacy: Tommie Smith, John Carlos, and Muhammad Ali**. Founded by Arshan 'Azzy' Azzam, it now boasted hundreds of members, Stompiano included. The group, comprised mainly of multi-millionaires, purported to fight what Dr. Martin Luther King, Jr. called the giant triplets of racism, militarism, and extreme materialism. Ms. Chan highlighted the irony of the effort. "Although certain members have gone to jail in this fight, they rely on high-priced lawyers to get them out."

I blinked at a full-screen mug shot of Azzy. He's the darkest man I know, but somebody still saw the need to refinish the photo, paint more midnight into his face, and make him mean-looking, too, find the snarl in his lips and the anger in his eyes. Ms. Chan mentioned his arrest the previous winter. Azzy and other athletes,

Stompiano and Mijango included, protested the efforts of private military contractors to "turn illegal aliens into soldiers for the War on Terror." I have a vague memory of the issue at the top of the news one night, gone the next. President Trent, despite numerous threats, had failed to force Mexico to pay for the beautiful wall he'd promised. Thanks to American taxpayers, more border agents had been hired, the wall had been extended, but it wasn't all that beautiful. In the meantime, the president settled on a more ambitious plan. U.S. Detention Centers were overflowing with illegal aliens. The president invoked executive privilege to allow private military contractors to train "male aliens of military age" for the wars in North Africa, the Middle East, and elsewhere. There was a big stink about it, a number of legal challenges, and the issue may eventually reach the Supreme Court. The president insists he has both the authority and the duty to make such a move. His mantra is, "I'm keeping us safe, I'm keeping America safe. That's my first job as your commander-in-chief."

Azzy faded from the screen and Ms. Chan appeared, her hair shiny and smooth, her skin fair, her delicate beauty at odds with all things dark and unruly. She'd teased and tormented me with history, Azzy and Wild Child's run-ins with the law, and she'd connected the dots to implicate other rebels, other times. She offered the news in layers, as if it were a meal with various courses. I wished she'd just come to the point and tell me if Johnny would be available for Game 2, or if—the news would jolt me worse than another war breaking out—he'd spend the World Series in jail.

Ms. Chan wore an earpiece, listened for cues, and proceeded with pauses. "Mr. Stompiano was arrested less than an hour ago. The Cub star, who is twenty-eight years old, has now been arrested twelve times. He has been in police custody as a minor. He has been in police custody as an adult. He is in police custody **now**." She leaned forward. "Tonight, less than an hour ago, he

vandalized a billboard and defaced an image of President Trent."
An apartment complex—it could have been anywhere—now lit
the screen. "On Chicago's North Side," said Ms. Chan, "security
cameras monitored illicit activity on a fire escape above Belmont
Avenue at 1:16 a.m. Mr. Stompiano and his accomplice, Ms. Janice
Oyakawa, were taken into custody minutes later. Our sources have
documented the crime and released this brief segment of film."

I sat up in bed. I didn't care what Johnny was arrested for,
the crime meant nothing. I wanted Ms. Chan to answer **Yes** to
one question—Will he play tomorrow? The crime, as recorded
on high-tech equipment, seemed to have occurred at high noon
on a bright day. At a glance I observed nothing original, a display
of lunacy, a flourish for the absurd. I asked myself the questions
that haunt the century: "What is real? What can we believe? Is
everything a ruse?"

Johnny, in a blue stocking cap, a Cub jacket and jeans,
fastened a rope to a fire escape railing. He clambered over the
rail, grabbed the rope and pulled it toward him, apparently to test
its strength. Janice, in black tights, crouched on the landing with
a paint bucket and brush. Johnny dangled eleven stories off the
ground. His girl dipped the brush, handed it to him, and leaned on
the rail. Her beau, holding the rope with one hand, used the other
to dash a wedge of black paint on a RE-ELECT MICHAEL J.
TRENT billboard. He confined his attention to the space beneath
the president's nose. Swaying, he winked at Janice, lifted one
foot free of the landing, and leaned out a bit farther. Death, the
pavement of an alley, was perhaps one hundred feet below. Johnny,
as lackadaisical as Tom Sawyer painting a picket fence, swished
the brush back and forth, darkened the moustache. His girl lifted
a hand to her throat. She leaned over the rail, called to him, and
then opened her arms as though to catch him should he fall.

The vandal never stopped smiling. A minute later, his work

finished, he climbed back to the landing and lifted his girl in his arms. Janice arched her neck and swooned. When he let her down she groped for the rail, stumbled, a dame dizzy with passion. Right there, I should've known this was 21st century vaudeville. The pranksters had choreographed the show, and rehearsed it, a center-stage arrest before a vigilant nation. Of course they planned to get caught, but I hadn't figured that out yet. One thing from this wasted night has remained lucid: the affection of kisses, the love not even I could deny. High in the air, they kissed three times, a spasm of spontaneity. I said aloud, "Whoa, Johnny," though I never wanted him to stop. A square moustache, a president, an election—who gave a damn? Those kisses were more real than any others I had seen on TV or in life.

They showed the lovers being cuffed in front of the apartment building where they'd committed their crime. Johnny, still smiling, twisted his hands into a thumbs-up position as two cops led him to a car.

*

Ms. Chan returned. She is regal in her beauty, an equal to Johnny's girl, but her voice is asexual, a mild clatter of machinery. My rage, this gut-wrench that can rise in an instant and steal every pleasure, is comprehensible. Each day I speak and hear others speak, but where is meaning? Where do we hide it? Where are words that are true? As I listened to Ms. Chan, I asked myself embarrassing questions: Is my voice an echo of hers? Am I mechanical? Am I broken? Am I worse than dead? There are times when I long to be lashed with a whip, pummeled. Or better, let me be struck by a ball, stung with cowhide. Lord, let me crowd the plate, let Azzy throw. Bring the heat, big boy. Play hardball. Let me open my arms to a pitch flaring hot and bright and in near the heart.

Ms. Chan: "Butch Malecki, the lead spokesperson for the Chicago Cubs, will soon issue a formal statement of apology. Mr. Stompiano and Ms. Oyakawa will be held accountable for their misdeeds. Anonymous sources have informed us, however, that the two will be released on their own recognizance within the next half hour."

My sigh of relief was loud enough for my North Side neighbors to hear. I suppose the authorities had no choice but to let Johnny play ball. He had too many fans, in Illinois and elsewhere. He could scrounge up money for bail, too, however high they set it.[2] A pauper, a nobody, might have rotted in the clink.

When Ms. Chan gave way to Dr. Gaines and Dr. Fuller, African American educators, light-skinned scholars from Liberty University, I should have switched channels. Gaines, who could have passed for white, identified **Live the Legacy** as "a socialist organization with direct ties to Khadijah Jamil." Books, thick and important, heavy with knowledge, formed a wall behind the scholars who sat at a long desk. Up high, the spine of a black book jutted from a shelf, and I bet it was the Bible. But the books were too many to name or wonder about and seemed to extend well beyond the edges of the screen.

Dr. Gaines warned of "a rising tide, a grassroots movement to advance the cause of Islam in our own backyards and among our own citizens."

I winked. If Stompiano's a Muslim, I'm the Virgin Mary. Azzy calls him "Wild Child." Chicago calls him "Steal Home Johnny," or—best of all—"Thief."

Dr. Gaines bemoaned "America's intellectual and moral deficiencies. I'd best put this in simple terms," he said, "because

---

[2] Like I said earlier, the Kid gives away most of his earnings, but he can always rely on Mijango or some other millionaire to go to bat for him.

it is simple. As a nation, we've been addicted to sports since the 1920s, and today we watch nothing more closely than the lives of celebrities on and off the field. A single athlete has the potential to shift public opinion faster than any politician or entrepreneur, or even the heroes who've put their lives on the line to fight for our freedom." He opened his hands, palms up. "Consider some recent history. In 1967, Muhammad Ali refused to participate in a war the United States would have won had a majority of citizens remained strong, vocal, and united. Viet Nam marks the darkest chapter of our history, but today the stakes are higher. It behooves us to wake up before the world as we know it is swept out from beneath our feet."

Dr. Fuller pointed out that Islam, the world's fastest growing religion, "now claims more than 1.6 billion believers. How many will embrace Islam next month," he asked, "or next year? And how many converts will become citizens of the United States? Ms. Jamil, in her bid for the presidency, claims to be an advocate for human and environmental justice, but she is—first and foremost—a Muslim. It is astounding and frightful to imagine this woman as our commander-in-chief."

What in hell were they worried about? The USA wasn't about to send a black Muslim woman to the White House. These doctors were conservative, cautious, taking nothing for granted. Dr. Gaines was right on one score, though: the entire nation—the whole red, white, and blue—is addicted to sports.

*

Nick called minutes later when I was nursing a whiskey.

"Dumb as a Cub," he said, "dumb as swamp mud. That's our centerfielder."

I had to grin. "He out of jail yet?"

"Yeah, I'd say he's on his way home, or let's hope so." He

groaned. "I just got off the phone with the front office. After Game 2, I have to force Johnny to give a public apology."

"Good luck."

"Luck, hell. I'm in charge of telling him what to say: 'I'm sorry, I did a dumb thing. No excuse.'"

"He won't say it."

"Well, he damn well better. Before the game, he'll receive his marching orders."

I kept quiet. I knew what was coming.

"Listen, think you could pull Johnny aside before the game? Talk some sense to him?"

I paused. "Did McPherson or Malecki ask **you** to do it?"

I heard a smacking sound, maybe a hand against his forehead.

"I'd like to help," I said. "If McPherson or Malecki wants me—"

"Screw it," he said, "screw this whole bloody mess. The rummies in the front office think I'm Wild Child's ventriloquist. Here, Johnny, say this, simple shit, nine words. Now shut up, zip it. No comments, no questions. Take a shower."

I sighed. "Well, they don't know the score, but they're not so dumb as to think you can control Johnny."

"Yeah, tell that to Malecki. You should hear the fat bitch. You'd think I was the one who committed the crime."

I didn't know what to say. I listened to the skipper rant, curse the front office, curse Johnny, curse Khadijah Jamil, curse the Democratic Party, and then back around to the front office. "You know how hard it is to manage a team?" he said. "You have any idea?"

"Maybe not."

"Flush the election down the nearest toilet. Who needs it?"

"Nobody."

"You know that Muslim lady's received some death threats?"

"Sure."

"You won't hear me crying if somebody shoots her in the head."

Nobody would shoot her because she had no chance to win the election. I told Nick to get some sleep.

*

Twenty years ago it was less difficult to distinguish what was real from what wasn't. Our nation was peculiar, full of gimmicks and oddities, but we still hadn't reached the point of general paranoia. At the turn of the century, few drones patrolled our skies because we were not, prior to 9/11, afraid of the world. I have known nights when I would trade all precautions for the innocence of a babe. Earlier, I took half an Ambien, and now I downed a full tablet. A saner man would have switched off the tube, but I surfed channels. The news, of course, was the same. Johnny and Janice. A kiss on a fire escape. The inscrutable Asian lifted off her feet. They stopped showing Johnny leaning out from an eleventh-story landing to paint a moustache on Michael J. Trent. The president, with his fondness for late-night tweets and litigation, had probably threatened to sue the networks. The tarnished billboard might have already been removed.

A CNN broadcaster, with no attempt to conceal a smile, said, "A Cub, a Cub in custody." I smiled too, but then I muttered, "You bum, you heartless bastard. Why don't you get a job?"

But he showed the last kiss once more. Hunched over, my back against the bed-board, I found myself blubbering like a babe: "Goddamn you, Stompiano, just give us a rest!" I never saw a man more alive. No wonder they arrested him, and his girl, too, for an excess of splendor. High in the air, at the rail of a fire escape, they kissed, coupled, till any idiot had to admit there was some beauty in this world, maybe even love. My experience is otherwise. My first marriage lasted three weeks. My wife, after she undressed on the night of our wedding, swore on a motel room Bible that the tongue is the strongest muscle of the body. This fact, if it is a fact, seemed irrelevant for us, but perhaps important for others. Johnny and Janice, for instance. Chicago's lovebirds. Reality TV taken to another level. After they vanished from the screen, I turned off the tube and lay in bed. My heart began to race, then petered out and seemed to stop. I opened my eyes to darkness. I said aloud, as if Johnny and his girl could hear me, "Don't grow old, kids," and then I remembered I was always old. My bed felt like a coffin, and was about the right size. A single, of course, but saggy in the middle. I cupped a hand over my mouth to make sure I was breathing. What the hell can you do when life passes you by? I slept, if I slept at all, in a state that passed back and forth between awe and rage.

PHOTOGRAPH

I watched Fox News all morning. Three times, once live, twice on replays, I suffered with Butch Malecki, our three-hundred-pound spokesperson, as he delivered the official Cub apology to—in Butch's words—"a stunned nation." Perhaps our ball club could double as a circus. Fire Escape Johnny could be our high-wire walker or trapeze artist. Nick Glouser could manage a troupe of clowns. Cub coaches and front office personnel could step into a ring and be chased by tigers. Butch, his forehead gleaming with sweat, his voice boyish, said, "All of us associated with the Cubs profoundly regret the lack of respect shown to President Michael J. Trent." A close-up showed bits of food in his moustache, blond crumbs. Who was in charge of editing? Three times Fox showcased Butch's dishevelment as he blurted empty and formal phrases, plus a promise not even God could keep.

"After tonight's game, in a live broadcast, Mr. Stompiano will offer an apology, not only to his teammates and to the great city of Chicago, but to **all** Americans who have watched this travesty unfold on national TV."

*

Jackie and Sam called at around 11 a.m. The older boy wanted to know if Johnny would play tonight.

"He'll play," I said. "If he can stay out of jail till game-time."

"I don't know why they arrested him, sir. Maybe he's innocent."

I didn't say anything.

"Sir, Jackie and me are wondering if you have our tickets. I mean, for tonight's game."

"Well, not yet, but you can stop worrying. I'll pick up your tickets in a few hours. Meet you and your brother at half past two, all right?"

"Clark and Addison, sir? Like we planned?"

"Like we planned."

He went silent a few seconds. "Sir, can I ask one more favor?"

I waited.

"What about the other games? Can Jackie and me get tickets if the Cubs play in Game 6 and Game 7?"

I grinned. "What do you mean **if**?"

"Jackie says we could win four straight and end the Series in Boston. This means we wouldn't play at Wrigley Field till next April."

I chuckled. "We'll see."

"But Jackie and me want seven, Cubs in seven. Johnny'll steal home to win the last one."

I rubbed the stubble on my chin. "Well, maybe I can scrounge some tickets if this whole show hasn't sold out in advance."

"Thanks, Mr. Donachio."

"Now get on down to Clark and Addison at two-thirty sharp. You hear me?"

"We'll be there, sir."

"Call me Coach Billy," I said. "And say a prayer for the Cubs."

*

Jackie and Sam were there when I arrived a few minutes late. They had Cub caps, baseball gloves, and were standing under the bright red marquee—WRIGLEY FIELD, HOME OF THE CHICAGO CUBS. I battle the blues daily, but just then—knowing how much a ballgame meant to them—I could almost imagine I was the grandpa they never had.

They thanked me around twelve times after I gave them their tickets and Game 2 programs. They kept calling me Sir, or Mr. Donachio. I was hoping they'd ask me to autograph the programs, but they didn't. Each boy shook my hand formally before hurrying toward the gates.

*

I was the first one in the clubhouse, so I turned on the TVs. The pundits—I mean buzzards—had spent several hours sharpening their claws and teeth, and now they tried to turn Stompiano into a carcass. He was "a ne'er do well, an anarchist, a misfit, a perennial malcontent." I half agreed and half didn't care.

I made some coffee and moseyed about. The lockers are open, no doors. Spikes on the floor, uniforms hanging. Bat racks above the uniforms. A white envelope was wedged beneath two of Johnny's bats. I remembered the slip of paper I'd found after Game 1, a note from Janice, and of course I wanted another. A small voice—"Whoa, Billy"—couldn't keep me from sidling toward Johnny's locker. Is finding different from stealing? "Well, yes," I told myself, "but which is better?" A desperate man perceives the propriety of each.

I took the envelope, found it unsealed, and opened to a wallet-sized picture of beauty now disturbed.

Janice in a one-piece bathing suit. Modest, almost Victorian, but the silk or cotton was the color of a fever. My nose came within inches of curves, cleavage (not enough), and an open-lipped smile. Behind her a rock loomed, yellowish, twice her height, and above the rock a white cloud. Johnny is a throwback. Every yahoo has a million pictures on his phone, but maybe the best ever taken is on this high-quality paper. I stared at it a long while, then turned it over and found a poem:

Between a rock, a cloud,

a whisper (Te amo),

the beauty of the world.

I knew at once who dashed this in blue ink—Johnny Stompiano. I recognized his writing because I'd seen his autograph many times.

I needed the picture more than he did. That's what I told myself as I found room for it in my wallet. He sees Janice every night, whereas I see no one. I tossed the empty envelope in the garbage. I felt a bit more chipper than when I arrived.

TRICKSTER

World Series

Game 2

Wrigley Field

Line-up Cards

Visiting Boston Red Sox

SS Domingo López
RF Kaido Miura
CF Moises de Dios Ovando
3B Bill Murphy
1B Maceo Mason
LF Preston Hollis
2B Jay McCreary
C Antonio Chévez
P Marty Haskins

Home Chicago Cubs

CF Johnny Stompiano
LF Jamal Kelsey
SS Rey Rodríguez
1B Jimmy Lieski
2B Jesús Mijango Cruz
C Junior Parker
RF Terrence Gumbs
3B Matt Creighton
P Mario Aguas

During batting practice, I stand in the dugout with high-powered binoculars. I know Jackie and Sam are in Row 9 of Section 534, but it takes a long search before I find them. In the far reaches of the upper deck south of right field, the boys tug at a snake of licorice. Sam comes away with the bigger half, but offers it to Jackie. Generosity—the smallest gesture—always takes me by surprise.

*

And Janice is in a box seat four rows behind home plate. No trace of the long night mars her face. She appears alert, dispassionate, a pillar of poise amid roused pilgrims. A bulky black coat shields her from autumn, but a scarf—flimsy, soft red—would match her bathing suit. The stolen picture is my most prized possession. I wouldn't trade it for a stack of hundred-dollar bills.

I employ the glasses with discernment. No peeping Tom wide-eyed at a window, but a master of circumspect glimpses. Janice sits with Isha Azzam, Azzy's wife, her two little girls, plus Jesús Mijango's beau, the one I call Cue Ball, and a wide passel of blacks fanned out in a circle. I recall meeting Isha at a pre-season banquet, a charity event. Her broad smile greeted me, then her warm hand in mine, and she sung out her name before I asked. She's a shade lighter than her husband, as is most of the world, Africa included. I frame her now through shined glass, but I realize I'll never know her when she leans back and laughs, her voice as bright as the flash of her teeth, a belly laugh that makes me feel I'm a million miles away. An instant later Cue Ball joins in, then Janice, and I wish I knew what was funny. Had I heard the joke, would I feign amusement or delight? Would I comprehend some fragment of what they comprehend? I have a hunch they communicate in code, in the vernacular of rebels. I again raise the glasses, zoom in, but who are they? We live in different worlds.

*

I sit on the bench and talk with Nick about the line-up.

"Why you hitting Jesús Mijango fifth? He had three hits in Game 1."

Nick says he knows what he's doing.

Sure, he does. He knows the earth is as flat as a table in a Kansas kitchen. A baseball is square and the Cubs always win.

I step out on the field with the glasses. I scope my orphan boys and try to feel hopeful. Jackie and Sam are up there in the rafters. Maybe they'll bring the luck of Charles Victor Faust.

*

Moises de Dios Ovando slams a slow curve onto Sheffield Avenue for a three-run homer in the first inning. As the ball arcs up and out, a moan follows its flight like the tail of a comet. I moan with forty-two thousand pilgrims. Pausing for breath, I moan some more, then pepper the moans with obscenities. Down three-zip in the first, I anticipate disaster. I tend to apply basic math to glum situations. If the Bosox score three runs every time they come to bat, the final score will be around 27-2.

But the Cubs don't fold. In the second, Junior Parker laces one down the left-field line for a two-run double. In the third, Mario Aguas, the Cub starter, begins to dominate. He and his counterpart, Marty Haskins, establish a snail's pace. They shake off signs, second-guess their catchers, their managers, step off the mound and talk to themselves, second-guess themselves, and the game is still 3-2 in the seventh when Matt Creighton beats out an infield hit and Terrence Gumbs slides home with the tying run. I holler, "That a way, Matty! Better lucky than good! Hell with good!" We need more hits, a big inning, but one run is all the gods give.

Dirk Rouda takes over for Aguas in the eighth. I hurry to

the clubhouse to relieve myself, begin to head back to the dugout, then stay where I am. All our TVs are on. I mute them—the sound unnerves me—and sit in a chair near Matt Creighton's locker. I've been associated with losers all my life. If we blow this game, then what? We'll arrive in Boston with our feet planted in a grave, our shovels poised to scoop the last few feet of loam.

I look at Dirk Rouda. The difference between watching him from the dugout and watching him here is that TV brings him closer. His porcine face is blotched with colors, purple and blue, smudges of gray, colors like bruises. I see tobacco gruel, dabs of slime on his lips, and the most remarkable thing is that he never stops spitting. How does he spit so much? What is he? A fountain? He and the batter, Moises de Dios Ovando, size each other up. They scowl. They spit. They drool. They stare. Either one appears rabid enough to kill.

An old tune skirls through my skull. "Baseball, baseball, ain't it a wonderful game?"

Rouda hurls one up and in. The Bosox slugger spins, staggers, and the ball seems to take a chunk out of his right shoulder. He's lucky he didn't get beaned. Shouting obscenities, he drops his bat and wags a fist at Rouda. The latter burps and gargles. The stuff that oozes from his mouth looks like the insides of a snail. Nobody intimidates Rouda. Dios Ovando, muttering, shaking his head, lumbers to first base.

Rouda cuts a fastball high and tight to Maceo Mason, then hangs a slider waist-high. Mason, a lefty, should be able to pull the ball, but he dribbles one to short. Rodríguez to Mijango, the latter airborne over the high slide of Dios Ovando, a spinning dancer who fires a flame to first—double play. Three pitches later the inning's history. We go to the Cub eighth, the top of the order— Steal Home Johnny. One more run could deliver the game.

I sidle over to Stompiano's locker. I should stop myself

before I become a kleptomaniac, but maybe it's too late. His street clothes are on hangers, and I pat the pockets in search of another picture, a note—anything. His Cub jacket, the same one he wore last night on the fire escape, may contain a treasure. I lift an envelope from a side pocket, stuff it down my pants, and mosey out to the dugout where I belong.

Nick gives me a where-you-been look, but he doesn't say anything. The Bosox have a new pitcher, a fire-baller—Theodore Laurent. He dutifully brushes Johnny back with a hummer, then breaks off a curve wild high. Nick claps, touches his left ear, his throat, and the third base coach relays the sign to the batter: swing away.

Laurent throws a slider up and in. At this point (3-0), he knows Johnny will get on base one way or other. No free pass, better to hurt him, or at least scare him, retaliate for Rouda throwing at Dios Ovando. He blisters the ball, a full heater that sends Johnny sprawling as though a scythe has struck him at the knees. Azzy, his voice a beggar's, says, "Get up, Wild Child, get up. You hear me?" Johnny seems small and distant. He lies on his back, shivery and moaning, then quiet as dirt. I thought the ball grazed his shin, but now he cups his hands over his right knee as though to stabilize broken bones.

I fire a glance into the stands as Janice rushes a hand to her throat. Isha Azzam is up and yelling, so is Cue Ball, but Janice remains silent. My vision blurs, but I can sense the worry in her face, the beauty that comes from love. Her Johnny is down. He pulls deep breaths and grimaces as two trainers extend his knee, straighten his leg. Mijango Cruz says, "Get up, Johnny. **Levántate. Corre.**" Pilgrims are waving fists, yowling, throwing cups, newspapers, programs. The animal shrieks turn to applause as the Thief rises, rubs his knee, and gimps his way to first.

He takes the shyest lead I've ever seen—maybe a foot. He

hunkers down, doesn't butterfly his hands, taunt the pitcher. Laurent throws over and Johnny gimps back. He can't flex his right leg. He has to drag it along, stiff as a steel shaft.

Never in my life have I seen a pitcher relax with Johnny on base. Now, with roles reversed, the Bosox reliever taunts the Kid, throws over to first three times, not to prevent a steal but to make Johnny use his leg, aggravate his injury. From the bench we remind Laurent this is the National League. Dirk Rouda says, "Yeah, hope you have to hit, Laurie. Your fucked-up face is history. A rocket between the eyes."

Chicago's Robin Hood has been reduced. Spitting and wincing, gritting his teeth, he's no more threatening than a one-legged grandpa. Laurent fires a strike to Jamal Kelsey. Johnny strays off the bag one step. Laurent, more a torture artist than a pitcher, throws to first to watch him suffer. "Stay put!" I yell. "Stay on the bag! Save yourself!" I yell loud enough that Johnny might hear me. He takes his lead, though, a full step, now a step and a half. Laurent throws over and the cripple is back.

Johnny cups both hands over his right knee. He spits, rubs his knee, and mutters something to the first base coach. On the bench I'm next to Franny Blair, our head trainer. I say, "Tell me how bad it is. Anything broken?"

He glances at Johnny, then looks away.

"Come on," I say. "We need a pinch-runner or what? Yes or no."

"No," he says.

"You sure?"

He nods. "He checks out fine, but he'll need x-rays later on."

I rub my right knee as Johnny inches off the bag. "Forget it," I say. "The only way he'll gimp his way home is if somebody hits one to the moon."

But when have I been more wrong? The Kid fools every pilgrim in the park. No, he fools the whole wide world. Maybe he could steal anything, steal Christ off the cross and come back at night to spirit away the nails. When Laurent slows his delivery, kicks high, throws a change-up, Robin Hood jump-runs for second. I mean he **jumps** more than runs, bolts like a beast. He could saunter to the bag, come in standing, but no, he dashes, dives, then lights to his feet and slaps his right knee to show the crowd it doesn't hurt, maybe never had. He trash-talks and stares arrows at Laurent till the pitcher turns to face him. The Thief tips his helmet. He gives Laurent his summer smile, big, loose lips, buckteeth, head cocked to one side, languorous and easy. He shrugs and talks some more, maybe informing the pitcher his knee's fine, Jim Dandy, the ball just grazed him. Squatting and rising, Johnny displays the strength and spring of his legs. "Hot damn!" says Nick. "Hot damn!" The Thief keeps bantering and smiling as he edges off second base.

A five-step lead, make it six. Now watch the hands start to move. They bend at the wrist and start flapping, flapping, quick wing beats, up and down, up and down, electric. Touch him at your own risk. You might get a shock, heat and sparks through your fingers. His chest heaves as he hollers at Laurent. I can't hear Johnny but I read him: **Legs say one thing—RUN, RUN, RUN! Hey, pitcha, pitcha, pitcha. Throw your speed-ball, your hummer. You throw your change I'll steal third base standing.** Laurent throws three hummers out of the zone that send Jamal Kelsey to first. A walk, is all. But Wrigley's pilgrims rise and wail as if the game is won.

The Bosox skipper emerges from his hole (the dugout) and signals for Armando Atecas. Laurent got stymied not by a batter but a trickster, a stunt man. The crowd, paying homage to Chicago's Robin Hood, chants, "Steal third! Steal home! Steal home!" The Bosox, despite their defensive prowess, have little chance of keeping Johnny from giving us the lead.

Rey Rodríguez sky-hawks a 1-0 pitch to deep right center. A lick of wind would carry it out, but the ball hangs and dies and the right fielder gathers it at the wall. Johnny tags and bolts. Once more he could come in standing, but for sport or spunk he arcs into a headlong dive. I suppose every pilgrim in the park knows he was up late last night, out on a fire escape with his girl, then in the custody of authorities. He must require less sleep than the rest of us. Being near him is like being near a snarl of sparks, a flame jittery and bright.

Runners at the corners, one down. Double-Play Jimmy taking warm up swings. I sit and mumble, "Don't choke, Jimmy. Surprise me. Do something right."

Nick flashes the steal sign to Jamal Kelsey. Johnny, inching homeward, has a short lead off third. He claps, shuffles his feet, and harangues the pitcher. "Come on, come on! Deal!" The Bosox third baseman straddles the bag to keep the Thief from straying too far. The shortstop and second-baseman are at double-play depth. Jimmy waits.

Jamal breaks on the pitch, a fastball hot and high. The Bosox catcher fakes a throw to second, fires to third, but Johnny dives back—safe by a heartbeat. Azzy wings his cap in the air and catches it one-handed. A rapper with a rhyme, he says, "Can't nab Wild Child, oh no! Better luck trying to catch lightnin' and ring it 'round a toe."

Stolen base for Kelsey. Both runners in scoring position. The Bosox need to tighten their net. As Atecas rubs up the ball, the infield—except the third baseman—moves in for a play at the plate.

Jimmy hits a high chopper to the right side. McCreary, the second baseman, tries to bare-hand the ball, but it smacks off his palm as the Thief flies home. Arms spread, Johnny swoops and dives, brushes a hand on the corner of the plate, then rolls sideways to avoid the catcher's shin guards. McCreary, scrambling, picks up the ball and clips Jimmy at first. Had he fielded cleanly, he might have gunned down the Thief who ignored the sign to hold. Maybe, though, Johnny's dash made McCreary botch the play, slap the ball instead of catch it. What can you do when someone runs the way Johnny runs? A jump of light, libido a blazin'. McCreary, a mere mortal, suffered a moment of distraction. He separated himself from a baseball god.

Enough noise in this park to wake the dead. Old Mordecai "Three-Finger" Brown, old Frank Chance, old Hack Wilson. Let's wake the Cub legends and give them box seats. Or better, let's roost them on the rooftops of Sheffield and Waveland Avenue. They can look down on a bowl of light where new legends are playing ball.

Bad Ball Jesús swings a black bat that looks too small, a toy. He's a bad ball hitter. Atecas would be wise to throw him nothing a bat can reach.

Jesús whiffs at a ball high and wide. Atecas, working fast, plants one in the same spot, but the Lord restrains his urges. A fan over the Cub dugout hollers, "You're the boss, Jesús, you're the boss." But a slim lead in late innings tends to shoot shivers down a pilgrim's spine.

Atecas tries to sneak in with a backdoor slider. The pitch starts out a foot outside, but breaks toward the plate, knee-high and falling. Jesús' strike zone (relatively speaking) is spacious as Wyoming. Arms extended, he whip-swings the bat and thwacks a comet down the right field line, extra bases. Kelsey jogs home to give us a two-run lead.

The pilgrims over our dugout sing a one-word psalm— "Jesús! Jesús! Jesús!" Sometimes we don't think of him as being gay. We just think of him as a player who ranks among the best. Sometimes Jesús Mijango is in Johnny's league in that he brings to hitting what Johnny brings to running. He can cold-cock a ball and light it up better than anyone who has donned a Cub uniform and reached for a bat.

Dirk Rouda slobbers on my shoulder. "Game's ours," he says, "game's ours. You can write it in the books."

In the ninth, the Bosox go three up, three down, and only the last out merits a brief mention. A deep fly to center backs Johnny to the wall where he makes a basket catch near the 400-foot sign. He has to add a flourish, you know, dash his initials on the game's final moment. He skies the ball into the bleachers, hurls it so high and far it almost strikes the scoreboard. Later on in the clubhouse, I'll give him some advice which he won't follow: "Save your energy, Johnny, smarten up. We've got three more games to win."

POST-GAME

In private, Nick would tell me they acted "like field niggers at a fair." Azzy Azzam lifted the Thief in his arms. Jesús Mijango tap-danced in front of his locker. Junior Parker wagged a finger, wriggled his hips, and said, "Turn to page twenty-three of your hymn books!" Dirk Rouda was Dirk Rouda. He chugged an Old Style beer, opened a fresh one, poured the contents in his cap, and put his cap on. He said, "Hey coach!" and trapped me with a bear hug. If losing is a quiet and depressing art, winning is mayhem. Jimmy Lieski waved and hollered at the cameras: "Cu-cu-cu Cubs win!"

Johnny, in post-game dishevelment, shirt un-tucked, cap in hand, stood near his locker, his glove and blond bats on the rack behind him. The skipper eyed him nervously. He said, "Let's stay on track, Kid," which meant, "Go on, apologize for last night, no diversions." Johnny, who'd jump every track in the world if given a chance, noted that Azzy would pitch Game 3 in Boston. "I look forward to that one," he said, "but it's not fair to Mr. Dios Ovando and his teammates."

Somebody snickered.

"Yeah, you're glad you're a Cub," said Johnny. "You don't have to step in against Azzy, wag your shank of wood in the air, come up empty."

"**Mareado**," said Jesús.

"Three swings," said Johnny, "and sliver your fingers, grab some bench. A base hit next time? An infield single?...Man, you'd have better luck riding out on the ocean to wrestle a typhoon."

The only typhoon I know is Johnny. Al Muscat, ESPN's main bottom feeder, complimented the Thief on his base-running, his coyote stunt, his "I'm hurt act," and then he got down to business. "Last night," said Al, "you were with your girl on a North Side fire escape. A brush and some paint. A messed-up billboard. Was this a coyote trick?"

Johnny grinned. "Afraid you'd ask."

"Tonight you've agreed to apologize. Am I right?"

"We'll see."

"Fine, then, base one. Tell us why you did it. Any special reason?"

Johnny hesitated. "No, no special reason. Right down the middle of the road. General as pudding."

Al looked confused.

"Ran out of paint," said Johnny. "I'd hoped to paint a fuller moustache."

"That's an apology?"

"No, but a start. I can say more."

"You should."

"Well, if you look at a picture of Mr. Trent—**any** picture— what's the problem?"

Al thought about this. "I don't know."

"The tough guy image," said Johnny. "I'm not sure I believe it."

Nick said, "Let's can the chatter. Just give your apology."

Johnny stared deadpan at the camera. "I'm sorry I ran out of paint last night. Mr. Trent's sort of puffy looking, but that's not my fault. I think he'd appear more formidable with a moustache. Sort of bushy, all black. A high-seas pirate."

Jesús clapped and whistled.

"Knock it off," said Nick. "Where's the apology?"

"It's around here somewhere," said Johnny, and looked this way and that. I expected the Kid to ham it up, entertain us with histrionics. Instead, his head cocked to one side, his right hand raised, palm up, he said, "Almost a winner, darn close. Another dab or two of paint and the president would look alive."

Jesús, smiling, said, "**Tan lindo, vato lindo.** Straight from the heart."

He and a few other Cubs burst into laughter.

"**Con duende,**" said Jesús. "**La alegría oscura.**"

I wished to hell he would speak English, **plain** English.

"**La verdad,**" he said, "**y nada más.**"

Nick positioned himself between Johnny and the cameras. "Forget the chatter," he said. "The thing to remember is that Johnny's sorry. He's not putting it right, but we know he's sorry."

Johnny nodded.

"Admits he screwed up," said Nick. "What else can he do?"

"Not much."

"Bone-dumb stunt, no rhyme or reason. The sort of stupidity a man might regret every day of his life."

Every muckworm in the joint grew excited. Tension and greed, a go-for-the-jugular instinct. A story, a headline. NEWS IN CAPITAL LETTERS. Muscat, a consummate bottom feeder, his camera crew behind him, other crews in the wings, took center stage.

"A question," he said. "You say the paint—"

"Skip it," said Nick. "We know Johnny's sorry."

"Yeah, but the paint. He said he ran out. Did I hear this right?"

"Doesn't matter. You heard what you heard. The main thing is the apology."

"He didn't—"

"He said he was sorry. How many times does he have to say it?"

Johnny, perched on a stool in front of his locker, raised one finger.

"Give it a rest," said Nick. "Non-baseball questions are for the front office. All legal matters are for another time and place."

The skipper asked the press to leave, but it took a while before he and I and some other coaches shooed Muscat and the other bottom feeders down the tunnel toward the dugout. Nothing's harder to slip free of than a school of bottom feeders enthralled by the smell of blood.

Nick turned to Johnny. "You have some explaining to do," he said. "In my office."

"**Cuidado,**" said Jesús. "No cage fits a coyote."

"Then we'll **make** one," said Nick, "I guarantee it." He hiked a thumb and waggled it at Johnny. "I thought coyotes were wise guys, huh? Well, this one hurled himself in a trap, didn't he? Whole goddamn world wonders what in hell he's smoking. A fire escape and a can of paint, a bad trip. Another Cub with a loose screw." Nick waved a hand. "There's stuff you guys don't know, stuff I wish I didn't know. You're ballplayers, privilege up the ass. Don't know a problem from a pile of hundred-dollar bills."

I was ready to head home and pore over the envelope I'd borrowed from Johnny's locker, but Nick called me aside. "Come on," he said, "you're my back-up. Two-against-one gives better odds."

So we made our way to the skipper's office, a comfy room

with two sofas and all the amenities. Nick and I wore starched uniforms, but Johnny's was mud-stained, his jersey hung loose, and he wore flip-flops, shower shoes rather than spikes. The skipper sat at his desk and motioned the Kid and me toward a small sofa. Johnny plunked himself down, lackadaisical, immune to the petty concerns of mortals like me and Nick.

The skipper opened the top drawer of his desk and brought out a fifth of Old Crow. He fumbled about for shot glasses, a tray, and seemed not to hear when Johnny said, "I'm fine, skip, none for me."

I tried to ease the tension by offering a toast. "To the Game," I said, "to baseball. And maybe it's time we forget the rest."

"In heaven," said Nick, "and we ain't there yet." He looked from me to Johnny. "Earlier today, do you remember we rehearsed your apology?"

Johnny nodded.

"**Your** apology," said Nick, "**yours**. 'I'm sorry. I did a dumb thing. No excuse.'"

"I remember."

"Didn't remember with the cameras rolling, though. Piled on some shit about running out of paint."

"Well—"

"Well, shit stinks, plain and simple. Damn it, Johnny, I told you what to say and how to say it. I showed you a door, a way out, and you built another wall."

The front office had compiled media reports, what they called "a fact sheet," and now Nick made us suffer by giving us excerpts of three articles. "Go on," he said, "jump in the shit. In less time than I can say, 'Fuck you, Jack,' all this and more circled the globe."

To: Andy McPherson, Chicago Cub General Manager

Cc: Butch Malecki, Nick Glouser, 74 others
Subject: Johnny Stompiano/Cub fallout

Excerpt #1

"Johnny Stompiano's late-night performance on a Chicago fire escape went well beyond the absurd. Through vandalism, a standard and infamous tactic of 20th century Nazis, the Cub icon tried to compare our president to Adolph Hitler. His unlawful act, recorded live on film and broadcast nationally and internationally, underscores his own disturbing tendencies toward anarchy and violence."

—Cindy Lang, Campaign Manager of President Michael J. Trent

Excerpt #2

Let's forget Johnny Stompiano, except when he's on the ball field. This election boils down to two issues that will shape the entire century—the economy and the War on Terror. Our military is capable of defeating any enemy in any lost corner of the world if—and only if—our will as a nation remains unshakeable. Daily, advances in state-of-the-art weaponry and surveillance technology give us added advantages in confronting Islamic extremists wherever they reside. Ms. Jamil, a devout Muslim, calls the majority of defense expenditures "pie-in-the-sky projects to invite the richest men on earth to press down a bit harder on the backs of the poor." Is this our future commander-in-chief? Every citizen who loves this nation, regardless of his race, class, or religious background, knows America is at a crossroads. We are now engaged in the struggle that will define the 21st century, the great world-wide military and moral effort to defeat the demonic forces who wish to erase God and goodness from the earth...

—Official Statement of Michael J. Trent Re-Election Campaign

Excerpt #3

...What can be said about the Chicago Cubs? They are arguably the finest team in baseball, but last night they ventured into new terrain—presidential politics. It seems that Johnny Stompiano, the best base-runner in Chicago since Lou Brock left for St. Louis, has cut a deal with Congresswoman Kadijah Jamil. Last night's performance on a Chicago fire escape played out like an underground comic strip, or a B-grade scene in guerilla theatre. Why all the attention? Well, because Stompiano's a professional provocateur who knows what he's doing. The candidate of his choice, Khadijah Jamil, has already received a modest boost in the polls.

Who is Ms. Jamil, and why is she running for president? She has repeatedly tried to present herself as "an environmentalist, a moderate, a friend of the working poor," but she is—first and foremost—a Muslim. In September, when she surprised us by choosing Aaron Kaufman, the Jewish governor of New York, as her running mate, the liberal media applauded. Days later, however, we learned they both oppose almost all military aid to every nation in the Middle East, Israel included. Again and again, they claim to be pro-Israeli and pro-Palestinian, as if such a stance were possible. The oldest question is the best question: Are they for us or against us? This is the question to take to the polls.

—The Weekly Standard

*

Johnny showed no interest in the reports. He seemed distracted as he rolled his right sock down to his ankle. A lump, pink and swollen, the size of a quarter, protruded from his shinbone. He glanced up and said, "Not bad, skip." He dabbed a finger along the edges of the wound.

Nick said, "So Laurent dinged you. You weren't completely

faking."

He smiled. "Well, I made it worse than it was, didn't I? I put on a show."

Nick reminded him the pitch was clocked at ninety-six-miles-an hour.

"Yeah," said Johnny, "but it just shook me a little. A dinger like this, hell, it's a boon. The best remedy is to jump around and run and get the blood flowing up and down your leg."

I fought back a smile.

"Fine," said Nick, "so you've got some smarts, some trickery on the diamond. Too bad everywhere else you've got some world-class dumbness."

Johnny's eyes crinkled into slits.

"Ever hear of Rube Waddell?" said Nick. "Philadelphia Athletics?"

"One of my favs, skip. Greatest southpaw before Sandy Koufax."

"And the dumbest," said Nick, "bar none. Before games he was scheduled to pitch, you know where his manager sometimes found him?"

"Fishing?"

"No," said Nick, "out front of the ballpark. Sometimes shooting marbles with kids, or waiting to hear the whistle of a fire truck." Nick downed his whiskey and replenished his glass. "So Connie Mack, Rube's manager, doubled as a baby sitter. He practically had to pull Rube by the ear to get him inside the park and out on the mound. The boy could pitch, though, if he stayed focused. Rube was obsessed with fire trucks, or anything shiny. So opposing players and coaches would try to distract him, break his rhythm by flashing bright objects from the dugout—marbles, toy fire trucks, chips of metal." Nick clucked his tongue and chuckled. "Distraction and dumbness, you notice they're cousins? Johnny and Rube, Rube and Johnny. See something shiny and forget about playing ball."

Johnny, after a pause, said, "Never saw anything special, skip. Nothing shiny."

"Yeah, then it saw **you**. Came up and shook your hand. Whispered your name. Kissed you."

"Not really."

"**Really**," said Nick. "Patted your ass, kissed you. Took you home to bed."

I doubt the old Rube had Johnny's poise. The Kid didn't apologize, didn't challenge Nick either, but eased back on the sofa, one leg crossed over the other. He looked as relaxed as somebody tuning in on a late night talk-show. I couldn't see any fear in him, a hint of boredom, sure, but no genuine discomfort. I wondered if Nick was feeling what I was feeling: admiration and hatred. Johnny's about my height, five-nine, but built like a stray cat who turns down most chances for a meal. I longed to bully him, rub his nose in his smallness, but how? I patted my gut, beer-barrel thick, and thought, "I outweigh you by fifty pounds." True enough, a plain fact. But God knows I felt trivial and small.

Nick and I exchanged glances. The skipper needed some help, a cheerleader on the sidelines. Up to now, all I'd done was sip his Old Crow.

"Johnny," I said, "what you did last night hurts yourself **and** your team."

He made no acknowledgment that I'd spoken.

"Vandalism," I said, "and for what? To make a point?"

Nick said, "He has no point."

"You didn't know you'd get arrested? Cameras up there taking pictures of every inch of Chicago and you imagine invisibility?"

"I wasn't worried."

"There's your problem," I said. "Nick and I wish you'd worried enough to stay home last night."

He shrugged.

"Wise up," I said. "Before you pull the whole goddamn sky down on yourself and your team."

He chuckled when I asked if Janice was the architect of the fire escape fiasco. Suggesting that I too was a man of experience, I told him the prettiest girls always had a middle name—**Trouble**. "Where'd you two meet?" I said. "Some political ho-down?"

"No, a West Side poetry slam. We were on the same team."

Nick grunted. "To hell with that," he said. "You're on **this** team, and you may have noticed we're in the World Series."

"I'm mostly enjoying it."

"**Mostly**?"

"It's been a pretty good ride so far."

The skipper tried to tell him how dumb he was, how he had to look for his own head, screw it back on, but who were the dummies? I'd needed almost twenty hours, plus a jolt of whiskey, to realize the Kid planned to get caught. Had he gotten away with his stunt, then what? No national attention. No spotlight. Nobody thinking about President Trent, who he might resemble. Keep in mind the star of the fire escape stunt wasn't some street punk, a wild hair up his ass, a brush in his hand, but a living legend—Johnny Stompiano. Was the Babe better loved than our Cub orphan? I don't think so. This kid with his shaggy hair and buckteeth was the best-loved ballplayer in the history of the Game.

For what it was worth—nothing in the end—Nick set limits. No talking to the press about anything but baseball. No embarrassing yourself and your team. No buffoonery. No off-field tricks. No wee-hour highlights. "In a nutshell," said Nick, "we need a moratorium on dumbness. You hear me?"

"Sure, skip."

"A moratorium," said Nick, "a goddamn moratorium. That's all this meeting is about."

The skipper sniffed his Old Crow, flared his nostrils, then tossed the whiskey down the hatch.

Johnny was looking at a picture on the far wall—Ernie Banks and Billy Williams standing near home plate, the centerfield scoreboard in the distance. I looked, too, and for a minute or more the tension lifted. Ernie, Mr. Cub, flashed a bright smile. I spoke my thought aloud: "Our chance, our year. Can you feel it?"

Johnny said he could.

"Then keep your tricks on the field," said Nick. "Can you do that?"

"Shouldn't be too hard, skip."

"Well, that's not good enough. I need to hear a promise, a swear-on-a-Bible promise."

The Kid cocked his head. "Whatever."

"Whatever won't cut it," said Nick. "Look me in the eye and promise me you won't do anything dumb till the World Series is over."

Johnny hesitated. "I won't do anything dumb."

"Fine," said Nick, "copasetic. That's all I need to hear."

The skipper filled his shot glass to the brim. He, too, gazed at the picture of Ernie and Billie. "Not much to ask, is it? Don't do anything dumb."

It was a great deal to ask. Dumbness, like beauty, is in the eye of the beholder. Johnny might turn our world upside-down before the Series ended. At some level, Nick, sober or drunk, knew this, but he still went through the motions of pretending to manage a player. Later, when Johnny further embarrassed the team, the skipper would call on me as a witness to inform the front office of his attempts to establish control. I understood my role. I would know what to say to the front office, and I knew what to say now.

I told Johnny to keep his nose clean. I told him the skipper and I had faith in him and the other captains. I went on to predict the Cubs would win the Series. "Well, why not?" I said. "Somebody's got to win this thing, so it may as well be us."

I drank and talked, drank and talked, and so did Nick. The skipper was mid-sentence—"a moratorium on dumbness"—when Johnny sprang from the sofa and lit from that room as swift as the wing-flap of a bird.

Nick, in his whiskey drawl, kept jabbering about the moratorium.

"Save it," I said. "He's gone."

"Huh?"

"Johnny's gone."

The skipper looked around. "So now what? I been talking to myself?"

I didn't say anything because I didn't count for anything.

"Well, wake me and shake me," said Nick. "I could use another drink."

BAD COACH?

I was woozy when I got home, but I had one little thing to do before I spilled into bed. At the kitchen table, under a strong light, I held in my hands the envelope I borrowed from Johnny's locker. I kept telling myself I borrowed this item and would return it, and if I didn't return it...well, why get upset about stealing from a guy who has everything? Was I a bad coach? A loser? I turned on the TV to counter the late-night quiet. I could still hear the trouble in my heart.

I opened the unsealed envelope and spread three pages on the table. All I wanted was to find something that **meant** something. A man my age—seventy-three—doesn't have much time left. I'd piddled away the days, the months, the years, and I couldn't get them back.

10.26

Dear Johnny,

I at times resent sending you fewer emails and text messages because of surveillance, but in one regard the authorities serve us well. As I write I feel the blood in my hand, the warmth of paper.

The shapes of letters are my own.

Yesterday, Khadijah Jamil began a speech in Philadelphia by reading the work of an Israeli poet. This poem for our time deserves a billboard. Isha and I think it belongs near the Liberty Bell, or else in DC. Azzy says, Why not both?

From the place where we are right
flowers will never grow
in the spring.
The place where we are right
is hard and trampled
like a yard.
But doubts and loves
dig up the world
like a mole, a plow.
And a whisper will be heard in the place
where the ruined
house once stood.

                    —Yehuda Amichai

No tragedy is greater than believing one knows everything. In this false "knowing," there is the appearance of "strength," the appearance of "security." But to appreciate complexity, ambivalence, multiple interpretations—this is life and requires a strong and nimble heart.

My current writing instructor believes I write for a small audience or no audience, but how is this possible? Li-Young Lee, another Chicagoan, addresses his poetry "to an all: the stars, the trees, the birds—everything." I, too, address my poems this way, and my letters, though they are nowhere near as successful as Li-Young's. People imagine that life differs from poetry, but they are wrong. We live—if we live at all—for everything. Stars. Trees. Cats.

Birds. Base-thieves. Presidents. Saints.

Khadijah received 3 more death threats yesterday. The media made no mention of this, nor of earlier threats. Isha told me Azzy has received 4 threats since he began 'campaigning' for Khadijah, and 3 of these mentioned "taking out your wife and your daughters." Several reports identify you as a "Muslim convert, a radical," though you have no more religion than a drop of rain.

Of course those in power are not seriously afraid of athletes like you and Azzy, but they do fear the millions who have never had a voice or a song other than one of lament. They fear a shared poem rising faster than tides of propaganda. They fear everything beyond the certitudes of fundamentalism, the crumbling cathedrals of capitalism, the doctrines of demagogues, the "safety" of frozen beliefs. They fear life and its counterpart—death. They fear all that breathes and all that is still.

I seldom know what you'll do next, or what I'll do.
And maybe this is why we're in love.

Janice

I didn't know what to make of this letter. I was almost sorry I stole it. I glanced at the TV, a late-night talk show. I said, as though the host and guest could hear me, "How about if you chumps say something that means something?" No one did.

I reread Janice's letter. A few words from Johnny's girl found a home in me: **As I write I feel the blood in my hand, the warmth of paper. The shapes of letters are my own.** I would have been happy to take her hand and feel the blood and place an ear to her pulse. A bad coach? A degenerate? Or must every man make a life raft of the buoys that float his way?

BLUE ANGELS

World Series

Game 3

Fenway Park

Line-up Cards

Home Boston Red Sox

Visiting Chicago Cubs

SS Domingo López
RF Kaido Miura
CF Moises de Dios Ovando
3B Bill Murphy
1B Maceo Mason
LF Preston Hollis
2B Jay McCreary
DH Flaco Méndez
C Antonio Chévez

CF Johnny Stompiano
LF Jamal Kelsey
2B Jesús Mijango Cruz
1B Jimmy Lieski
SS Rey Rodríguez
C Junior Parker
RF Terrence Gumbs
3B Matt Creighton
DH Mick Gutowski

During batting practice, I slip back to the clubhouse and gravitate to Johnny's locker. I let my eyes browse the bat rack, blond bats (extras), street clothes on hangers, towels, lean shadows warm with possibility. I frisk the pockets of his jeans, jangle his keys, peruse a ballpark pass, a business card from a lawyer in North Chicago. A scavenger, I search for a scrap of paper, a few words from Janice. I kneel to check beneath the insoles of his sneakers— nothing. Perhaps he's more careful about what he leaves behind.

When I was a child, I was addicted to those toy dispensers that let me drop a coin in a slot, turn a dial, and receive a surprise. Say a plastic cowboy with a six-gun, an Indian smoking a pipe, or a miniature rifle almost as small as the coin that fed the machine. Sure, I knew the toys were junk, but they stirred my curiosity. By and by, I discovered a deeper pleasure: stealing. I pilfered prize marbles (cat eyes) from friends, spare change from my father's dresser, and countless "gifts" that filled loose pockets. In eighth grade, I homed in on essentials—girlie books from Frank's Cigar Store, lighters, rare and coveted baseball cards, cigars dipped in brandy. Old Frank, blind, accompanied by a golden retriever, was an easy touch, but I would have eluded him even if he had 20/20 vision. I stole things all through my teenage years and never got caught. I'll tell you a secret: my hands still quicken in the swell of desire.

I nose around Azzy's locker, but what could he give me? His long, dark coat hangs from a rack. A yellow envelope, unsealed, its contents secured by a rubber band, is in the breast of the coat, the security pocket, which is the first place I check. I would like to pat down his suit coat, his trousers, but I've barely begun when I hear someone flush a toilet. I stuff the envelope and what feels like eight or nine pages down my shirt.

I make my way to our dugout and watch Jesús Mijango take batting practice. He and this ballpark have something in common—they're freaks. Mijango smokes line shots off The Green Monster, the leftfield wall that rises thirty-seven feet over the playing field. Yes, thirty-seven feet, painted green, the highest wall in baseball. Instead of trying to lift one into the seats, Mijango punishes the wall, puts some new dents in it. This gay boy from South Central LA is so good he scares me. His black bat burns each pitch with a bolt of devil's light.

*

At game-time someone blares a radio over our dugout. Sam Foley, the Bosox play-by-play man, refers to Stompiano as "Fire Escape Johnny, America's Last Hooligan."

Mike Madson, his sidekick, says, "He's got more nicknames than I have cousins, so let's loan him one more—No Rules Johnny. And just now he's out of jail, out on bail, leading off the game."

I wish I too had a colorful name—No Rules Billy, or Fire Escape Billy. Nobody's ever called me anything out of the ordinary. I'm Billy, or plain old Bill.

I lean toward the playing field, toward Johnny. He spits on his hands to better his grip. No batting gloves for this huckster. He stands in, bat cocked, fingers twitching. With a stance, an attitude, he pesters the pitcher. I can almost hear the Kid muttering, "Come on, come on, come on. Lay one in."

The Bosox ground crew brought their own rain. Earlier, they'd run their hoses and left the infield muddy, especially near home plate and first base. The aim is to slow Johnny down, gum up his spikes, ruin his traction. I'll bedevil my diction by saying I want a rule in the books to help No Rules Johnny: **Rain must fall from heaven**. All year long every home-field opponent has brought their own rain.

Johnny gets behind in the count, then slaps a soft single to left-center.

"Cheap hit," says Foley, "but he'll take it. Fire Escape on first and let's see if he runs."

He leans into his lead...five steps, five and a half, less than usual. Bent over, arms dangling, his hands dart and twitch as if battered by sparks.

Madson says, "A bit swampy near first base now. A duck might like it, or a pig, but not No Rules Johnny. He's a few inches shorter sinking in the mud."

Swamp or no swamp, I believe he can steal. That's what I want—a steal. I want it more than a homerun that sails for the seats.

Nick, cautious bastard, calls for a bunt that moves Johnny to second. So up steps Mijango, our best hitter, but I know what's coming—an intentional walk.

Jimmy Lieski, Double-play Jimmy, pigeon-toes toward the plate. Before he steps in the box, he goes through a routine I've seen more than five hundred times during the regular season. Gripping the meat side of the bat with both hands, he shuts his eyes, bows his head, and prays. His batting average for the season and post-season (.231) suggests a lack of divine intervention. Jimmy keeps praying, though, and he believes. The Lord must have a reason for setting him down more than three times out of four.

To say nothing of the double plays.

He whiffs at two sliders that slide well out of the zone.

Nick says, "Come on now, Jimmy. You're the clean-up hitter. Show us why."

Ball one, up and in. Detrick's toying with Jimmy. Give him a little heat near the chin, a little brush back; shrivel the balls, tighten the sphincter. The next pitch will be nasty. I predict a cut fastball breaking low and biting the dirt. The nastier it is, the better it is to run on. The catcher will need to make a clean grab and quick throw to have a chance to nip Johnny. Nick, who seems to read my mind, flashes the sign for a double-steal: a hand to his mouth, a finger to his chin, a hand brushing his chest, the Chicago Cub emblem. But Bob Detrick smells something. He glides into his stretch, then steps off the rubber to see if Johnny leans toward third. No, no leaning, no showing his cards. The Kid lazies back to second, kicks the bag, and says something to Detrick. The Bosox pitcher needs the resin bag. He paws it a while, then tosses it aside like something he hates.

Sam Foley says, "Detrick's more worried about the runner on second than the batter. He gives Stompiano a long look, another, and..."

The pitch is filthy and fast as sin. It skirts the outside corner, dives, rakes the dirt, hot to handle. The catcher scoops, but his off-balance throw is too late to nip Johnny. And Mijango takes second base.

Azzy, at the rail of the dugout, calls to Johnny. "Wild Child, you're ninety feet from home."

We forget Jimmy Lieski till he sort of swings. Confused, he check-swings, dibs the ball, bloops it over the infield. The shortstop runs out, the left fielder runs in. The ball—look at it slice and sag and stumble through the sky to green pasture. A stranger to religion, I remember one line from my Catholic childhood: "He maketh me to lie down in green pastures, He restoreth my soul." Here comes Johnny, now Jesús; the Cubs lead 2-0. Credit Jimmy with the cheapest clutch hit of his cheap career.

*

The game's ours for five innings. Azzy Azzam is throwing bullets. He's got nine strikeouts. He's hitting corners. He's Cy Young with a tan. As we take the field in the sixth, still clutching a two-run lead, Dantel Hood says, "Hot strikes, Azzy! Hot strikes! For Khadijah and Satch!"

Sam Foley says, "Top of the order, Domingo López. Miura and Dios Ovando waiting in the wings."

Floodlights illuminate the near sky. Before López steps in, Blue Angels, fighter jets, swoop over the field, flare over the Green Monster, and rise in V-formation toward a half moon. I tell myself V is for Victor, Victor Faust, and Game 3 is ours. I'm not the least bit spooked by the rush of sound. Planes are planes, a common World Series attraction, a show of power. A kind of wild hurrah for the Red, White, and Blue.

But Azzy looks rattled. He asks the home plate ump for a new ball. He gets it, rubs it up, sticks it in his glove, and grabs the resin bag. His hands sweat, his face, his back, his chest. Planes or no planes, pressure or no pressure, the man's a river. Blue Angels generally fly before the National Anthem, and sometimes they buzz the field for the seventh inning stretch and another song—"God Bless America." Azzy has often been skewered on newscasts and in blogs for more than once calling the display of might and right "an expensive way to broadcast ignorance to the heavens." Now he glares at the sky as though it bodes him bad fortune. Did they send the planes an inning early to break his stride, addle his wits? All I know is he pitched to the next four batters with no more poise than a wild stallion with cloudbursts and lightning licking his tail.

Sam Foley, enamored by planes, says, "They're out there in the yonder, you can hear them. F-22s, fighter jets, staking their claims in the sky."

They're gone, but the roar lingers. Those 22s shook the rafters of this old yard and the bedrock beneath it. I can still feel the vibration in the soles of my feet.

Azzy walks Domingo López on four pitches, Kaido Miura on five. Moises de Dios Ovando takes a practice swing with a weighted bat.

Ovando is ugly. The Bosox, as a team, are ugly. The same

can be said for the Cubs, except for pretty boy Jesús and a few others. The Bosox are worse, though: swarthy fellows, shadowy, unshaven. I wonder if they wash their hands. Ovando, for instance, has fingers like those of a mechanic, cigars of grime and grease. You want to give him a jumbo jar of Pep Boy and say, "Dab on the cream, kid. **Scrub**." Outside the ball-yard, though, he and Azzy and all the Cub rousers are pals, members of **Live the Legacy**. Hell, it's a new world, you know. In some ways I miss the era when all the great athletes were spoiled brats.

Sam Foley says, "Let's see if Moises de Dios Ovando can do some damage. He's a natural born Cub killer, or at least has the potential." He thinks he's come up with a catchy phrase, so he repeats it—"natural born Cub killer." Now his sidekick repeats it, so he too can be clever. The radio chatter swoops over our dugout at full volume. We might as well be inside the contraption—the wiring, the tubes, the speakers. My body quivers with the rumble and roll of bullyrag announcers having too much fun.

Azzy shakes off a sign and goes with his mainstay, a four-seam fastball that shoots in at ninety-nine-miles-an-hour. Dios Ovando blisters it with the heat of his bat. The ball scuds, soars, and it's not coming down any time soon. Foley, in his high-faluten style, dabbing butter on bacon, says, "Watch it while you can. That ball's tailing a jet, a Blue Angel, and gaining ground, or I should say **sky**. Sails over the Green Monster and gone, gone, gone...Wave your goodbyes!"

Mike Madson says, "A fast ball, straight heat. Some Red Sox fan will find it in the Charles River."

He, too, takes butter with bacon.

"So grab your scorecards," he says. "López is home, Miura's on his heels, and here comes Moises de Dios Ovando. Tally it on the board—Red Sox three, Cubbies two. Let's get a few more."

They get more than a few. After Azzy walks the next batter,

Nick brings in our best middleman, Eddie Jeffries, and the Bosox cheap-hit us to death. At one point, the bags loaded on infield singles, we almost staunch the wounds, but Jimmy Lieski fields a bunt and berserks the ball, hurls it wild high and into the seats. Hell with it. I won't relate the three thousand and three nuances of defeat. I'll just say by the time the inning ends, fifty-six minutes have passed, eight runs have scored, and five Cub pitchers are in the showers. On the bench I sit between Dantel Hood and the skipper. The latter keeps mumbling what I'm feeling: "Well, fuck it then, fuck this whole ballpark. Flush it down the pot."

But Foley and Madson rub Cub noses in Cub failure. They recap the inning, stick our heads in the pot, these raconteurs of insult and frippery. Goddamn it, I can still hear Foley's voice in my head: "Moises de Dios Ovando gave us the lead with one swing. After his three-run sky-shot, well, we sat back and let Cub relievers and Jimmy Lieski pad our advantage." I can almost see the little guy's face lit up, his nose red as a pimple. "I have to say the Cub bench looks sorrowful now, heads hanging in the vicinity of knees, no chatter about a come-back." He sighs and chuckles. "So here's an idea, a suggestion. Maybe after the game No Rules Johnny and other Cub personnel can find a tall building with a fire escape. What hotel are the Cubs at? The Hyatt? Well, we'll need some security on those fire escapes to make sure no one takes the leap."

The one thing that might give me pleasure just now would be to silence that radio with a sawed-off shotgun blazing from the hip.

*

Jimmy Lieski hits a long homerun—a solo shot—in the seventh. He's a dangerous hitter when a game is already lost.

SOUTH SIDE NEWS

Nick stayed out on the field for an interview. He tolerated questions for maybe a minute, then barred the press, bottom feeders one and all, from the clubhouse. He stormed in, beet-faced and breathless, and kicked a Gatorade cooler against a wall. "Garbage game," he said. "They want me to talk about it till I stink."

After a game, a tough loss, my own company, though unpleasant, is the best option. I begged my way out of a post-game meeting with Johnny and the skipper. "This headache's a doozy," I told Nick. "Feels like somebody struck the back of my skull with a hammer." I did, in fact, have a headache, but it was mild. I wanted to clear out so I could peruse the materials borrowed from Azzy in the privacy of my room.

After telling Nick, "Go easy tonight, don't drink yourself sloppy," I took a cab to the hotel. From my sixth-floor suite, I ordered spring water, a bucket of ice, and a pint of Jack Daniels. I would need a quick bracer before I examined the borrowed materials. I set Azzy's envelope on my nightstand with a certain tenderness. These chubby hands can be delicate now and then.

So this was my secret life, maybe my only life. I downed

a couple drinks before I rolled the dice, scattered the contents of Azzy's envelope on a white bedspread. Along with a pamphlet, *South Side News*, I found a child's drawing of a sun and a tree, and—thanks to colored pencils—a letter that damn near glowed.

Dear Daddy
    I do my job I make the world pretty. U say that why we here even Minnah. She not the best sister but she sometime pretty. I like her drawings.
    Mommy pretier than evry woman. Warm all over and big like a tree or a star.
                Luv U & Mommy & sometime Minnah
                                      Rasheeda

I sipped my drink. I knew Azzy had daughters, but I didn't know their names till now. Rasheeda used bright colors in her picture for her Daddy. She made the sun red, the tree green and gold. Her writing was like a bunch of sparks—yellow and orange—and the first letter of every word was red.

I picked up *South Side News* with less enthusiasm. I was eager for something intimate, not some publication meant for mass distribution. I felt a little better when I noticed some quotes from Azzy in the lead article. I'd never heard of *South Side News*, but I whet my curiosity by telling myself I was the only white guy, except maybe for Steal Home Johnny, to read such a rag.

PEACE FORCE REPLACES POLICE FORCE
IN SOUTH CHICAGO
By Dexter Bennet

Chicago, Oct. 13—Shortly after midnight at Halsted and 87th, a four-person Peace Team responded to an urgent call.

Carrying no weapons, the team entered the residence of Robert and Lanette Lawton. They found Robert at his kitchen table, a jackknife poised at his left wrist. As two team members approached him, he thrust his knife forward and issued a threat.

Marcus Foster, a team leader with eight years' experience, said, "We responded to a call from Lanette. We've known the family all our lives, and we know Robert's been struggling since he lost a job he held for sixteen years. A minute passed, maybe two, before he handed me his knife."

Peace Force, founded by Khadijah Jamil eleven years ago, has met with considerable success in South Chicago, but the Chicago Police Department has consistently been at odds with its methods. Told of the incident at the home of Robert and Lanette Lawton, Chief of Police Dick Kowalsik said, "A man brandishing a knife belongs in jail, but what will Peace Force do? Invite him to a meeting. Come one, come all, mugger or murderer—it's one big family. What has happened to the law? Nine times out of ten, when there's an emergency in South Chicago, nobody tells us. Nobody calls."

Marcus Foster emphasized that Peace Force does not hesitate to report dangerous criminals to the police. "We know our own Hood," he said. "We know who we're dealing with. Our job, more often than not, is to approach a man and remind him of who he is. If you know someone well, if you can stand in his shoes, you can mirror what is best in him. Violence ends where love begins. These might serve as pretty words for the press, but they also happen to be true."

Arshan "Azzy" Azzam has been involved with Peace Force since its inception. Long before he became a household name, he was—and still is—an active member of the organization. In recent weeks, his support for Congresswoman Jamil's bid for the presidency has resulted in four death threats. Peace Force Teams *regularly patrol the area around his home.*

Azzy, in an interview before Game 1 of the World Series, said, "I don't know what to make of it. I brushed aside the first threat, which was addressed to me alone, but the last three mentioned Isha and our daughters in the first line. In daylight hours, I believe the threats are just words, but sometimes at night I lay awake and wonder. The threat that worries me most comes from a Wahhabi who believes 'Khadijah and other heretics share a set of beliefs that are a desecration of Islam.' Well, he'd like to straighten us out, show us the true path, or else put us in graves. So—among other things—he told me in detail how he'd kill my kids.

"I forget how many death threats my friend Khadijah has received. This world's been dizzy for a long, long while. Race, religion, sports, politics, power—it's all in the mix. Hank Aaron received countless threats back in '74 when he was trying to pass Babe Ruth and become the Homerun Champion. Lewis Grizzard, then the sports editor for the Atlanta Journal, *feared Hank would be dead before he could be the champion of anything, so he quietly had somebody write up the slugger's obituary in advance. Well, Hank became the champ anyway, and survived all those threats. Where are we all these years later? For better or worse, this country's more addicted to sports than ever, and this is why players like me and Mijango and Steal Home Johnny can make a difference. Hank walked a more dangerous road than we'll ever see. Mijango's received just two threats, Johnny none. They'd take down the whole team before they went for him. Let me add, though, that he's no less courageous than Mijango and me. He just sets in some different skin."*

I freshened my drink. I didn't know about Lewis Grizzard and the obituary that waited in vain for Hank. I knew about the threats, sure. Everybody knew Hank's life was on the line.

"I'll tell you what irks me," said Azzy. "I've heard a question, an echo, countless times in the span of my career—'Why can't you just play ball?' Well, I learned to play hardball on cracked sidewalks and cinders and broken glass. Wynton Marsalis wrote a song— 'From the Plantation to the Penitentiary...' You know I got seven pen pals in jail? America has written off pretty much all the people in my Hood.

*"Bill Russell, the old backbone of the Boston Celtics, said, 'You're not going to reduce me to an entertainer.' When I'm told I'm political, controversial, I say, 'No, I'm just human. I'm just trying to help whoever I can.' Fighter jets buzzing ball yards and stadiums to add to the World Series hubbub, the Super Bowl hubbub—now **that's** political, and should be controversial. I love this country enough to be offended by its violence. Like Khadijah says, 'A whole lot of people got to change their hearts before the world's gonna change.' Me? Steal Home Johnny? Jesús Mijango? We're just three players trying to liven things up on and off the field."*

I stared into my drink. What did I want from Azzy? Something to salvage a sliver of the night? Or something to change me altogether? I envied the man for being important enough to have his life threatened. I worried about Rasheeda and Minnah, though. I don't know why anyone had to bring the man's kids into this mess.

I fixed another drink, then kicked off my shoes and got in bed. I bunched some pillows behind me so I could drink and read in a slouch. The thrill of stealing, or borrowing, is that it is pure possibility. Word by word, I awaited a shock, a tingle, or just something to keep me awake.

Several pages of *South Side News* featured Khadijah Jamil in an interview with Jeffrey Baines, the editor of this rag. Azzy had underlined about half of it. I had the whole night to kill, but I just read what he underlined, which was plenty. I figured these streaks of blue ink signaled what the big man cared about. I wanted to know him at least a little. I wanted to know someone in this world besides Nick Glouser, who reminded me of myself.

Jamil: I have to wonder if people will fight their own selves all the way to the grave. When nothing's sacred, nothing's safe. It don't matter to me whether Joanne Bland, who taught me this, is Muslim or Jewish or Christian or Holy Roller or agnostic or whatever—she got it right.

Baines: You've received forty-one death threats since you were nominated for president. Most of the negative campaign ads directed against you cite your Muslim beliefs. Why are so many Americans afraid of Muslims, and you in particular?

*Jamil (after a long pause and a wink): I'm a little like Shirley Chisholm, un-bought and un-bossed. She was the first black woman to run for president, and that was way back in '72. Well, if I, a Muslim from South Chicago, ever walk in the front door of the White House, I guess we'll call the event **historical** (Laughter.) The big question, though, is how more than 300 million Americans are going to live their lives. I mean, who do we give our power to? Who are we afraid of? If we say, 'Oh, the big players got so much money, they make the laws, they can crush me, they can crush everyone, they can take the whole earth, package it in plastic and Styrofoam and sell us the air we breathe, the water we drink,' I say, 'Yeah, that's right, they been doin' just that and more. So come together in community, stand tall. DO NOT RENDER YOUR LIVES IRRELEVANT.' I don't deeply care if I walk in the front door of the White House, but I do care about how we live. We* *don't have much time to turn ourselves around.*

Baines: What about the death threats? I mean, you can't just ignore them.

Jamil: I don't. My whole family's been threatened, my husband, my little girls, and even two nieces and a nephew. I've received in the mail three nooses, seven bullets, a bushel full of epithets, but a few of the threats are borderline apologetic. WE DON'T WANT TO KILL YOU PEOPLE, one person wrote, BUT WE'D BEST GET IT DONE BEFORE YOU KILL US. By YOU PEOPLE, he means Muslims of every stripe and color. If Islam is perceived as a violent religion, its elimination can be perceived as a civic duty. The world always tends to get real simple any time a group of people is persecuted. Nazis railed about the inherent violence and corruption of Jews. Things are nowhere near as bad for us, but the winds trouble me. Day after day, in what we call 'the news,' we hear about 'the inherent violence of Islam.' That's one of many things that needs to change.

I sipped my drink and stared at the ceiling. Is anything more out of place in this world than sincerity? Jamil was trying to open hearts or something, but she was on a long, rough road to nowhere. Dead end is a mild way of putting it. Every sign on this road is blank.

Baines: But haven't some of the most serious threats to you and your family come from fellow Muslims?

Jamil: Yes, they have. I'd say at least a third have come from Muslims who sincerely believe they must protect the purity of Islam from contamination. Over and over, I'm accused of being a western Muslim, progressive, out of sync, but I say Islam is—at its core—egalitarian, committed to social justice, and relentless in its reverence for life. The Qur'an—if seen in its entirety—points

133

straight to this truth.

Baines: Are you saying your interpretation of Islam is superior to others?

Jamil (scowling): No, that big bad word—superior—is not one I wish to own. I'm just stating the obvious. It's common that those who profess to believe in a particular religion know little or nothing of its core values. Most people are told what to believe by some power figure, paternal or tribal or whatever, and they take it in—no question asked.

Baines: Could you give an example?

Jamil: I could give several, but I'll start with the Hadith, the narratives and sayings of the Prophet, peace be upon him. My favorite unheralded scholar, Asma Barlas, notes that the Hadith began to be compiled more than a century after Muhammad's death and was not completed until more than 300 years later. Some of the sayings attributed to the Prophet are fabrications. It is the Hadith that introduced into Islam images of women as 'evil temptresses, the greatest fitna (temptation) for men, unclean over and above menstruation...weaker intellectual powers, and therefore unfit for political rule...' This is nonsense. The puritan school of Islam, dominated by men, selects apocryphal passages from the Hadith to sanctify their bias. In Saudi Arabia, for example, an interpretation of Islam that oppresses women—and really everyone but The Royal Family and the clerical establishment—has been enforced since the birth of that nation after World War I. The notion that women must be veiled and secluded is not Qur'anic. The puritans often cite the Hadith to override the Qur'anic principles of equality and social justice. In Saudi Arabia and elsewhere in the Middle East, leaders have abused Islam by forcing it to suit the whims of authoritarian rule.

Baines: I suppose the Saudi Royal Family is worried you might win the American presidency.

Jamil (laughter): They should be, but I'd guess they sleep well at night.

Baines: Your candidacy came out of nowhere. You were unknown outside Chicago's South Side two months ago. Now you're a household name. How does that feel?

Jamil (smiling and cross-eyed): Household? Most people can't pronounce Khadijah, but that's okay. What I'd like, though, is that they learn a little about my namesake, the Khadijah who was Muhammad's wife for twenty-five years. She was unusual for the seventh century, or maybe any century. Khadijah ran a caravan in Arabia at a time when women had almost no power or responsibility outside the home. She became prosperous, and she hired Muhammad, who was among the poorest men in Mecca, to see that her wares reached their destinations safely. She found him trustworthy, capable, and highly intelligent despite his lack of education. At age forty, widowed, she proposed to Muhammad, who was then about twenty-five. No, we're not talking here about a meek woman; we're talking about a woman who had a life in this world. We're talking about a full human being.

After Muhammad, Khadijah was the first Muslim. Most of his followers, however, came from the ranks of the poor, the have-nots, and they were many. Mecca was ruled by a few wealthy and corrupt individuals. The Qur'an was a direct challenge to their power.

I downed my drink and fixed another. Religion bores me. Politics bores me. History bores me. I trolled to the next page.

Baines: You call yourself an environmentalist more often than you call yourself a Muslim. How—living in the heart of South Chicago—did you become an advocate for the earth? I mean, there isn't much earth where you and me come from.

Jamil (smiling): True, but we got more gardens now. We got a community garden on almost every block and more than a few on rooftops. I'm an amateur naturalist. I love birds and have studied them since childhood, yet I must admit that—after more than fifty years—I don't know a single species in great depth. And to take this further, there is always this fact, which is perhaps the only fact: however much one studies a creature or a religion or a stone or a leaf or a person, the unknown territory remains vaster than the known. Complexity is what comforts me, and the mystery of life. One has to be strong and humble to glimpse truth.

This was all Azzy underlined. The interview went on for two more pages, but I let it rest. I turned on the TV and tinkered with the remote. A thousand channels or more, a viewing menu as long as a medieval scroll, yet nothing of relevance. Through the chatter, the shifting images, all I thought of was Azzy, his dizzying quest to make things better. What I had in this sprawl of pages, this newspaper I'd never heard of, was a borrowed glimpse of the man, what he cared about and what he denounced. I was halfway sure I knew him a little. Best of all, my mood improved. What I mean is I wasn't way down in the dumps now. Sure, I was down there a little, but at least I could see.

I rearranged my pillows and reread Rasheeda's letter to her daddy. Was she safe now? And Minnah? How would I respond if Jackie's life were threatened, or Sam's? I barely knew these kids, yet I needed them. Nobody—not even a creep—wants to live and die alone.

I had their phone number. It was 10:35 in Boston, 9:35 in Chicago...A good time to call? I dialed up and a woman answered on the fifth ring. I assumed this was Jackie and Sam's foster mom. I introduced myself, apologized if I was disturbing her, and asked if she and the boys had seen the game.

"They saw every second," she said. "I didn't."

I heard some chatter in the background.

"Are they awake?" I said. "Is it all right if I say hello to them?"

She stayed quiet. Maybe she was half deaf.

"I'm calling as a friend," I said. "Maybe we can all talk if you put them on another line."

Nothing feminine in this woman. She barked the boys' names—"Jackie! Sam!"—and seemed to drop the phone on a hard surface. I doubted she was much of a mom. I pictured an elderly hag who wore the same faded clothes each day, who had no greater pleasure than stepping out onto a dingy porch in slippers and robe to pluck monthly foster care checks from the mailbox. If she was screening calls, why did she let the boys speak to me? Did she set the bar so low that everyone jumped over? I needed a pause, a beat or two, to fix her in my mind: poor white trash from head to toe.

Sam came on, his voice high and excited. He started jabbering about the first inning, how Jesús and Johnny stole second and third, then came home after Jimmy hit a single.

"That was some single."

"And Jimmy hit a homer, too, six innings later. I still don't believe we lost."

I did.

"We'll win tomorrow," he said. "Dantel Hood's pitching."

"Against Matt Perlow."

"Perlow's good?"

"Off and on. A wicked slider."

"Well, Johnny can hit a slider, and Mijango hits everything. We might score a lot of runs."

He put his "brother" on the phone. Jackie said the Cubs would win either tomorrow night or on Sunday.

I said, "Why not both nights? Can't we put together a little winning streak?"

"No, not in Boston. The Cubs will win the last two games at Wrigley Field."

I winked. "You're my Charles Victor, you and your big brother."

"Sir, we'd be luckier if we saw each game at the ballpark."

I hesitated. "Sure, kid."

"Remember Game 2? Wrigley Field?"

"How could I forget?"

"Me and Sam were in the upper deck and the Cubs couldn't lose."

A bit drunk, I promised the kid he and Sam would have tickets for Game 6 and Game 7, but my mind drifted to a deeper concern. While Jackie jabbered non-stop about his number-one hero, Johnny Stompiano, I had to wonder where I fit in. How would I mean anything to these boys a year from now? How well would I know them? Would I somehow find out where they lived, jimmy a window, slip inside, and steal some treasure tucked away in a pocket, a drawer, a closet? To know someone requires a miracle, or at least special circumstances. I never knew my mother till she was dead.

Louise was her name, and she was quiet and pretty. I was eight when she died in a hotel fire in downtown Pekin. My father said he never knew her at all.

He found a stack of love letters in a shoebox. They all came from one man, Danny Murton, her secret lover. Danny's profession of love broke my old man's heart more than my mother's absence. Once, late at night, I heard him talking to himself. "Did I ever know her? Did I...?" We were on the sofa watching a ballgame, and he thought I'd fallen asleep.

He kept the letters, but he never meant for me to see them.

138

Every day I came home from school to an empty home, and I began to rummage around in drawers, cupboards, closets—whatever might hold a secret. I found the letters in the chest that housed my father's rifles. My mom's lover praised her "for staying in a bad marriage to raise a son who needs you. You've got gumption," he wrote, "and that's one reason I love you. Most women would cash in the chips and run."

I felt bad for my father. Why didn't she love him, and why did she stay in "a bad marriage" for me? My father and I had never talked much, and soon we lived in silence. He fed me TV dinners, spent a lot of time at taverns, but he still played catch with me in spring and summer. By age nine, I was the most talented Little League second baseman in Pekin, Illinois. By age twelve, I began to believe I could redeem two lives—mine and my dad's—if I got better and better and made the Major Leagues.

Sometimes I riffled through my dad's belongings for whatever he was hiding. I would scrutinize scraps of paper—bills, lists, scribbles—but nothing fit together to make a story I could understand. Three albums of wedding photographs—why did he keep them? My mother was beautiful in white, and he looked handsome and confident. What happened? Did they ever know each other? Did they love me? Answers never came and they've been gone for years.

*

After Jackie rattled off every Stompiano story he'd ever heard, Sam came on to thank me for calling. "I told my mom you're the Cub bench coach," he said, "but she doesn't believe me."

Why should she? Why believe anything?

"Will you call again, sir, when you're back in Chicago?"

"If you stop calling me sir."

"I'm sorry."

"No," I said, "let's skip the apology. You're doing your best to be polite."

I heard him breathing. Once before, I'd asked him and Jackie to call me Coach Billy or grandpa. The latter would be swell, I preferred it, but I was nobody's grandpa and never would be. I remembered a line from Groucho Marx that summed up my life: **I wouldn't belong to any club that would have me as a member.** I was a hard man to please. Had someone invited me into his family, I would've grown suspicious. What? You want me? Maybe you need a pet.

I asked Sam to call me coach. "Last name's Donachio," I said. "If you need to be formal, call me Coach Donachio."

He said, "Okay." A moment later he said, "Coach Donachio."

"Swell," I said, "perfect. Now you and me are pals."

I wanted to talk late into the night, but about what? Sam said, "Good night, Coach Donachio," I said, "Night, pal," and that was that. The click of a phone is a lonelier sound than a foghorn. Sometimes it's so abrupt it takes away your breath.

ROACHES

World Series

Game 4

Fenway Park

Line-up Cards

Home Boston Red Sox

Visiting Chicago Cubs

SS Domingo López

RF Kaido Miura

CF Moises de Dios Ovando

3B Bill Murphy

1B Maceo Mason

LF Preston Hollis

2B Jay McCreary

C Antonio Chévez

DH Flaco Méndez

CF Johnny Stompiano

LF Jamal Kelsey

2B Jesús Mijango Cruz

1B Jimmy Lieski

SS Rey Rodríguez

RF Terrence Gumbs

C Junior Parker

3B Matt Creighton

DH Mick Gutowski

Before the game, lounging in the dugout near Azzy, I eye his brood behind home plate. He looks, too, at his wife Isha twelve rows back, her arms curled over her girls, Rasheeda on one side, little Minnah on the other. Rasheeda's say seven or eight, and Minnah—sucking her thumb—looks like a kindergartener. I remember Rasheeda's drawing of a tree and a sun and her boast to her Daddy: **I make the world pretty.** Well, these kids take after him, their faces blue-black, no sign of dawn, but they're cute the way most kids are cute. Janice and Cue Ball sit with Azzy's brood, and I have to wonder who made the glue that holds this clan together. I mean, Janice is pale and pretty, keen on poetry. Cue Ball's in love with Mijango. He's black, so he sort of meshes with Azzy's people, but I doubt he's Muslim. The way Isha curls her arms over her girls makes me recall the threats her husband mentioned in *South Side News*. The one that worries the Cub ace most came from a Wahhabi, which must be a really conservative Muslim who wouldn't mind chopping the heads off less conservative Muslims or any chump who offers his neck. Well, the world's always had these types, whether we call them Wahhabis or whatever. You'd have to be younger than I am to glimpse a ray of hope.

*

The game is scoreless for five innings. In the sixth, the Bosox—who fail to hit the ball out of the infield—scratch a run out of nothing. I have a bad feeling this game is history. We look beat already, or I look beat. Last night, I slept maybe three hours. I feel like a pile of sludge wrapped in a package. Nick's kicking the Gatorade cooler. He often does this when we're getting our ass beat for no reason. He's old, but he has a lot of pent up energy. I think he sleeps well at night.

*

Seventh inning.

Bosox fans over our dugout are blasting their radios. Sam Foley and Mike Madson refer to our leadoff man as "Fire Escape Johnny, No Rules Johnny," as he makes his way to the batter's box. Foley says, "What's missing in this picture? Shouldn't there be an electronic monitoring device around a wrist or an ankle?"

"I'm all for it," says Madson, "but another idea's a curfew. Put Johnny in a crib—sides raised high—before the moon comes out."

These shock-jocks are part of a new generation of broadcasters whose ratings rise as the volume of jokes and insults rise. What I'd like now, after their cheap badinage, is to see Johnny turn on a Matthew Perlow slider and deliver it to the neighborhood of comets. Johnny hasn't homered this post-season, but he's capable. He's strong for a kid who weighs in at maybe a hundred-fifty pounds.

He gets behind in the count, 1-2, then surprises us with a bunt. Before Foley can say, "Lays one down," Johnny's half way up the line. The first baseman charges, bare-hands the ball, turns, but throws late to the bag. Foley, after a breathy pause, says, "What's he doing bunting with two strikes? No Rules Johnny burns another rulebook. He's out there with his squib single and there's nobody out."

Go ahead, Bosox bums, blast your radios. Blast them louder when Johnny comes home.

He takes a modest lead. Jabbering at Perlow, he leans toward second, flicks his wrists, flutters, leans toward first. Foley says, "He's got his two-way lead, his usual. No Rules Johnny might dive back to first, might break for second. Might wink and smile and stay where he is."

I eye Johnny, watch a smirk come and go, then home in on his girl. I often calm myself by observing a spectator rather than the field at a crucial time.

"Perlow's cranking his clock," says Foley. "He checks the runner, checks again, and here we go."

Janice shakes and shouts, leaps to her feet, her black hair fanned like a lion's mane. The hot crack of the bat rends the air.

"Line shot," says Foley. "Juiced down the right-field line, extra bases. Fire Escape Johnny's running as from a blaze."

The ball skims the grass near the warning track and bounces off the wall. The right-fielder plays the ricochet, but has trouble digging the ball from his glove. "Stompiano rounding third," says Foley, "heading for home. Miura finds the handle, cannons the ball in, and holds Jamal Kelsey to a double. Red Sox 1, Cubs 1. A runner on second and nobody out."

I am confident we will take the lead until I see something that remains difficult to believe. The Bosox catcher calls for the ball and tags Johnny. The ump, Lanny Burjack, one of the best, clenches his fist, pumps his right arm, which can mean but one thing—the Thief neglected to touch home. I moan till my lungs hurt. In the dugout, we're all studying the replay, and it seems the Thief—sprinting—grazed home plate with his left foot. We're hopeful the call will be overturned, the run will count, after the play is reviewed. Hell, Johnny had time to kiss home plate, put his arms around it, but he was flying so fast he barely brushed it with a spike.

A minute later, Burjack raises his fist again. Johnny's out. Case closed. Nick knocks over a Gatorade cooler. I press my hands to the sides of my head.

Sam Foley says, "No Rules Johnny is finding out about a rule—you need to touch home plate to score a run. He's moping now, talking with Burjack, shaking his head, the stunned look on his face as clear as a scream—**I don't believe it!**" He yuckles. "Well, **I** believe it. The Cubbies tie us, or seem to, but then they give the run back, trade it in for an out. Well, thank you, dear Cubbies, and come again. No Rules Johnny is out at home."

He says all this in the wake of Bosox cheers. These blood-sucking fans, forty thousand or so strong, are a rousing and barbaric display of lowlifes who love nothing more than receiving undeserved gifts.

Nick storms out to jaw with Burjack. His face is heart-attack colors. He waggles a fist near Burjack's chin. He kicks up dirt, spins, tosses his cap, kicks it when it lands, kicks it again, plays soccer with his cap. "The Cub skipper's begging to leave this game," says Foley. "He's kicking his cap this way and that, and now he's in Burjack's face, spit and venom. The Cub skipper seems to have forgotten the umps on the field have no role in the review of a play other than to relay the decision of the review team studying the video feeds in New York City. Well, up comes Burjack's arm—you're outta here. Nick Glouser kicks his cap again, gives it a boot. Better send this rag to a seamstress and patch the holes, the spike marks. In the meantime, the Cub skipper can go cry his grief to a concrete wall."

The office of the visiting team's manager is nothing but a concrete pillbox. Before Game 4, Nick found a cockroach beneath a stool. The bug, on its back, was dead. Nick was sure some Bosox thug had put it there. "Some flunkie," he said, "trying to mess with our minds."

Nick keeps kicking his cap. Now he stoops, digs up handfuls of dirt, showers the dirt in the air, then heads for the clubhouse. This puts me in charge, Second Lieutenant Donachio. I'm still trying to get an angle on what happened: Steal Home Johnny out at home.

The Bosox skipper orders an intentional walk for Jesús Mijango. Two on, one out. Jamal Kelsey, at second, stole nineteen bases during the regular season; Mijango stole twenty. Jimmy Lieski hit into thirty-one double plays.

Mike Madson says, "Challenge him, come right at him. After you catch a break, after you see the other team hanging their heads, play hardball. Matt Perlow should go straight for the kill."

Perlow catches Jimmy off balance with a roundhouse curve—strike one. I expect his next offering will be a tease, a slider close enough to the plate that the batter swings, and mean enough that the catcher works hard to keep the ball from bounding to the screen. When a hitter swings through a mean pitch, the catcher is challenged. He has to field the ball cleanly, set himself, throw, and by this time the runners, more often than not, are ninety feet closer to home.

I flash the double-steal sign to Jamal and Jesús. My first decision as the Cub skipper spikes a shiver up my spine.

Sam Foley says, "Perlow's ready to deal. He's looking in, he's looking...A glance at the runner on second and here he comes."

As the runners fly, Lieski lunges at a slider, misses, and his momentum carries him out over the plate. The catcher scoops, but our clean-up hitter—tall and still holding his bat in front of him—blocks any attempt to throw. Jamal had a jump, had third base stolen, Jesús had second, but the home-plate ump makes the only call he can make—**batter interference**. This sends Jimmy to the bench, out number two, and forces Jamal to return to second base, Jesús to first. "Son of a bitch," I mutter. "Son of a whore." I rap my knuckles against my chin.

Sam Foley calls us "old-time Cubbies, loveable losers in a train wreck." He snaps other insults, one more distasteful than the other. I go out to argue to get away from the damn broadcast. If the ump gives me the boot, well, I won't have to listen to these radios over our dugout. The fact that Burjack made the right call makes no difference now. I'd like to watch the rest of this game on a muted TV.

Before I start in on Burjack, I look over his shoulder at the fans behind home plate. Janice is standing, looking me over, it seems, which is a good reason to put on a show, stick up for our club. Nobody's too old or tired to display lunacy. I have studied the late Billy Martin. I know how to spit, how to scream. I know how to kick up dust storms, throw my cap in the air. I know how to get booted out of a ballgame. For as long as Burjack lets me, maybe a minute, I tell him he's the sorriest, dumbest, and ugliest this and that to ever set foot on a Major League ball field. When I'm running out of gas, just about the time he gives me the boot, I look behind home plate and see Janice and her companions. Is the girl watching me out of the corner of her eye? Does she care? No, she's chatting with Isha and Cue Ball, and no one seems the least perturbed. A minute ago, I thought Janice would appreciate a manager—or acting manager—showing some spunk, trying to fire up his team. I was wrong, though, and should've known better. Young silver-backed apes are impressive. Old ones get bloodied every day.

I join Nick in his office. He's cursing Burjack—"Dizzy motherfucker, blind bat"—and watching the game on Fox. I hunker down on a metal chair, no pads. Nick sits on a stool behind a small desk.

We let out a whoop as a wild pitch skips past the catcher. Kelsey skates over to third, Jesús Mijango to second.

"Now let's hit the damn ball," says Nick. "Let's see some yahoo knock in a few runs."

After an intentional walk, Terrence Gumbs, a power hitter, steps in with two down and the bags loaded. Nick, hunched on his stool, claps his hands and says, "Come on, Gumbo, flex your muscles. Let's lift one over the Green Monster as easy as baling hay."

Gumbs cold-cocks a 2-1 pitch to the deepest part of the yard. At the crack of the bat Nick hollers, "Bingo! Clear the bases!" but Moises de Dios Ovando makes an over-the-shoulder catch on the warning track near the 420 sign. Nick jumps to his feet and hurls a trashcan at a wall. He kicks his stool, spins, kicks it again. Nothing in this office is easy to harm. Concrete walls, concrete ceiling. The trashcan is metal, as are the legs of the stool.

Between innings, I tell the skipper how Sam Foley described the interference play. "Poured salt on our wounds," I say. "Opened a barrel and couldn't stop pouring."

"Why be surprised? He's the biggest asshole in baseball."

"Bosox fans love him."

"Assholes love assholes."

"Every other fan over the Cub dugout is blaring a radio. After a big play, after Foley and Madson get going, you can hardly hear yourself think."

Nick slides open the bottom drawer of his desk and takes out a fifth of Old Crow and a stack of soda cups. "In hell or high water," he says, "there's one thing that helps."

He opens the bottle and fills two cups half way. "Now we're in business," he says. "I propose a toast to Sam Foley's death."

Maybe he had a nip or two before I joined him. Leaning over his desk, his eyes dart one way, now another. I look, too, but all I see are the TV, a radio, a trashcan tipped on its side, a file cabinet in a corner. Nick's eyes are busy as a hawk's.

"I saw a roach," he says. "At least one."

"Where?"

He points to the file cabinet, the shadow it casts.

"Little fuckers dig in," he says. "They lay flat and still as a platoon of Marines."

I strain my eyes, then relax. Odds are I'll see one soon enough.

We do what we do best: sip Old Crow, look for bugs, and watch our team suffer. In the bottom of the seventh, after the

Bosox score twice, Nick picks up the trashcan and stares into it. "Little fucker's in there," he says. "He knows he can't get out."

Before things get worse, I excuse myself by claiming I have to urinate. I know in my heart my team will lose this game. The only way I might salvage anything from the waste is to prowl around the clubhouse. If I can riffle through a few lockers, I might leave Fenway with some memento of recompense.

I've never received a fan letter, or even hate mail. Johnny receives letters in bundles, boxes, so why shouldn't he share the bounty? I flip through a tall stack and choose a letter he's already opened. A post-it note blocks the sender's address and says, *Important—don't recycle.* I recognize Johnny's handwriting. The fact that he plans to save this letter is proof of its value. Maybe I'll return it to his locker before tomorrow's game.

I am doubly drawn to a letter that bears a salutation—*Johnny, Mon Belamour*—in green ink. The handwriting, unmistakable, is that of Janice Oyakawa. A small, neat script like a watercolor wash of leaves and light.

I go to my own locker and stuff the booty in the case of my laptop. I gather the materials borrowed from Azzy, *South Side News* and Rasheeda's drawing, and return them to the security pocket of his overcoat. I frisk the other pockets and find three tickets for tomorrow's game, plus a computer disc the size of my thumb. I leave the tickets, but I can't help wondering what's on the disc. Instead of taking it, I boot up my laptop and save the documents on my hard drive. Copying is different from borrowing or stealing. I can keep these documents as long as I wish.

*

I mosey back to Nick's office and find him listening to Bosox radio, WEEI. Sam Foley's saying something, then Madson, and Nick's making little marks on a blank scorecard. I start to protest

149

("What the hell's this?"), but he tells me to hush. He's muted the TV, so we just have the radio racket, the abuse of shock-jocks. The Bosox have extended their lead to five-zip, and Foley and Madson take their time recapping the inning. When they finish, when the commercials come on like a blessing, or a relief from torture, the skipper informs me he plans to sue Sam Foley for calling the Cubs suicidal. "He said it twice," said Nick, "and Madson laughed twice. I'll sue these cornholers till they laugh themselves dead."

His pen skirls across the scorecard. I glance at squiggles and curlicues that look like bugs.

*

In the final innings, no one wearing a blue helmet hits the ball out of the infield. We look like a team of sleepwalkers, a team that has tossed down a heavy dose of Quaaludes. In the ninth, after we go down in order, Sam Foley starts singing an old Simon and Garfunkle song—"I'd rather be a hammer than a nail." Nick, heavy-lidded, half in the bag, says, "Yeah, fuck you, Sam, fuck you and your hammer." He reaches for the bottle and takes a long swig.

*

Can we be saved? Is hope a disease? I have a message from Janice, an envelope labeled *Important—don't recycle*, plus a few stray documents from Azzy. Before I leave Fenway, I need one more item—tickets for Game 5. I'm thinking of Charles Victor Faust, the luckiest man in the history of the Game, and I'm thinking of my orphan acquaintances, Jackie and Sam. I'd like to call these kids **friends**, but I know better. If the Cubs lose Game 5, the World Series is over and I doubt I'll coach in another one before the world itself is over. I mean, kaput. Belly up. Like the roach Nick found earlier under a stool. Even an idiot knows this world—or at least the human side of it—probably won't be around much longer. No world, no World Series. There you have it. I might be dizzy and drunk, but I know who's lucky and who's not. Nick's still at his desk making marks on a scorecard. Me? You know about me. Case closed. Jackie and Sam, though, these boys are fresh. Maybe they're a little like Rasheeda and can make the world pretty, or at least more tolerable. Hell, even a drunk knows there isn't much time left for good things to happen. I need two tickets for Jackie and Sam.

DARK LIGHT

In the locker room, quiet after a loss, I went around asking for tickets. "I'll pay double," I said. "I'll pay triple. I need tickets for tomorrow's game."

Cub personnel generally make advance reservations for friends and loved ones, but I seldom use the service due to a lack of human relations. Earlier in the eve, had I sunk lower, I would've filched the tickets from a locker while the rest of the team was busy losing Game 4.

Azzy, naked but for a white towel at his waist, said, "How many you need, coach?"

"Two," I said. "I'll pay double."

"You won't pay a penny. I got three giveaways."

I groped for my wallet. "I'd like to reimburse—"

"No, maybe one day you can thank Sami Slyde. His trio would be here tomorrow if they weren't playing a gig in D.C."

Never had I stood this close to a near-naked giant. As Azzy bent over with his towel wrapped tight, I worried the white fluff might slip free and reveal him in his fullness. The man was too much for me, too alive or something. I looked past him toward the neutrality of a wall.

His uniform and big-and-tall-man clothes hung in his locker. When he reached a hand into a pocket of his trousers, I was pleased I hadn't stolen from him earlier. "Yours for the asking," he said. And his face—circular, blue-black—was the darkest eclipse of the darkest sun.

He stood near enough to embrace. He swayed, turned, and something inside him or around him shone so bright I raised a hand to push it back. Sure, I was drunk, but what happened next had nothing to do with whiskey. Blinking, I saw him slide three tickets in my left hand. "Yours," he said. "Tell your friends to bring us some luck."

I leaned back to see his face, my left hand a cup near my chest. Light poured from Azzy, light and heat, and swung over me like a summer sky. I had no chance to slink toward a wall, grope for a shadow. No one, not even Fire Escape Johnny, was fleet enough to outrun the man's brightness. Midnight led to noon, but I wasn't afraid now. For too short a span—drum a finger on your heart, breathe—the sun of one man was more potent than any fear.

My voice broke the spell. "Azzy," I said, "let me pay you."

"No, these are courtesy of Sami Slyde. Don't make me say it again."

"I don't know him."

"Well, he'll be in Chicago in about three weeks, playing a weekend at Nikki's."

I didn't know Nikki either.

"He's old," said Azzy, "about your age. But he's still the best jazz violinist in the world."

*

I checked the tickets when the euphoria passed. They were wrinkled, folded in half, but nonetheless genuine. I checked the date, the specifics. Everything was right.

Three tickets! It should have occurred to me sooner that Jackie and Sam's foster mom would have to allow her boys to come to Boston. If she was worth a nickel of what the state paid her, if she was any sort of mom, she wouldn't let either of her charges hop on a plane and fly off to a distant city. Now, with three tickets, I could invite her to come along. I would make it clear that the whole package—airfare, restaurants, hotel, taxis, ballgame—was paid for. If necessary, I would sweeten the deal with some money on the side.

I went to my locker, brought out my laptop, and tried to book three tickets for a plane leaving Chicago the next morning. I got stalled when the form asked for the full names of those in my party. I remembered the white boy's last name (Moriarty), but what about Sam's? As for their foster mom, their pseudo-mom, I didn't know her from Eve. I told myself, "Damn it, Billy, sober up a while." My hand was trembling as I reached for my phone.

Sam answered my call, so I went straight to work. "Young fellow," I said, "let me pose a question. How would you and Jackie and your foster mom like to see Game 5 at Fenway Park?"

I heard an in-breath. I bet his mouth hung wide open.

"Tickets courtesy of Azzy Azzam," I said. "One for you, one for Jackie, and one for your mom."

He blurted, "Jackie! Jackie! We're going to Boston! We're going to Boston! We're going to see the game!"

So Jackie got on, had me tell him three times what was what, then left me to deal with the foster mom. Being cordial isn't my nature, but at least I discovered her name—Sonia. After I put the whole thing in a nutshell, the ballgame, the free trip, she said, "What's the catch? Who are you?"

"Billy Donachio," I said, "Cub bench coach. We spoke briefly last night."

But the old hen was suspicious. Who wouldn't be? A call on a dark night, a stranger offering her and her boys coveted gifts. To compound matters, I couldn't divulge my motives. If I spoke of luck, of Charles Victor Faust leading the New York Giants to three pennants before dying, she would dismiss me as a loony. I couldn't wonder aloud if Jackie and Sam were the Charles Victors of the 21st century, nor could I admit that my sole friend in this world, Nick Glouser, was still in his office looking for roaches. I had one thing in my favor: neither Sonia nor her boys knew me. My stars were crossed, heaven had fallen, but what if no one looked up? I wanted new friends. I wanted to belong. I was like the Cubs in their sorriest years.

"Sonia," I said, "the tickets are from Azzy Azzam. I didn't pay a nickel, but I have three tickets. Tomorrow morning all you and your boys have to do is catch a cab to O'Hare."

She said, after a lengthy silence, "This is nuts."

"No, call it generosity, a genuine offer. Do you know Johnny Stompiano's an orphan?"

She stayed quiet.

"He'll grin like a fiddler when I tell him two orphans are coming to the game."

She said she had to give it some thought.

"Well, there can't be much to think about. Your boys want to see this game? Am I wrong?"

"No, but—"

"I already reserved a hotel suite for the three of you," I lied. "Just one thing, though. I can't book with United Airlines until I provide your full names."

Extracting these was as tense as trying to extract eggs from a worried and roosting hen. Sonia pecked at me, questioned my motives, backed me toward a wall. Three or four times I told her generosity was not completely defunct. "I wish I could introduce you to Azzy," I said. "He's the most generous human being in the world."

I was about to give up when she blurted the boys' birth names (Jackie Moriarty, Samuel Calvillo), and her own (Sonia Melgar). To avoid mistakes, I coaxed her to spell the last names twice.

"One more thing," I said. "I'll book your flight for around 10 a.m. Does that suit your schedule?"

"This is crazy."

"Well, is Azzy Azzam crazy? Is generosity crazy?"

She hesitated. "A lot of things are crazy."

"Yeah, but this is up-front," I said, "all cards on the table. I'm sure you and your boys would like to see the game."

I told Sonia I'd click on my laptop, book the flight, and call her back. The old hen hung up before I could say goodbye.

The next time I called she let the phone ring around twelve times, probably to fray my nerves. I bet her boys were begging her, "Please, mom, please! Pick up the phone!"

When at last she did I heard Sam's voice in the background. "He's nice, mom, don't worry. He just wants us to see the game."

Sonia was taciturn, almost spiteful, but she took down the flight number, the reservation code, and confirmed the departure time in Chicago and the arrival in Boston. I heard Jackie and Sam whistling and whooping. Sam shouted, "We're going to Boston! We're going to the World Series! We're going to the game!"

I said to Sonia, "Check in around two hours early at O'Hare. Might as well give yourselves some breathing room."

She gave me silence.

"I'll be waiting in the baggage area, okay? Logan Airport in Boston."

"Fine."

I smiled. "Your boys call me Coach Donachio, but call me

Billy if you like."

I sometimes reach for mountaintops when standing in a cellar. She didn't call me anything, unless **Bye**—spark-quick on this lady's lips—might pass for a name.

CALIPHATE CUBS

The room-service waitress, Asian, pale and pretty, wore a plaid skirt, a white blouse, and shiny black shoes. I gave her a tip and watched her bow five times, once for each dollar. Her pronunciation was a work in progress. When she said, "Tank you, sir, tank you," I said, "No, tank **you**!" I felt mean the moment I mocked her. "Here," I said, and sent her away with another five in her hand.

I fixed a stiff nightcap, JD with a dash of water. After the booze set a small fire in me, a moderate glow, I opened the letter from Janice. I bent over and sniffed the paper, the ink. I let my longing linger a little while.

Dear Johnny,
To see one thing clearly—a ball with red stitches, a brown leaf, a cloud—changes everything. And to write one true thing reinterprets the world.

A cloud? I've seen more of those than anyone and nothing changes. Janice is fanciful, optimistic. I'd lay down some hard cash to see through her eyes.

I believe every community has its own language, its own poetry, and it is kin to common speech. It grows in this place of commonality, it moves through it, in the way that a rose expands in the circle of its scent. It is more natural than special, more found than discovered. The poems on Wrigley Field billboards are our North Side poems. But poems are in soil, color, light, breath, song, flesh, fire. They are born in silence, in spaces barren of names.

Our East Coast friends will soon post two poems on DC billboards. On 11/03, as planned, you and Azzy and others will meet KJ on a Wrigleyville rooftop—more on that tomorrow. President Trent's comment has gone viral. Nothing the least bit original, though it's being treated as 'news.'

Steal a base for me, steal my heart,

Janice

I did some basic calculations. If the Cubs could tread water and stay alive, Game 6 of the World Series would be played at Wrigley Field on November 3rd. Would the event with KJ (Khadijah Jamil?) be held after the game, or would there be no game to interfere with poetry and politics? I smiled at the thought that Janice was scheming, maneuvering, cutting deals on the side. As for President Trent's comment, he said the Republican Party was "in trouble if all the blacks and browns and Muslims and women and gays and freaks and mental cases show up at the polls this time around." He was in an elevator, chatting with aides, and didn't realize he was being recorded. The old crank hasn't apologized, and why should he? He tells it like it is, crude and bare.

I delayed reading the second letter, the one marked *Important—don't recycle.* I had that to look forward to, plus the contents of Azzy's disc that I'd stored on my laptop. To finish everything of interest early in the eve would leave too much time to kill.

I turned on the tube to check the news. FOX, in their special coverage of the election, gave Khadijah Jamil maybe thirty seconds. In Memphis, addressing the issue of poverty to a crowd of paupers, some of them homeless, she predicted victory in November. Her eyes shiny, her face as dark as the night above her, she stood on the top step of a church and sang a Negro spiritual from the time of slaves.

> Go down, Moses.
> Go down to Egyptland.
> Go tell ol' Pharoah,
> Let my people go!

The black people sang with her, the browns too, and even some whites. I wondered if Jamil's handlers gave her permission to sing an old slave song. I had a hunch she received a lot of advice which went to seed.

The remainder of the newscast was devoted to Michael J. Trent and his bid for re-election. In an address to a military audience at Fort Myers, he named several countries that were "freedom's enemies, Satan's eternal companions." Mr. Trent's a bit pudgy, but at one point he shared the microphone with a retired Marine Corps colonel who stood on his left. This colonel **looked** like a colonel. He'd obviously seen a war or two because he had around thirty medals on his chest, rows of rainbows, and he was tall and hard, a man's man, sleek and muscled as a shark. He spoke of "terrorists losing ground on all fronts, from the Middle East to South Asia." President Trent asked a question and the colonel knew the answer. "The United States, led by a strong commander-in-chief, will continue to light the way and assist everyone everywhere who yearns for dignity, self-determination, and a God-filled way of life."

The president invited his campaign manager, Cindy Lang, onto the stage. A blue-eyed blond in a red skirt, a red sweater, she was drop-dead gorgeous. If she and Janice Oyakawa were in a beauty contest, the judges might have to toss a coin to choose the winner. Anyway, Ms. Lang and our commander-in-chief crisscrossed the country in Air Force One, touched down in battleground states, and they seemed to be having the time of their lives. In her presence Mr. Trent looked—I tend to choke on this word—happy. They were unbeatable, unstoppable, and they knew it. One had money and one had looks.

I thought Ms. Lang might say something besides, "USA! USA! USA!" but maybe this was all she needed to say. Soon the colonel joined in. He and Ms. Lang worked the crowd into a frenzy, and those three letters—USA—seemed to create a universe, or at least an empire. Maybe it was a trick of the lighting, but the president's face turned really orange now, and his hair too. Despite his age, all the ruckus agreed with him. "Turn up the volume!" he seemed to be saying. "Let's go crazier than crazy!" Never in my life had I seen a man more at home in the bedlam of center stage.

Now Trent's VP, Gerald Price, came up and shook his boss's hand. Price, the darling of evangelicals, never needed to say much since his beliefs were known. He and the president and Cindy Lang had to be the most photographed threesome in history, and tonight—as always—Trent was the man in the middle, the nation's flag behind him. I have to admit the president looked good for an old man. He was American sexy, if you know what I mean. One could see at a glance he had complete command of the stage.

*

It was getting late, so I brought out the letter marked

Important—don't recycle. Was it possible this was also from Janice? Hope is usually a mistake.

Dear Johnny,

We met several times at gatherings in support of my wife's candidacy, and I've always admired your sly humor, your wit, your street smarts, and your caring for endeavors larger than yourself.

I, like others on the South Side, am amused by what we now call "Johnny's Fire Escape Antics." Neighbors shake their heads, smile, palaver, but later come the questions. Did you paint the moustache with such precision as a reminder to some, an alarm to others? Did the end product refer to all of us, or just one man?

The day Khadijah turned 21, her grandmother took her aside and woke her ears with a song of complexity: "All that is humanly possible is possible in me." At first, in mind and heart, she could feel Khadijah leaning toward the sublime, contemplating all the wonders she might perform, the countless beings she might help, but by the time the day ended she knew her grandchild had enough grit to consider the pain she might cause if she failed to see her flaws. If I sing to you, Johnny, "All that is humanly possible is possible in me," will you comprehend? America's tragedy is and has always been a tragedy of innocence misperceived. O, the white, the pure, the cross, the sheets, the chains, the rope, the trees, the needles, the jails, the bombs, the $, the dope, the hope are not mere skeletons of history but current crucifixions. Many wish my wife dead for a variety of reasons: her blackness, her religion, and—last but not least—her understanding of history's influence on the present. Money men can't buy her, fundamentalist clerics can't scare her into submission, so nooses arrive in the mail, her name and the n-word—or the M-word (Muslim)—scrawled in red and taped to blond ropes. A common life, this century and others: soot for air, rubbish for earth, bars for sky. No vote-hungry *politician comes down to the streets, the shelters, the jails, but this is where you'll find Khadijah. I'd better back-step before you think she's some sort of saint, the Mother Teresa of Islam. If you were to set a halo on her head, she'd say, "Wild Child, get that thing off me," and she'd laugh till she filled the room. So, Johnny, no halos for the candidate, and no devil's horns either. Every truth is half humility, half wonder. My wife's only perfection is her awareness of flaws.*

You are 28, I believe. Khadijah, another quick learner, began to wise up on her 21st birthday. All that is humanly possible is possible in me. One who perceives the range, the capacities, is far less likely to bring harm to our world. This, it seems, is all the wisdom I have garnered in 58 years.

Sincerely, and with a smile for you and Janice and every tender wish,

Ahmed Jamil

What was I to do with this? At first I was sorry I read Ahmed Jamil's letter, but then I went back and read it twice. **All that is humanly possible is possible in me**...It dawned on me that I'd spent my life courting the nether-side of phenomena. I resided in suffering, made dates with depression. A white guy supposedly enjoys advantages, right? But the advantages vanish in a heart made of sludge.

I tried to ease myself to sleep with late-night TV. How was it that a thousand channels or more had merged into the same dead channel? I thought of calling Jackie and Sam, but I checked the time—1 a.m. My boys needed their sleep before their big trip to Boston tomorrow morn.

I got out my laptop and opened Azzy's file, the stuff that I'd downloaded from the disc he kept in his locker. I trolled through several documents, nothing all that captivating, but it was better than TV. Most of what Azzy saved on disc was about Islam, which has two meanings: peace and submission to God. I didn't know the Cub ace was an author, a sort of amateur historian. I'd never known a ballplayer who had serious intellectual pursuits.

Azzy, in his essay for an on-line journal for "moderate Muslims," began with an apology for the brevity of his analysis. "This is merely a sketch," he wrote. "For a fuller account of the history and evolution of puritanical Islam, see Khaled Abou El Fadal's *The Great Theft: Wrestling Islam from the Extremists*." I scrolled through twenty-one pages of text and read maybe a third of what Azzy wrote. Brevity? I don't think so. Anyway, I just read this bit about "the birth of Wahhabism" and "The Islamic State."

*

Abd al-Wahhab was an 18th century preacher from eastern Arabia. After visiting Basra and observing the rich diversity of Shi'ism and Sufism, he strove to strip Islam of superstitious innovations and restore it to its "original purity." Wahhab and his disciples embarked on a violent crusade, tearing through the Arabian Peninsula demolishing sacred tombs, cutting down sacred trees, and massacring whoever disagreed with their vision. They banned music, flowers, poetry, coffee. Under the penalty of death, Wahhab and his "Holy Warriors" forced men to grow beards and women to be veiled and secluded.

I shrugged. Did Azzy think he was relating something new? Lunatics create history while the rest of us twiddle our thumbs.

Al-Wahhab made a pact with Muhammad ibn-Saud, the leader of a minor tribe in the Arabian Peninsula. Ibn-Saud would wage war against infidels and idolaters; in turn, al-Wahhab would provide religious "guidance." This alliance eventually changed the course of Islamic history, as well as "the geopolitical balance of the world."[3] *The Saud tribe became increasingly powerful and Wahhabism spread throughout much of the Arabian Peninsula.*

During World War I, the British, "eager to control the Persian Gulf," provided arms and money to help the Saudis in their rebellion against the Ottoman Empire. The plan worked. After the war, the Ottoman Empire was dismantled, the Caliphate abolished, and the leaders of the Saud tribe reigned in Mecca and Medina. They renamed the Arabian Peninsula the Kingdom of Saudi Arabia, imposed Wahhabism on the entire population, and publicly executed about 40,000 men.

Who was Azzy trying to impress? Sure, the world's brutal, always has been. 40,000? That's the minor leagues compared to the Nazis. Numbers can't reach me, nor can historical facts. I finished my drink and poured another. My heart was pounding for no reason. I scrolled to the next page.

Oil revenue made Saudi Arabia a world power, and some of its vast wealth has been spent in the service of "religion." More than one hundred billion in Saudi money, funneled through the charities the government established, has brought the Wahhabi doctrine to the far corners of the world. Across the globe, mosques, primary schools, secondary schools, and universities are built free of charge, but with a catch—adherence to the Wahhabi vision. Scholars critical of Wahhabism—its brutal simplicity, its denial of Islam's rich intellectual history—are outlawed. Instead, authors and publishers who promote puritanical Islam in the Kingdom and throughout the world are awarded lucrative contracts. In addition,

---

[3] See Reza Aslan's excellent *No god but God.* (Of course this is Azzy's footnote, not mine. —Billy D.)

the government imports large numbers of workers from other countries to work in the oil fields. They, too, are indoctrinated with the Wahhabi view, which they bring back to their countries after their work contracts expire. In this way, Abd al-Wahhab's obsession to strip Islam of religious diversity has continued into the 21st century.

ISIS has attracted recruits from at least seventy-four countries to wage "holy war" against infidels. Saudi Arabia has joined the fight against ISIS, but—more than all else—it is the Saudis' worldwide promotion of the Wahhabi doctrine that created ISIS to begin with. The religious and political ideology of Saudi Arabia and ISIS have more similarities than differences. Both are completely totalitarian. Both strive to destroy the impetus toward social justice and equality, the main tenets of the Qur'an, which are the very heart and soul of Islam.

In ISIS-controlled areas of Afghanistan, children begin their religious training at age three or four. Eight-year-old boys know how to fire weapons. In primary schools, male students are shown violent videos—beheadings, public executions, battles—as part of their training to become ISIS fighters. Suicide bombers are as young as twelve. ISIS calls these armies of children "The Caliphate Cubs."

Up went my brow. The Caliphate Cubs? According to Azzy, some of these children were orphans. Others were kidnapped. The Nazis had the Hitler Youth. What's new in the world? ISIS has the Caliphate Cubs.

In Afghanistan, ISIS fighters are paid approximately $700 per month. In this war-ravaged nation, work is scarce, stability merely an ideal, and many men join ISIS not out of any religious or political conviction but because they have no better way to support *themselves and their families. James Baldwin reminded us that no one is more dangerous than the man who has nothing to lose. In Douar Hicher, an impoverished suburb of Tunis, numerous young men have left their homes to give their lives to "the Caliphate." A Muslim friend of mine calls this "religious adventurism." These men have no access to classical Islam. Their circumstances have left them with a crude and inaccurate understanding of their religion. The consequences could hardly be more tragic.*

*

Azzy went on for several pages about The Global Marshall Plan to alleviate poverty and hunger, repair the global environment, and make groups such as ISIS irrelevant. The Cub ace spoke as from clouds. **We can, by working directly with and for the poor, develop sustainable economies in areas that have been devastated by conflict.** The plan, modeled roughly on the Marshall Plan that pulled Germany and Japan out of the dregs after World War II, would be funded by a small slice of what Azzy called "excess" (1-2% of the GNP of advanced industrial nations). Good luck, Azzy. You'd be in business if you were asking for an additional 1-2% to buy more military hardware for the wars in South Asia, North Africa, and the Middle East.

In part, The Global Marshall Plan was the brainchild of Michael Lerner, an American rabbi, but it supposedly had backers from all religions. Azzy wrote, *Every Christian and Muslim I know in South Chicago supports this plan. Neither the United States nor any alliance of nations can kill its way to victory over ISIS or the Taliban, etc. Those who fight and die in "the Holy War" become martyrs in their communities, heroes to emulate, so that for every dead terrorist perhaps ten more are born. Muslims who truly understand the beauty of Islam can—with the help of all caring people—wrest Islam from those relatively small bands of fanatics who have transformed a great faith into a cult of coercion and killing. Puritanical versions of Islam must be challenged. To succeed, our effort must alleviate poverty and establish basic civil rights.*

Azzy noted that Khadijah Jamil's efforts to gain some traction for The Global Marshall Plan in Congress had been thwarted for more than a decade. Did he really believe Jamil had a chance to become America's commander-in-chief? Was he **that** out of touch? I worried for his sanity, and mine too, because I was in somewhat of a tizzy. I'd been reading about Islam—**Azzy's** Islam—for almost an hour. I longed to sleep, to slip free of this world and its hallucinations, but I couldn't even close my eyes. Why did Azzy care so much? What if his ideals killed him? What if Wahhabis harmed his family? I found myself muttering, "Give it up, Azzy. Let someone else be a sucker." I had to admire him, though, for going against the grain, and for caring about something other than baseball. Azzy Azzam—he was my opposite. I had no religion. I had fuzzy values. I'd be the last chump in the world to go against the grain.

*

My sorrows were so small, so personal, but I was dying for someone to talk to. I took a half-finished drink down to the lobby. I exchanged pleasantries with a girl working the front desk, but her good looks unsettled me. Beside beauty I am shy, forlorn, an eternal stranger. Will I be shy at the age of eighty? At ninety-nine? Don't put anything past me. I may blush on the morning I'm lowered in a grave.

I wished her a pleasant eve and sat on the sofa facing the front entry. Three limos were parked on Beacon Street. A wall about waist-high, an anti-terrorist barrier, prevented vehicles from driving up the cul-de-sac to the doors of the hotel. Had management asked my advice, I would've said, "Build the wall higher! And build a moat!" It's no use, though. On a given night, the best they can do is keep some crazies out and others inside.

I looked up from my drink as a taxi pulled up behind the limos. I couldn't see well, but I knew the girl stepping out on the curb was Janice Oyakawa. A moment later, Johnny hopped out of the taxi and closed the door.

I should've retreated to my room and taken a sleeping pill. Johnny waved to the cabbie, took his girl's hand, and they walked up the cul-de-sac toward the hotel. Another cab pulled up on Beacon Street. Someone short and bulky got out the back door.

Split a second twelve times, no, twenty times. One-twentieth of a second was all I needed to recognize Al Muscat. The words of an old song crossed my mind: **How can I miss you if you won't go away? How can I miss you if you stay and stay and stay?** A newsman, a bottom feeder, Muscat will stir up trouble till he dies. Like a walrus, he would move more naturally belly-down, his appendages employed as flippers. I've often wondered why a ballplayer or a team of ballplayers hasn't sealed him in a sack and tossed him in a river. I discredit Muscat for helping to establish the main rule of modern-day sports media: Use every waking moment to create or reveal sins.

Worried that Johnny would embarrass the team, say something to get us all in trouble, I got up, drink in hand, no coat, and ventured outside. He and Janice came up a pathway beneath a tall tree. Muscat called, "Johnny! Hey, buddy!" The walrus waddled forward and grabbed the Kid's arm.

"Muscat," I said, "that's enough," but he ignored me. Even Johnny ignored me. Janice? She was looking at the sky, so I looked too.

Dim stars over a maple tree, a half moon. Beauty is in the last inning. In the twenty-first century even the stars appear caged.

Down here in the dark, the noise, Muscat wanted to speak with Johnny off record. "No tricks," he said, "no gimmicks. None of this will see the light of day."

Muscat was Muscat. He would trouble a stone to hear its voice, chip and scrape until sparks flew. In a perverse way, he was Johnny's accomplice. Our centerfielder would pretend to be fooled. He would ignore a gag order, speak "off record," and later express surprise and outrage when private comments became public. The Kid knew as well as anyone that whatever issued from his mouth would be instant news, pretty much the only news left. If he spoke in whispers, the world would hear thunder. Or at least the sports' world of America would amplify and repeat his words till they nagged us even in our dreams.

So Muscat and Johnny were in cahoots. Me? Hunched under an awning, a few steps beyond the main door of the lobby, all I could do was watch. Johnny still held his girl's hand. Mine were sweating, despite the chill in the air. Muscat gave Johnny a playful punch to the shoulder. Deck him, I was thinking. Smash his teeth.

Muscat, getting down to business, mentioned a front-page article in yesterday's *Chicago Tribune*. "Your night on a fire escape is well-remembered," he said. "Johnny the Vandal—how's that sit with you?"

"It sits fine."

"Your target was President Trent, and you may be hearing from his lawyers."

"I already have."

"Defamation of character, defamation of an image."

"I did nothing wrong."

"Johnny, let's cut the crap. You turned our president into a symbol. You had a gallon of paint, enough to blacken the whole billboard. But all you did was paint a moustache."

Johnny shrugged.

"You remember what you told me after Game 2?"

"More or less."

"You ran out of paint. You wanted to give the president a fuller moustache, but ran out of paint."

"Al, everybody knew I was joshing."

"Joshing?"

"Yeah."

"Well, how about if you surprise me and tell the truth?"

Truth, in the mouth of Muscat, sounded like a disease. I took one step backward. Light-headed, eyeing Janice, I edged back near a wall. She let go of Johnny's hand and came up the walkway. If she hadn't approached me, or if she'd passed by me and into the lobby, I might have recovered. A coach's job is not only on the field. Right now, for instance, I should have been threatening Muscat and those who employed him with litigation, restraining orders, a whole regiment of lawyers yapping like Chihuahuas. Would this have stopped him? No, not for a second. But it would have left me with a sense of purpose, a shred of meaning. It would have given me the illusion that I had a role on this team.

Janice stepped in front of me. "Sir," she said, "it's alright. Johnny knows what he's doing."

I nodded.

"So let them chat a while," she said. "It can't do any harm."

In black boots, snug jeans, a sweater, she was elegant. A purse hung from her left shoulder, its flimsy strap angled between her breasts. The smell in the air—what was it? Blood and salt? A woman? And where did it come from if not from her?

I coughed. I made croaking sounds, dumb as a frog. Janice touched my right forearm; I remember the pressure. "Come," she said, "let's go inside. Johnny will join us soon."

A minute or so later the roustabout sauntered into the lobby. "Hey, coach. Up late, aren't you?"

I cleared my throat. "You too, Kid."

"No, this is more or less the norm."

DILDOS

Nick woke me with a phone call before sunrise. "You hear it?"

"Hear what?"

"Hell's bells," he said. "They bang louder every time Johnny opens his mouth."

The skipper cursed his managerial duties, his bad nerves, his lack of sleep. The front office had called him at four in the morning. "Butch Malecki wants to know why I can't control Johnny," he said. "Why can't I snap on the cuffs, be his jailer? And why can't I lead us to victory as easy as blinking an eye?"

I heard a computer or a TV in the background.

"Malecki's the fattest bitch in show-biz," said Nick, "and the dumbest."

I agreed.

"But Johnny's a hellcat, a one-man circus." He groaned. "He won't get hurt by this, but I might. My ass is in a sling."

So it was. I went up to Nick's suite to listen to the latest news on his laptop. I expected to hear a voice-script of Johnny's conversation with Al Muscat, but ESPN delivered the whole kit and caboodle—audio and video, sharp contrasts, well-defined color. I suppose mini-cameras had been mounted in bushes and trees, on light poles, fire hydrants, curbs, walls, awnings. What's the world coming to? We'll all be sorry if no sin or shame can be buried in the night.

But Johnny grinned. In baggy jeans, a Cub jacket open at the collar, he communicated ease and warmth, and maybe even trust. At a glance, a normal person might see him as normal (I'm OK, you're OK), but let me give you the low-down. Johnny has a tattoo, a red coyote—running—at the center of his chest. This is his true portrait. The Kid will trick you every time.

On this new day, ravaged, hung-over, I received a rare gift: Muscat and his editors had left me where a reluctant witness belongs, the cutting room floor. I might have been fired had Nick or others in management found out that I'd waited in the wings while Johnny embarrassed the team before a national audience. "Why didn't you stop him?" they'd ask. "Why didn't you drive off Muscat with a stick?" Well, Muscat was Muscat—unstoppable. Management could understand obsession, Muscat's or their own, but I was well beyond the pale. In the presence of Janice Oyakawa, I became as helpless as an insect sucked dry and pinned to a board.

*

The day's top story began with Janice letting go of Johnny's hand and walking off-camera. No witnesses now, no promise from Muscat—"This is off record." The bottom feeder asked Johnny if he thought the Cubs had a chance to win the Series. Were they dead, out of luck, or would they bounce back from a three-game-to-one deficit?

Johnny, head cocked, said, "I'm not worried about it, Al. We've been the comeback kids all year long."

Muscat smiled. "Seeing is believing," he said. "Cub fans, near and far, say, 'We'll win three in a row the way we did in '16.'

Red Sox fans say, 'No way. We'll clinch this Series tomorrow.' Less partisan observers say off-field fiascos have hurt the Cubs, all but ruined their chances. A few nights ago on a fire escape, for example. Johnny, nobody in his right mind believes you ran out of paint."

The Kid nodded. "It doesn't matter, Al. I used all the paint I needed."

"Well, maybe you did, but most people say it's a damn shame that a great athlete demeans himself with vandalism, off-field stunts."

"Whatever."

"Face the facts, Johnny. Most people are tired of world-famous athletes who think they can do anything they want."

Thus far the news was tame enough to put me in a slumber. Johnny jabbered a bit about his notion of "theatre, the value of spontaneity, the fact that creativity has to be provocative to mean anything at all." The artsy talk lasted around thirty seconds, which was all I could stand. Johnny shocked his audience by referring to President Trent and Company as "a bunch of dildos." The Kid had a whole list of grievances: the systematic trashing of the environment, the refusal to do anything about climate change; the abuse of immigrants and Muslims and people of color; the giving away of billions to the Defense Department, which was once called the War Department; the obsession with big money, big wars—the more wars, the more money, the more racism, etc. Except for the mention of dildos, it was standard issue. Just another leftwing rant.

Muscat has snake-slit eyes, but these widened a bit. "Okay," he said, "what else? What else about President Trent?"

I soon heard the influence of Ahmed Jamil's letter, the fire, the insight, but with the compassion withheld. According to Johnny, President Trent posed as "America's innocent, our white

lamb, our white knight, our homerun-hitter in the 9th inning."
He made a mockery of the man, a mockery of "innocence," and
seemed to be just getting started when they muted his mike.

"Let me ask you something," said Muscat. "Are you a
ballplayer in the World Series, or are you running for office? Most
people, including your coaches, think you should stick to playing
ball."

They turned his mike back on. "I don't listen to most
people."

"No, but you might learn some respect for the Game. We
needed more than a decade to crawl out of the steroid scandal, so
why dig a new hole with politics?"

Johnny shrugged. "Al, you wouldn't notice politics if I were
your Great White Hope."

"I don't see—"

"Well, then, try lifting the damn blinders. There's a world
out here, Al, and it's begging to be seen."

Old Muscat, the veteran bottom feeder, was speechless. He
took one step back and listened. Johnny claimed the Game couldn't
be stuffed in a box of crackerjacks, a Yankee Doodle Dandy. "And
as to its purity, Al, I wouldn't worry about a myth." While the
base-thief cocked his head and talked trouble, a single word kept
banging my brain—**dildos**. Johnny didn't say it again, or need to,
but it came forth as loud as the clash of cymbals. I remembered
my odd cowardice, my inability to speak in the presence of his
fiancée. Between his legs, Johnny must have something vital and
raw, whereas I have…well, something less. What's a dildo? A shaft
of rubber, I guess. Or some sort of plastic, a by-product of oil.
My inadequacy has nothing to do with age, everything to do with
malaise, a distrust of my own life. Johnny seemed to be offering a
cure, fresh blood, perhaps his own, but who could take it? Sitting
in Nick's suite, my hands limp between my thighs, a great wall of

178

vexation swept over me. The truth was crippling; the truth was simple. I could not imagine being fearless in the presence of beauty. I could not imagine watching Janice take off her clothes.

JUMP

World Series

Game 5

Fenway Park

Line-up Cards

Home Boston Red Sox

Visiting Chicago Cubs

SS Domingo López
RF Kaido Miura
CF Moises de Dios Ovando
3B Bill Murphy
1B Maceo Mason
LF Preston Hollis
2B Jay McCreary
DH Flaco Méndez
C Antonio Chévez

CF Johnny Stompiano
LF Jamal Kelsey
2B Jesús Mijango Cruz
1B Jimmy Lieski
SS Rey Rodríguez
C Junior Parker
RF Terrence Gumbs
DH Mick Gutowski
3B Matt Creighton

During batting practice, a motley bunch of Bosox fans parade through the park with signs:

WHO ARE THE CUBS? DILDOS! MINIS!
FIRE ESCAPE JOHNNY'S DUMB!

The Kid is unflappable. In batting practice, he laces line drives all over the yard, singles and doubles, then sky-hawks a ball into the fourth row of seats over the Green Monster. On his last swing, he drags a bunt down the first base line and sprints to second. Does he ever do anything half way? No, he's a gamer, a trickster, on and off the field.

*

First inning.

An 0-2 fastball almost nicks Johnny's chin.

"Close," says Sam Foley, "but no cigar. Early Wynn claimed he'd throw at his mother on Mother's Day, but only if she crowded the plate."

Bosox bums must have a dozen radios setting on the roof of the Cub dugout.

"Stompiano's nobody's mama," says Mike Madson.

"No, he's fair game," says Foley, "whether crowding or bailing." He chuckles. "Buster Levine licked his whiskers, cleaned him up for bedtime. But look at Stompiano digging in, still crowding the plate." He pauses. "You know his IQ, Mike?"

"Not off-hand."

"Divide his batting average by ten, subtract three hundred, and don't worry if you get a negative. Bosox fans near the Cub dugout are carrying a banner: FIRE ESCAPE JOHNNY'S DUMB."

He gives his whiskey laugh, a low rumble. "Levine winding and here he comes."

The batted ball makes a sound as sharp as a whip on a hard surface. Sam Foley, his breath stolen, gasps to get it back, then talks fast to catch up with the play. "That's belted down the right-field line, fair ball, and knocks up against the wall...Miura plays the bounce, throws, but Stompiano dives into second with a lead-off double." He huffs a breath. "Nothing wrong with that pitch from Buster Levine. A fastball, up and in, but Fire Escape Johnny swung blind and gave it a lucky ride."

"Lucky?" I say aloud. Johnny set the table with a whip.

Azzy, up against the rail of the dugout, calls, "Waste no time, Wild Child, waste no time. Now let somebody bring you home."

Jamal Kelsey almost does. He jiggers an 0-1 pitch between short and third, but Domingo López backhands the ball and fires across the diamond—out number one. Stompiano, who broke for third the moment López released the ball, is now ninety feet from home.

Nick and I sit side-by-side in a corner of the dugout.

"Don't skip out on me," he says. "Not tonight."

I look at him.

"You know damn well what I mean. No hanging out in the locker room, no disappearing. Is that clear?"

I nod.

"Use the crapper between innings. Don't set up camp."

I tell him not to get kicked out of the game.

"I won't," he says, "unless something weird happens."

Something weird always happens.

"I'm staying," he says, "through hell and back. I'm staying till the final out."

Sam Foley says, "We'll pitch around Jesús Mijango, throw him junk balls. Jimmy Lieski on deck. The Red Sox looking for a double play."

The free pass for Jesús won't go into the books as intentional, but it should. Four balls nowhere near the plate.

Jimmy.

He says his prayers. That's what he's good for. And he's good for taking a fastball, strike one, over the heart of the plate.

"Mijango with a good lead off first," says Foley. "Stompiano, edging down the line, eyes home plate. Levine's trying to split his vision, keep an eye on both runners. He throws to third, Stompiano in diving...Now look at Mijango dancing off first, trying to draw attention. Jimmy Lieski, the Cub clean-up hitter, keeps saying his prayers."

Now Levine hurries a pitch that bounces in front of the plate and ricochets off the catcher's shin guards. The ball skips down the first-base line as Johnny canters home, scores standing. I whoop it up, pump my fists, snigger till my nose runs. These Bosox bums can turn up their radios full blast. They can eat crow. They can shit and go blind. They can go to hell in a hand-basket. They can roast for a million years.

Sam Foley, after a pause, says, "Cubs draw first blood. But this game has a long way to go."

*

Between innings, I get out the binoculars and scan the crowd. No Cub fan has a choice seat behind home plate this time around. I find Janice beyond the right field wall, almost twenty rows back, with Isha and her girls and a bunch of blacks—mostly women—gathered in a circle. This circle includes my good-luck orphans, Jackie and Sam, and Sonia, the old foster mom, who sits between them. She and her charges are with Azzy's clan because Azzy provided their tickets. I guess the big guy trusts me, trusts whoever I might invite to a game, and shouldn't he be more careful? If Azzy knew I'd borrowed a few things from his locker, read his daughter's letter and browsed *South Side News*, he might wonder what I'm after. Well, what **am** I after? I hardly know who I am anymore. I do things that make no sense.

Jackie rests his head on his foster mom's shoulder. Maybe Sonia's all right for these boys, not just fostering for the money. One thing for sure—she's not the lady I thought she would be. Several hours earlier, at the airport, I shook her dry, cold hand. The Sonia in my head—white, dumpy—was replaced by a Mexican, or maybe an Indian, a woman damn near as dark as Jesús Mijango. A chaos of lines near her eyes and mouth, a slight rasp in her throat, placed her in her mid-sixties. Later, months later, she would trust me enough to tell me she'd been Jackie and Sam's foster mom for seven years, and the one and only husband of her life, Joseph Melgar, had died the previous winter. Today, however, upon meeting me, she was taciturn, subdued. Her gray coat and dark slacks reminded me of rain.

*

After retiring the first nine batters, Porfirio Guevara walks Domingo López to lead off the fourth. Kaido Miura sacrifices, moves López into scoring position, and up steps Moises De Dios Ovando. Fans near the Bosox dugout hold up religious signs:

MOISES LEADS US FROM WILDERNESS!
RIVER JORDAN, PART YOUR WAVES!

Sam Foley says, "Come on, Moises, let's hit one to the Charles River. Or at least bring in Domingo from second base."

Well, Nick could order Porfirio Guevara to walk the bum with first base open. On deck, though, is Bill Murphy, and his last time up he hit a ball that Johnny caught near the 420 sign in right-centerfield.

"Guevara glances at the runner," says Foley. "The big fellow's talking to himself, he's got the habit. I remember an old Bosox pitcher, Frank Sullivan, was once asked how he pitched to Mickey Mantle. Frank spoke the plain truth: 'With tears in my eyes.' Right now Porfirio Guevara is reaching up to wipe away the tears."

Foley prefers fiction to facts. Guevara, dry-eyed, didn't reach for anything. I put the glasses on the Cub pitcher. Sure, he's talking to himself, maybe asking questions. But his eyes are dry as mine.

He gets behind in the count, 2-1, and comes in with a slider that doesn't slide. Sam Foley says, "Moises drives one deep! That ball will leave a fresh scar in the Green Monster, bounce toward leftfield, and here comes López with the tying run. Moises makes a wide turn around first, draws a throw, but he'll have to settle for a single. Let me tell you something: the Monster, shallow in left, thirty-seven feet high, can help you or hurt you. A routine fly sometimes goes for a double, or even a round-tripper, and sometimes a cannon shot, a homer anywhere else in the world, slams off the wall—no different in the scorecard than a scrub single. But this one **is** different, a game-tying World Series RBI, and listen to these fans." He shuts up long enough to make way for Bosox cheers. "Fenway Park has come alive," he says. "Red Sox one, Cubs one. Let's see if we can knock Guevara out of this game."

They don't. Talking to himself, no tears, mumbo-jumbo in Spanish ("**Bien hecho, amante**"), Guevara keeps us tied.

*

The game I want—a Cub rout, a cakewalk—never materializes. In the seventh inning, the score still tied, Flaco Méndez loops one down the right field line and into the third row of seats left of the foul pole. Sam Foley calls it "a drive, a hot smash," but maybe a breeze carried it, plus a Bosox prayer, and it is one of the ugliest homeruns I have seen in more than fifty years of baseball. "Méndez laid into a change up," says Foley, "jacked it down the line, see you later." The crowd is roaring. "Circle the bases," he says, "mark your scorecards. Red Sox 2, Cubs 1. Maybe that's all the runs we need."

He fails to mention the right field foul pole is three-hundred-and-two feet from home plate. He fails to mention this goddamn ballpark is a tinderbox of tricks.

*

Ninth inning.

After Ruben Romero, the Bosox closer, walks Mick Gutowski, Nick calls on Drexel Rountree to pinch run. Matt Creighton, trying to bunt a 2-0 pitch up near his eyes, pops the ball to the pitcher. This brings up Johnny, our best hope to scrounge a run and keep the World Series alive.

I would've headed for the clubhouse if Nick hadn't chided me earlier. No bailing out, no disappearing. No sitting on the crapper while a ballgame is being decided. My secret pleasure is that no one knows about my stealing. No one knows about my needs.

Johnny drags a bunt. The ball rolls up the first-base line, picture perfect, till it hits an unseen pebble or a sky-high curse and squirts foul. Sam Foley says, "No harm done, strike one to Stompiano. Let him bunt another foul ball, and another, and we'll ring him up for out number two."

While players and coaches crowd the rail, I sit alone, eyes closed, head bowed. I hear the ball bury itself in the mitt of the catcher. Sam Foley says, "That's ball one, just missed the outside corner." I glance toward home, but I can't see beyond the players and coaches standing in front of me. They look desperate the way they clutch at the rail, gripping it hard as if it's the last thing that keeps them from keeling overboard into a boiling sea. After ball two smacks into Chévez's mitt, I grab my binoculars, stagger to my feet, and slink in between Nick and Azzy. I suppose every soul in Fenway Park is standing. I try to home in on my boys, Jackie and Sam, but where are they? Peeking out between shoulders, I suppose, fighting for glimpses. The faces I see are not my lucky charms.

The Cubs...I cannot bear to watch them. But I spy Sonia through the glasses, her face of boding. She claps once, her dark hands under her chin. For an instant it seems that I stand beside her, that I hear the slap of her hands. I don't see Johnny hitch and swing. I don't see the ball fly like a spark off the meat of the bat, soar up and out like something shot from a cannon. Nick says, "Hot damn!" and flares an elbow into my face. The glasses gouge my eyes, turn the world black, then bright, set it whirling. Players and coaches jump and jive. I hear one voice—Azzy's—that swells out over the moans and groans of deliverance: "Oh, Wild Child, oh baby. You hit that ball a ton!"

I take shelter in his heat, his largeness. No one can run Azzy over. No one can reach high enough to throw an elbow into his face, knock him senseless. Bleary-eyed, I hold the man's forearm and peer out at Johnny rounding second, cruising, enjoying the regal pace that dovetails with just one play—the homerun. Sounds burble from my throat, tears shame me. I want to hold this imp in my arms, give him my life, what is left of it. "Take it," I would say, "take it. I never knew what to do with it. I'm old. I'm beat. I've been a beggar all my life."

When Johnny is carried down the steps of the dugout all I can do is touch his shoulder, feel him for a second. This is life, flesh and blood, the vitality I long for. I remember seeing Sonia through the glasses, her dark hands. Clap! Home run! As if she gave a command. I didn't see Wild Child swing for the fences, but she did. Later, on replays, I'll watch over and over as Johnny lights into a Ruben Romero fastball and sails it out over the Green Monster. As the ball leaves the yard I expect Wild Child to raise a fist, leap in the air, but he appears relaxed, almost subdued. A close-up shows a slight grin, lips closed, a hint of mischief as he rounds the bases, the volcano of his heart contained.

"Cubs 3," says Foley, "Bosox 2. Let's get out of this inning and start swinging the bats."

*

Bottom of the ninth.

Sam Foley lulls us with facts ("Dirk Rouda's on the mound facing a pinch-hitter—Leonel Hernández"), and in the next breath bullies us with fiction: "The Cubs—if you want a prognosis—are headed for a train wreck. Hernández is pesky enough to jangle Rouda's nerves."

The Cub closer has little use for nerves or intelligence or things of this nature. Chewing on tobacco soaked in Kahlúa, the stuff trailing like jism from his lips, he sets down Hernández on three pitches. Rouda has the hands of an executioner. Reddish slabs, stumpy fingers. Splotches of blue and purple on the knuckles when the skin stretches tight. He burps and spits, lets loose a steady drool. I wonder how he keeps hydrated. I wonder if he soaks his pillow with spittage while asleep each night.

Up steps Domingo López. He crouches till he's around four-foot-two, and works Rouda for a walk. Sam Foley, his voice as harsh as the hack of a crow, says, "The tying run's on base for our right-fielder—Kaido Miura. Moises de Dios Ovando grabs a weighted bat. Only a double play will keep him from coming to the plate."

I grab the glasses and hunt for my boys. Sam must be hidden

in shadows, but Jackie—mouth open, Cub cap set at an angle—is in the arms of Sonia. She's lifted him so he can see the field, peer out over shoulders. Cub and Bosox fans are on their feet, and maybe never sat down since Johnny's round-tripper. I watch Jackie sway in the arms of his foster mom. Come on, pal, bring us some luck. Send a signal to Charles Victor Faust.

Miura lunges at an 0-1 pitch and bloops the ball into leftfield. "Base hit," says Foley. "López, the tying run, pulls up at second; Miura, the winning run, is on first. I can see from here these fellows are thirsty for a World Series. Why haul the champagne to Chicago, right? And no one's thirstier than Moises de Dios Ovando, the man at the plate."

On this he goes astray. No one's thirstier than me, Billy Ray Donachio. I may be a new phenomenon: a coach, a fanatic, who doubles as a locker-room thief.

Dios Ovando lifts a high fly ball into leftfield, an easy play for Jamal Kelsey. The Bosox, stripped to their last out, eye their clean-up hitter—Bill Murphy. Sam Foley reminds us "he's a dangerous hitter, especially in the clutch." I wish I could slink back to the clubhouse and prowl. Even if I came up empty, found nothing of value, the hunt would distract me. Why is nothing more difficult than watching the Cubs when a tight game must be won?

Murphy check-swings at the first pitch and loops a Texas-Leaguer. I moan when I see it arc over first base, hug the line, a floater with **Cheap hit, bye-bye Cubs, wait till next year,** burned in leather. But then I see the ball hanging, Jesús Mijango catching up with the ball. I see the Lord near the foul line, his bright glide and spring, and I strain against the rail of the dugout and blurt a one-word prayer—"Jump!" At a full sprint, the Lord leaps, flies, his left arm flung forward, quick as the tongue of a snake, and he snares the ball, closes the webbing of his glove, and keeps running. I grab a deep breath and use it to holler: "Jesús! Jesús! Jesús!" He is more beautiful than a panther bounding across a field.

Sam Foley starts whining. He says, "In this town we call it robbery, a criminal violation. Jesús Mijango took away extra bases. He ran out into right field and took away the game."

The Cub Lord slows to a trot as he crosses the foul line. He tosses the ball toward a smattering of blue hats, outstretched arms—Cub fans. Squeezed between Nick and Azzy, I'm woozy as a drunkard. I manage to say, "Sweet Jesus, sweet Jesus." My heart is a runaway train.

For a second or more I let Azzy hold me. I don't hear Sam Foley. I don't hear Mike Madson. I hear Azzy say, "Come on, coach, come on," and he helps me up the steps of the dugout. A half dozen Cubs have run down the right-field line and are jumping with Jesús. I see Terrence Gumbs, Rey Rodríguez, Dirk Rouda, Fire Escape Johnny. I see Junior Parker and Jamal Kelsey, and here come Matt Creighton and Jimmy Lieski. You would think the Cubs had won the World Series, shored up Game 7, all over but the shouting. And here I come, my feet raking the earth, hustling behind Azzy and Drexel Rountree and players decades younger. Soon I'm amid the ruckus, near Rountree and Azzy and Fire Escape Johnny. We lean inward on the circle of players and coaches, the joy and high feeling and blood lust hubbing out from the man in the middle—Jesús Mijango Cruz.

JUDAS

What is more disorienting? An important Cub triumph or a hint of happiness for no reason? The skipper allowed every bottom feeder but Al Muscat to join us in the clubhouse. Blame elation. Blame the aura of high feeling. Blame the glow of victory that buoys a man before gravity brings its blows.

The media bellied up to Johnny and Jésus. Cal Reese, who often works with Muscat, asked the Kid about his ninth inning blast over the Green Monster. "Pure luck," said Johnny. "I forget the pitcher's name. Romeo...?"

"Ruben Romero."

Johnny nodded. "Yeah, Romeo's a stud. He knows I can hit a curve up and in or a slider low and away, so he tried to fool me with a pitch that flattened out over the heart of the plate."

Reese smiled. "Nice way of putting it."

"Yeah, stir your stumps," said Johnny, "do a dance. We're taking this Series to Wrigley Field."

Reese and his brother bottom feeders ate this up, but before Johnny's banter could segue to something beyond baseball, Nick called him to his office. "You all have a good time," he said to

Reese and the players. "Right now Johnny can use some rest."

The Kid did a double take as if **rest** was not a word in his lexicon. I began to follow him and Nick to Nick's office, but the skipper took me aside. "You're in charge of the clubhouse," he said. "In two minutes give Reese and these bums the boot."

The post-game show descended into the white noise of predictable conversation. Yes, Jesús Mijango "made a beautiful catch," Porfirio Guevara "pitched a brilliant game," and Dirk Rouda "gutted his way through the ninth inning." I suppose hundreds of thousands of viewers were sipping beer, nodding off on sofas, or chitchatting, making phone calls ("How about those Cubs?"), with the TV as background. Reese and his brotherhood needed to up the ante, reengage a drifting audience. After what could be said about Game 5 was said, he elicited comments about the unusual signs seen at the ballpark. "One sign, for example, read—FIRE ESCAPE JOHNNY'S DUMB."

Jesús snapped his fingers. He stood beside his locker, his black bats, his black glove, and looked straight at the cameras. "Johnny has **duende**. That's the main reason you don't understand him."

"**Duende**?" said Reese. "Can you define it?"

Jesús paused. His eyes fluttered as if following the flight of a bird from branch to branch to the crown of a tree. "Maybe it's everything," he said. "Or at least everything you've missed."

Reese, white as a blind man's cane, turned his attention elsewhere. Nick said to give him and his clan two minutes, but I would've needed a gun to follow the directive. Reese homed in on Jimmy Lieski. Aware of our weak spot, or one of them, he said, "And you, pal? Do you step in line with Stompiano's off-field antics?"

Jimmy swallowed. "Me?"

"Not your shadow, and not your momma. Just tell me what

you think."

Jimmy, perched on a stool, head down, seemed to be aware of his hands, his fingers curled near his groin.

"You with me?" said Reese. "You awake?"

"Yes, sir."

"Stompiano made a certain comment last night in a live interview. You've heard the news, right?"

Jimmy nodded. "Sure."

"And it's okay for him to speak this way? Slander whoever he wants?"

"I—I—"

"No slander involved," said Jésus. "A coyote keeps howling till the deaf begin to hear."

Dogs were on my mind more than coyotes. Trying to shake free of the media is like trying to shake fresh shit off shoes with webbed soles.

Reese gave way to Doug Laird, a colleague who had weaseled his way to the center of the clubhouse. Laird had his main line written on a slip of paper. "Tell us if you agree with this statement," he said, speaking not only to Jésus and Jimmy, but to the team, the Chicago Cubs, players and coaches. "Early this morning," he said, "John Farnsley, the commissioner of baseball, summed up your teammate's off-field behavior as follows: 'The speech and actions of Cub outfielder Johnny Stompiano are unbecoming and unacceptable to every responsible person in the game of baseball.'" Laird, in an auctioneer's voice, read the summation a second time, then asked who agreed with the commissioner. "Stompiano will be fined," he added. "The exact figure—yet to be named—is certain to be steep."

Jesús whistled. "Aim the camera over here," he said. "The commissioner gets paid to keep his voice small. Otherwise, they'll withhold his salary."

"You don't agree with him?"

"**Mierda y mierda.** If you can't smell it, well, breathe a bit deeper."

"Let's keep this civil."

"Civil?" said Jesús. "Johnny's a coyote, so the commissioner wants a cage."

Laird ignored him. "What about you?" he asked Jimmy. "What about the rest of this club? Is the commissioner on track? You with him?"

Jimmy cupped his hands near his groin. "He—he's doing his job."

"And he's right?" said Laird. "You agree with him?"

Jimmy nodded.

"That's enough," I said. "Let's not beat a dead horse. This clubhouse is closed."

I couldn't keep tabs on all the voices. Laird and Reese and the other bottom feeders, plus players, coaches, everyone speaking at once. Laird's voice was loudest. "Let's see a show of hands," he said. "How many of you support the commissioner? Who agrees with his statement?"

I glanced at Joe Peralta, the pitching coach. Up went his right hand, not high, but conspicuous. I hesitated, then raised my right hand, swear on a Bible. Posture was important, principle wasn't. Any coach at odds with the commissioner would cut his own throat.

"Who else?" said Laird. "Any more coaches? Players?"

Pete Carnes and Josh Safranski and the other coaches raised their hands.

"Jimmy," said Laird, "should I count you up or down? And you—Rouda, Creighton, Delaney—which way? Up or down?"

Nobody said anything. Nobody moved.

"That's it?" said Laird. "No vote?"

Jimmy raised his right hand but dropped it so fast Laird wasn't sure he could count it.

"So the commissioner's wrong?" said Laird. "Is that what you're saying?"

Jimmy wagged his head. "Nuh—no, sir. No. I support him."

"Then let's see a show of hands," said Laird. "How many support the commissioner? How much energy does it take to raise your hand?"

Jimmy's right hand rose to the level of his nipples. Mine rose higher, as did those of the other coaches. After our votes were tallied, I tried to lead Laird and company to the door.

Jesús blocked my way. "Let's see a show of hands for Johnny. Who's with Johnny?"

"Save it," I said. "Skip the drama."

"**Vatos lindos**," said Jesús. "Let's see who's still alive."

My hand came down slow, a motion like swimming. Many reached high, but none belonged to a coach, nor any pale face other than Dirk Rouda, Mick Gutowski, and Paddy Delaney. Jesús raised a fist. Certain Cubs—Azzy, Kelsey, Gumbs, Guevara, Rodríguez, Aguas—brought their hands up in a casual way as if taking a stand was an everyday occurrence. Jesús began tallying the votes. "Okay, one, two, three, four..." The Cub gay boy proved he could count to nineteen.

Azzy called from across the locker room. "Maybe you can shift the cameras this way," he said. "I'm with Wild Child, you know I am, and no one can or should tame him. There's one thing I need to say after casting my vote, though, and say it with my might. To walk down a new road, to join hands, we need not humiliate **any** man—president, sinner, banker, thief. This was Martin's way, and this is what Khadijah Jamil believes."

Azzy, his arms wide as though to gather us in, said, "Hang with me a little while, hang with me." He grabbed his phone and danced his thumbs across the screen. "Keep in mind Khadijah Jamil grew up where I grew up—South Chicago. I first met her when I was eight years old."

In a voice deep as a preacher's, bright with hope, he began reading an excerpt from "Jamil's most recent speech," but the bottom feeders lost interest within thirty seconds. Cameras clicked off; equipment was gathered, packed, and soon the feeders dispersed. I made a mental note: The next time the media sets up camp, sticks like shit on webbed soles, invite Azzy to read as from a pulpit whatever suckles the sadness from his heart.

As the players began heading for the showers, I knocked on the door to Nick's office, ducked in, and asked if he or Johnny had an extra ticket for Game 6 at Wrigley Field. "I need it bad," I said. "I'll pay twice what's it worth."

I would have paid tenfold. I remembered watching Sonia through the glasses in the ninth inning. The split second before Johnny hit a homerun her hands rose and joined—clap, bang, and the rest is history. Had the old girl brought us some luck? Had she and her orphans kept this World Series alive? Havoc and loss, ordinary cousins, require no contemplation, but winning is the stuff of wonder. I'll tell you the Game's oldest secret, a secret I've carried through the mist for fifty years: A baseball man is comprised not of cells, but of superstitions, ephemera. A game-winning homer blows foul one night, fair the next. In mid-summer, drunk after a tough loss, I told Al Muscat the Cubs seldom caught a break on the night of the new moon.

At heart I'm a Judas. I'd just betrayed Johnny, raised my hand to support the commissioner, but here I was asking a favor. I had Game 6 tickets reserved for Jackie and Sam, Game 7 if needed; to complete my trinity of good fortune, I needed to take care of Sonia. Johnny had a larger retinue than any Cub except Azzy. Furthermore, he hadn't seen me betray him, couldn't yet hold it against me, which gave me a small window of time to cut a deal. Within minutes after he left Nick's office, he would hear about the fiasco in the clubhouse. Nonetheless, I counted on the Kid to display a quality that I lacked: integrity. If he made a deal, I reasoned, if he shook on it, fair and square, he wouldn't go back on his word.

He said he'd reserved around thirty seats. "We'll see what jives," he said. "Some of my people might not be able to make it."

"Then I'm one of your people," I said. "I'll pay double for a spare ticket."

"Skip the money."

"No, I didn't pay Azzy for three tickets for tonight's game. I ought to pay for something."

He waved a hand.

"Why bellyache over chump change?" said Nick. "If we win the Series, pool our salaries, we can buy Bolivia." He sipped whiskey. "Way I see it, all that can stop us is a lack of focus. I was just telling Johnny we'll have no distractions, no press in or around the clubhouse before or after Game 6."

I nodded. "A wise move."

"The Kid here, he's just going to play ball, play hard. Do what he's paid for."

"Good."

"Two more games," said Nick. "That's all we need to win."

Johnny hunched over on a straight-back chair, elbows on his knees, hands dangling. I pressed a pile of greenbacks into the palm of his left hand. "A ticket for Game 6," I said. "A deal, okay?"

"It's already paid for."

"Yeah, and this time I'm picking up the tab. Who needs to argue?"

"Well—"

"No well or but or anything. Just take the money and call

it a deal."

I shook the Kid's hand, pumped it twice, patted his shoulder.

"Okay," he said, "call me tomorrow when we're back in Chicago. If one of my people cancel, the ticket's yours."

*

I called the Kid around twenty hours later. He had two extra tickets, and one was for my "friend." By now he knew I'd betrayed him, but he sounded jolly. At the end of our conversation I told him how sorry I was about last night. "I got caught in the middle," I said. "Any coach going up against the commissioner is like a wave against the sea."

He chuckled. I suppose he was sharp enough to know I'd prepared my excuse in advance.

"That's a good one," he said. "But maybe some day that sea you're looking at will seem like a pond."

MY LAST THEFT IN BOSTON

Before we left Fenway, when no one was looking, I snitched a magazine from Jesús Mijango's locker. I eyed Johnny's street clothes, but I had neither the time nor the privacy to frisk his pockets, pick and choose. Players bustled about—in and out of the showers, the trainers' room—and soon we would board a bus for Logan Airport. I dusted a hand over some papers in Azzy's locker, but I already had reading materials. The magazine, wadded and rolled, stuffed down the inside pocket of my trench coat, felt as hard and menacing as a gun.

On the plane, I sat with Nick, had a few drinks, and we talked about the incident in the clubhouse. The other coaches had briefed him, and of course he was peeved that the ball-club had again spun out of control. "Now what?" he said. "Will I be a punching bag for the front office, or do they need a dart board?"

I shrugged. "At least we pulled off a win."

"Yeah, but my nerves are shot. Where do I get extras?"

"I wouldn't know."

He twirled a swizzle stick in his whiskey. "I could pray to Mary Magdalene," he said, "the whore of Israel. But I'd give my left nut to get this club to stick to playing ball."

Well into the flight, over Ohio, I made my way to the restroom. I didn't even know the name of the magazine I borrowed, but I was curious. Why is the unknown a balm, a blessing, and also a fear? Trench coat still on, I locked the door, and wrested the magazine with both hands. *Presente*, it was called, *The Magazine for the 21st Century*. The large photograph on the cover was of a pink house near a quiet sea.

Bent over, an overweight gnome, I browsed at my leisure. I should've known Jesús' rag would show pictures of men posing as couples, men embracing, holding hands, men intimate with kisses. One pair strolled along a beach in Hawaii, the hills behind them a shimmering green. They had a pet, a poodle, for Christ's sake, and it was happy as hell to be unleashed and skittering over the sand near blue waves. I shook my head and thought—"Family?" They had a doggy, so all they needed was an adopted kid.

I was relieved there was no nudity, no obvious bulges in swimming trunks. The plane swayed me, slight turbulence now, so I removed my coat, lowered the toilet seat, and sat with the garment folded on my lap, a desk for the magazine. I moaned when I saw the feature articles were about the election. Khadijah Jamil this, Khadijah Jamil that. How much would I have read if the act of stealing hadn't added a certain zest?

I knew a bit about the first article from the materials I'd borrowed earlier from Azzy. Khadijah Jamil lived dangerously, received nooses in the mail, bullets too, and the most serious threats came from radicalized Muslims. Jamil, when asked if she was afraid, said, "Oh, yes, at certain times, but I will never retreat to a 'safe haven.' No one lives long in this world—a hundred years is not long—and when you know fully your vulnerability, an odd thing happens—fear starts to fade. Yes, death will come, you know not when, so you lean toward what is larger than any woman or man—love and compassion. We all come from something larger than life."

Jamil dismissed the notion that the Western world and the Muslim world are incompatible. "No, you will not hear me talking about the so-called 'battle between civilizations.' Almost one-fourth of the human species is now Muslim, and I'd guess 99 percent of us have no sympathy whatever for ISIS or other groups of extremists. Separating Muslims from the rest of humanity plays into the hands of ISIS, for they thrive on separation and long for the final battle between 'good and evil,' the Apocalypse that sends 'them' to 'heaven' and 'us' to 'hell.' Certain American politicians in **both** parties also thrive on separation, on endless military and economic expansion, an expansion that concentrates wealth and resources into fewer and fewer hands, and they too must be stopped. Don't think for one second that I present myself as the catalyst, the mover, or some such thing. No, we need **communities** to be the catalysts, the movers and shakers. The best I can do is give voice to the concerns of a wised-up people. I'm one lean fish in a wide-open sea."

It was hard to bend my mind around any of this. Did Jesús Mijango read this bedevilment? Did he take it in? Since when did star athletes care about anything more than their salaries, personas, perks, poodles, pricks, girls (boys for the Cub Lord), cars, endorsements, adoration? Through Azzy and the tri-captains, I knew of Tommie Smith, John Carlos, and Muhammad Ali—a so-called "legacy of conscience." All said and done, though, so few stars or for that matter so few nobodies care about anything beyond the sound of their names.

The smell in this sky-high toilet, the damn deodorizer or whatever, was getting to me. I breathed little sips of it, the less the better. I made the mistake of glancing at my face in the mirror. I wore a pained, forlorn expression, a septuagenarian orphan. A vein bulged above the raised line of my brow.

I thumbed through Jesús' magazine till my vision blurred. I felt dazed, defeated. What the hell was going on in this world? And why was I sitting on a perfumed stool on the far side of the clouds? I was a deranged human being, a fellow in the throes of disintegration. I asked myself what—if anything—did I care about. Jackie and Sam came to mind, then Janice, then Azzy and Jesús and Johnny. I knew the Cub captains were freaks, weird as a blizzard in July. But I also knew—despite my condition—they were better than all the men I had ever known.

I rose from that perfumed hellhole, wallowed up the aisle, and sat down beside Nick. He looked me over and said, "Billy, you may as well admit you were playin' with it. You were gone how long? An hour?"

I shivered. "Maybe five minutes."

"Hell, you were shinin' the old shank. Put on your seatbelt!"

"Knock it off, Nick."

"Shinin' it up and down, all three inches."

"Spare me."

"Or else you about fell down the hole and drowned."

On this he was halfway right.

DARK HORSE

Late Saturday morning, game day, I called Sonia and made arrangements. I would stop by a Wrigley Field ticket booth at noon, then meet her and Jackie and Sam at The Dark Horse Tap and Grill on Sheffield Avenue. She insisted on paying for her ticket, the boys' tickets, lunch for her family, but I doubted her sincerity. "No, let me treat you," I said. "Don't give it another thought."

I had trouble rousing myself. I picked up the tickets a half hour late, arrived late at the Dark Horse, but did Sonia and her boys have the good sense to wait for me inside? No, they were Cub fans, believers in sacrifice, so they stood in the cold and suffered. The wind hawked fallen leaves. Death colors—bright orange, red, yellow—whirled toward Wrigley Field. The boys, in thick winter coats, huddled with "mom." Up shot Sam's arm, then Jackie's, when they saw me approaching. "Mr. Donachio!" called Sam. "Mr. Donachio!" Why couldn't he drop the formality and call me Coach?

Sonia, in a white coat, looked like a Catholic headed for Mass on Resurrection Sunday. "Well, Happy Easter," I thought, "praise the Lord. Please give us two more victories." In this moment how many pilgrims were praying for the Cubs? How many for the Bosox? Had I believed in God, a big, bearded fellow in the sky monitoring and answering prayers, I would have sympathized with His workload. I believed in common staples—old age, death, the decay that awaits all of us, humble or sublime. I couldn't help opening my arms, though, as Jackie and Sam ran toward me. These boys were—and **are**—the sun of July.

Sonia, in Easter white, would have appeared virginal but for the darkness of her face. Erect, bespectacled, she had the pious mien of an avid churchgoer. She let me shake her hand—dry ice—then turned away. The day was raw, the wind blustering, and after the thrill of meeting Jackie and Sam the prelude to a Midwest winter was a force to reckon. The wind bent me at the waist. As predicted, it swept in off the lake, and if it kept up, tonight's long, towering drives would be outs rather than homers. An hour ago, when I first stepped outside, the air was a spiked drink, something to elevate the senses. Now, however, I was haggard, shivering, and might have bet money Game 6 would be a Cub funeral. I rubbed my hands, then cupped them to my mouth and blew. Gamblers ready their dice this way, blow on them full steam. Maybe luck is something warm.

*

The Dark Horse was noisy and crowded. I could have led my trio down the block to a quieter joint, but I enjoy the ambience here, the old ceiling fans, the muted lighting, the wooden bar that looks worn enough to have been here when the Cubs won the World Series in 1908. Behind the bar they have a faded picture of Frank Chance, nicknamed Husk, the most successful skipper in Cub history.[4] The wall to the right of the bar features modern-

---

[4] Mr. Chance had a winning percentage of .664. Good luck trying to find a Cub skipper who topped this mark.

day heroes: Johnny diving head-first into second, a comet of dust behind him; Jesús on-deck, two black bats resting on his right shoulder, his grin imperious; Azzy on the mound, his left leg kicking high, his right arm back, the ball almost completely hidden in the largeness of his hand. In early August, I ate lunch at the Dark Horse before Azzy threw a one-hitter against the Pirates. More importantly, I ate here before Johnny stole home against the Cards and made the Catch that gave the Cubs the pennant. In recent months, I'd avoided the food in the clubhouse. Eating out was lucky, especially at the Dark Horse. The Cubs had tallied six victories and one loss, a winning percentage of .857, when I holed up here before games.

We warmed ourselves at a table in a back corner. Despite the ambience, the good cheer of the boys, my mood turned sour. I recalled raising my hand against Johnny, helping to lead the charge—coaches versus players—and now I felt like a schoolboy ratting on a pal. After Game 5 no other choice seemed possible. All said and done, I had to back the commissioner, stay on good terms with the czar of baseball. At some level Johnny knew this, but I still felt like a Judas. My mind emptied when I tried to recall a time in my life when I'd acted with courage. I couldn't dredge up a single instance, one brave act to elevate above others. Was I a coward at birth, or did I lose myself in a life-long descent into drunkenness and sloth?

The two TVs over the bar were tuned to different stations. Channel 9, WGN, showed World Series highlights. CNN had election news, polls and graphs, talking heads, the format so familiar you could close your eyes and still see the screen.

Sonia and Jackie sat across from me. Sam, the brown boy, was at my side. The silence was awkward, so I said, "How about tonight's game? Will Johnny steal some bases?"

Jackie said, "He has to."

"How many?"

"Two. Maybe three."

"That's asking a lot."

Sam said, "He can do it. He even steals on pitch-outs."

I nodded. "If he gets a jump."

"And Azzy Azzam's on the mound. He knows we have to win."

After our waitress took our orders, I brought out the tickets for Game 6. I set them on the table, slid one to Jackie, one to Sam, and one to the old lady. Each ticket was an ace from my deck of good fortune. The Cubs were the home team now, down three games to two, but at home. The World Series would live or die at Wrigley Field.

Sonia opened her purse. She had the boys show the price on their tickets, then counted out cold cash, nine-hundred-and-ninety dollars—full payment for three tickets.

"No, that's not in the cards," I said. "I aim to treat you."

She pushed the greenbacks to my side of the table.

"The Cubs pay me well," I said. "More than I'm worth."

"We won't accept your offer."

"Why?"

Her color heightened. "The money's yours, so keep it. We wouldn't be sitting here if we couldn't pay our own way."

The old girl—look at her. She had blood in her cheeks, fire in her eyes. She was as riled up as a moon-sick teenager mad at her date.

"Well, then, somebody pinch me," I said. "Three tickets for the World Series but I can't give them away."

Old Sonia. She was witch-thin, stingy in the flesh, save for the roundness of her bosom. I sensed her anger gathered there, in her chest, and flaring up to her face, her eyes, her elf-like ears. The Easter coat—all but the top button fastened—could not hide her femininity. She started to say something, then fetched a long breath through her nostrils. She unfolded her napkin and placed it on her lap.

I pocketed Sonia's money, money I didn't need. "What are you? A banker? Some relation to Rockefeller?"

She looked toward the bar.

"She's a librarian," said Jackie.

"Retired," said Sam.

I smiled. "Well, I never before knew a wealthy librarian. Tell me, how does a librarian get on Easy Street? Steal the fines? Pocket loose change for forty years?"

She tilted her head and looked past me.

"Yeah, all right, a lame joke. But why make a fuss? Can't I treat you and your boys? Everywhere else my money's good."

Queen-like, she dismissed me with the wave of a hand.

After the waitress brought coffee for me and Sonia, Cokes for the boys, I found out why gifts from me were as unwelcome as touch from lepers. "Sir," said Sam, "you raised a hand against Johnny. We didn't think you'd do that."

"But I—"

"We thought you were for him. We were sure of it."

"I **am** for him."

"But we saw you, sir. You raised your right hand. You were on the news three or four times."

Was I no longer a nobody? Had I left the wide, gray zones of Limbo? I tried to explain my predicament. I had certain duties, contractual arrangements, which were locked in place. I sided with management because, in part, I was being managed. "Besides," I said, "there's every reason to support a commissioner who's trying to keep the Game from turning into a sideshow." I glanced at the boys. "You and how many other kids see Johnny as a hero? Well, shouldn't he watch his language, show some respect, conduct himself as a gentleman? The commissioner has a responsibility to defend the family spirit of the game."

Sonia stirred her coffee. "That's weak."

"What?"

"Weak."

I looked down. "**Weak**? What in heavens are you talking about?"

"You know."

"No, I honestly don't. I have no idea. I did the one and only thing a coach could do."

But I felt the word worm its way through my ribs, my heart—**weak**. I couldn't look at the old girl. Nor could I have looked at my eyes in a mirror. I used my last wisp of energy to try to recover lost ground.

"Weak?" I said. "What about realistic? When's the last time a bench coach challenged the commissioner of baseball? Can you tell me?"

"I haven't counted the days," said Sonia.

"Well, count the years, count **all** of them." I lay my hands palms up on the table. "Weak?" I said. "You don't understand the rules."

But she did understand. In her white coat, her Sunday best, she'd played me for a sucker. Here was a lady more offended by my "propriety" than by a young Cub calling President Trent and Company "a bunch of dildos." For a few seconds I forced myself to look at her. She pulled in a deep breath, huffed, then added sugar to her coffee. "How about that?" I said to myself. "Sugar! Must I sip bitterness all my life?"

Lunch was mostly silent. Now and then Jackie or Sam said something about tonight's game, predicted stolen bases for Johnny, a home run for Jesús, a complete game for Azzy. At one point, I added my two cents worth: "The tri-captains are terrific,

210

you're wise to admire them. But I still say Johnny should watch his tongue."

Maybe Sonia was the ice queen. We'd been in the Dark Horse at least thirty minutes, but she still had her coat on as if she might rise any moment and bolt for the door. What did she think of me? That I was what Stompiano would call a dildo? A loser? A bum? I suppose no one could blame Sonia for assuming the worst. Over lunch, I dared to look at her twice. The last time she met my glance, let out a sigh, and twirled a spoon in her coffee. She turned to Sam and said, "You know what I want tonight?"

"What?"

"I want to see Johnny steal another base."

She paid most of the bill, but let me cover my burger and fries, my coffee, plus the tip for the waitress. I laid out two twenty-dollar bills, tipped like there's no tomorrow because maybe there was no tomorrow. The Cubs had to win Game 6 before they could win Game 7, right? I said to my difficult but lucky trio: "I want a World Series triumph, a **Cub** triumph, more than anyone in the world."

Sam said, "No, I want it more," but he high-fived with me, as did Jackie.

Sonia? The old girl didn't crack a smile.

BARE

I needed to recover from the beating I took at the Dark Horse. The ideal remedy would have been to wander alone in the clubhouse, to stray upon a letter from Janice, or a note, a poem, a wayward treasure. Today, however, security officials swarmed the ballpark, manned entrances and exits, and they eyed me as though eying a thief the moment I entered the gates. I spouted a greeting, "Good day, gents," which they countered with grim silence. A dozen or more cops surrounded the clubhouse, and if one had stepped forward to read me my Miranda Rights before snapping on the cuffs, I might have offered a confession. "Yes, you've got the right man, the clubhouse thief. Lock me up, toss the key, but at least bring me my laptop so I can watch Game 6!" Had the tri-captains reported missing items? If so, why had modest plunder—a letter or two, a photograph, a few notes, a magazine—led to such a resonant response by the keepers of the law?

I sidled by the clubhouse cops and opened the door to Nick's office. I'm often the first one in the park, but today I found the skipper at his desk filling in a scorecard with a stubby pencil. He glanced at me, all smiles, and I wondered what he knew. Did he suspect I was the clubhouse thief? Were there clues? I sat across from him in a folding chair.

I said, "What's with all the security? Somebody murder somebody?"

"Keep your voice down."

"You'd think Jack the Ripper was on the loose."

I noticed he was clean-shaven, no stubble today. Perhaps Nick had benefited from a good night's sleep.

"Can you keep a secret?" he whispered. "Can you hold onto it till game-time?"

I shrugged. "Seal me up. Where's the duct tape?"

"Billy, how about if you drop the jive and just listen. President Trent will be in the Chicago Cub pressroom fifteen minutes before the game."

"Holy—"

"Holy rigmarole and shut the hell up. If Johnny and his gang find out in advance, we'll have hell to pay."

"Who else knows?"

"Nobody who shouldn't. In the pressroom, it'll just be you and me, the president and his campaign manager, plus Butch Malecki from the front office."

"A photo op?"

"That's the idea. The president will pose for pictures, say a few words, and then he'll be chauffeured onto the field to throw out the first ball."

I hung on this. "But the players—"

"Yeah, they'll see him on the field, that's okay. How much mischief can they plan in three or four minutes?"

A lot, I thought.

"After the National Anthem, after throwing out the first ball, the president will be whisked away."

It sounded simple, but it wasn't. Junior Parker is our starting catcher. Would he pose for a photo-op, catch a ceremonial first-pitch thrown by President Trent? No, Junior would refuse, as would everyone under the spell of Johnny, Azzy, and Mijango, which meant most of the team. When I mentioned this to Nick, he said, "Who are you forgetting? Who's at the helm of this club?"

I tipped my cap. "You've been great."

"I'm the number one catcher for our commander-in-chief."

The skipper left the worrying to me. I returned to the clubhouse, where security personnel outnumbered the players. Johnny, sitting on a stool shuffling a deck of cards, said, "Why all the sheriffs? I haven't done anything wrong yet." He winked at one of the officials. "Can't you see I need more time?"

He bandied and joked, but the sole laughter came from Azzy and Jesús Mijango. The security officials never smiled, rarely blinked, and I wondered how long they could clamp their jaws before they milled their teeth to mouthfuls of dust.

*

During batting practice, I stood between the dugout and the on-deck circle while Jesús Mijango roped line drives to all fields. I began to relax till Azzy, furtive, came beside me, said, "Hold still, coach," and dropped to his knees. A white napkin in one hand, a hanky in the other, he swept something up from the raked earth. "Here we go," he said, "up and easy." He rose and passed by me with a worm, a night-crawler, in the bed of his hands.

"Can I move now?" I said.

"Yes."

This man the size of two took slow, careful steps, and stopped near the brick wall that separates the fans from the playing field. He plowed the dirt with his spikes, prepared it as for planting, and bent down to release the worm. I raised my brow to a mute heaven. Was it not enough to cheer for the underdogs, my Cubs, for example? Must we concern ourselves with the fate of a worm? Azzy's largesse saved the creature from being spiked by batters moving from the dugout to the on-deck circle. Beside the wall, in dirt softened for burrowing, the favored one would survive.

Front-row fans, quiet at first, began to beg for autographs. Azzy, stepping wide of the spiked earth where he'd set the worm, greeted the rowdies with handshakes and grins. He signed programs, pennants, Cub caps, jerseys. He might have lingered had I not reminded him it was time to warm up.

Moments later, as Azzy headed down the left field line toward the bullpen, I sidled up near the wall and looked at the lucky worm. I, though a Cub, stood alone, for no one called for an autograph or in any way acknowledged my presence. Perhaps the worm was more alive. I bent down and watched it wriggle, the segments of its body moist and pink, and then I turned toward the field, the sky, the scoreboard. Was the score 0-0 before the first pitch, or were the Cubs already losing? Taking into account all the baseball I'd played and watched and suffered over for decades, I was sure of one thing: There was never a single instance in which tenderness for small things contributed toward a win.

In Chicago we call the wind the Hawk. It would be a force in Game 6, and now it raked the grass, spat clouds of dust toward home plate, and feathered a chill into my legs, my groin, my heart. I could've spiked the worm, reduced it to mush, but my legs stiffened. Bent forward by a gust of wind, I glanced down the left-field foul line at Azzy, a man as strange as he is large, a black Samson who walks the earth with steps almost silent. On another night I would've killed the worm, or any being this vulnerable, but now I withdrew. Azzy was big enough and good enough that some shred of him had to enter me against my will.

*

Michael J. Trent's secret visit to the pressroom was well managed. A film crew showed him shaking hands with Butch Malecki and the skipper. The president shook my hand, too, and even patted my shoulder. He was shadowed by his campaign manager, Cindy Lang, in a red dress and matching scarf. Gorgeous is too mild a word.

Trent seemed somewhat shorter than the showman I'd seen on TV every night. Rounder too, pudgy and pink, though he managed to exude an aura of firmness and camaraderie. The strength of his handshake rivals that of Jesús Mijango Cruz.

Nick, beaming, said, "Four more years, four more years." The skipper shot me a glance, so I had to say something: "Best wishes, Mr. President, for victory at the polls."

Not only a lifelong depressive would get depressed by what happened. Butch and Nick kept leaning in to get themselves on TV beside our commander-in-chief and Cindy Lang. The cameras weren't live, but maybe the rubbernecks would make the news, or YouTube, later in the eve. The president spoke of the Game, how splendid it was, how wholesome, and how it still defined "the irrepressible American spirit." The director of the film crew said, "Good, excellent. Now shift the angle." After instructing Nick, a long-legged bone of a man, to stoop to the president's height, he had Mr. Trent repeat his lines.

The pressroom, a large bunker beneath the grandstands, has no décor save for the Cub logo pasted on blue walls. Michael J. Trent, a suit coat in one arm, his shirtsleeves rolled up, praised "the unrivaled uniqueness of Wrigley Field. A splendid park," he said, "an American monument for over a century. I've said it before and I'll say it again: You can't get better than this."

He slid an arm over Nick's shoulders, and Nick was so happy he crouched a bit lower. Mr. Trent said, "Let's give credit where credit's due. What skipper Nick Glouser has done for the

Cubs this year, what Butch Malecki and the front office have done, is nothing short of miraculous. Success comes from strong leadership, bold strategies, and a willingness to rock the boat. My first term as America's commander-in-chief is a case in point. At first, some members of my own party worked against me, saw me as a disrupter rather than a uniter." He shook his head, incredulous. "What they forgot is that someone had to re**make** the party, brush away the cobwebs. The Silent Majority—believe me—is silent no more. America is back. American pride is back. The White House is back. The support I've received is incredible, just incredible. Everybody's saying, 'What can I do, what can I do?' to help you win another term."

Mr. Trent rolled his shoulders and gritted his teeth. Minus the puffy hair, he resembled an aging thug itching for a fight.

"Let's review the last four years," he said. "My presidency has turned this country inside out and right side up. People looked to me for change and I'm **still** that change. We've made tremendous progress, unbelievable progress, but there's more work to be done. In my next term we'll make our cities safe, clear the streets of provocateurs, clean up the garbage. We'll make our universities part of our movement rather than clubs for anarchists and misfits.[5] We'll secure our borders, strengthen our military, defeat the terrorists. And if the Washington elite, the media, the career politicians, the hangers-on, can be silenced, our movement will be unstoppable." He jabbed a finger at the cameras. "One flag, one God, one America. We now have the power to make the United States the greatest country in the history of the world."

He shook Nick's hand as though to close a deal. The lengthy pause was a stage ploy, a way to highlight sincerity. He was a

---

[5] Laquan Langford, an African American comedian, encouraged the president to make education great again by reopening Trent University.

pretty good showman overall.

"Cleaning up our cities, defeating the terrorists, building our military, our economy—it's all one battle."

Nick agreed.

"We're at a crossroads," said the president. "We're in new territory."

"That's right."

"But I have faith—**complete** faith—the American people know which way to turn."

By now he was short of breath, puffy with emotion. I doubt he could've said much else, so the cameras clicked off, a photographer took a few shots, and that was that. The Secret Service ordered Nick and Butch and me to "stand in place" till the commander-in-chief and his campaign manager made their exit. I was itching to slip free of that room.

*

The green of Wrigley Field, a pleasure to the eye, was a brief respite from politics. Standing near the dugout minutes before the game, I looked toward the left-field wall as the utility doors swung open, and I took a deep breath as a Cadillac Escalade, white and gleaming, roared onto the field. I expected the president to instruct his chauffer, a black man, to cruise the warning track, circle the yard, but the car sped straight for the mound as ballpark speakers blared the news that Michael J. Trent would "throw out the ceremonial first ball in Game 6 of the World Series." The announcement—as with anything involving the president—drew boos and cheers. The Cadillac slowed as it reached the infield and glided to a halt in the grass behind the mound.

Two Secret Service agents, toughies I'd seen earlier in and around the pressroom, emerged from the Cadillac. A moment later the taller one reached a long arm into the vehicle to help Mr. Trent rise from his seat.

Johnny, who'd been standing with Jesús and Azzy near the third-base line, called, "Hey, Mister Trent, Mister President. One question, sir."

The old man should've known better than to acknowledge him with a glance.

"Where's your orange jump-suit?" said Johnny. "Give me a minute and I'll find you one."

Jesus' quick-fire Spanish sounded like claws on bark, but Azzy calmed him. "Hold steady," said the big man, "hold steady. Stay with me." Cub players and coaches were queuing up along the third-base line, getting ready for the National Anthem. In the east, soon to join the World Series hoopla, we could hear Blue Angels practicing loops and turns over Lake Michigan. Azzy waited till the planes tailed off before he sent a signal to his teammates. "Ralph Boston," he said, "Ralph Boston. You know what to do."

I had no idea what to do. The Chicago Christian Choir— schoolgirls in white gowns, boys in white tuxes—stood in rows near home plate. The president, his right hand on his chest, his left curled around a baseball, lumbered to the top of the mound. Nick must have given him the ball.

Johnny cocked his head, aped a grin, and I thought, "Here comes trouble." I learned later that Ralph Boston was a black Olympian who stood barefoot to accept a bronze medal in Mexico City in 1968.

We Cubs toed our foul line, the Bosox toed theirs, and we removed our caps before the choir began singing. At the phrase "dawn's early light," the Blue Angels swooped down with a burst of speed and sound that shook Wrigley Field from fundament to flags. I glanced over my shoulder to see the planes pass and veer and wheel, majestic acrobats, sparks of light, and when I turned and looked down, my heart racing, I saw Johnny on my left, Azzy on my right, the two of them shoeless, sock-less, or as Nick would say later, "Barefoot as pick ninnies in a field." I blinked and saw other field-hands: Barefoot Jesús, barefoot Junior Parker, barefoot Dantel Hood, barefoot Jamal Kelsey, and five others. I didn't know what to think, what to do. No barefoot Cub looked toward the president or the fans, the choirboys and choirgirls, the American flag over the centerfield scoreboard. Each looked, with mad fascination, it seemed, at his simple and humble feet.

The choir, oblivious, continued to sing. I glanced at Nick and the president, their right hands over their hearts, their eyes on heaven, two patriots unaware of what was occurring on the ground. Secret Service agents stood at attention, however, and glared at our barefoot players as through the crosshairs of rifles. I sang louder—"the rockets' red glare, the bombs bursting in air"— till the Angels roared by one last time and buried every voice in the yard.

I looked at Azzy, his feet dark and leathery but for streaks of pink between his toes, and I looked at his face, his eyes downcast but proud, his breath coming deep and full through flared nostrils. No, the planes hadn't shook him tonight; nothing had shook him. Azzy appeared as determined as a fisherman working something big, working slow and careful, letting his catch circle beneath his boat, letting it take out some line and go deeper, deeper, to where it vanished in darkness. My mind circled, too, and groped for answers, or at least clues. What did Azzy want? And these other shoeless Cubs—what did they want? My mind ran a race to nowhere. A strong jolt of whiskey might have settled my nerves.

After the Christian Choir finished the Anthem, the ballpark speakers again blared the announcement that President Trent would "throw out the ceremonial first ball in Game 6 of the World Series." Nick was at home plate already, pounding a fist in a catcher's mitt. The president's hair was blowing. He patted it down with a hand, then got ready to deal. He rocked back and forth on the rubber, looking in, looking. Nick, a clown, flashed a finger (fastball), and the president nodded. The old stager went into his wind-up, kicked his left leg as high as he could, and damn near threw the ball over Nick's head.

The skipper made a little jump-step and snared it. The president, his face flushed, shook a fist and shouted, "Good grab! Good grab!" There was no applause, however, as most pilgrims were staring at barefoot Cubs.

The president's men escorted him into the Cadillac. I suppose he saw barefoot players out his window, but what could he do? Good riddance, sir. The Caddy and the president glided across the field and disappeared through the open doors of the left-field wall.

The umpires huddled at home plate. Punishment was in order, but what? The barefoot Cubs were now putting on their socks, preparing to play. I looked across the field and spotted other malcontents, four or five Bosox players who still stood barefoot. Their captain, Moises de Dios Ovando, gave a nod, and they too began to busy themselves with their foot-ware. In the coming days, in a circus of publicity, these Cubs and Bosox would be skewered by media moguls, dismissed as "rebels without causes, performers of cheap theatrics." For now, though, I knew the umps would do nothing but issue a warning and let the game proceed.

Nick came over and grabbed my arm. "What the hell's going on?"

"Too much. I would need years to explain it."

"You'd better start."

"Start where?"

"At the beginning."

"The players did something dumb."

When I told him what I could his face turned pink, then blue and pink, and then a gray and blue that worried me. "You're kidding," he said. "Barefoot as pick ninnies in a field?"

I nodded. "They stood shoeless, sock-less. We don't know what it means."

In truth, I perceived a glimmer of meaning. I remembered Ahmed Jamil's letter, a cogent observation: **A common life, this century and others—soot for air, rubbish for earth, bars for sky.** As for Mr. Trent's performance, I understood everything. I shared a fellow feeling with the old showman as I too longed to convince myself and others that I was genuine, inimitable, a force of nature. The president, with more devices than the average depressive, could take center-stage and sing the National Anthem with a Christian choir as jets sailed by, and he could climb the mound to throw out the first ball in Chicago, the home of his nemesis— Khadijah Jamil. Old Trent had the wherewithal to do things **his** way. Money and fame are a potent mix.

Nick hurried over and started jawing with the umps. Trevor Doyle, the Bosox skipper, was already there, and they were apologizing, no doubt, for the foolishness of the players. Nick would later hound the Cub captains about who was responsible for "the insanity, and what in God's name did it **mean**?" In the end, no one took blame or credit, or explained any motives. Azzy said, "Sleep on it, skip. It was a silent gesture, to which you add your own song."

When the home-plate ump called, "Play ball!" I sat on the bench, my legs weak, my heart weak, and tried my best to concentrate. Game 6? I almost forgot we had to win tonight and win tomorrow to bring home the crown.

HANDYMAN JESÚS

World Series

Game 6

Wrigley Field

Line-up Cards

Visiting Boston Red Sox

SS Domingo López
RF Kaido Miura
CF Moises de Dios Ovando
3B Bill Murphy
1B Maceo Mason
LF Preston Hollis
2B Jay McCreary
C Antonio Chévez
P Bob Detrick

Home Chicago Cubs

CF Johnny Stompiano
LF Jamal Kelsey
2B Jesús Mijango Cruz
1B Jimmy Lieski
SS Rey Rodríguez
C Junior Parker
RF Terrence Gumbs
3B Matt Creighton
P Arshan "Azzy" Azzam

Azzy has what Dantel Hood calls "the blue-note-two-strike blues." Domingo López bloops a 1-2 change-up down the left-field line for a leadoff double. Kaido Miura misses a bunt, falls behind 0-2, then slaps a broken-bat single beyond the reach of a diving Jesús Mijango. Speed on the bases, first and third, nobody out. Moises de Dios Ovando looks hungry enough to devour a child.

Hood says, "You best throw your Trouble Ball, your Bat Dodger. Blaze one home for Satch."

What can you say about a cheap-hit circus? Dios Ovando, on an 0-2 count, check-swings and pops the ball up on the left side. Creighton runs back, turns the wrong way, and the ball flutters down on the white line—fair by what, a centimeter? First inning and Nick and I are already bowing our heads, muttering curses. Domingo López scampers home to give the Bosox the lead.

Seven minutes, three batters, and a cheap hit later, we go to the bottom of the first trailing two-zip.

*

Behind the Cub dugout, a small restroom sets in a dark cove. I hear whispers, peer in, and see Nick crouched in shadows. His words, muddled with the noise of the crowd, are gibberish, but he's cursing, no doubt, cursing two cheap runs, and every rot-gut word he can think of is at home in the gloom. I can't count how many times a Cub has ducked into this cove and muttered to himself. A stink has welled up, a permanent stink, but it seems I'm the only one who minds. Players and coaches, except for me, use this restroom during games rather than retreating to the clubhouse. Nick has a satellite radio on the floor between the piss bowl and a stained sink. During the season, he sometimes listened to the Cardinals and whispered foul invectives when they caught a break.

Now he fiddles with the dial till he finds Bosox radio, WEEI,

Mike Madson and Sam Foley. The latter, his voice chipper as a bright morning, says, "The Red Sox have taken the lead on the shoeless Cubs. Now let's see if we can humble them further, set them down one, two, three, and get a few more."

I'm beside Nick in a jiffy. "What the hell's this?"

His eyes are wild. "Don't touch it."

"Nick—"

"Don't touch it. Don't even look at it. This is my radio. **Mine**. You can go and get your own."

The skipper turns down the volume. "We'll piss on Sam Foley's party," he says, "send him bad luck." He glances toward the bench. "I'll make you a deal right now. If we don't score in the first inning, I'll turn this thing off."

I grab him by the elbow. "You promise? First inning? No more?"

He nods. "First inning, lieutenant, all or nothing. This bugger's off and stays off 'less we catch a break."

The fact that his key players stood shoeless during the National Anthem may have set his mind off balance. On any given day, though, Nick tends to be superstitious. If things go wrong, he'll juggle the line-up, make sudden switches, sit on a certain spot on the bench, close one eye, fling his hands away from his chest, and so on. As a general rule, the longer a man stays in baseball, the more he is ruled by superstition. Manager Dusty Baker used to sit in his office before a lighted candle. Nick? That's not his style, he'd piss on a candle. No New Age hoodoo for Nick.

*

Johnny bumps a fist to his chest as he steps in the batter's box. His spikes ruck the earth, slice narrow grooves, anchor his heels. Like no one save Jesús he owns the space between the lines, the dimensions—give or take inches—of a backyard play-box or a boy's coffin. He's facing Bob Detrick, Wild Bob and his ninety-nine-mile-an-hour fastball. Johnny has nothing but a shank of wood, a blond bat held loose in his hands. He'll squeeze hard only in that split second when wood meets leather. Right now a pretty girl could sneak up behind him and free the bat from his hands.

Nick and I have come out of the cove and sit side-by-side on the bench. We can still hear the radio. The smell of urine is faint. There are worse hells than this.

"Red Sox playing for a bunt," says Mike Madson. "Murphy's well in on the grass. Mason, edging toward home, is daring Stompiano to swing the bat."

"And let him swing," says Foley. "The wind, blowing in off the lake, has enough spank to knock down a homer. This is a night for short-ball, not long-ball. The Red Sox showed how to do it with two runs in the first."

Johnny shows bunt, then pulls back, half-swings, and high-hops the ball past a charging Bill Murphy.

"That's down the line," says Foley, "fair by inches. Preston Hollis runs the ball down, looks at it, and there it is, written between the seams in capital letters—CHEAP DOUBLE. Stompiano pulls into second, and he has his shoes on. Nobody out, first inning. The Red Sox trying to hang on to a two-run lead."

Mike Madson, the straight man, says, "Give Stompiano some credit. He shortened his swing and put the ball in play. He picked his spot."

"Or maybe the spot picked him," says Foley. "He hit a cheap double down the left-field line."

Nick pipes up: "Fuck you."

After Jamal Kelsey moves Stompiano to third with a grounder to the right side, the Bosox walk Jesús Mijango intentionally. The cheering of Cub pilgrims would be louder if someone other than Jimmy Lieski were stepping to the plate.

Detrick leans into his stretch, checks the runners. He holds the ball a good ten seconds before he comes home.

Jimmy pops the ball sky-high. I'm muttering curses, Nick too, but Azzy yells, "Tag Wild Child! Strike the peddle!" López, the Bosox shortstop, drifts back and makes the grab some ninety feet behind second base as Johnny heads home. **Baseball is lightning**. You can read this on the electronic billboard over the leftfield bleachers. You can see it, too, as Johnny hightails for home and the ball shoots home and Johnny dives and is safe by a margin so small you can call it luck. Nick says, "Jesus H! Jesus H. Christmas!" I wonder what H stands for as Johnny trots toward the dugout slapping the dust from his thighs.

Sam Foley says, "A little pop-fly leads to an undeserved run. And now some dizzy scorekeeper—where are you, Diz?—will have to credit Jimmy Lieski with an RBI."

He splashes bright paint on every Bosox triumph and seals every Cub sunbeam in a dustbin. The sharp glance I give Nick is quicker than words. "Hell no," he says. "My radio stays on as long as the game's close."

*

At the end of six and a half, the Bosox leading 2-1, Nick says, "Who you bird-dogging?"

I was watching Sonia through the glasses till he spoke. "Nobody."

"You watch the stands more than you watch the game. Which is more interesting?"

No way to answer that.

"Well, don't strain your eyes. A septuagenarian shouldn't birddog a girl more than a few innings a week."

I try to keep my hands and voice from shaking. "I watch a certain fan for luck."

"Luck? You once told me you didn't like that word."

"I don't."

"Well, luck's the key," he says. "You have my permission to watch her till we win."

Sonia's in the upper deck beyond the right field foul line, though not as far back as Jackie and Sam. On TV she saw me vote against Johnny, saw my hand go up, and this turned me into his opposite—a loser. Maybe I've come to respect her because she's perceptive, even clever. Had she kissed up to me, admired me in some way, I would have dismissed her as a chump.

I can't find Janice and Isha and Jesús' beau behind home plate. Johnny, due up third this inning, has already grabbed a bat.

"Where's your girl?" I ask. "I haven't seen her tonight."

He shrugs. "She's not here, coach. She got busy with something else."

A double-take, a triple-take. Busy with something other than baseball? And Azzy's wife? Her too? And Jesús' beau? They're occupied with something more pressing than Game 6 of the World Series? I'm stumped till I recall a note I stole, a message from Janice regarding a meeting with KJ (Khadijah Jamil?) on the evening of November 3rd. After Game 6, win or lose, you can count on more shenanigans. Johnny and his gang have any number of trump cards and jokers stuffed up their sleeves.

The skipper and I sit side-by-side, arms folded to our chests. The only warmth in my body is in compressed molars. My bones say winter is near, my teeth say we're losing. The wind's blowing in from centerfield at twenty-five miles an hour.

In the Cub seventh, Johnny comes up with one out and one on. For a few seconds I watch Sonia, her Easter coat a white flower in a field of Cub blue. These glasses focus so well I can zoom in on lips the color of raw liver. My girl is cold, everyone's cold, except certain players. I lower the glasses as Johnny raps a fist to his chest, spikes the dirt, rolls his shoulders. I remember Game 5, ninth inning, when he jacked a Ruben Romero fastball over the Green Monster. No hope for a home run now, not with the wind misbehaving. Maybe the Babe in his prime or Hammerin' Hank or Barry could challenge the Hawk and drive one to the seats. As for Johnny, he'll shorten his swing, maybe loop a single. Stick out his blond bat and put one where they ain't.

Sam Foley says, "There's a strike to Stompiano. Matt Creighton, the runner on first, hasn't stolen a base all year."

I steady my elbows on the top rail of the dugout. I spy Sonia again, her hands under her chin, her lips moving. Is she praying? I lower the glasses as Johnny drives a clean single into centerfield.

"Creighton pulls up at second," says Mike Madson. "Two on, one out. Bob Detrick in a jam."

Sam Foley, the Scrooge of baseball, calls Creighton "a one-man blockade to keep Fire Escape Johnny from lighting the base paths." He says, "Tip your caps to a snail. The Cubs may need a long double to even the score."

Jamal Kelsey breaks his bat and loops a lazy fly ball to the right fielder.

"That's two down," says Foley. "Let's give the shoeless Cubs one more breath, a short one. Here comes Jesús Mijango Cruz."

He steps in the box and his shoulders start twitching, his hands moving. As if the bat were shooting spurts of electricity into his fingers and up the length of his arms.

"Have to pitch to him," says Madson. "A walk will put the go-ahead run in scoring position."

"Keep the ball off the plate," says Foley. "Mijango will swing at anything. That's why they call him Bad Ball Jesús."

I hold the glasses steady and spy Sonia with one eye. The old girl's on her feet, clapping and ballyhooing with the congregation. The day we met she insisted she tolerated baseball but was no fanatic. Well, tonight she seems to have joined the fold, the die-hards Sam Foley and Mike Madson call "the Baby Bear faithful." Is she my opposite? Is she lucky? She might shout herself warm if she keeps at it. I give her a nod, then turn my attention to the field.

"Ball one high and away," says Foley. "Mijango was tempted."

"Tempt him again," says Madson. "The wind's gusting, blowing straight in. That last pitch from Detrick topped a hundred-miles-an-hour."

But Detrick—however fast his next pitch flew—is less than dear. I see Mijango sway and swing. I see the wood in his hands, a stick of charged light, black and bright, ringing. The crack of the bat says **Yes**. A single up the middle says, **Good enough**. A hard double says **RBI**. A home run, if hit on the line, is a long lightning of **Yes**, a **Yes** that splits the air and breaks the wind's back. Sam Foley says, "Mijango crushes one...Dios Ovando back-peddling. He's at the wall..." And Dios Ovando does what we do—he watches. At the track the Bosox centerfielder looks up and maybe listens, the crowd restrained for a moment, breath held in, the ball sizzling, a frying pan sound, and then up and out and Dios catches nothing but the sound of its leaving. That ball's gone, it's gone. On a windblown night what does Jesús do but part a gale.

We got a rapper in the dugout. Azzy says, "Handyman Jesús, picked up a hammer. Hit a three-run slammer."

Dantel Hood looks at the sky and moans.

The scoreboard says Cubs 4, Red Sox 2.

Azzy, eyes wide, says, "Is it a sin, a **sin**? To hit a ball so hard you hurt the **wind**?"

Hood's rhyme is a bit weak. "Can't lose with Mijango Cruz."

But the truth is we got two more innings to go.

I'd like to hear Sam Foley cry-babying his eyes out, but I

can do that later on YouTube. I'm trying to feel I'm part of this crowd, part of this spectacle at Wrigley. Everybody in this ballpark is going crazy if they weren't already crazy. Sonia is out there in her virgin coat. I can see her without looking. What do I need with high-powered binoculars? What do I need with eyes? Jackie and Sam are out there. Lady Luck is closer to the field. The three are among the pilgrims now raising the rafters, bending the beams.

*

We carry our 4-2 lead into the ninth inning.

Dantel Hood snaps his fingers, bobs his head. "Satch and Khadijah, Khadijah and Satch."

Hoodoo mantra from the bench.

Azzy Azzam looks like he's ten-feet tall when he takes the mound. He catches Kaido Miura looking at a 1-2 fastball, a flare that shaves the inside corner. Moises de Dios Ovando should be the next victim. He fouls one back, misses one, takes a pitch inside, then loops a soft single into left field. Sam Foley calls this "a fine piece of hitting," but all he did was hold his bat over the outer edge of the plate.

Bill Murphy, adjusting his batting gloves, spits, shrugs, scowls, grouses. Sam Foley reminds us the tying run is at the plate.

Azzy teases a slider to wriggle in over the outside corner. The big man's choosing his spots, throwing what he wants where he wants. Before games, Satchel Paige used to fine-tune his control by using a matchbook as home base. Standing sixty feet and six inches from a little slab, he'd throw strikes and chip away at corners. By game-time home plate—seventeen and a half inches across—would seem ocean-wide. Right now Azzy's a matchbook man, he's that fine. Buzzing pitch after pitch over the black, the thin strips of rubber at either side of the plate.

Murphy lunges at a fastball and slaps a soft liner to center.

Fire Escape Johnny lopes in, makes a basket catch, and runs the ball back to the infield. I hold up two fingers, but everyone from here to hallelujah knows we need one more out to play Game 7 at Wrigley Field.

Johnny places the ball in Jesús' black glove, eases it down as though he's delivering the Lord an egg. Why has he run the ball back to the infield instead of tossing it? For luck, I assume. What else? Bent over, he rubs Jesus' glove like rubbing an oversized bead of a rosary. He nods at Azzy, pats the Lord's glove once, twice, then hustles back to medium-deep centerfield.

"Hocus-pocus," says Sam Foley. "The Cubs are praying for luck."

"We need it more than they do," says Madson.

"Luck and hits," says Foley. "Maceo Mason at the plate."

He swings late, strike one, and goes to the dugout for a new bat. The bat's the problem? He better find one wide enough to cover the strike zone from bottom to top.

Azzy lights the outside corner and Mason shunts the ball up the middle. Sam Foley says, "Mijango dives, backhands the ball," and then I can't hear him. Mijango, sprawled on his side, flicks his glove, opens the flaps, and up comes the ball in a smooth arc, waist high for Rey Rodríguez, force-play at second, game over. I'll remember Game 6 this way, Mijango diving, stealing a hit from Mason. And I'll remember how Fire Escape Johnny ran the ball back to the infield, stuck it in Mijango's glove, then patted the glove for luck. Baseball gods are fickle, often cruel, but tonight they've shown mercy. They let Mijango break the wind's back, pick up a hammer, hit a three-run slammer. And they let Azzy, despite a sore shoulder, an achy arm, pitch nine strong innings. Right now I'd like to hear Sam Foley pissing and moaning, recapping Cub heroics, but the pilgrims have ascended. Wild demons and dogs, saints stunned by rapture, lunatics suddenly free, make less noise than Wrigley's faithful. Bellevue? Fenway Park? Yankee Stadium? No, they're second-stringers. This is the capital of noise.

Look.

The skipper bent over beside a urinal. He picks up the satellite radio, cradles it, and puts the speaker to his ear. I take two steps toward him, then turn back. I need some air; I need something other than a urinal. I mutter, "Later, Nick, catch you later. I'm getting the hell out."

As fast as these old man legs will take me, I head for the huddle of jumping jubilance behind second base. I hear one man above the others, and soon I lean on him—Azzy. Like an old-time preacher he raises both arms, his voice gospel-deep, bell-deep, and I feel a shudder under my ribs as he spouts a six-word sermon: "Jesús the Miracle Worker, Jesús Mijango!" I don't often get close to Azzy. Why should I? I'm not afraid, though, at least not for now. Because his body is as warm as any home.

BABEMBA

Despite the jubilation, the skipper stuck by his decision to bar the press from the clubhouse. At a team meeting he insisted that all players, not only the tri-captains, refrain from communicating with the press till the World Series was history. Nick said, "Let's show some common sense for a change. No more politics. No more media stunts. No more barefoot ballplayers posing for cameras." He gave Azzy a sharp glance, then cut his eyes toward Jesús and Johnny. "You're paid to do one thing," he said, "play ball. So go on home—no detours, no sideshows—and rest up for the biggest game of our lives."

Everyone seemed to agree. The players, the tri-captains included, left soon after they showered. The skipper and I headed to his office for a nightcap. He brought out a fifth of Old Crow, two cups, and pretty soon we sported our post-game glow. A widescreen TV showed Cub highlights. We sat on a blue sofa side-by-side.

"Dantel Hood in Game 7," said Nick. "Pour me another stiff one and I'll believe the son of a buck can win."

I freshened his drink. We clinked cups.

"To victory," he said. "None too soon."

He began cursing when ESPN featured the pre-game shenanigans of barefoot Cubs. "Pick ninnies," he said. "Let them pick cotton in the fields."

After he calmed down, after the station broke for ads, I asked if he had an extra ticket for Game 7.

"For your gal?" he said. "The one you spy through the glasses?"

I fidgeted with my hands. "She's not my gal."

"Well, she'd better be by game-time. One ticket for Lady Luck—is that all we need?"

I half believed it was.

"Just one thing," said Nick. "Are you sure she's lucky? You don't have a hard-on for nothing?"

I felt the heat at the back of my neck. "What the hell you hawing about? You drunk already?"

"No."

"We just happen to win every time she's in the park."

Why was I blushing? Did I have designs on Sonia? Did I anticipate certain favors? A man in ruins, forever beyond romance, should fear no one and nothing. Let the old girl wear a chastity belt, iron skivvies. Could luck be asexual, antiseptic as surgery? For no rational reason I saw Sonia as the luckiest lady in the world.

Nick said, "She can't watch on TV? Hole up in some bar?"

"It's not the same."

"Well, then you got yourself a problem. I'm nobody's savior."

He didn't need to tell me.

"Let her listen to Bosox radio, Sam Foley."

"It won't help."

"Works wonders for me," he said. "Set him near a urinal where he can smell his own stink."

So I knew we'd be listening to Sam Foley in the dugout in Game 7. During the off-season, I might hear the bastard in my dreams.

Nick finished his drink and poured another. He said, "Here's to Lady Luck, whoever she is." He cocked his head in what seemed to me an imitation of Johnny. "Don't worry, Billy. Later on I'll make a few calls, see what shakes. I might find a way to get your gal in the park."

Two drinks later, no phone calls, he said, "Lady Luck will have a ticket, but it will cost you."

"I'll pay anything."

"I can seat her behind home plate for around three thousand dollars."

"I'd pay more."

He chuckled. "I bet you would. Lover boy in a pinch, huh?"

I felt the sweat break out on my forehead.

"Leave your binoculars in the clubhouse, lieutenant. She'll almost be close enough to touch."

Once more he tried on his imitation of Johnny, head cocked, eyes half closed, a jazzman digging music. Subtract fifty years or more and he might have fooled someone. Nick was never Johnny, though, not even as a rookie with fresh dreams of conquering the world. Johnny took chances at every step. He stole bases no one should have stolen. He hit safely when he should have been out, and some of his biggest bets were beyond the white lines. Nick? He was my Siamese sidekick, a mere watcher. We were a couple codgers suckled by loss.

Head cocked, cup raised, I said, "To you, Nick, to you and Johnny," and mirrored his paltry imitation. Maybe his sad smile meant he understood the facts. We longed to be original, unpredictable as weather, but had somehow become the opposite. We could admire Johnny in secret, Jesús and Azzy too, but we could not imitate them any more than we could imitate the roar of the wind. I knew just one thing—we were in the thralls of mystery. You ever watch a storm blow in over Lake Michigan? A bulwark of clouds on the roam, churning and rolling, shooting light, hot and bright, sky booming. It can look like a movie set, but it's not for show or anything but truth. If you pay attention you might feel something begin to shift, the base you stand on no longer solid. The thunder and light of creation, the boom and sparkle. **Come on, Johnny. Come on, Jesús. Come on, Azzy**. Black winds and water and light a mockery to the mildness of common shores.

We had another drink, then another, and were well oiled when the phone rang. Butch Malecki, calling from the front office, wanted to know what in hell was going on in Wrigleyville. "Didn't you tell your players to stay away from the goddamn media? Didn't you **order** them?"

The receiver, which Nick held some ten inches from his left ear, was like a speaker blaring at full volume.

"I damn well **did** order them," said Nick. "I made things so clear even Johnny understood."

Malecki told him to turn on MSNBC. "Johnny understood nothing," he said. "Right now we got nineteen Cubs on a Wrigleyville rooftop. Khadijah Jamil is at center stage."

Nick started cursing. Malecki cursed louder before he hung up.

After I grabbed the remote and changed channels, Nick mimed his right hand into a pistol. His face, grizzled, streaked with blue, worried me. "Go easy," I said. "There's nothing we can do."

MSNBC shined their show-time lights. The kind that blaze enough heat to lather your face in sweat. Nick pointed the barrel of his finger at Khadijah Jamil. "Boom," he said. "You'll be dead soon." The candidate stood at a podium on a nearby rooftop in front of Azzy Azzam and Jesús Mijango Cruz.

Now the show-time lights widened to include others, most notably the candidate's family. Ahmed Jamil and his two daughters sat with Isha Azzam and her brood, plus some blacks and whites I didn't recognize. I'd seen Ahmed and these girls in the news several times, posing with the candidate as a family. He was a slender, friendly looking fellow, though no less dark than Khadijah. I remembered his letter to Johnny, which I'd saved along with some other things I'd stolen. **Everything humanly possible is possible in me.** I suppose I'd proven this in my own crooked way.

Khadijah wore a dark blue suit with a red scarf. We knew which rooftop she and her followers were on when the TV showed a hundred or more seats (all occupied) rising in rows, and above the seats a billboard that had run the same verse all year long—**I BELIEVE A LEAF OF GRASS IS NO LESS THAN THE JOURNEYWORK OF THE STARS.** I once mistook this poem as an ad for lawn fertilizer, but that was before the first game of the season. Anyway, Khadijah, a mike clipped to her lapel, seemed to be midway through a speech.

Nick tossed some whiskey down the hatch. "Hell's bells, I'm going up there. I'll bust up the show before it goes any further."

"They won't let you in."

"Hell they won't. Worse comes to worse, I'll throw myself off the roof."

He grabbed his coat and Cub cap, but I knew he wouldn't go anywhere.

"The door to that roof's bolted," I said. "You'd need a key to get in."

"Or an axe."

"Calm down for Christ's sake. There's nothing we can do."

Nick cursed. He threw a chair against a wall, but he knew I was right. I freshened his drink, then mine, and we sat on the sofa and watched the tube. In seats and in aisles, near the candidate and

241

her family, the faithful had gathered. Besides Jesús and Azzy, who now stepped to the side, I saw every colored guy on the team salted by four whites—Paddy Delaney, Dirk Rouda, Mick Gutowski, and Fire Escape Johnny. I had to catch my breath when I spied Janice waiting in the wings. She wore a Cub coat open at the neck, a blue scarf, blue slacks, high heels. A thought slipped from my lips before I could edit: "That flower in her hair, what is it? Morning glory?" Nick moaned and rubbed his eyes, his forehead. I almost felt sorry for the old wretch. He feared beauty and danger, the way they often merge.

The wind tugged at scarves, riffled hair, and flapped a large banner over the podium, red letters on a blue background—**LIVE THE LEGACY: TOMMIE SMITH, JOHN CARLOS, AND MUHAMMAD ALI**. Did Jamil indeed wish to be president? It seemed to me that Middle America, with its hand on the remote, flipping channels, keen on entertainment, would flash forward to something—anything—**white**.

At first, Khadijah made little sense. She might as well have spoken in tongues, babbled to an unseen god. I leaned forward, but all I heard was some chatter about a lost tribe—the Babemba. I know now she never called them lost, but the name alone conjured carcasses, relics, mummified cultures long devoid of meaning. The Babemba—she made the name sound like a drum—were not Americans. They were South Africans, and they had a custom Khadijah deemed important. Whenever a member of the tribe caused suffering, he or she was brought to the village square and surrounded by every man, woman, and child, every neighbor, every acquaintance, and though she made no mention of dogs I saw some, and though she made no mention of stones I saw some in clenched fists, and the offender—some thief or thug—was tied to a pole and shivering. I would have inverted every spoken word had Khadijah not circled back to tell her story in a different way.

She sounded the three Bs into a drum roll. She'd told the story once, and then she came around to tell it like this.

Babemba.

They were a people, a tribe, in South Africa. When someone caused suffering in the community, he or she was taken to the village square and surrounded. "That's right," said Azzy, "the village square," as though to mark the story true to this point. The culprit was surrounded, but no one held a stone, a knife, a mean thought, a barbed tongue. The people gathered "to bring back the good."

The Babemba spoke one by one, careful and calm. In testimony that sometimes went on long past midnight, long past the rise and fall of the moon, long past dawn and sunrise, the Babemba convened. Khadijah seemed to believe what this tribe believed: every sinner has his virtues, every louse his Sunday suit. I could feel myself beginning to sweat. The Babemba were good, maybe too good. As the moon rose and fell, as the sun came out, they reminded some thief or thug of his own kindness in times past, and of his contributions—large or small or immeasurable— that helped someone live. And after the ceremony, or "blessing," as Khadijah called it, the man was welcomed back to his home and his tribe.

I leaned toward the TV, but for a time I shut my eyes. I imagined myself at the center of a circle, surrounded by everyone I had known in my seventy-three years. Of what good deed could the most generous man or woman remind me? Could beauty return if it never existed? What virtue, what act of spontaneity, might justify my life?

I wondered if those circling me would be silent for days, months. In the end, would they see some good in me, or would I defeat generosity and watch the villagers slink away, heads down, stumped by my ignorance, greed, wrath, the ten thousand ills of the mind and heart that gut every gift of grace? I was a thief, a kleptomaniac—petty in some ways, but with enough desire to saturate a city. I stole this and that—words, ideas, a picture of a girl—and I loved what I stole. Thievery let me know Janice a little, plus Azzy, Jesús, Ahmed Jamil, Fire Escape Johnny. I stole life itself, odd fragments that I sewed into quilts, arranged in collages, in an effort to discern patterns. Was it possible to know someone without stealing? As for the boys, Jackie and Sam, and Sonia—who might never in her life say anything good of me—they were strangers of a distant village. I knew almost nothing, except to know I needed them. A family of sorts, a small circle. Something salvaged from the wreck.

Babemba.

The TV made odd sounds. It seemed a choir had begun to hum, sing, in voices barely audible. Were the airways playing unintended riffs, or had a tribe begun to gather? Khadijah, stepping out from behind the podium, began to sway, sashay, the first would-be-lady president to suggest in her body the necessity of a dance.

"We've brought South Africa," she said, "to South Chicago."

Azzy nodded. "Talk it to Dearborn Homes. Or else sing it."

"South over rooftops," said Khadijah, "where there's no money, no fame, but this other thing—a song not before sung on these shores."

"A song," said Azzy.

"When a disturbance occurs, when someone steals, for example, or causes anyone deep pain, we do what the Babemba do—surround the one who brought harm to remind him of his goodness."

Azzy hummed and nodded. "A sun of words."

"Yes, there are such words," said Khadijah, "and we know them."

"Amen.

"A sun of words sung to the roundness of a man's heart."

Was I foolish enough to want the rooftop revelers to circle me? Yes. But I had no idea what even the most magnanimous would say.

One last thing happened on this night of victory. I saw Janice near the podium between Khadijah and Johnny, and I remembered a note I had stolen: **To see one thing clearly—a ball with red stitches, a brown leaf, a cloud—changes everything. And to write one true thing reinterprets the world.**

Janice read a short poem by a Palestinian, and another by an Israeli. She added that these poems would appear on D.C. billboards later in the evening. I remembered the Israeli poem of Yehuda Amichai because I'd stolen it from Johnny's locker. Nick, with no hankering for poetry of any kind, said, "All she needs is for someone to throw her on her back."

I sat as though alone, bent forward, my hands on my belly. I tried to contain my longing, yet here it was, in this loose flesh, and in the heat of my face, the sweat at the back of my neck, the beat of my heart. I wanted to rise to a Waveland rooftop and a poem about a leaf of grass and the journeywork of stars. I wanted truth to be less embarrassing, desire more attainable. I wanted to be welcomed by a sun of words, by Azzy and Khadijah, Johnny and Janice, and everyone else large enough to help me overcome my shame.

Babemba.

A drum.

A song.

A poem.

ONE TRUE THING

The next morning I found a note on my kitchen table. Green letters, perfectly formed, generous—a tree of words, if not a sun of words. They came to me as from the light of a dream.

Dear Johnny,

I would carve our names inside the wide heart of a wide oak if knives were subtler tools. You know the lovely tree we've sat beneath in Grant Park? On a Monday in spring, we whispered our names into craggy bark—who needs knives? Standard tools, however honed, lack subtlety, and divide wholeness. A whisper is plenty. And sometimes a mere breath can be a balm for a wound.

Steal a base for me, steal my heart.

Love,
Janice

I tried to recall pilfering this note from Johnny's locker. Drunk, leaving Wrigley, I must have slipped it in a pocket, carried it home, and placed it at the center of my table the way another person might set a vase of fresh flowers. I sat now with my hangover, my coffee, and waited to fully waken. I read the note again and again, in silence and in whispers. A room of flowers, wall-to-wall roses, would have failed to greet me with as much pleasure as this note from a girl.

But a night of drunkenness comes with a price. For my pounding head I took Tylenol, for my stomach Maalox, and I had a hard time rising from a chair. The morning was half gone before I mustered the strength to dress myself and make a few calls. Nick surprised me, answered on the first ring, but he had no recollection of promising me a prime seat for a lucky lady. I jogged his memory by pushing the highlight button of our conversation. "The Cubs have never lost," I said, "when this woman was in the park."

Nick hesitated. "She's that lucky? You're sure of it?"

"Positive."

"I reserved that seat for an in-law, but it's yours for three thousand."

"I'll pay more."

He chuckled. "She's a shark, huh? The kind who gets luckier as you empty your wallet?"

"Not really."

"Well, write me a check for three grand. I'll tear it up when we win, make confetti."

"I'll pay either way."

"You mean we might lose?"

I coughed. "I don't think so."

"Then meet me in my office. Bring a check. Be there at half past twelve."

I got Sonia on the line and set up the logistics.

"Same place as yesterday," I said, "one o'clock. I'll have tickets for you and your boys."

*

So I again met the little family at the Dark Horse Bar & Grill. The place was jammed, the TVs going at full tilt. The noise, the chatter, shoved my nerves through a grater. What I needed was a hot toddy, a nip from the dog that bit me. The Babemba, the glow of last night's victory—where were they? I'd smothered the good feelings in a batch of Old Crow.

Sonia wore her Easter Sunday garb, a coat as white and harsh as a new refrigerator. Are women sane? Sara, my second wife, used to spend hours trying on clothes and asking me, "How does this look? What do you think?" The unscheduled fashion shows stung my eyes to tears.

Men stood three-deep at the bar, and the line for tables stretched out the door. Smells wafting from the ovens and plates— meat loaf, roast turkey, home fries—woke no hunger in me. One eye closed, the other blurry, I watched the TV mounted on the wall behind the bar. Eddie Bray, Channel 9's meteorologist, was decked out in a blue suit. "Tonight at Wrigley," he said, "we can expect apple cider weather, cool, clear autumn. Fierce winds, white stars. Look for Johnny and Jesús to brighten the heavens with every breath they blow."

I'd never heard Eddie speak this way. Was he trying to be poetic, elevate the weather report to the height of a billboard poem? Maybe he and everyone else in town was changing, or at least making an attempt. I thought of drab-looking caterpillars, worm-like things that transform overnight into butterflies. One day we watch them belly along over a battered earth, and the next we see bright wings ply morning sunlight. A few years back Johnny was an unproven rookie, consistent in one category—eccentricity. Jesús? He had the fiercest swing in the National League, but he struck out too much and earned the name Bad Ball Jesús. Azzy was a fire-baller who lacked finesse, as was Porfirio Guevara. Now all of the above had not only sprouted wings, but spread them wide enough to inspire multitudes. It seemed everyone, even a prosaic meteorologist, longed for new altitudes, new language—**Fierce winds, white stars.** As for me, I was sick enough to puke, but I told myself, "Damn it, Billy, shape up!" I remembered I used to write poetry in grade school. Hell, in 7th grade Sister Mary Michael presented me with a blue ribbon and told me I had talent. Strange things happen at any juncture. Maybe I'd write some new poems if I survived the self-abuse.

*

We sat in silence till a waitress took our orders. Old Sonia had barely given me a glance, but I thought a gift priced at three thousand dollars might change her tune.

I lay the tickets on the table.

"I wish I had three seats behind home plate," I said, "but for Game 7—Cubs and Bosox—it's a miracle to have any seats at all."

I pushed Jackie and Sam their tickets, but let Sonia get her exercise—reach. She put on her glasses, held the ticket in the light, mumbled something, and then she said, "I'm sorry, but this is well beyond my means."

A gift from me was the last thing she wanted, so I told her the ticket was bought and paid for by Johnny Stompiano. "He knows about you and your boys," I said. "He arranged for all of you to see the game."

She inspected the ticket. We live in a time when generosity, plus the goodwill that allows for generosity, are suspect. "Johnny paid for this? A ticket for me?"

I nodded. "That's right."

"But Johnny doesn't know me."

"He knows you and your boys because I told him about you."

She shook her head.

"Here's an idea," I said. "Just see this as a gift."

Upon meeting Sonia, I soon grew accustomed to a pinched look, a dark tension in her eyes, a grimness in her mouth, a stock reaction to my presence. She wore this look now, and she haggled. "How can I accept this? A ticket to a ballgame is one thing, but this is extravagant."

I shrugged. "What's the fuss? Stompiano's extravagant. He **invented** extravagance. Why's it hard to believe he wants you to see the game?"

She bit down on her lower lip and pulled a long breath through her nostrils. I could feel my bluff starting to work, taking the desired effect. Sonia hemmed and hawed, expressed numerous reservations, but I knew I had her. "Oh, all right," she said finally, "but what's the catch?"

I raised my brow. "Catch?"

"You know what I'm talking about. It's beyond me why a ballplayer I admire but never met would give me an expensive ticket to a game."

Lady Luck impressed me. She was spunky, dignified, and keen on the most lonesome thing in the world—truth. Anyone hunting for truth, be it large or small, was anchored in another century. It bothered me that I had to spoon-feed her a story. "Well, you know Johnny," I said, "Mr. Unpredictable. He walked up to me and said, 'Give this ticket to the boys' foster mom. I won't accept one red penny in return.'"

What a stickler. After accepting Johnny's "gift," she paid me in greenbacks for Jackie's ticket, then Sam's—eight-hundred-and-fifty-eight dollars. Try and talk the old girl out of anything. You'd be better off trying to tame a tornado. She glared at me till I inserted the bills in my wallet. "Fair enough," I said, to acknowledge the rule she played by: Do nothing that in any way indebts you to this man.

After the haggling was over, I asked Sonia and her boys if they'd heard Khadijah Jamil's latest speech. They hadn't, so I told them about the Babemba, about Jamil and nineteen Cubs on a rooftop, but I had trouble matching the event to language. The more I tried, the more convinced I became that Sonia saw through me—a man who desired forgiveness. Had I deemed myself worthy of forgiveness I might have risked a revelation. To say I've wasted my life is an understatement. I've botched every breath, squelched every truth, and how does a man of my nature make amends? At present, all I could do was invite my lunch-mates to go on-line and see what I saw some fourteen hours earlier. "If you get a chance," I said, "try MSNBC's homepage. I'm sure they'll have a link."

I had no appetite for the food that arrived. Sonia seemed to be vegetarian, a rabbit with her herb salad, Italian dressing, but her boys began to devour a full meal—roast turkey with mashed potatoes and coleslaw. I barely glanced at my burger and fries.

The Dark Horse had four TVs, each tuned to a different channel. I looked at one, then another, a dull-eyed drunk forever doing penance. News. The election. The ballgame. The world. I was rubbing the base of my skull, a place where pain itself seemed to originate, when a barkeep, at the request of a patron, put all TVs on one channel—FOX.

A thin man in a gray suit reported that two poems in the nation's capital—one by Fady Joudah, the other by Yehuda Amichai—had been removed from billboards early this morning. I remembered Janice, in the wind of a Wrigleyville rooftop, made brief mention of two poems destined for D.C. billboards. They'd been posted last night and already they were gone.

The thin man, a chimera, disappeared from the screens, and in his place we saw empty slabs—billboards—over a three-story building on Constitution Avenue. Surfaces were scraped to a brilliant white.

Sonia and her boys and I picked at food and watched TV. A voice-over—the thin man—again told us the poems had been removed early this morning. A cut to footage of workers on billboard walkways peeling away scrolls of paper, the sunrise behind them. Who ordered the poems removed? The thin man? The president? Homeland Security? Guys at the bar heckled and harped as at a four-eyed ump who'd made a bad call.

The thin man, at a podium now, and with the nation's flag behind him, claimed that the poems, in themselves, were appreciated in the nation's capital, but not the misguided goals of certain celebrities. "The poems were posted illegally," he said, "as no one filed for permits."

I waved a hand. What the hell was he afraid of? You would think a poem was a loose grenade, a bomb.

"New security ordinances have been in place for a year," he said. "Only ads or messages that have been screened and pre-approved can be posted within a three-mile radius of the White House. This is the law."

I thought to myself, "Soon we'll need a permission slip to wipe our asses. And they'll tell us what dumb-fuck book we can read as we sit on the stool."

A moment later I found myself standing, pushing back my chair, and pointing to the TV mounted over the bar. The thin man still cajoled, jabbered, justified, and I said, "What's this? You take center stage? You rob us of poems and give us garbage? What's next? You steal our stories, too? Then what? We wander around like zombies? Will that make you happy? What the hell do you want?"

A couple drunks at the bar started cheering me on. The thin man was saying something, but I talked over him. "You want to steal another poem?" I said. "You want a story? Okay, then. Pay attention. 'To see one thing clearly—a ball with red stitches, a brown leaf, a cloud—changes everything. And to write one true thing reinterprets the world.'"

I'd read this note from Janice so many times that I knew it by heart. Before I sat down, I recited it again and some of the Dark Horse rowdies, plus a waitress or two, a barkeep, thanked me with a cheer. For a moment I felt the way Fire Escape Johnny must feel when he steals a base, or how Jesús must feel when he hits a ball with everything he is made of. Best of all, Sonia was looking at me with the most wondrous perplexity I had glimpsed in decades. With her eyes, her mind—spark quick, almost audible—she assessed me, and I read the results as clearly as if she'd spoken. "He's a man, a fighter of sorts. He's not a doormat." And for the first time I saw her smile come my way.

She was, I recalled, a retired librarian. Unintentionally (the only way possible), I'd made a good impression, and of course I wasted no time in spending unearned revenue. I referred to other choice lines from Janice, insight gleaned from youthful wisdom. I told Sonia and her boys of Li-Young Lee, a Chicago poet who addresses his poetry to an all—the stars, the trees, the birds. "People imagine life differs from poetry, but they are wrong. We live—if we live at all—for everything. Stars and trees. Cats. Birds. Base-thieves. Orphans. Saints." Orphans was my addition. The rest was a stolen jewel.

The poetic overture bewildered the boys. They glanced at Sonia, at me, at one another, their eyes as alert and guileless as those of deer in a deep forest. I flashed a wink, a smile. "Relax," I said. "And don't feel left out if my rambling gets hard to follow." I cocked my head. "You're young," I said. "You have plenty of time. Some day you'll know a thousand times more poems than this old man."

The only poems I knew came from looted lockers and Wrigley Field billboards. I could've told myself, "You're a faker, a thief," but in this moment I felt genuine. When Sonia kept smiling, I began to believe there was—is—a man in me deserving of a smile. Or at least a wink, a nod. A wish-me-well to ease the chill of the coming night.

Sonia added no comment to my poetic performance, except, "Li-Young is generous, at times exceptional," to which I nodded. I feared she would ask me to name a favorite volume of poems, a favorite passage, or to speak of other poets. She said nothing more, though, and in time I grew almost calm in the presence of her smile.

I said to her boys, "Okay, so you already know poetry and baseball are secret twins. Right?"

Sam nodded. Jackie picked at his turkey.

"Jesús is a poem," I said. "Johnny's a poem. Who can stop them?"

"Nobody," said Sam.

"And the three of you in the park, the three of you at Wrigley. Who can stop you?"

"Nobody!"

I clapped and winked. "Well, there it is, fans, there it is in capital letters: THE POEMS ARE WHAT WINS IN THE END."[6]

*

Janice sees knives as unsubtle tools, but are they? Some lover had carved initials into the wooden tabletop.

T.C.
&
L.W.

I ran a fingertip across razor-thin scratches. Such small details, small and perfect. The grooves warm on my skin.

---

[6] In a crooked way, I was right. The poems banned in D.C. became an overnight sensation. In case you haven't seen them, or have but need a review, turn to the Appendix of this book.

COME HOME IN THE DARK

World Series

Game 7

Wrigley Field

Line-up Cards

Visiting Boston Red Sox

Home Chicago Cubs

SS Domingo López

RF Kaido Miura

CF Moises de Dios Ovando

3B Bill Murphy

1B Maceo Mason

LF Preston Hollis

2B Jay McCreary

C Antonio Chévez

P Juan Bartholome

CF Johnny Stompiano

LF Jamal Kelsey

2B Jesús Mijango Cruz

1B Jimmy Lieski

SS Rey Rodríguez

RF Terrence Gumbs

C Junior Parker

3B Matt Creighton

P Dantel Hood

Where is the boundary between baseball and religion? In the box seats, in the bleachers and grandstands, pilgrims sing hosannas with signs and banners:

CUBS IN HEAVEN IN GAME 7

JESÚS & JOHNNY & AZZY—HOLY TRINITY!

WORLD SERIES—EXPRESS TRAIN TO THE PROMISED LAND!

WE ARE FORGIVEN! WE ARE ALL FORGIVEN!

JESÚS, BRING US HOME!

So for Game 7, a rough, autumn night, the wind a bruise, white stars overhead, pilgrims have brought promises of salvation, prayers, songs, pleas—flowers for Wrigley's altar. I spy Sonia in her Easter coat four rows behind home plate. Lady Luck claps and shouts, her breath a thin cloud. The temperature at game-time is thirty-seven degrees, close to what Channel 9 predicted. I use my binoculars to find Jackie and Sam in the upper deck of right field, the blue rim of turtleneck sweaters knurled above winter coats.

"Boys," I say to myself, "let you and your mom be my Charles Victor Faust."

*

Before the Cubs take the field, players and coaches are cramped together in the dugout where Pastor Jimmy Lieski tries to convince us the high winds are a sign from Christ.

Jesús Mijango says, "You mean like an omen? **Un presagio?**"

Jimmy's stuttering, but he manages to say something about the Rapture.

"Nothing to be afraid of," says Jesús. "It means **los vatos lindos** will appear."

Jimmy speaks of Christ rather than Jesús so we the fallen, his captive dugout audience, won't associate the true Christ with Jesús Mijango. It's Christ this and Christ that, prayers and supplications. Things will get worse before they get better. I should have plugs of cotton for my ears.

In the lair behind our dugout, between the urinal and the sink, Nick tunes his satellite radio to WEEI. Sam Foley and Mike Madson, insult artists, bastards both, hurl pre-game punches. Foley calls Dantel Hood, the Cub starter, "a champion of mood swings, a package marked Fragile."

Nick talks back to him. "No problem," he says. "If you bend down a little, you can kiss my ass."

We won Game 6 while listening to WEEI in the dugout. Nick isn't the first manager to be ruled by superstition, but he takes it to another level. He'd be the last skipper in the Bigs to admit he's psychotic. Nick sounds more or less sane when he talks with reporters, or even his players. Just under the skin of reason is the bedlam of a madhouse. Trust me. I know the man as well as I know myself.

*

First inning, two down, the Bosox threaten. Kaido Miura's on third, Moises de Dios Ovando on second. Why not walk Mason, load the bases for McCreary? I fire this question at Nick, who shakes his head.

He squats down between the radio and the urinal. Like me, he's hung-over, jug-bitten, messy as pig-slop. Azzy says, "Hey, skip, turn that noise down a notch." Nick looks from the big man to the radio, starts to reach for the dial, then shakes his head.

Hood offers a change-up. Mason, a lefty, starts to swing, pulls back, and the ball breaks low and inside. Parker, from a crouch, burns the ball to Creighton at third. Miura almost steps into the tag. He skids, pivots, then—Creighton chasing him—hightails for home.

"Run-down!" says Foley. "Miura in a run-down! And look at him go!"

Creighton hurries a throw that glances off Miura's helmet and ricochets toward the Cub dugout. Nick, couched in the stink, the gloom, snivels like a beat-up dog.

"Well, here comes the first run of the game," says Foley, and lets out a cackle. "Oh, man, they had Miura in their gun sights. Junior Parker whipped Creighton a laser. No way Miura could dive back to the bag, so he broke for home and let Creighton help him. The throw—from a Bosox perspective—was on the money. Banged off the back of Miura's helmet, then rolled toward the Cub dugout." He snorts his pleasure, a nose-full. "By the time Junior Parker could retrieve the ball, Miura had scored and Dios Ovando sailed over to third." A sound like bones sliding on bones, cracked knuckles. "The Red Sox draw first blood," says Foley, "and there's more where this came from."

"A lot more," says Madson.

"We could open a blood bank in this park."

Now Nick shoots me a look. "So where's Lady Luck? Late for Game 7?"

"No."

"Well, she better be worth it. I have an in-law who could be sitting in her seat."

The Bosox score another run on a wild pitch. I glare at Sonia as though it's her fault. This game's barely gotten its wings and we're down two-zip.

*

In the Cub fifth, the score unchanged, Johnny comes up with two outs and Junior Parker on second. The wind, tingling, howling, elemental, blows straight in from centerfield, and no one—not even Jesús Mijango—can grab a bat and drive one to the seats. I'm still struggling with the effects of last night's booze. My head feels swollen, trodden upon, but even teetotalers might sense something fierce in this sky, something unrestrained beyond the vagaries of weather. Jimmy Lieski says, "Behold, I am coming," and stands at the rail of the dugout. A Cub awaits deliverance, the Rapture of Christ's coming? To fend off temptations, worldly influence, he quotes scripture from memory: "But outside are dogs and sorcerers and the sexually immoral and murderers and idolaters, and whoever loves and practices a lie."

And Johnny.

He strides to home plate with the ease of a satisfied cat. While he digs in and goes through his paces—waves a blond bat in the air, bumps a fist to his chest—pilgrims rise and wail. Azzy, leaning over the top rail of the dugout, yells, "Wild Child, you bring Junior home now, you bring him home!" His tone is that of a father giving his son an important task.

Straight heat, high and tight. Ball one. Bartholome, working fast, breaks off a slider, a diving bullet, but Wild Child heeds Azzy's call and socks the ball up the middle. The shortstop's headlong dive is pure show. The ball's by him and clips the grass in centerfield before he hits the ground. Junior Parker lopes home, cuts the lead in half. Bosox 2, Cubs 1. Johnny's on first base clapping his hands.

Jamal Kelsey takes strike one. After a pitch-out evens the count, Johnny starts jawing, ragging the Bosox pitcher, the first-baseman, the second-baseman, bumping a fist to his chest to punctuate.

"Fire Escape Johnny," says Foley. "Let's crown him king of jabberwocky, king of trash."

"What's he hollering?" says Madson.

"He's a one-trick pony," says Foley. "He keeps telling us he's out of jail, out on bail, come what may."

Juan Bartholome, stooped, dark, crow-like, spies the runner over his left shoulder. A stillness on the mound, a gaunt profile, a study of vigilance. Neck sunk into his shoulders, he sights the baserunner as a hunter sights prey. He waits for Stompiano to gamble, lean an inch too far, or at least stop shouting. **Goddamn you, can't you shut up!** Quick as a cartoon on fast-forward, Bartholome kicks and fires.

"Runner going!" says Foley, and then the hubbub of this ball yard buries his voice. A fastball from Bartholome sails high and outside. The catcher, cat-quick, plants his right foot and zips the ball across the diamond. Johnny dives, latches onto the front edge of the bag with his left hand, the tag coming down hard on his neck. Had the throw been level with the base, six inches lower, they'd have nipped the Thief for out number three.

Head down, Juan Bartholome rubs the ball, tries to shine himself some luck. Dust devils, miniature tornadoes, whirl across the infield and over the mound. Jimmy Lieski says something about the Rapture. Sam Foley says, "It's wild out here, a witch's brew. All the winds of the ages are stirred up for this final showdown at Wrigley Field."

Bartholome nips the outside corner, strike two. Before the catcher can snap the ball to the mound I hear a sizzling sound— electrical, hot wires sparked and snarled—and then all is lost. At first I am too stunned to see it—the dark. A man beside me moans. I hear a guttural **Ahh** in the stands, a rumble of wonder and disbelief, the tone of a question that fears an answer. I hear Jimmy Lieski beg his great wish—"Christ take me." In the stands pilgrims call to each other, or to something less dark, but there are no words, or none I hear, only the rumblings beneath the wind, the moans that become part of the wind, the human part tame and trivial. Jimmy does not cry or shout for deliverance. In his mind's eye maybe he's already risen to light, Rapture Jimmy spared hell on earth, the redundancy of plagues and floods and wars, the torments of Revelation. I, barren of religion, believe all and nothing. The world as I knew it is over, or never existed. I have no wish to mock any man. Not now when the edges of my flesh seem to be slipping away in vapor. I tell myself the blackout may be comprehensible. A mechanical failure, a Cub failure. A power grid out of commission. Two months ago, across town, a blackout interrupted a game between the White Sox and Twins for almost an hour. Comprehensible or not, the darkness and wind **now**, in the fifth inning of Game 7 of the World Series, spawn awe and terror. A blast of wind shoves me to the back of the dugout. Gasping, I swallow a kernel of the storm, dust and grit, madness like a spice. It seems I have sampled my own flesh.

When the lights come on the first one I see is Johnny. Arms akimbo, he stands still and straight, not on second base, though, on home plate, the rubber slab—the Thief stole two bases! The lights boom and the noon-like glare snaps at my eyes, blinks me awake. Johnny nods at the home-plate ump and then angels his arms, spreads them—**Safe!** The ump, frozen in position, masked and crouched, comes alive. His arms start to rise, then float down, hands to thighs, the pose of a thinker. Chévez, the Bosox catcher, still holds the ball in his mitt. He tags Johnny—a gesture, a way to get back in the game. How long were we in darkness? Thirty seconds? A minute? Two? Five? In the gloom that held us, in the wind that extinguished every spark from every match, the Thief smelled home base.

Wrigley's faithful call to him, their voices at first tentative, but soon rising to full pitch, as brash as the halo of light returned to our ball yard. I wag a fist and shout, "That's right, baby! That's right! Tie game!" I stomp and shout until the home-plate ump shakes his head and points Johnny toward second base.

It's the right call, sure, it is. But I can't help feeling Game

7 should be tied. **Johnny came home in the dark, he came home.** These words sing through me as powerful as the wind.

"A charming ballpark," says Foley, "a touchy-feely museum. But these bozos didn't pay the light bill."

"No, they didn't," says Madson.

"Spent too much on Fire Escape Johnny's salary," says Foley. "Spent too much on a guy who should be in jail."

Nick slips out from the shadows behind the dugout. Holding the rail, a bit wobbly, he climbs the dugout steps and goes out to argue the call.

He sidles up to the home-plate ump and I can guess what he's saying: "The ball was in play, no one called time; Stompiano, free to advance, stole two bases." The ump points out the obvious— special circumstances. Being able to see or smell one's way through darkness does not translate as a run.

I can't hear Nick, but you can be sure he's stinking the place up with curses. The wind at his back, he kicks dirt at the umpire. A dust devil whirls around home plate, then heads straight for the Cub dugout. Nick throws his cap off the ump's shins, plays the ricochet and tries it again. He ignores the big thumb waved in front of him—**You're outta here**. The skipper fetches his cap and hurls it to the wind.

Johnny and Jamal get between Nick and the ump and in a minute or so, order—such as it is—returns.

"Let's get the score right," says Mike Madson. "Red Sox two, Cubbies one. Stompiano, head down, is making his way to second base."

The skipper, as he trundles by me and heads for the showers, says, "Don't touch that dial. You hear me?"

I nod.

"Hell or high water," he says, "my radio stays on."

I'm too superstitious to cancel someone else's notion of luck.

Nick is less than whole, I know this. But so was Charles Victor Faust.

Bartholome, his poise stolen by a blackout, a thief, walks Kelsey. So first and second now, two down. Jesús Mijango Cruz is flicking his bat.

The Bosox, with a measure of wisdom, would walk him to load the bases. Lieski's on deck, Rapture Jimmy, shaky as a drunk on a bad morning. He's probably wondering what he did wrong, why he's still on this Earth. Sharp twitches in his arms, his shoulders, his eyes unsteady. For once I'm glad Nick's in the clubhouse early. Jimmy could be struck blind and the skipper would still let him hit.

I tap Drexel Rountree and say, "Grab a bat, Tree. You're on-deck."

Azzy helps Jimmy down the steps and into the shadows.

"Nice and easy," says Azzy, "that's right. Just set yourself down and breathe."

Pitch.

"Ball one," says Madson, "way outside. Mijango, itching for contact, leaned over the plate and almost took a rip."

Bartholome tosses the ball to first. Kelsey, the go-ahead run, had a good lead. He's thinking about scoring on a double, flying home behind Johnny. The middle infielders play back on the grass. The outfielders, despite the wind blowing in, are a few long strides from pressing their backs to the vines.

Jesús swings at a ball he couldn't have reached with Jacob's ladder.

"Beautiful," says Foley. "Feed him two more in the same spot. Let Bad Ball Jesús swing and miss and put this inning to bed."

But the Cub Lord is argumentative at the plate. Chin up, bat cocked, his fingers drum a troubled riff. The pitcher, wind and dust swirling behind him, calls time and grabs the resin bag. Bartholome

ponders the location of his next pitch: high, low, outside, inside…
graze the chin? Jesús Mijango will not see a strike.

Azzy, at the rail of the dugout, says, "Swing away! Swing
away! For Khadijah and Satch and your mama in LA!"

Bartholome burns one low and inside. A hard slider
that might have grazed a kneecap had Jesús not anticipated its
trajectory. Bailing out, the Lord swings his bat like a sickle felling
weeds. Bartholome's head snaps back. He stumbles to his right,
his head craned toward a ball scudding past third and down the
line, extra bases. Foley says, "That's trouble, that's trouble…" And
that's all he can sputter before the rising pandemonium, the roused
pilgrims, bury his voice beneath a sea of noise.

Johnny wings home and plants both feet on the rubber. **Tie
game, count it. Can't send me back to second.** Pete Carnes, the
third-base coach, runs up the line wind-milling his left arm. Jamal
blurs by him, legs like wild pistons. I'm wind-milling same as old
Pete. Beside me, Azzy's wind-milling, and then Junior and Dantel
and Porfirio Guevara, a wide sweep of arms waving our man
home. A strong throw from the left-field corner cannot catch Jamal
as he slides in, spins past the catcher, rises to his feet and bumps
fists with Fire Escape Johnny. Notch another run, make it 3-2.
Cubs take the lead. And across the windswept diamond, on second
base, Jesús Mijango Cruz jabs a finger at the sky.

The skipper, once, to me alone, said, "LA Mexican? I doubt
it. Ornery and dark as a Gullah nigger. Carolinas got thousands
dark as him."

But how does he shine so? Give me an answer. Henry
Chadwick said, "Baseball is lightning," but there is more—
lightning is life. I know best the shady side of things. I mean
depression, stoppage, lightning a drizzled line on a far horizon. But
it's still true, isn't it? The lightning, I mean. Look at Jesús Mijango,
Azzy Azzam, Fire Escape Johnny. Some folks hold the brightness to

their hearts and gift you with a glimpse.

"Bartholome missed his spot," says Madson. "Chévez set up high and tight, but the pitch came in low and inside."

"Better to have thrown the ball four feet off the plate," says Foley. "That's the only way to keep Bad Ball Jesús from taking his rips."

The Bosox pitcher is bent over behind the mound, his glove covering the lower half of his face. Trevor Doyle takes his time walking to the mound.

"Bye-bye, Bartholome," says Foley. "Jesús Mijango wrote him a ticket to the showers."

*

That wraps up the scoring till the eighth inning when Terrence Gumbs and Junior Parker pad our lead with back-to-back doubles. Going to the ninth, the score 4-2, I bring in Dirk Rouda. My heart starts pounding so fast I have to sit on the bench, close my eyes and call for a trainer. After checking my vitals, Franny Blair advises me to stay seated. Everybody else is standing. I can't see my players. Hell of a way to manage a team.

I ignore the advice and make my way to the rail of the dugout. Franny cuts me a look, then flits into the clubhouse and comes back with a folding chair.

"Sit," he says, and I obey like a puppy. My eyes peek out an inch or two over the dugout wall.

"Three outs from winning the World Series," says Foley. "Can the Cubs hold on?"

"I doubt it," says Madson.

"They already have Azzy Azzam, their ace, loosening up in the bullpen."

"They expect trouble."

"No, let's put it plain—they **are** trouble. No one torments them as well as they torment themselves."

Dirk Rouda slavers and spits as he looks in for a sign. Kaido Miura, his eyes narrowed in concentration, black bat jerking, alive in his hands, shags a deep breath and waits, waits, waits.

He shanks a first-pitch slider into shallow right-center. Stompiano bursts in, snares the ball ankle-high, on the fly, and whips it to Mijango Cruz.

"One out," says Sam Foley, "but stay tuned. The Red Sox have come from behind all year long."

Dios Ovando, on a full count, takes a pitch that looks like strike three. The ump points him to first base, a free pass, but I'm too weak to argue. Up comes Bill Murphy, the Bosox clean-up hitter. Blow Hawk, blow. Rake with claws anything headed for the seats. Fling back the long ball, hell with the homerun. Catch it in a fist of wind and drop it in Steal Home Johnny's glove.

Jimmy Lieski is the only Cub extra sitting on the bench. Swaying, clutching his arms to his chest, he mumbles incoherent prayers. Sorry, Jimmy, no Rapture tonight, or not yet. You'll have to wait for two more outs.

Rouda bends one low and outside, a split finger fastball that coaxes Murphy to lunge. The ball caroms off the bat, bloops over first and falls a foot or so fair down the right field line. Terrence Gumbs bare-hands the ball, winds and fires, and holds Ovando at second base.

"Now we'll call it a rally," says Foley. "Two on, one out, and the go-ahead run coming to the plate."

Can't something be easy for the Cubs? Just once before I die? I look toward the stands, a sign from Lady Luck. Should I let Rouda pitch? Let him face one more batter? Maybe she should be the one managing this team.

"Rouda's ready to throw another spitter," says Foley. "That's his one pitch."

"He has a curve," says Madson, "and sometimes a slider."

"Same thing," says Foley. "He goobers it with spit."

Mason wings at a slow curve and wallops the ball sky-high. Johnny and Jamal Kelsey converge in left-centerfield, back-peddling near the 368 sign. "Stompiano calling for the ball," says Foley, "waving off Kelsey. He drifts to his right, now his left...and he races in and makes the grab for out number two."

He huffs a breath. "On a normal night that ball would have landed on Waveland Avenue," he says. "And a three-run homer would have given the Red Sox a 5-4 lead."

I steady my eyes on Sonia as she shakes her fists. Her mouth opens, wide and dark, and stays open. Maybe every sound her body can make pours up and out, a homerun of sorts, and she's getting some notion of how much mania we can squeeze between the field of play and the sky. Johnny made a fine catch. The wind spun that ball into a devil's dance, so he out-danced the devil. This Kid has nerve, I mean nerve. I may never fully believe we're on the same team.

Jay McCreary at the plate. Mean in disposition, a junkyard dog, small but with teeth. Rouda tries to rattle his chain with a fastball high and tight. McCreary, elbows up, leans into it, lets the pitch plunk his left forearm. The scorer will mark HBP, hit-by-pitch, because there's no shorthand to say a Bosox mutt broke free of his leash, leaned over the plate, and put the Cubs in a bases-loaded jam.

Joe Peralta, the pitching coach, nudges me. "Put in Azzy," he says. "One more mistake and we're up Shit Creek."

So I hoist myself up the steps of the dugout and walk toward the mound. The umps probably think I'm stalling, giving Azzy more time to warm up, but I can't move any faster. Preston Hollis, the Bosox leftfielder, is waiting to hit.

Never has the mound seemed this steep. I clamber up, hold

out my hand, but Rouda won't give me the ball.

"I can finish," he says. "Goddamn it, that's what I'm paid to do."

Azzy's already lumbering in from the bullpen. I made the call. I can't reverse it. And I wouldn't if I could.

The infielders gather on the mound. Junior Parker says, "One more out, one more," and I wish he hadn't spoken. I can't imagine the final out that gives my team the World Series. It is a mirage to one dying of thirst, a pool of false water gleaming in a desert littered with bones.

Rouda won't give me the ball, but he gives it to Azzy. He glances over his shoulder at the batter taking practice swings. "Blow his goddamn lights out," says Rouda. "And don't waste any time."

I make my way to the dugout, my folding chair, and attempt to observe. Sometimes my eyes close, sometimes they fail me. It frightens me to wonder what I might give to win this game.

My first wife tried to persuade me to donate my eyes, my heart, my liver to any chump who might need them at my death. The thought of organs torn from me, plucked from cavities, was a bit much, but Janet reassured me. "You'll be dead, ya dummy; you won't have any nerves left." Now I feel odd pressures in my head, my chest, my gut. In one dazed and dizzy moment I might trade everything—eyes, heart, liver—for a World Series win.

"McCreary's jabbering at the pitcher," says Madson, "trying to distract him."

"The same thing Stompiano does to pitchers," says Foley. "So let's serve the same medicine at a double-dose."

Azzy comes home with a hummer, a strike. I can tell from the look in his eye, the long breath rounding his chest, he'll feed Hollis nothing but flames.

McCreary with a good lead off first. He dances, claps his

hands, hollers at Azzy. He represents the go-ahead run, so he lets Azzy know. He's playing Johnny's game, not as well as Johnny, but shifty and mean.

"Hollis in his crouch," says Foley, "digging in. An extra-base hit may give the Red Sox the game."

Azzy leans into his stretch, checks the runners, fires. Ball outside, a quick throw to first by Junior Parker. McCreary dives, claws his way toward first base. Rountree slaps the tag on his left hand and the first-base ump rattles a fist.

I hear a voice soft as a candle: "Don't say it 'less it's true." I hear my rag-tag heart, a rumble starting up. I hear breaths being drawn, the breathers not quite believing, not yet, and at last, when Jesús Mijango raises his arms and shouts at Azzy Azzam, shouts at Junior Parker and Drexel Rountree and Rey Rodríguez, shouts at Wrigley's pilgrims, shouts and keeps shouting, no one—not even Coach Donachio—can deny that the Chicago Cubs are once more baseball's champions of the world.

Steal Home Johnny does a cartwheel as he makes his way in from centerfield.

AFTERMATH

Phalanxes of cops equipped with clubs, cuffs, masks, and stun guns are no match for Wrigley's pilgrims. The field is stormed, occupied, and I half expect devotees to pitch tents, spread sleeping bags, start campfires, settle in for winter. A man with a red beard stands on home plate, his face biblical. Bloodshot eyes stare out beneath deep ridges, scars, inscriptions of suffering. Is this pilgrim about to cast off the yoke? Arms raised, he yelps, howls, beckons. I'd like to pat him on the back and say, "Easy, buddy. Don't blow your circuits." I am the brother of every man who's been a loser all his life.

I rise from the dugout as from a grave. In widening rings around the mound and first base Cubbies are hopping, hugging, jumping on each other's back. I want to shout in Azzy's ear, "World Series! World Series!" but before I can reach him six pilgrims wedge their way in and hoist him on a bridge of shoulders. A leviathan, a breached whale, he towers and sways over the mound as stout pilgrims—legs splayed, feet pawing the turf—weave and bow with his weight.

"Azzy!" I holler. "Hey Azzy!"

Tomorrow I'll see a picture of myself taken by a *Chicago*

Tribune photographer: my face beet-red and white foam spurting from my mouth.

I push through the crowd until the crowd pushes back. Every Cub, even the lowliest, has become a baseball legend. Pilgrims embrace me, lift me in their arms, and soon I am aloft, riding as though on horses. My bearers turn and veer toward home plate. I spot Sonia in the box seats four rows back, a lady too dignified to scale a low wall and face off with the cops and guards who are lining up again, hoping to clear the field by midnight. I raise a hand and call to her and whoever may hear, "Hallelujah! Hallelujah!" Have I ever uttered a paean of praise? No, my life has been a mantra of moans, sighs, sniffles. **Hallelujah, then, hallelujah.** A wave-like word that makes me feel easy to carry, buoyant as a boat of light.

Those bearing me begin to glide, accelerate. I holler at Sonia through cupped hands, "Meet me outside, meet me on Waveland!" I catch my breath and say, "Bring Jackie, bring Sam! Meet me on Waveland!"

Maybe her smile means she has heard me and agrees.

FLAG

Did Lazarus speak his first night back?

After the field was cleared, after players and coaches filed into the clubhouse, after the champagne was uncorked, Cub heads anointed, I offered a toast "to the men who put poems on billboards, to the tri-captains who Live the Legacy, who enliven the Game in and beyond the ball yard."

Nick made a cutting motion near his throat.

"No, put me on record," I said. "The only way I'll die a loser is by refusing to play."

On camera, on record, I paraphrased Janice Oyakawa, Ahmed Jamil, and even *South Side News*—the freebie newspaper that I'd borrowed from Azzy's locker. I jumbled everything up. I spoke with fervor when I told ESPN that our tri-captains, like the great Bill Russell, the great Muhammad Ali, could not be reduced to entertainers. I said, "Azzy learned to play ball on cracked sidewalks and cinders and broken glass. Let's remember that." I said, "Wynton Marsalis wrote a song—'From the Plantation to the Penitentiary...' Azzy's got how many friends in jail? If they're his friends, they're **my** friends. You hear me?" I opened my arms like an orator firing up his admirers. "'Violence ends where love begins'" (*South Side News*). "And as for the big boys in D.C., the playmakers on Wall Street, I'll tell you what they fear—a poem." I went on in this vein as if the words were mine, and they **felt** like mine in the heat of the moment. I paraphrased Janice. I waxed poetic. I needed every sound and syllable, stolen or whatever. I even put in a plug for Khadijah Jamil.

Several reporters appeared skeptical, including Al Muscat. If Johnny and Azzy, who were on the far side of the clubhouse, had heard my outburst, they would have known I'd been snooping around their lockers. Muscat said, "Okay Billy, that's enough," and tried to interview Nick. Jimmy Lieski stepped in front of the camera to thank Christ for the victory. The magic of the night was beginning to fade.

I showered, rinsed off the champagne, donned street clothes, and prepared to leave. By now, the tri-captains were gone, as were their teammates, except Jimmy Lieski and Matt Creighton. A week earlier, I would've been lame enough to cower in the Friendly Confines through half the night.

Creighton said, "You best wait for an escort, coach. The fans are still out there."

I cocked my head. "Tell you a secret, pal. My **family's** out there. I've kept them waiting long enough."

*

No car or truck could budge its way through the crowd. The *Chicago Tribune*, the *Special Edition*, arrived on the backs of bicycles. Boys hawked papers for ten bucks each, a fair price in that some of us would have paid twenty, even thirty. Pilgrims streamed toward vendors like spawning salmon. The boy I bought from yelled, "Extra! Extra! Cubs win the Series! Cubs win the Crown!" Hunch-backed, he snatched my twenty, stuffed it in his coat, and tossed me two papers. One was mine, a keepsake, and the other was for Sonia and her boys.

It occurred to me that I'd left Wrigley Field without stealing a note, a letter, a last tribute to the season. Had I taken enough? Would I pilfer more at some point? The notion that theft can birth a man—cleanse his eyes, jump-start his heart, strengthen his spine—is original in me.

At Waveland and Sheffield, hunched under a street lamp, I read the headline—CUBS WIN WORLD SERIES! At this wee hour, almost midnight, the streets bore more ache than wildness. Hundreds of cops and guardsmen mingled with pilgrims. Only the newsboys hawking papers made more noise than the wind.

"Coach," I heard. "Coach Donachio."

I turned to see Jackie and Sam, their mother between them and holding their hands. Jackie slipped free and came toward me. "I knew we'd win," he said. "I knew it."

"You bet!"

"And Johnny stole two bases in the dark."

I stooped and he came into my arms. I hugged the boy, lifted him, and he gave no resistance. "World champs," I said. "Isn't that something?"

"Yes!"

"And Steal Home Johnny lives up to his name."

I held him to my chest, then set him down near his mother. Sam, in offering a handshake, created a polite distance. He was old enough to have a certain shyness about a hug.

I glanced at Sonia. "Hope I didn't keep you waiting too long."

"Not at all."

"I got out here as soon as I could."

From Waveland and Sheffield, one could see a white flag hanging from a pole over the centerfield scoreboard. The wind, blowing in off Lake Michigan, made it snap, ripple. The cold bucked into me, late October spliced with winter. The streets and walkways belched their dregs. After-the-game smells of spilled beer, peanut shells, salt, tobacco. The four of us huddled for what warmth was available. In the west, waning, the moon had begun its downward arc. I said to myself, "More ache than wildness, am I right?" But my old heart turned, jostled, still very much alive.

I brushed Sonia's left arm.

"You see that flag over the scoreboard? The victory flag?"

She squinted.

"A white flag," I said, "but there's a blue W at its center."

"I don't see anything blue."

"Well, the wind's having its way, so all we see now is a flash of white. Whenever we win a ballgame—steal it or whatever—we raise the white flag."

She looked confused. "But a white flag means surrender."

"Not at Wrigley," I said. "At the flag's center, invisible from here, there's a W. Can you guess what it means?"

She let Jackie answer for her. "Win!"

"That's right, pal. At a glance, or from a distance, a winner sometimes looks like a loser."

They all looked at me.

"Never mind," I said. "There's a W in that flag."

I had two copies of the *Tribune*, the *Special Edition*, tucked under an arm. "Boys," I said, "I've got a surprise for you and your mom."

I gave one copy to Jackie, one to Sam, for I decided I didn't need one. "You can read them when you get home," I said. "Or in the morning at the kitchen table over bacon and eggs."

But they couldn't wait for morning. Right there, at the corner of Sheffield and Waveland, the boys squatted side by side, each with a paper draped over his knees, wind rippling its edges.

I stood with Sonia, who leaned toward me, almost touching. I wondered, "Should I take her hand? Should I?" I almost did, but then I hunched down near Jackie and Sam.

In the hazy light of a streetlamp, we studied pictures and captions. Look at Steal Home Johnny straying off second base. The next photograph frames darkness, a black-out. Nothing. In the next, Johnny angels his arms, stands on home base, and calls himself safe. The Thief smiles like the game's already ours.

Caption: *Stompiano steals home in pitch darkness, but umpire sends him back to second.*

True. But a few pitches later he came home for good.

Jackie and Sam asked some of the same questions they asked the first night I met them: What's Johnny like in person? What's Jesús like? And Azzy Azzam? What are they like? I thought about these players, but thinking didn't help. A long time passed before I spoke.

"Azzy's the best human being I've ever known," I said. "Jesús and Johnny?" I shook my head and glanced at the moon. "I don't think they themselves know what they'll do next."

I invited Sonia and her boys to the Chicago Cub Victory Parade.

"When?" said Sam.

"I'm guessing this weekend, Saturday or Sunday. Soon as I get word, you'll be the first to know."

Sonia wanted to get her boys home, but we had to walk all the way to Sheffield and Belmont before I could hail a cab. They lived near Garfield Park, a long way from Wrigley. Sonia made no effort to stop me when I gave the driver enough money to ferry them home. She waved to me until the cab turned a corner and I was alone.

KHADIJAH JAMIL

I woke late the next morning, made coffee, and sat at my kitchen table with notes and letters. I'd marked the items with green tabs (1st note from Janice 10/27, 2nd note from Janice 10/28...), and on this new day I read sequentially as one reads a story from start to finish. How often did she return to Pablo Neruda's "Ode to My Socks" to orient herself to splendor? **Johnny,** she added, **we are alive in our bodies and in language, and who is luckier?** I gave them a smile they would never see, but then I brooded. Was I alive in my body or in language? Would Sonia love me if I lived only as a thief?

I reread Ahmed Jamil's letter to Johnny: **Everything humanly possible is possible in me.**

*

In the late afternoon, I went out for a bite to eat. I stopped in at the Dark Horse, but I didn't have a pick-me-up, just a bowl of soup and a cup of coffee. I imagined Sonia and her boys beside me at the table. "Today I'm drawing a line," I said. "No more whiskey, no binges. Nothing." I pictured their smiles, their nods of approval. Despite shaky hands, an uncertain heart, I resisted the urge to bury myself in booze.

After my meal, I snatched the *Chicago Tribune* that someone had left at another table. It was smack full of Cub news, photos and articles, at least a dozen pages of mementos. I drank more coffee, sucked up every word, and then trolled for other news. Buried in the bowels of the *Tribune*, I saw that President Trent was in trouble. A security camera in a luxury hotel in Orlando had caught him kissing an admirer, pawing the young man's crotch and pressing him to a wall. The president, after "denying any and all wrongdoing," claimed that the film had been altered and was "nothing but fake news." The alibi would have worked, case closed, except that Trent's VP, Gerald Price, had witnessed "the obscenity" and found it "disgusting beyond words." Price, a heavyweight in religious circles, said his "resignation was forthcoming, as only a hypocrite would serve knowingly in an administration led by a homosexual." If the Cubs hadn't just won the World Series, this would have been front-page news.

Nothing Michael J. Trent did could surprise me, but this did: What if right here, in the United States of America, we elected to the presidency a black Muslim from South Chicago? Well, I was glad she was no Wahhabi. I still couldn't imagine Ms. Jamil walking in the front door of the White House, or **any** door, but it might happen. If the evangelicals, the social conservatives, boycotted the election, the president would go down in flames.

*

I was itching for a drink. I ordered a draft beer, no whiskey chaser. I was giving myself a little test. Could I stop at one, walk away from this place? I told myself, "One beer, Billy, and then head for home."

I was half way through a Guinness when there was an uproar in the joint. The Dark Horse has four TVs, and the barkeep now put them all on the same channel. Live TV, real time—that's the lingo. As if to say most time is neither real nor alive.

The sound of automatic weapons in Detroit.

A community health center, a low brick building.

> (I don't know where the shooting's coming from.
> Maybe from inside the building, maybe from a
> low wall in front of it, or maybe from the roof.)

Blood on a cement walk, several bodies.

A blast shakes the air.

> (I duck as if I'm there, in Detroit. Who's shooting
> who? And why?)

A woman dives on the ground and shields a child with her body.

Police officers, SWAT teams.

Weapons point every which way.

As if the enemy is the air we breathe.

*

I learned what happened minutes after the ordeal ended. Khadijah Jamil was making an appearance at a nonprofit health center for women and children. Before she could address her crowd of supporters, two shooters started shooting. The woman who shielded a child with her body was Jamil. The child survived unscathed, as did the candidate. Two women died, though, and one man, two girls, two sisters, nine and six years old. The assailants were also dead. I wouldn't know till the next day that they were ISIS-inspired, two brothers. As for now, I bent over and moaned and gripped the sides of my head. "Enough," I said, "enough," as if someone could hear.

I wished Azzy were at the scene. I wished he'd step in front of these jittery cameras, these cameras cutting every which way—blood pools, bodies, people scurrying—and say something we would never forget. No violence surprises us anymore. Azzy's big, though, and the man's spirit is bigger, and he might give us something to remember. I'd thieved my way into his world, **this** world, and now I felt the raw pain of it for perhaps the first time. I was shaking real hard. Two women dead, one man, two girls, two grade-schoolers, and murders like this could happen any time, any place, and they did. Khadijah Jamil, in a silent gesture, had sheltered a child with her body. Well, we'd better pay attention. They'd replay this scene over and over for at least the next hour or so. If we let ourselves see it, with eyes and heart in sync, we wouldn't need any speech.

PARADE

The day after the massacre in Detroit, I began making phone calls for Khadijah Jamil's campaign and contributed $300, the limit of what she and her people would accept. At times I was dizzy enough to count myself among her people, but I knew I was just beginning to enter a world ripe with meaning and intention. The stuff I'd stolen or borrowed from Azzy and Johnny and Mijango had accidentally given me an education. What to make of it? I mourned the dead in Detroit far more than I'd mourned the deaths of my mother, my father. By and by, though, I began to feel a bit of sympathy for my folks, too. They'd stumbled through every day of their lives, but maybe they'd done their best. Neither one had access to a real education. Neither one had any luck.

*

The parade to honor the World Champion Chicago Cubs took a route never before woven.[7] Beginning at 10 a.m. at Wrigley Field, marching bands followed by nine double-deck tour buses

[7] You probably remember that the 2016 victory parade cut over to Lake Shore Drive; this time we kept going straight down Clark St. through the heart of Cubdom.

headed south on Clark Street. Cops and guardsmen tried to confine pilgrims to walkways, but this was like trying to keep a roaring river from slipping through splayed fingers. On the roof of the first bus, the one for coaches and several players, plus a few mucky-mucks from the front office, I shuffled back and forth in front of the tri-captains. We basked in the praise of pilgrims, the wave-like roar of jubilance. I watched a teenage girl scrawl in blue chalk on the side of a building:

Flying free from a branch, Mr. Bird?

Love the tree at its roots

So I studied my shoes, black wingtips, then turned my face to the light. It was one of those brisk autumn mornings that invite an old man to shed a few years, to straighten his crooked spine, stand to be measured, and to breathe the sun—every last spark—to make up for days of lunacy and loss, bitterness and folly. I, however, had lost decades rather than days, which meant there was but one way to play. **Up the ante, Billy, bet the house. No more excuses. No whining. You're an educated man.**

Chicago had come to a near standstill. Every street corner had wheelers and dealers hawking memorabilia: Cub caps and jackets, t-shirts, team photos, pennants, buttons, and a special edition of the *Chicago Tribune*, photos from all seven games of the Series. I wished Sonia and her orphans could have ridden on the first float, front and center, but this was forbidden. They waited for the team in Grant Park.

Every few seconds Azzy clapped and sang out, "Thank you, Chicago, thank you and bless you." Look at Jesús in a black silk sport coat, pockmarked Jesús, the Cub Lord, serene and watchful. Johnny in jeans and jacket, sneakers, dark shades, his Cub cap turned around, brim to the back, flashing the crowd the peace sign.

From the lead bus, moving at a pace slower than a stroll, the world appeared safe, but I knew better. For once in my life my concern was for others. I kept telling myself, "Be ready for anything, Billy, good or bad."

The big news this morning was that our players, in a 19-6 vote, had invited Khadijah Jamil to meet the team at our destination—the Petrillo Music Shell in Grant Park. The front office responded by reiterating rules, official by-laws: No speeches, no politicking, no endorsement. Jamil would be granted a brief photo-op with the team, but she would not address the audience. Due to security concerns, the candidate would miss the parade and arrive in Grant Park at an unspecified hour.

Had I ever seen so many black folks on the North Side? There were hundreds, no, thousands, and they were not merely here for a celebration. In certain faces I saw signs of fatigue; in others, a hardness that could have been worry or rage, hope or despair. These people had to know someone might die today. The knowledge was in my gut, but they knew it first, and knew it better. They knew it before I was born.

I felt dizzy, disoriented, as if the weight and structure of my body were a new phenomenon to balance and hold.

*

Almost 1 p.m. now, more than an hour past our scheduled arrival, and for as far as I could gander Grant Park was a sea of pilgrims. Nobody had stayed home today, not even Sox fans. An outdoor stage awaited the World Champion Cubs, and in front of the stage—on a strip of asphalt—pilgrims strained against police barricades. I said to Johnny, "Let's hope all these revelers behave."

A parade crowd is different from a ballpark crowd. In Grant Park, for instance, no one passed through a metal detector or had his bag searched. At Wrigley Field, every man, woman and child would have been checked at the gates.

After Johnny helped me down the steps of the bus, he led me aside and we stood near a leafless tree. The team began to gather in front of us on a ramp that led to the stage. I said, "Let's go, Kid," but he held my arm. He said the team would stay put till Khadijah Jamil arrived.

On stage, the Chicago Youth Ensemble played a Sousa march, brassy and bold, all bangs and booms, as if to greet a victorious squad of Marines rather than a ball club. A skinhead conductor flapped his arms, cymbals clashed, trumpets blared, and I found myself fretting. Where was Jamil? Had she found a safe hideout? Maybe she was hunkered down behind the cement wall that curved up in the shape of a shell at the rear of the stage. Cops and guardsmen stood behind waist-high metal-link gates that separated us from the crowd.

When the music died down, Johnny told me he'd been missing a few things from his locker.

I swallowed. "What things?"

"Letters," he said, "notes. And it seems I'm missing a picture of Janice."

I flushed.

"Well, it's hardly worth mentioning. I'd read the letters and notes and I see Janice every night."

I leaned against the bole of the tree.

"You know you're a star on YouTube, coach?"

"**Me**?"

"Yeah, after Game 7 you had a lot to say. You reminded me of Janice when you went into that rap about poetry."

I winced.

"You didn't quote her exactly, but you were close."

I did my best.

"Well," he said, "no hard feelings. I seldom stay angry at a thief."

I curled an arm around the tree to steady my balance. Could I convince Johnny that I stole to save my life? Would he forgive me for stealing notes and letters as he'd forgive a starving man his bread? By chance, I made off with life's essentials. I fed from the bounty of strangers—Johnny, Janice, Azzy, Jesús, Ahmed and Khadijah Jamil—till they were almost like friends. No, I didn't know I was trying to save my life when I first plucked an envelope from Johnny's locker. I knew—if anything—a vague but powerful desperation. A man blind and starving frisks a hand among loaves, fruit, fishes, then steals the whole basket. Greedy? Insane? Who is to judge?

I said, "Sorry, Kid. I didn't mean any harm."

"I know."

"I took this and that and then things got out of hand."

Hunched, head down, I made of my body a question mark. What else could I do with it? But Johnny, loose and light, jabbed me in the arm.

"You surprised me, coach. I didn't know you were a fan of poetry."

"Neither did I."

"Pretty soon we'll have poetry all over this city."

I tried to smile. "Good."

"We need sponsors, though, the more the better. Let me tell you what's in the works."

So while Andy McPherson, the Cub general manager, was on stage palavering about the greatness of the Game, the greatness of our nation, our military, I bent my ears to Johnny. The Kid spoke of "a new scheme that might liven things up. By spring training," he said, "we'll have poems on buses, trains, poems on every side of this city." He grinned. "You feel guilty about ransacking my locker? All right, then, sponsor a poem. The plan is to put poems on every bus and every car of every train by the 1st of March."

I stood straighter. "Mark me down," I said. "I'll sponsor a whole fleet of buses. A long train, too."

"And you can choose the poems," said Johnny. "Just remember they need to be short to fit on the placards that are normally full of ads. Janice and Isha are the editors."

I grunted.

"If you want to browse," he said, "go to the website— openbook.com. You'll find poems from Chicago and every side of the world."

I told him I'd get back to him on the specifics. "I'll choose one poem," I said, "but I'll sponsor dozens, maybe hundreds. I'll let Janice and Isha choose the rest."

My ignorance might have shocked him. At age seventy-three, I still grope for the names of things. What is a poem? What is not a poem? Who has the power to decide?

I asked the Kid if he had time to meet a couple orphan boys, Jackie and Sam.

"Sure."

"I scrounged backstage passes for them and their foster mom." I grabbed his arm. "Can you wait here a few minutes? Stay put?"

"I'm not planning to slip away, coach."

"I'll round them up and be right back."

So then, as Andy McPherson gave way to The Chicago Youth Ensemble, as forty musicians blared yet another Sousa march, I weaved through the backstage multitudes, the mayor and his entourage, front office mucky-mucks and friends of mucky-mucks, and I found the little family waiting where I'd asked them to wait— behind the south wall of the stage. They wore passes safety-pinned to coats, brand new Cub coats for the boys, the Easter coat for Sonia. Jackie and Sam jumped and waved the moment they saw me. "Coach Donachio!" said Sam. "Coach Donachio!" I paused to catch my breath, to listen. Sam called again, and now Jackie: "Coach Donachio!" Go on, I thought, scatter me—name and title—amid the glare of trumpets, bugles, and sun.

I led my lucky trio to the players: Johnny and Jesús, Azzy and Dantel, plus a score of others. The boys were too timid to speak. Jesús patted their shoulders, Azzy too. And then Johnny lifted Jackie into his arms and up onto his shoulders so the boy—at Azzy's height—could take in the crowd.

"How many people?" said Johnny. "Are there a million?"

The boy beheld a spectacle. Mouth open, eyes blinking in sunlight, he said, "At least! At least!"

"Take a long look," said Johnny, and began turning in a slow circle. He invited the boy to gape in all directions before he brought him back to earth.

Minutes passed, but these pleasured themselves, stretched, and felt more like hours. I relaxed till I saw Khadijah Jamil, flanked by Secret Service agents, coming up behind us. She was followed by her entourage: Ahmed Jamil, her husband, Cue Ball and Janice, Isha Azzam, and a number of others, mostly black folks. Neither Ahmed nor Isha had brought their children along. I remembered the little girls, ages nine and six, who died in Detroit.

Khadijah mingled with players and coaches. Cops were everywhere, as were guardsmen. I tried to ease my concerns, but I edged forward a few steps to help form a shield around the candidate. Someone sidled up to Azzy and clipped a mike to his blue blazer. The Chicago Youth Ensemble played "Take Me Out to the Ballgame," some of us sang, and then the players and coaches and Khadijah Jamil began to move up the cement ramp and onto the stage. There, as we were following each other—Azzy, Khadijah, Jesús, Johnny, me—Azzy turned to the crowd, his right hand high but not waving, and he said, "Stop, don't do it! Don't do it!" His voice boomed as loud as a kettledrum.

One shot snapped the air. I saw blood on Azzy's hand, bright red, and then it gushed like a fountain. I heard him say, "Don't hurt him, don't hurt him no more. That's enough!" Just then I didn't know someone besides Azzy was hurt. I didn't know what was enough.

Khadijah Jamil repeated Azzy's words: "Don't hurt him, don't hurt him no more." Arms raised, she stood between Azzy and the crowd.

She told Azzy to lean on her, ease himself down, but the big man continued to stand with his hand raised higher than that of a witness taking a solemn oath in a court of law. Yes, he stood, he towered, and the blood came down from his hand.

A long time seemed to pass before he leaned on Jamil and a few others and let his body be cradled. She and Johnny and Mijango and me eased Azzy into a sitting position, his legs stretched before him. Jamil wrapped a white hanky around Azzy's hand, the entrance and exit wounds, but the blood kept coming. Mijango, arms slightly raised, head back, fought back tears, and then they came. Jamil said, "That's right, Jesús. Tell the sky. Tell the lake. Tell the rivers." Was the candidate the prime target? Had the bullet strayed?

I looked around.

I held Azzy's good hand.

I said, "What happened? What happened?"

His voice, I'll always remember, was weary, so weary I sometimes want to lie down when I hear it, and I've heard it in my head any number of times these past few weeks. "White guy with a gun," he said. "Just the other side of the fence."

I wouldn't know more till I saw a replay of the event on TV. A young man in a Cub cap, Cub jacket, buttons open, a Blackhawks T-shirt showing underneath. At a glance he was any fan till you noticed his face. A fixed glaze in his eyes, no emotion, a machine with its buttons pressed, its movements automatic. Crouched on the fan-side of the fence, he drew a gun from his jacket, and Azzy, on guard, saw him before he fired. The big man raised his right arm (Stop! Don't do it!), but the automaton fired one shot before he was mobbed. Black folks body-slammed him, bashed his head with fists, and might have killed him had they not heard Azzy calling for restraint: "Don't hurt him, don't hurt him no more. That's enough!"

The bullet severed a bone (metacarpal #3 I found out later), but Azzy kept his hand raised for several seconds. The world as his witness, he saved the man who tried to lay him in a grave.

Sonia stayed with me after the shooting, Jackie and Sam too. An ambulance, escorted by seven squad cars, took Azzy to Northwestern Memorial Hospital. For security reasons, the team and the candidate were not allowed to follow. Isha flagged a taxi and made her own way to the hospital. She would be there for her husband when he came out of surgery in the late afternoon.

*

Sonia and her boys and I and who knows how many pilgrims and players ended up at a Michigan Avenue hotel. We filed in past the doormen, past security, and we scuffed up plush carpets and made our way to a backroom bar. A half dozen TVs were going. Maybe everyone in the nation, or at least Chicago, was watching the latest bulletin. We saw Arshan "Azzy" Azzam, a giant with pink, sunlit palms, creased black face, one hand bleeding. And we saw Jesús Mijango, the badass who could stare down any pitcher who ever lived, tremble before he burst open, a slab of stone split down the middle, tears in the fissure. We saw Khadijah Jamil and Jesús and Johnny and me ease Azzy down, two of us holding him under the arms, the other two bracing his back. Jamil pressed a hanky to the wound, and this simple act seemed as salient as anything that could happen. Maybe we understood that if we didn't know something in this moment we never would, we were dead. But I think most of us knew things, big, unspeakable things, and what we knew would never again allow for smallness. I never before saw Jesús cry. I never before saw truth jump like a star over a mountain, enough light to re-make the world.

"Don't hurt him," said Azzy, "don't hurt him no more. That's enough."

Sam, beside me in the bar, gesticulating, speaking to everyone and no one, spun out the words in his head and heart so fast I could barely keep up. "Azzy tried to stop the man from shooting," he said. "He saw him first, saw him before anyone else." The boy raised his arms, staggered, and made a ripping sound—the flight of a bullet. "But I didn't hear the shot, not then. I heard everyone yelling, everyone going crazy. I didn't hear any words, just a lot of noise, and then Azzy's voice, no one else's. He must've shouted so loud even God could hear."

Maybe so.

RIVERS

Two hours after the parade and the shooting, President Trent held a press conference. He expressed "profound regret for the violence in Chicago," but warned the nation's voters "that violence on a far vaster scale might soon be our daily bread from coast to coast."

The president reminded us around twelve times that Khadijah Jamil is a Muslim. He dismissed questions about the sex scandal as "propaganda, a mere distraction." He claimed that he loved women, always had and always would, and that all else was a lie.

The scandal proved to be more than a distraction. The election was three days away and pollsters called it "a dead heat."

We learned that the shooter in Grant Park, Adam Logan, is a Christian fundamentalist who thought he was "doing what Christ wanted" him to do. In Detroit, two Muslim extremists went after Jamil and her supporters and killed five before they blew themselves up. Where would this end?

*

President Trent was all over the airwaves on election eve. Over and over, he promised that Khadijah Jamil, if elected, would "usher in one hundred years of darkness, one hundred years of economic misery and violence and denigration and chaos," etc., etc.

The old crank chose his words carefully (darkness, misery, violence, denigration), but he was a ruined man with bloodshot eyes, cotton candy hair, and a glare that no longer worked. The Republican base—the social conservatives, the white evangelicals, the Deep South—boycotted the election. The support of Wall Street wasn't enough to carry Trent to victory. Blacks voted. Latinos voted. Asians voted. Muslims voted. And—for the first time in more than forty years—Billy Ray Donachio voted. Yes, in the early morning I walked a straight line to my polling place and cast my vote stone sober. This, too, is historical. Anything can happen in this world, and I mean **anything**. I was beginning to feel good about myself.

Late in the night, propped on pillows, I sat in bed sipping Martinelli cider and watching the returns. It was almost dawn when the networks—even FOX—called Congresswoman Khadijah Jamil "our president elect." I fought off the urge to open a bottle of JD. "Well," I said to myself, "it's a new ballgame, first inning." Yet how could anyone—Steal Home Johnny, Azzy, even Jamil herself— know what would happen next?

A religious man would have prayed for our president's safety. I bet Azzy was praying right now, but all I could do was stumble out of bed, go to my window, and watch the light seep into the sky. I WANT JAMIL TO LIVE. I felt this inside me in capital letters. Well, to vote is easy enough, but then what? I didn't know how to help Jamil, how to help **us**. There I was looking through the glass and saying, "Don't hurt her, don't hurt her," as if the world's madmen had convened and could hear the smallest whisper. The light went from deep gray to silver. I was a madman, too, or at least knew the terrain. Azzy was probably praying for peace, but I was just hoping we humans would shoot each other a little less.

*

After Azzy underwent surgery to reset the broken bone in his right hand, medical progress reports became front-page news in Chicago. Jackie and Sam, assuming I had the inside-scoop, called me on a Wednesday night.

"All I know is in the morning paper," I said. "I don't want to bother Azzy with too many phone calls."

"Well, what about next year?" said Jackie. "Will he be ready for spring training?"

"The doctors are optimistic."

"Does his hand hurt? Can he do things?"

"I'm sure he's feeling better."

"Sam and me send a card to the hospital every day."

I smiled. "Well, Azzy's home now, I know that much. The other thing I know is that he never complains."

I asked to talk with his mom, but as soon as I heard her voice I turned shy as a schoolboy. I did manage to say I was among the sponsors of "a new scheme to put poetry on every bus and train in Chicago. Hey," I said, "what's money for? The least I can do is support a project everyone can enjoy."

I told her I would sponsor forty poems, but then I upped it to fifty.

"Really?"

"Yes, line up the buses, hitch the trains. Toot the horns. Blow the whistles."

She chuckled. "And will you choose the poems? All fifty?"

I hesitated. "No, there are editors for this project. I'll let them choose every poem but one."

I could feel her smiling when she asked which poem I would choose.

"I haven't quite decided. Are there more poems in the world than people?"

"Well—"

"The fact that there are so many poems makes it difficult to choose."

I told myself, "That's enough, Billy," but I said a few other things to give the impression my knowledge of poetry matched that of a retired librarian. "How to choose?" I said. "How to choose from the millions of poets and poems that deserve greater recognition?" By the time we said goodbye, she must have wondered how and where a baseball man had learned so much about poetry. And I, too, had something to wonder about—**Does she love me a little?** The question took my breath away.

*

Baseball is the poem I know best. Give me white bases ninety feet apart, grasses bright as fire, a mound where the pitcher stands—sculpt the earth American. The Game is made of colors, configurations, smells and sounds (raked earth, a batted ball), and every inch—grass or dirt—is carved, tended, a wordless poem. As for poems made of language, they leave me hungry for something solid, a world I can grasp with my senses. For a baseball man what is a poem? What should it do? Steal a base? Hit a home run? Make a diving catch in a green alley? My secret wish was to become the man I presented to Sonia, the one for whom poetry is song, pulse, drumbeat. Studious late in life, I pored over Janice and Isha's website for hours, days, weeks. I read hundreds of poems, perhaps thousands, but where was the one I needed? I understood little of what I read.

*

Johnny sent me an email in mid-November.

Coach, Janice & Isha have gone to bat for you. As requested, they've chosen all but 1 of the 50 poems you've so generously sponsored. Please choose #50 by Thanksgiving if you want it posted on a bus or train by March 1.

I wrote back, *Any suggestions, Kid? Might you choose a passage for me?*

He replied minutes later.

Try the website Janice and Isha put together—openbook. com. You'll find poems from every country, but a hunch tells me you'll want something American. What can I say, coach? Click the 'USA' link, or 'Chicago,' and see what happens. Keep reading, keep hunting. If I come across a poem that makes me think of you, I'll send you an email or give you a call.

*

I was bug-eyed from staring at my computer, so I went out and bought *Leaves of Grass*. I'd never bought a book of poems, never in seventy-three years. Maybe I had to do this before I died.

At North Side donut shops and cafes I began to plow through it, but the length—nearly five hundred pages—was daunting. I found the part called "Song of Myself," some fifty pages, and recognized myself in certain passages—"Be at peace bloody flukes of doubters and sullen mopers." So Whitman knew me, or knew the old Billy, but sent good tidings nonetheless. Would I have enjoyed his book had I stolen it, or ripped out a random page and stuffed it in a pocket? In mid-November, the days cloudy and cool, I wandered from one donut shop and cafe to another. My eyes hurt, my teeth, my bowels. Depression started to weigh down on me, but I couldn't stop reading. If I quit now, then what? I'd just go back to being a moper. The book lay heavy in my hands. Each page bore down on me like a full day's work.

I was not the only one mining the poetic. In part, the North Side lived from poems, or so it seemed. In Clark Street cafés, in joints on Halsted and Sheffield and Lincoln and Broadway, highbrows and lowbrows and bums hunched over coffee and tea—hot with steam—lips sometimes moving, whispering, a hand sometimes sliding over a page, grabbing a pen or pencil to mark passages, jot notes in margins, the reader sometimes holding the book near his nose (Does a good poem **smell** good?), and then reading and rereading, plumbing, reconsidering, taking in poems with sips of coffee, tea, or an occasional donut or cookie or dish of ice cream in these libraries that allow treats.

Was I the only one who suffered? Yes, I suffered with "Song of Myself," suffered word by word because the "bloody flukes of doubters and sullen mopers" seemed most intimate. I scrawled the line in a notebook, plus this—"And as to you corpse I think you are good manure," and this—"Preferring scars and the beard and faces pitted with smallpox over all latherers..." If my fellow readers suffered, I failed to notice. I drank coffee by the pint, as if it were beer, and induced headaches, diarrhea, hints of ulcers. Others, I was certain, never suffered this way. They must have believed poetry would save their lives.

I, a recovering alky, am also a thief. In a Clark Street café, I tried to steal a poem. A sweet-looking brown woman rose from a table and went to the restroom. Her book lay open, a slip of paper angled across it—enough to tempt me. I hurried to the counter for more coffee. As I returned, I passed her table and noticed she'd written something on the paper. Trembling, I snatched it, but I spilled some coffee and burnt my fingers. "Christ!" I almost shrieked. "Christ!" I smothered the exclamation in long, hot breaths.

She communicated in a neat, narrow script that might be called calligraphy: *"All that has black sounds has duende... And there is no greater truth. These black sounds are the mystery, the roots fastened in the mire that we all know*

and ignore, the mire that gives the very substance for art."
                              —F. G. Lorca

I remembered Jesús Mijango using this word—**duende**. Maybe I held some in my hands.

"What the hell you doing?"

I turned.

The husky red-haired kid who worked the counter glared at me.

"I'm just—"

"You were nosing about Lucille's table. You took something."

I shook my head. "Took what? This little slip of paper?"

"Put it back," he said. "Put it back and get the hell out."

I let the slip of paper flutter down on the open book. It belonged here, a bookmark (homemade), a poem within poems. Lucille was reading poetry in Spanish, or what looked like Spanish to my unschooled eye. I was lucky she wrote in English as if for me.

"Go on home, old man."

"Yes."

"Grab your book and leave."

                              *

I'm surprised I didn't head for a bar and drink myself silly. I stood on a corner near Eddie O's, a joint Nick and I used to frequent, but I somehow found the strength to turn my back to the door. The streetlights had come on. It was Happy Hour, and I could hear men laughing, carrying on, sucking a bit of cheer from glasses, bottles, tumblers. I used to belong in joints like Eddie's, but now I was stranded, unmoored. The sky had gone from gray to dark gray. It was cold enough to snow.

Eyes half closed, I walked at an old man's pace. I noticed my hands and saw Azzy's hand, his wound, and I saw Khadijah Jamil take a handkerchief from her pocket. I and millions had

301

witnessed a shooting, ordinary in most ways, but extraordinary if seen through a lens that neither magnified nor diminished. Azzy stood to his full height, his hand raised. He bled and kept bleeding after Khadijah and others helped ease him down and she wrapped his wounds, front and back, entrance and exit. Jesús cried as a man cries, his face to the sky, the sun, his arms beginning to rise. Frame a moment, any moment, and there is enough light to remake the world.

Or enough darkness, enough "black sounds." I stopped to listen. I held my book near my chest.

*

A few days before Thanksgiving, I called Sonia and the boys and invited them to meet me at Wrigley Field. I told Sonia I wanted to see if the victory flag was still flying over the centerfield scoreboard. "I'll bet you three season tickets to next year's Cub games," I said, "that by now they've taken it down."

Of course I believed the opposite. I intended to lose the bet and give her and her boys season tickets for the coming year.

I reviewed the system for Sonia. The white flag, embossed with a blue W, heralds victory; the blue acknowledges defeat. "All year," I said, "after each loss, they took down the blue flag lickety-split, sometimes in a matter of minutes. They let our victory flag sail a while, play the wind, but by now—three weeks after Game 7—I'll bet you my shirt plus three season tickets the scoreboard crew has packed away the flags."

I suggested meeting at Waveland and Sheffield at 6:30.

"Seven," she said, "after the boys have dinner. Don't be late."

*

For once in my life I was early. As expected, our old flag was up, bucking a stiff wind, and I knew it would stay up all winter

302

unless a storm tore it from the pole.

The night was clear, the temperature in the high teens—almost cold enough to keep everyone indoors. Two brown boys, the scoreboard towering above them, played Pepper with the old ballpark. They fired tennis balls at a brick wall, snared the rebounds, and threw hard and fast as though to gun down runners. The taller one had scattered small stones near the wall so he could practice fielding bad hops. He was a whiz, ate those balls up, never missed. At one point he spun to his right, backhanded the ball, and threw from his knees. "Bravo," I said, but he didn't hear me. He called to mind a young Jesús Mijango Cruz.

*

Sonia showed up at seven o'clock sharp, but I didn't see Jackie or Sam. The old girl wore a Christmas coat, red with a white collar, and her eyes were happy and bright.

I stepped forward, almost swept her in my arms, but drew back at the last instant. "So where's your boys?" I said. "They didn't care to come to Wrigley?"

She told me they preferred to stay home tonight.

"Really?"

"They need a break from me," she said, "or at least Sam does. He's almost thirteen."

I tried to remember that far back—thirteen. My mother was gone. My dad was good as gone. I've been an honorary orphan for most of my life.

I pointed to the victory flag over the scoreboard. "Well, here's for Sam's birthday," I said, "and an early Christmas for you and Jackie." I flashed a smile. "You and your boys win," I said. "Three season tickets to next year's games."

The wind tossed the flag, a crisp sound, a ripped breath. Shy and jittery, I told Sonia the Cubs were worthless in bygone years, but I had the sense to interrupt myself. "Never mind," I said, "look at our victory flag. Up to me, she'll kite the winds all winter. Through snow and sleet, Chicago blizzards—I mean old-time blizzards—let her fly the heavens. On New Year's Eve, maybe we'll walk out to Waveland and Sheffield and salute the flag, right?" I glanced at her; she was smiling. "So keep her up in the breeze, I say. If next April we blow the home opener, fine, we'll bring her down and kite the blue. But let our victory flag fly for as long as she can."

Those two brown boys looked like they could play all night. Tennis balls bounded off bricks and made quick hollow sounds, soft echoes. I glanced at Sonia and said to myself, "We're fifty years past our prime." I envied the lithe movement of the boys, the effortless concentration. Achy and stiff, I hugged my arms to my chest.

Sonia was mumbling.

"Speak up," I said. "I'm a bit hard of hearing."

"Jackie and Sam asked me to thank you for all those games we saw."

"Thank Johnny and Azzy."

"No, we'll thank **you**," she said. "You went through some trouble."

I glanced at the flag. "Trouble?" I asked. "This is trouble? You and your boys brought the luck of Charles Victor Faust."

She didn't ask who Faust was.

"Are you serious about the bet?" she said. "Three season tickets?"

"Why not? I can afford it."

"But the boys have school. They'll have to miss quite a few day games."

"I suppose."

"I can bring them to the playoffs, the night games."

"Good."

"They'll have my permission as long as they do well in school."

She gave me a sidelong glance. "You know I never used to like baseball?"

You're forgiven, I thought.

"All the money, the hype. And I'm supposed to care about a bunch of millionaires running around a ball yard?"

"I know."

"But now I care about some of them," she said, "because they aren't the brats I imagined."

"That's right."

"Azzy, for example. Jesús Mijango. Johnny Stompiano."

"Three aces."

"And I was wrong to judge you," said Sonia, "the way I did in the beginning."

I fetched a quick breath.

"It seems crazy now, but I took you for a fool. I mean, a guy who cares about nothing but the score of a game."

I tried to swallow.

"I was wrong," she said, "**completely** wrong. You're as generous as any man I've ever known."

The compliment stunned me. Generous? How could I live up to the billing? At age seventy-three, I had learned of the Babemba tribe of South Africa, but I was skeptical that I, an American thief, could ultimately be forgiven. Forgiveness comes from truth, and where did this leave me? I should've whispered to Sonia a few shadings of truth, the fact, for example, that I knew next to nothing about poetry and "black sounds," that I was—at best—a thief of poetry, too. I love what I steal, I thought, so how can I be forgiven? I have no black sounds, no **duende**. I steal from those who have.

Sonia spoke of the parade, the shooting, the courage of Azzy and Khadijah. "Here's what I think," she said. "We're a young species, a creature just beginning to evolve. Every moment is forgiveness, compassion—nothing else—but we still need outstanding moments—heroes—to glimpse our generosity."

My nod was tentative.

"When Azzy was hurt," she said, "you held his hand. You stayed."

I swallowed. My throat was sore.

"From that moment on I knew you were good."

I reached for her hand, but pulled back before I had it in my grasp. Given a choice, I would've put my paws in my pockets, a reflex, then lowered my head, another reflex, and stood as still as a corpse had the old girl not taken the initiative. Sonia grabbed my left hand and gave it a squeeze. "Come on," she said, "come on. What's with you?" A good question, fundamental as flesh, but **what** did she want? Sonia lifted my hand, or we both lifted, I might have helped, and I touched her throat. I felt something, a vein, the push of blood, warm, and became more addled. Sonia was what, around sixty-five-years old? I was her senior, I couldn't be far from a grave, so what did she want? The blood at her throat, the thick vein, surprised me. The old girl was alive. She was no cardboard cutout. Her blood ran strong and true, a river that shook my fingers. Eyes closed, I traced the surface of a vein, no, an artery, and then she kissed me. Quick and cold, wintry, but on my lips— no doubt about it. On Waveland Avenue I held her for maybe a minute, and I kissed her, or was kissed, drawn to her body. I vowed to make fact from fiction, to become the man she admired. Why not? I thought. Why not? She was correct to see me as a good man the day Azzy was shot.

On Waveland we said Goodbye because we—I—didn't know what more could be done. She hailed a cab, got in, but I said something, my voice loud through the back door still half open, her right hand gripping the handle. "Tomorrow, I mean Sunday, we'll do something. Okay? Maybe dinner."

Familiar words sounded strange—**maybe dinner**.

"Yes," she said. "I would like that very much."

Her cab sped away. The color—bright yellow—blurred like a comet. I watched it round the corner and disappear.

I gave myself an order: "You'll call her tomorrow, Billy. You **will** call her. And it doesn't matter if you're afraid."

*

Hours later, at home, I tried to recall the specifics. Had I held Sonia in both arms? Had I pulled her close? At the kitchen table, a cup of coffee before me, I lifted a hand to my throat and fumbled for a pulse.

*

Long past midnight, I opened *Leaves of Grass* to a random page. Eyes half closed, vision narrowed to a small passage, I read a poem that would soon be posted on a North Side train.

> There is no virtue, no beauty in man or woman, but as
>   good is in you,
> No pluck, no endurance in others, but as good as in you,
> No pleasure waiting for others, but an equal pleasure
>   waits for you.
> —Walt Whitman

Did Lazarus wake to a poem? Did he sit up straight? The old vessels, the rivers asleep in me for years, began to stir, rise. And I could feel the push of blood and light before I lifted a hand to my throat.

Acknowledgements

The poem in the first chapter (Left behind/ By the thief/ The moon in the window) is from *Dewdrops on a Lotus Leaf: Zen Poems of Ryokan* (Shambhala).

The information on Hank Aaron and Lewis Grizzard in the chapter titled "South Side News" comes from Lewis Grizzard's *If I Ever Get Back to Georgia, I'm Gonna Nail My Feet to the Ground* (Ballantine Books).

The Global Marshall Plan is briefly outlined in the chapter entitled "Caliphate Cubs," pages 168-169. For a fuller description Google *tikkun global marshall plan*.

The following books on Islam informed parts of this book:

The Great Theft: Wrestling Islam from the Extremists, by Khaled Abou El Fadl
The Muslim Next Door: The Qur'an, the Media, and that Veil Thing, by Sumbul Ali-Karamali
No god but God: The Origins, Evolution and Future of Islam, by Reza Aslan
"Believing Women" in Islam: Unreading Patriarchal Interpretations of Islam, by Asma Barlas
Qur'an and Woman: Rereading the Sacred Text from a Woman's Perspective, by Amina Wadud.
The Koran, translated by N.J. Dawood
Approaching the Qur'an, by Michael Sells
The Butterfly Mosque, by G. Willow Wilson
Green Deen: What Islam Teaches About Protecting the Planet, by Ibrahim Abdul-Matin

Thanks to author Mushreq Abbas of al-monitor.com for the article, "The Caliphate Cubs of IS," which describes the Islamic States' recruitment and training of children in Iraq and Syria.

Thanks to George Packer's essay, "Exporting Jihad," in the March 28, 2016 issue of *The New Yorker.*

The following works of Dr. Martin Luther King, Jr. informed parts of this book:
Why We Can't Wait
The Strength to Love
A Call to Conscience
A Testament of Hope
Stride Toward Freedom
"Letter from Birmingham City Jail"

Dave Zirin's books on sports informed *The Clubhouse Thief.* I am especially grateful for *What's My Name, Fool?: Sports and Resistance in the United States* and *A People's History of Sports in the United States.*

Silent Gesture: The Autobiography of Tommie Smith with David Steele also informed this work.

Ken Burns' documentary, *Baseball*, provided many glimpses into the history of the Game; I'm especially grateful for the stories of Charles Victor Faust, Cool Papa Bell, and Satchel Paige. Peter Golenbock's *Wrigleyville: A Magical History Tour of the Chicago Cubs* is the best book about the Cubbies that I know of. Tim McCarver's *Baseball for Brain Surgeons and Other Fans* and George Will's *Men at Work* are excellent guides to the intricacies of the Game. *Baseballs's Greatest Quotations* by Paul Dickson and *505 Baseball Questions Your Friends Can't Answer* by John Kingston were also helpful.

Thanks to Kim Kolbe and Sarah Elizabeth Kidd and everyone at New Issues Poetry & Prose. Thanks to Nancy Brink, Jim Coleman, Vicki Dern, Ellen Greenblatt, Bob Jecmen, Michael Job, Earll Kingston, and Mike Levine for reading various versions of this novel. A bow to Robin Rose, the Zuni Mountain Poets, and the Veteran Writers' Group led by Maxine Hong Kingston. Thanks to my friend John Bielenberg for treating me to Cub games. And a deep bow to my wife, Uong Chanpidor, for her patience and her kindness.

Any shortcomings in *The Clubouse Thief* are my own.

Appendix

Fady Joudah's "Mimesis" and Yehuda Amichai's "The Place Where We Are Right" became famous and inseparable after they were removed from D.C. billboards for "security reasons."

MIMESIS

My daughter
                    wouldn't hurt a spider
That had nested
Between her bicycle handles
For two weeks
She waited
Until it left of its own accord

If you tear down the web I said
It will simply know
This isn't a place to call home
And you'd get to go biking

She said that's how others
Become refugees, isn't it?

THE PLACE WHERE WE ARE RIGHT

From the place where we are right
flowers will never grow
in the spring.

The place where we are right
is hard and trampled
like a yard.

But doubts and loves
dig up the world
like a mole, a plow.
And a whisper will be heard in the place
where the ruined
house once stood.

Works Cited

Amichai, Yedua. "The Place Where We Are Right" from *The Selected Poetry of Yehuda Amichai*, copyright 2013 by Yehuda Amichai, used by permission of University of California Press, http://www.ucpress.edu/.

Aslan, Reza. *No god but God*. New York: Random House, 2006.

Baldwin, James. *The Fire Next Time*. New York: Vintage International, 1992.

Barlas, Asma. *"Believing Women " in Islam: Unreading Patriarchal Interpretations of the Qur'an*. Austin: University of Texas Press, 2002.

Berra, Yogi, with Dave Kaplan. *What Time Is It? You Mean Now?* New York: Simon & Shuster, 2003.

Bontemps, Arna. *American Negro Poetry*. New York: Hill and Wang, 1995.

Burns, Ken. *Baseball*. TV Documentary. PBS, 1994.

Dickson, Paul. *Baseball's Greatest Quotations*. New York: Harper Perennial, 1992.

Francis, Robert. "The Base Stealer." *Baseball Almanac*. http://www.baseball-almanac.com/

"Go Down Moses," Negro Spiritual.

Goodman, Amy. "'Nothing was Sacred, Nothing was Safe': Selma Historian Recalls Bloody Sunday in 1965." *Democracy Now* Interview, March 7, 2000. https://www.democracynow.org/

Hicks, Dan. "How Can I Miss You If You Won't Go Away?" Original Recordings, 1969.

Joudah, Fady. "Mimesis" from *Alight*, copyright 2013 by Fady Joudah, used by permission of Copper Canyon Press, www.coppercanyonpress.org.

Kaminsky, Ilya, and Katherin Towler. "The Saint, The Murderer, All of It: Li-Young Lee's Poetry of Reconciliation." *The Sun Magazine*, August 2005.

King Jr., Martin Luther. *A Call to Conscience: The Landmark Speeches of Dr. Martin Luther King, Jr.*, Clayborne Carson and Kris Shephard, editors. New York: Grand Central Publishing, 2002.

King Jr., Martin Luther. "How Long, Not Long." Speech, Montgomery, Alabama, March 25, 1965.

Lardner, R. W. (lyricist) & White, G. Harris (composer). "Gee, It's a Wonderful Game."

Marx, Arthur. "Groucho is My Pop." *Collier's Magazine*, 1951.

Milosz, Czeslaw. *The Collected Poems*. New York: The Ecco Press, 1988.

Ryokan. *Dewdrops on a Lotus Leaf: Zen Poems of Ryokan*. John Stevens, translator. Boulder: Shambhala Publications, 2003.

Soto, Gary. *New and Selected Poems*. San Francisco: Chronicle Books, 1995.

Stainton, Leslie. *Lorca: A Dream of Life*. London: A&C Black, 2013.

Veeck, Bill. "Baseball is a Boy's Game that Makes Grown Men Cry." AZ Quotes. http://www.azquotes.com

Whitman, Walt. *Leaves of Grass*. London: Penguin Classics, 1981.

Will, George F. *Men at Work: The Craft of Baseball*. New York: Harper Perennial, 2010.

Zirin, Dave. *What's My Name, Fool?: Sports and Resistance in the United States*. Chicago: Haymarket Books, 2005.

Photo by Uong Chanpidor

James Janko refused to carry a weapon while serving in Viet Nam as a medic in an infantry battalion commanded by Colonel George Armstrong Custer III. Janko's medals include the Bronze Star for Valor, which he returned to the U.S. government in 1986 to protest their military involvement in Central America. In 2008, Janko gave away other medals to Vietnamese victims of Agent Orange: Mrs. Dang Hong Nhut, who suffers from thyroid cancer and has had numerous miscarriages, and Ms. Tran Thi Hoan, who was born without legs due to her mother's exposure to the chemical.

Janko's short stories have appeared in *The Massachusetts Review*, *The Sun*, and many other magazines. He won a 2002 Illinois Arts Council Award for Fiction, and his earlier novel, *Buffalo Boy and Geronimo*, received wide critical acclaim and won the Association of Asian American Studies 2006 Prose Award and the 2007 Northern California Book Award for Fiction.

www.jamesjanko.com